SOLAR FURY

SOLAR FURY

Shattered Sunlight Series Book I

E.A. CHANCE

ALSO BY E.A. CHANCE

Shattered Sunlight Trilogy

HUNTING DAYBREAK

HOPE IGNITES

Omnibus Edition

SHATTERED SUNLIGHT SERIES COLLECTION: BOOKS 1-3

ACKNOWLEDGMENTS

Thank you to Joseph Nassise, my mentor/editor/*Sensei* and prolific NYT bestselling author, for his invaluable guidance and encouragement, and to my award-winning cover designer, Timothy Barber, for his immense talent and ability to see into my mind and create the covers I envision.

I'm grateful to my supportive and loving sister, Jill, who stayed by my side and kept me going through one of the most difficult years of my life. You are the best sister and friend a person could have.

Last, and most importantly, thank you to all of you, my readers. None of this would matter without you. Your kind and enthusiastic support means the world to me.

In loving memory of Dad, my example, best friend, partner in crime, and hero. I miss you every day.

CHAPTER ONE

DR. RILEY POOLE pressed her forehead to the rear window of her father's SUV and stared at the pile of neatly stacked luggage. "I can't do this," she whispered as she fought a wave of panic and reached for her mother's arm.

Marjory gently peeled her daughter's fingers from her wrist. "Take a breath, dear. It's too late to back out of the medical conference, and this is a minor hurdle compared to the ones you've overcome since Zach's death."

Riley turned and searched Marjory's eyes, desperate to believe her. Traveling to a conference half a continent away felt more like diving off a cliff than scaling a minor hurdle.

Her father tossed her carry-on onto the backseat and scratched his head. "What's with all the suitcases? You and Julia are only going for a week."

Marjory elbowed his ribs before Riley could answer. "It's her first time leaving Colorado in more than three years, Thomas, and Julia's never been to Washington, DC. They need to be ready for any adventure."

"Then, I'll defer to your expertise, Marjory. What does a weathered old rancher know about such things?"

Thomas enjoyed passing himself off as a country bumpkin, but he was one of the most brilliant men Riley had ever known. He'd been a respected physician in the region for decades and was loved by the community. She marveled that he'd been content to leave his career and putter around their small ranch since his retirement.

Riley twisted her unruly red hair into a knot and leaned against the liftgate. "It's Zach's fault I always over pack. He never used to let us leave the house without preparing for Armageddon."

"That explains the bug-out kit," Thomas said. "You're going to a luxury hotel, not a war zone."

Riley gave a nervous laugh. "It's my security blanket. Don't judge."

He winked, and Riley felt her panic fade. She owed him so much and wouldn't have survived the trauma of losing her husband without him.

As she reached up to hug him, her daughter, Julia, burst out of the house and let the screen door slam behind her. She bounded down the steps and gave each of her grandparents a quick kiss, then hopped into the front seat of the SUV. Riley's two younger children, Emily and Jared, followed Julia and came to a stop in front of their mother.

Emily tossed her curly red ponytail and glared at Riley. "Why can't I go with you, Mom? It's not fair," she said in her signature, high-pitched whine. "Julia gets to go everywhere, but I get abandoned at home with Jared."

Emily was nine going on thirty. Riley found it exhausting having to justify every decision to her.

"I'm not abandoning you. You know I'm only allowed one guest. Work on the attitude, and I'll consider taking you next time."

"Give it up, Emily," Julia called from the car. "You're not worming your way onto this trip."

Not to be ignored, Jared pushed past Emily and hugged Riley's legs. Burying his face in her thigh, he said, "Don't leave me, Mommy. You'll never come back."

Riley rubbed his silky brown hair and fought her tears. Jared had been glued to her since Zach's helicopter was shot down on the Afghanistan border three years earlier. During those early traumatic months, it had comforted her to have Jared close. When her leave-of-absence ended, and she returned to her practice, it became a daily challenge to get out of the house without traumatizing him. Riley had taken care to prepare him for her week-long absence, and he'd put on a brave face, but when the moment arrived to say goodbye, his courage vanished. She looked at her father and mouthed, "Help."

Thomas pried Jared from Riley and swung him onto his shoulders. "Hey, buddy, don't you want to stay with me? I've got lots of fun adventures planned."

Jared giggled and nodded. "What are we going to do, Papa?"

"That's a surprise for when I get back from the airport." Thomas swung Jared back to the ground and said, "Emily, hug your mom, and take your brother in to wash up so you can help Nana get lunch ready."

Emily rolled her eyes and gave Riley a half-hearted hug before taking Jared's hand to lead him into the house. Riley was grateful when he skipped along with Emily and didn't look back.

Marjory folded her arms and watched her grandchildren walk to the house. "You'll have your hands full with that Emily, when she's older."

Riley nodded. "She reminds me a little too much of her aunt Lily for my comfort. Are you sure you can handle those two while I'm gone?"

"We raised you and your sister just fine. Well, maybe not your sister," Marjory said with a grin.

Lily was two years younger than Riley and the free spirit of the family until she married Kevin, a loving man who was a steadying influence for her. Their first child, Miles, was six months old. Lily was a wonderful mother, and Riley's kids loved their new little cousin. She was grateful Lily only lived twenty minutes away and visited a few times a week.

"If you need a break, have Lily bring Miles over to distract the kids. It'll give you a chance to put your feet up."

"We'll be fine. Get going. The airport's going to be a zoo this soon after the holidays." Marjory shooed Riley toward the car, then headed into the house.

Julia clapped as Riley climbed in the backseat and said, "It's about time, Mom. I thought you were going to make us miss our plane."

Riley smiled at her thirteen-year-old daughter. Julia always looked at the world in joyful wonder. She was so much like her father. Her steadiness and positive outlook had sustained their family for the past three years.

Even though Julia had suffered Zach's loss as profoundly as the rest of them, she was convinced he was in heaven looking out for them the way he always had before he died. Riley wished she could believe that, too, but she was riddled with doubts about the meaning behind his death. She did her best to push those feelings aside and soak up Julia's optimism while it lasted, hoping that navigating the teenage world wouldn't crush her spirit.

Riley slid her carry-on to the other side of the seat and hooked her seatbelt. She preferred to ride in the front, but Julia tended to get carsick on the twisty roads leading into Denver. As her father backed out of the driveway, she caught a glimpse of Jared's sad face as he waved to her from the kitchen window. She waved back, fighting the urge to jump out of the moving car and run back to her boy.

Riley relaxed her white-knuckle grip on the armrest as the shining Washington Monument came into view against the night sky. Though she'd been married to a pilot, flying had always made her nervous. Zach had taught her the dynamics of flight and assured her it was one of the safest forms of travel. While what he said made logical sense, it did nothing to quell her fears. She wouldn't have been able to even step onto the jetway without therapy and sedatives.

After an uneventful drive to the five-star hotel where the conference was being held, Riley led Julia to their elegant, two-bedroom suite, equipped with a living room, full kitchen, and breathtaking balcony view of the monuments.

"I feel like a movie star," Julia said as she stared wide-eyed at their room before kicking off her shoes and picking up the guest information binder. "I'm starving. Can we order room service?"

Riley pulled off her boots and dropped onto the overstuffed sofa. Too tired to go searching for a restaurant in the chilly air, she readily agreed. Their outrageously overpriced meal arrived forty-five minutes later, and after they ate, she ordered a pay-per-view movie Julia had been begging to see.

"I have to go downstairs and sign in for the conference but shouldn't be gone for over fifteen minutes," Riley said and kissed Julia's forehead. "I'll take my phone and key. Don't open the door to anyone and bolt it behind me. Call if you need anything."

"I'm old enough to handle being alone for fifteen minutes, Mom. You're just going downstairs, not to another state."

Riley stuffed her phone and room key into each of her front pockets. "Sometimes, I forget how grown-up you are, but you know how I worry. And I don't care how mature you are, bolt the door behind me."

Julia followed her to the door, and Riley waited until she heard the bolt click before walking to the elevator. She took a deep breath as she stepped inside and the doors slid shut, grateful for her few seconds of solitude.

Riley scanned the busy lobby for signs leading to the conference registration desk. She glanced at her conference map and almost plowed into the woman in front of her when she stopped abruptly. Riley threw her arm out to steady herself and knocked over an easel holding the conference welcome sign. The easel bumped against a small table, sending a lamp and vase of flowers crashing to the floor. Two guests jumped out of the way to avoid the shattered ceramic and backed into another table, tipping it over. Hotel staff appeared from all directions, fussing and asking if anyone was hurt.

A man leaned against the wall, watching the entire fiasco with folded arms and a smug grin. "If anyone's hurt, they're in the right place with a lobby full of doctors," he said. Riley smiled at his comment as she scurried toward the hallway to escape unnoticed. "And where do you think you're going?" he asked her.

She squared her shoulders before turning to face him, feeling her cheeks redden with each step he took toward her.

"Nice performance," he said, making a sweep of his arm toward the pandemonium.

"Kind of you to notice. Were you entertained?"

Instead of answering, he burst out laughing. When Riley scowled, he caught his breath and said, "Forgive me, but how did someone so tiny cause all this chaos?"

His comment caught her off guard, and she laughed despite her effort to be offended.

He extended his hand and said, "Coop. Nice to meet you."

She raised an eyebrow. "Coop? What does that mean? Like, chicken coop?"

"My nickname. What my friends call me, and I hope you'll be calling me Coop."

"Too soon to know. I'm Dr. Riley Poole, orthopedic surgeon."

She grasped his hand while keeping her eyes locked on his. "What does everyone else call you?"

"Dr. Neal Xavier Cooper III."

"You're Dr. Neal Cooper? *The* Dr. Cooper? The surgeon who invented the Xavier cardiac procedure?"

He gave a slight bow. "One and the same. If you're an ortho. How come you've heard of me?"

"Are you serious? Every doctor's heard of you. Are you presenting at the conference?"

"Yes, and worse, I'm in charge of this little shindig."

Riley was embarrassed for not knowing that but was also awed to be in the presence of the doctor who'd revolutionized cardiac surgery and helped save hundreds of thousands of lives.

He was nothing like she'd imagined. She'd pictured him as a contemporary of her father, but he was much younger, possibly no more than her age of thirty-five. He was just under six feet, with an average build and light brown hair that stuck out in all directions. He had an easy manner and seemed amused at the way she studied him. Everything about him said *boy next door*, but Riley sensed more running beneath the surface.

"Did I pass inspection?" he asked and glanced at their clasped hands.

She released her hold on him and crossed her arms. "Too soon to know that, either. So, you're in charge of the conference?"

"Yes. I was on my way to check on registrations when a little redheaded twister started wreaking havoc in the lobby. I had no idea this conference would be so dangerous."

"My husband always said to be prepared for anything." The words tumbled out of her mouth from habit. She found herself wishing she could suck them back in.

Dr. Cooper's tone changed slightly. "Sorry. Didn't notice the ring. Is Mr. Dr. Poole here? He's not going to come after me for flirting with you, is he?"

"He died when his helicopter was shot down in Afghanistan three years ago. I still forget he's gone sometimes." She pressed her lips together and shifted her feet. It was the most awkward and unpredictable conversation she'd ever had.

Dr. Cooper extended his hand again. "Can we have a do-over?"

"Yes, please, Dr. Cooper." She took a breath and squeezed his hand. "I'm from Colorado Springs. I have three children. Two girls and a boy. I brought my thirteen-year-old daughter with me. I should probably sign in and get back to her."

"I'm Coop from Chicago, divorced with no children. My wife decided five years ago that her acting coach was more fun than I was and took off with him. Honestly, our relationship was never anything to write home about, so it was no great loss. Since then, I've mostly worked, *a lot*."

Riley got into step beside him as he walked toward the conference room. "Seems like your ex was wrong about you. You have a good, if not odd, sense of humor, and I'd wager you're lots of fun. That's the first time I've laughed that hard since..." Her words trailed off. It still hurt to recall that former life, the one where Zach made her laugh every day. "Well, I haven't laughed that hard in a long time."

She couldn't seem to stop herself from revealing her intimate secrets to this stranger. Famous or not, she knew nothing about him as a man.

"Trauma. That's why I need a good sense of humor," he mumbled. "But you're familiar with trauma."

They walked the last ten feet in silence.

The mess in the lobby was cleared up, and a new vase and lamp had magically appeared by the time they reached the conference rooms. Though it looked like the incident had never happened, Riley felt a slight shift in her world.

She signed in for the conference and took the tote bag filled with materials from the registrar. When Coop stopped her as she headed for the lobby, she said, "Sorry for all the trouble earlier."

"I'm not," he said, holding her gaze. "Join me in the lounge after your daughter's asleep."

Riley was flattered by invitation but wasn't ready for anything so cozy with a man she'd just met. She wondered if he hooked up with a different woman at every conference.

"It's been a long day and I'm exhausted. Would you like to join Julia and me for breakfast?"

Before the words were out of her mouth, he brushed past her and strode off without another word. *Rude*, she thought, assuming he hadn't approved of Julia tagging along to their tête-à-tête. She pressed the elevator button and tapped her foot while she waited. *So much for the famous Dr. Cooper.*

Riley called Julia on the way back to the suite to ask her to unbolt the door, but she didn't answer. She tried two more times and felt the panic stir in her gut. She stopped at the hotel phone in the hallway near their room and tried again. Julia answered on the third ring.

"Hello?" she mumbled.

"It's Mom. Let me in, please."

Julia hung up, and the door swung open a few seconds later.

"I've been calling your cell. Why didn't you answer?" Riley said as she followed Julia inside.

Julia yawned. "You were gone for a long time. Where were you?"

Riley felt her face flush and hoped it was too dark for Julia to see. "There was some confusion downstairs. You didn't answer my question."

"I turned my phone off because everyone kept bothering me. Emily texted me like five times."

"Emily? Where'd she get a phone?"

Riley had given Julia a phone for her twelfth birthday because she knew she'd need one in middle school, but there was no way she was giving Emily a phone, maybe ever.

"She has Papa's phone," Julia said. "She called you, too, and was ticked that you didn't answer."

Riley forgot she'd silenced her ringer and pulled the phone from her pocket to switch it on. "Don't turn your phone off again, Julia, even if Emily is annoying you."

Julia crossed her arms and tilted her head. "You mean like you did? What if I had an emergency while you were downstairs?" She had a good point, but Riley didn't want to admit that to her. "Emily's texting will drive me nuts. Ask Papa not to let her have his phone."

"I'll call him before I go to sleep."

"Thanks, Mom. I'm going back to bed."

Riley gave her a quick hug and kiss on the cheek. "Night, sweetheart."

When Julia closed her door, Riley went to her room to change for bed and snuggled into bed. After her long, anxious day of travel, she'd expected to drop off as quickly as Julia had, but found herself staring at the dark ceiling, trying not to fantasize about Zach lying with her in that enormous bed. She hadn't been plagued by such thoughts in many months and blamed her encounter with Dr. Cooper.

There was clearly an attraction between them, but the way he'd run off baffled her. If he hadn't wanted Julia to join them for breakfast, all he had to do was say so. She'd have been willing to make other plans, but he hadn't given her a chance.

She groaned in frustration and pounded her pillow into a ball while shutting out thoughts of him. She'd brought Julia along to spend some one-on-one time and create new memories. The last thing she wanted to do was let some random man interfere with that.

Riley stepped onto the balcony at six the next morning and quietly closed the door to keep the street sounds from waking Julia. Breathing in the fifty-degree air and letting the sun stream onto her face, she savored the warmth that was unheard of in Colorado on a January morning. She hadn't slept well and hoped the sunlight would rejuvenate her.

She looked over the brilliant, bustling city and smiled, excited to show Julia the sights. She was looking forward to the conference as well, despite Dr. Cooper, and hated that he was part of the reason for her restlessness in the night. The only solution was to keep her distance from him. There would be hundreds of doctors at the conference. He could undoubtedly find someone else to annoy. She took another breath and headed inside to enjoy a bubble bath in her elegant jetted tub.

Julia was still sleeping an hour later. Riley hated to wake her, but if they were going to have breakfast before the conference orientation, she had no choice. She looked so serene sleeping there, and thirteen or not, Julia was still her angelic little sweetheart. Riley wished she could stop her from growing up. Losing her father had forced her to face more than her share of the harsh realities of life.

Riley sat next to her on the bed and brushed a strand of soft brown hair from her face. Riley had always envied Julia's thick, straight locks that were so like Zach's and not her red, unruly ones. Poor Emily had inherited Riley's hair and blamed her almost daily. Julia was tall and wiry like her father, too, not puny like Riley.

Julia stirred and grinned at her. "What time is it? Feels like I just went to sleep."

Riley kissed her forehead. "It's seven-thirty, so only five-thirty at home. It'll take a day or two to adjust to the time difference.

Do you still want to go downstairs for breakfast, or would you rather eat in the room?"

Julia flew out of bed and grabbed a handful of clothes from her suitcase. "If I have to be locked in here all day, I better get out while I can. I'll take a quick shower."

"You won't be *locked* in here the entire day," Riley said, as Julia ran past her into the bathroom and slammed the door. "I'll have breaks and we'll have lunch together. And we're going to tour the monuments after dinner."

Julia opened the door a crack and stuck her head through. "I still wish you'd let me go to the seminars with you."

"You're not allowed to, sweetheart, and you'd be bored to tears. You need to stay here and do your homework."

"I could take my homework with me," she said and closed the door.

"We've been through this. Please, don't behave like Emily. I don't have the energy."

"How dare you call me that?" she said over the sound of the shower.

Riley chuckled and got up to prepare her materials for the day. She scanned the list of workshops she planned to attend and ran over her notes for the seminar she'd be teaching. The room phone rang as she slipped her laptop into the tote.

"This is the front desk," a man said when she answered. "Dr. Cooper has asked me to relay his apologies, but he's unable to join you for breakfast this morning, as he has conference duties to attend to."

"Didn't know he'd planned to join me for breakfast," she said, "but thank you for calling."

"My pleasure, Dr. Poole. Is there anything else I can do for you?"

"No, thank you," she said and hung up.

"Who was that?" Julia asked as she came out of the bathroom.

"Front desk. It's nothing. You ready?"

Julia nodded and headed for the door. Riley followed her, more confused about Dr. Cooper than she'd been the night before. She'd taken his behavior as anything but an acceptance of her breakfast invitation. She followed Julia out to go for breakfast, determined to avoid him for the rest of the conference.

CHAPTER TWO

THE MORNING SPED by as Riley absorbed the material presented in her seminars. She reflected on how caught up in the microcosm of her hospital she'd been. It was refreshing to remember the larger medical world that existed. Physicians from dozens of countries had arrived for the conference. She looked forward to meeting them and learning new cutting-edge technologies and treatments.

She was making her way to the next session after morning break when Dr. Cooper called out to her. She was tempted to pretend she hadn't heard him but didn't want to be rude like he'd been to her the previous night. She pasted on a smile and turned to face him. She was surprised to see his crooked tie and unruly hair sticking out in all directions. Apparently, someone as rich and famous as Dr. Neal Xavier Cooper III didn't need to worry if his necktie was straight. Despite her effort to dislike him, she found the obliviousness of his appearance charming.

He grinned and moved toward her. "There you are," he said. "I've been looking for you."

"It's break time. I was in the break room. Where else would I be?"

Dr. Cooper raised an eyebrow and seemed confused by her coolness. "I was busy putting out conference fires and didn't check the time. How was breakfast with your daughter?"

"Lovely," she said flatly.

"That's it? Just lovely?"

"Yes."

He studied her for several seconds before scratching his head. "Good. Are you enjoying the conference?"

"Very much. I should get to my next session."

As she turned to go, and Coop reached for her arm but caught himself. "Can I have a minute?" She hesitated before nodding. "What's wrong, Riley? What happened between goodnight and now? Is this about me missing breakfast?"

We didn't say goodnight, Riley thought, but said, "I need to go, or I'll be late. See you around."

Her lips curled into a smile as she turned and left him staring. *Now you know how it feels.*

———

Julia was a prisoner in one of the most amazing cities in the world. The novelty of their suite had worn off, and she got bored thirty minutes after her mom left for the conference. Itching to get out and explore, she grabbed her phone, room key, and some cash ten minutes after her mom called during her morning break and headed for the elevator. Crossing the lobby like a girl on a mission, she was on the crowded sidewalk before she knew what was happening.

People rushed past and jostled her in their hurry to get wherever they were going. Some stopped and stared at her like she was a Martian. Others, mostly men, eyed her in ways that made her uneasy. Realizing her mistake in leaving the safety of the hotel, she dashed back inside and was back in their suite two minutes later.

She dropped onto the bed, feeling like an idiot. What had she been thinking, heading out into a strange city without a plan? Her dad always hammered how vital it was to know your surroundings and have a route before going on an adventure. She didn't even know where the hotel was. Finding the address in the guest information binder, she typed it into the maps app on her iPad. She was surprised to see they were only a few blocks from the White House. Their balcony faced the opposite direction, so she hadn't noticed.

Her mom had ordered tickets for a White House tour before they left Colorado, so that tour was covered. In fact, she and her mom had plans to see all the major sites and monuments. She made a list of other sites within walking distance since she didn't dare venture onto the Metro alone. With list in hand, she raced back to the concierge desk that she'd passed in the lobby. She'd seen enough TV shows and movies to know the concierge was her best source for information. She slowed and almost lost her nerve when she saw the hot guy behind the desk, but she'd gone too far to quit. She walked up to him with fake confidence and flashed a smile.

He returned the smile. "May I help you, miss?"

He was wearing a name tag, so Julia said, "Yes, thank you, Evan." She slid the list across the desk. "Which of these places should I visit first?"

He glanced at the paper. "This is a well thought out list. Most people overlook these sites when they tour our city. My personal favorite is the Smithsonian Museum of American Art. Are you interested in art?"

Julia scrunched up her nose. She'd only added the art gallery because it was so close to the hotel, but she didn't want Evan to know that. "I'd like to learn more about it."

"This is the perfect place to start. I'm an art student. I'd be happy to give you and your parents a tour after my shift."

"It's just me and…"

"Julia," her mom called from across the lobby.

She cringed and said, "My mom." She turned and smiled. "Hi, Mom."

Her mom practically flew to close the space between them. "What are you doing out here? I told you not to leave the room. What's wrong?"

"Nothing's wrong. Calm down. I just needed some air. I was asking Evan about sites we can visit near the hotel."

Riley's gaze flicked from Evan to Julia. "What you're doing doesn't matter. I expected you to be in the room. What if I had gone there and found you missing? I need to know your whereabouts at all times."

"She's safe inside the hotel, Dr. Poole," Evan said. "I was just offering to take the two of you on a tour of the art gallery after my shift."

Riley glared at him, then softened her look. "That's a kind offer, but we're occupied tonight. I'll see if I can fit it into our schedule later in the week. Come on, Julia, I'll walk you back to the suite."

As Julia's mom pulled her toward the elevator, she turned and mouthed a sorry to Evan. He dipped his head and turned to help another guest. Once she and her mom were in the room, she dropped onto the sofa and folded her arms, refusing to look at Riley.

"I'm the one who gets to be angry here, not you," Riley said.

"You were rude to Evan and embarrassed me. I did nothing wrong. I was just talking to the concierge, not running around DC alone. Why can't you just chill out and not overreact like always? We're on vacation."

Riley sat on the sofa and turned Julia to face her. "I don't always overreact. I may be more vigilant than other parents, but I have my reasons."

"You mean your PTSD?"

Riley looked away and gave a slight nod.

"You don't have to hide it or be ashamed, Mom. Lots of people have anxiety, even some of my friends, and we learned about it in health class. My teacher said people with PTSD should be open and talk about it."

Riley sighed. "I'm not hiding it. It's just hard for me to talk about. This isn't about my PTSD, though. You disobeyed me. For me to concentrate on the conference, which is the reason we're here, if you remember, I need to know that you're safely tucked in the room. I'm sorry if you don't like those conditions, but I made this clear to you before we left Colorado."

"I didn't know how boring it would be."

"It's only been a few hours. You can't be that bored already. How much homework did you get done?"

Julia looked at her laptop and notebooks stacked on the little desk. She'd only finished one math assignment, but it was too hard to concentrate with all the excitement going on outside the window. "Not much. Now that we're here, can't we make a new plan that we're both happy with?"

"What new plan? Aside from what Evan says, it's not safe for you to wander around the hotel on your own."

"I'm not five, Mom. I feel safer here than I do at school. Are you sure I can't come to your classes and sit in the back to do my homework? I won't make a peep."

Riley brushed a lock of hair out of Julia's face and tucked it behind her ear. "I'm sorry, sweetheart, but that's not allowed. I'll ask around to see if the hotel has a supervised area for you to study, but don't get your hopes up. Until then, promise me you'll ·stay in the room. I'll get you at lunchtime."

Julia frowned but nodded.

"Say it out loud."

"I promise."

Riley kissed her cheek and stood. "Good. I'm late for my next seminar, but I'll see you in an hour. I love you."

"Love you, too," Julia mumbled as she watched her leave. At least she'd gotten her to agree to find somewhere for her to study, but she still wasn't happy about being locked up in their suite.

She was relieved they'd finally had a conversation about her mom's PTSD. She'd wanted to talk about it for a long time. Her mom had taken them all for counseling after her dad died, and it had helped Julia. Even though she missed him every day, she'd moved on with her life and was afraid her mom never would. Julia was so over her being scared of every little thing and often felt more like a parent than a daughter.

Julia grabbed her school materials and carried them to the balcony. At least she could watch the world go by from there, even if she couldn't be part of it.

The incident with Julia left Riley feeling distracted, and she heard little of her next seminar. She asked the instructor if he'd mind emailing his notes before she went to pick Julia up for lunch. If they ate quickly, it would give them time to look into a place for Julia to study. Riley doubted there was one, but she'd promised to ask. She called to let Julia know she was on her way and found her waiting in the hallway.

"I'm starving," she said and headed for the elevator like nothing had happened earlier.

"When are you not starving?" Riley asked, wondering if she *had* overreacted earlier. She put the incident from her mind and enjoyed their meal as Julia chatted about what she'd seen from the balcony while she did her homework.

Riley swallowed a spoonful of delicious butternut squash soup and said, "Sounds like you did more people-watching than studying."

"People-watching is a kind of learning. Plus, I did my homework and finished today's assignments. What else am I going to do all afternoon, watch boring hotel TV?"

"It'll only be three hours until I'm finished for the day. Then, I'm all yours."

Julia clapped and gulped down the rest of her milkshake before getting up to go. "Let's go ask Evan if there's somewhere I can hang out while you're in class."

Riley gulped the rest of her soup and ran to catch up with Julia.

"We don't have a teen center," she heard Evan tell her. "There is a video-game room. Not sure how much studying you'd get done." When Riley reached the desk, he said, "One of us will always be at this station, Dr. Poole. Julia is welcome to sit at that desk behind me to do her homework. We'll keep an eye on her."

Julia folded her hands and looked at Riley with such hope in her eyes that she couldn't refuse. The area around the concierge desk was open and busy. It seemed safe enough. She gave a nod of approval and Julia kissed her cheek.

"I'll get my stuff," she said and ran off before Riley could protest.

"Thank you, Evan. That wasn't necessary, but I appreciate it."

"Our pleasure. Julia seems like a bright girl. She'll be fine. Have her check out the game room when she's done studying. There's always a hotel staff member present."

"I'll do that."

Riley checked on Julia twice during the afternoon. The first time she was typing away on her laptop at the small desk. The second, she was draped over an easy-chair near the concierge desk, absorbed in a novel from her required reading list. After her final seminar, Riley retrieved her so the two of them could dress for their big night on the town.

Before they headed out for the evening, Riley called her aunt and uncle, who had a horse ranch in southwestern Virginia. She'd allowed time in their itinerary to fly to Roanoke for one night before traveling back to Colorado. Uncle Mitch was her mother's older brother, and Riley hadn't seen him since Zach's funeral. The ranch had always been one of her favorite places to visit as a girl. It was a picturesque five-hundred acre estate, nestled in the rolling Blue Ridge Mountains.

"Hello, Pumpkin," he said when he heard Riley's voice.

"That's Dr. Pumpkin to you," she said with a laugh. "Will it work if we fly in early on Saturday? Were you able to convince the kids to be there? I'd love to see the cousins and catch up."

"They'll all be here. Holly can't wait to see Julia. What time does your flight get in?"

"I was waiting to talk to you before I made the reservation, but I'll do it before bed and text you. We can stay until Monday morning. Tell Aunt Beth I can't wait to see her."

She hung up with a smile, then double-checked the address for the trendy restaurant near the hotel where they had reservations for dinner. Armed with directions, she and Julia grabbed their sweaters on their way out. Evan called out as they passed his desk.

"You'll need more than sweaters. There's a cold front moving in, and the temperature has dropped ten degrees in the last hour. Calling for snow tomorrow."

Riley and Julia groaned in unison. "We'd hoped to escape the snow, but thanks for the heads up," Riley said as they turned back to get their coats.

They'd almost reached the elevator when Dr. Cooper stepped into Riley's path. She steered Julia toward the bank of elevators at the far side of the lobby, but Coop followed. When he called her name, she sighed and stopped to let him catch up.

"Evening, Riley. You'll need warmer coats if you're heading out tonight. Cold front moving in."

"We heard," Riley said. "We're just on our way back to the room. We have a dinner reservation, so we need to hurry."

Coop ignored her and held out his hand to her daughter. "You must be Julia."

She took his hand and grinned. "Yes, I must be Julia. Who are you?"

Riley elbowed her and said, "This is Dr. Cooper. He's in charge of the conference. We really do need to get going."

"Nice to meet you," Coop said, and winked at Julia. "Where's your reservation?"

None of your business, Riley thought, but Julia blurted out the name of the restaurant before she could stop her.

"Excellent choice. Mention me. The maître d' will give you the best table and treatment. What are your plans after dinner?"

Riley tried to catch Julia's eye to keep her from divulging any more of their plans, but it was too late. She rattled off every item on their itinerary for the rest of the week.

"Allow me to give you Coop's Deluxe Monument Tour after dinner. I'm very familiar with the city. I lived here when my dad was a senator."

Annoyed with herself for being impressed, Riley said, "Your father was a senator?"

"Yes, from the great state of Illinois. He was one of the youngest senators ever elected. He was a great man. We thought he'd serve for many years, but he died unexpectedly when I was eleven. Aortic aneurysm. That was what motivated me to become a cardiac surgeon. I wanted to save other children from losing their fathers so young." Julia lowered her eyes and stared at her feet. "Your mom told me about your dad," Coop said softly. "You understand that kind of pain."

Julia looked at him with glistening eyes. "He was a great man, too."

"He was," Riley said, and squeezed her shoulder.

"Sorry. Didn't mean to kill the mood," Coop said. "How about that tour?"

"Sounds fun," Julia said without looking at her mom.

"Perfect. Text me as soon as you're done eating. I'll meet you right here."

He was gone before Riley could protest. *What an odd man,* she thought as Julia tugged on her arm to get her moving to the elevator.

Riley was tempted to drop Coop's name at the restaurant but decided against it. As curious as she was to see what clout he carried, she didn't like the idea of being indebted to him, even in such a small way. She gave her name to the host, who immediately motioned for the maître d'. He came forward and bowed.

"Good evening, Dr. Poole. Dr. Cooper called and told us to expect you. Follow me, please."

Riley gave a weak smile before falling into step with him and heard Julia giggle behind her. The restaurant staff hovered and fawned over them throughout the meal. Riley just wished to be left in peace, but she had to admit it was the best meal she'd ever eaten. When she asked for the check, the server said Dr. Cooper had taken care of the bill. So much for not being indebted to him, and the night was far from over.

She toyed with not texting him after dinner and going sightseeing on their own, but she didn't want to seem ungrateful or have to explain her actions to Julia. She texted a quick note that they'd meet him at the hotel entrance. He was eagerly waiting when they arrived and guided them toward a limousine parked at the curb.

"This is too much after paying for our dinner. I have a rental in the garage we can use," Riley said.

"Not my doing. The conference sponsors provide the limo. We might as well make use of it."

He helped Julia into her seat before motioning for Riley to get in before him. She wasn't sure she believed him about the limo, but once again felt trapped into cooperating. She climbed in and sank into the soft leather seat.

Julia fidgeted excitedly in the seat across from her as she looked out the window. "I've never ridden in a limo. Where are we going first?"

"I always start with the Lincoln Memorial, since it's my favorite. Then onto the Jefferson. Those are the only two we'll get out to see tonight since it's so cold, but we'll drive around to get an excellent view of the city without all the traffic. You'll want to see the other monuments and museums during the day."

Riley pulled her coat tighter. "I'm freezing already. I don't understand it. I tolerate much colder temperatures in Colorado. This cold goes right through you."

"It's the humidity," he said. "It makes the heat hotter and the cold colder."

"We learned about that in science class," Julia said. "I don't mind. I want to see everything. We have forever to get warm."

"Excellent attitude. Never pass up an adventure," Dr. Cooper said, as the driver pulled as close to the memorial as he could. "We'll have a bit of a walk, so bundle up."

They got out of the limo and made the journey to the base of the memorial. No matter how many times Riley stood on those steps, it was an awe-inspiring sight. She stayed back to get the full view and only half-listened as Dr. Cooper gave his spiel to Julia, who hung on every word. Riley was pleased to see Julia's enthusiasm, knowing she'd always remember the experience.

When Dr. Cooper finished giving the history of the monument, he left Julia to explore and joined Riley. "What was that about this morning? I'd appreciate an explanation," he said.

Riley wondered how he still had no clue what he'd done to upset her, but her mood had softened, and she wasn't up for playing more games.

"You walked off so abruptly last night after I invited you to breakfast. I thought you were miffed at the idea of Julia joining us. Then you stood me up this morning. You didn't bother to apologize when we ran into each other later. When you asked how breakfast was, I thought you were being sarcastic."

He scratched his head and stared into the distance while he mulled over what she'd said. He seemed genuinely baffled by her explanation, but eventually, a light flickered in his eyes.

"One of my staff members waved me over last night when we were talking by the elevator. I should have explained instead of just walking off, but it looked urgent. About breakfast, didn't you get my message that I couldn't meet you?"

Riley crossed her arms and shuffled her feet. "I did. I assumed it was an excuse to get out of my invitation."

"I didn't want out of it, and especially not because you were bringing your daughter. She's delightful, by the way." He stopped and looked into her eyes. "I wouldn't lie to you, Riley. Not my style. As I said, I had to put out fires. I've been dealing with a thousand micro-crises all day. It's harder than performing a complicated surgery."

"Now, don't I look like a fool. I'm sorry for making assumptions. I'll put it down to being flustered after the lobby incident. Maybe we should start over again. *Again*."

"No need. We were both at fault. How was your dinner?"

Riley chuckled. "Incredible, thank you, Dr. Cooper. It was kind of you to take care of the bill."

"My immense pleasure. So, still calling me Dr. Cooper? Please, it's Coop."

"Fine, Coop," she said, allowing herself a small grin.

"Remarkable dimples, Riley. Can we give breakfast a second shot? As long as you promise not to get offended if I get called away to put out fires."

Julia ran up to them before Riley could answer. "I know what I said about having forever to get warm, but I'm frozen. Can we go back to the limo?"

"Yes," Riley said, and turned down the walkway to the car. "Dr. Cooper, I mean Coop, has invited us to breakfast. Interested?"

"Awesome," Julia said, and ran ahead of them.

"That's a yes," Riley said.

"Because apparently, I'm awesome," Coop said, and reached for Riley's hand.

She stopped and stared at his outstretched hand. She'd just met this man and wasn't even sure how she felt about him, but she was cold and tired, and the desire to feel a connection to him sent a thrill through her. Taking his hand didn't mean it had to go any further, and in less than a week, they'd return to their respective lives and never see each other again.

Her heart raced as she wove her gloved fingers into his. He beamed and moved closer until their shoulders touched as they walked to the limo. She let go before Julia saw, but the warmth of him lingered for the rest of the night.

They didn't return to the hotel until midnight. Julia was asleep within minutes of climbing into bed, but Riley stayed awake for two hours, googling everything she could find about Dr. Neal Xavier Cooper III. She uncovered no skeletons, and everything she read was positive. His patients sang his praises, and the thousands of followers on his social media accounts painted him as a god. The only slightly less-than-perfect thing she learned about him was that he was a bit of an absentminded professor and tended to retreat into his own world while doing research. *No one is that perfect,* Riley thought, and closed her laptop.

She lifted the hand Coop had held and examined it in the darkness. It had been years since she'd known romantic intimacy. Zach had been gone for months before he was shot down. The four-year mark since she'd been with him was only weeks away. Four years. It didn't seem possible.

Her parents had been nudging her to start dating. She'd had plenty of invitations, but in her mind, no man could ever measure up to Zach. Maybe it was time to consider that other men didn't have to be Zach. They just had to meet her standards. She snuggled into the blankets with a smile, imagining the possibilities. What could be the harm in enjoying a few days with Coop before returning to her celibate life?

CHAPTER THREE

JULIA WOKE before her mom and tiptoed into her bedroom. She kneeled on the carpet to watch her mom sleeping so peacefully. Julia wondered if that was how she'd been before her dad died. It had been nice to see her enjoying herself during their night with Coop, but then again, it was impossible not to have fun around him.

Julia stifled a giggle over the fact that her mom thought she hadn't seen them holding hands, but she didn't need to see to sense the spark between them. It was the same spark she felt around Dustin McClain, even if he was totally oblivious to her.

Her mom stirred and rubbed her eyes. "What are you doing?" she asked.

"Watching you sleep like you used to watch me when I was little."

"You must be really bored. What time is it?"

Julia folded back the covers and tugged her mom's legs over the edge of the bed. "Time for us to get up and get ready for breakfast with Dr. Cooper." Riley tried to hide a grin at the mention of his name, but Julia saw. "You like him."

"He's a brilliant and kind man. Who wouldn't like him?"

"Then get up, and let's go, but you have to see this first." She dragged Riley to the balcony doors and pulled back the curtain. The ground was covered in four inches of snow and flakes were still falling.

"Not what I wanted to see," Riley said, "but we won't let it stop us. What are a few inches of snow?"

"We're supposed to get at least two more. It makes the city prettier, though, don't you think? Almost romantic."

Her mom laughed and gathered her clothes to take into the bathroom. "It'll only be romantic until we have to go out in it. Turn on the local news so we can listen while we get dressed."

Coop was waiting for them in the dining room by a table laden with what looked like every item on the menu.

"I didn't know what you liked, so I ordered a little of everything," he'd said.

Breakfast was relaxed and uneventful, other than the buzz about the snowstorm. Julia devoured plates piled with pancakes smothered in syrup between unending questions to Coop about DC. Riley was grateful that he was patient and charming with her. What he told them was fascinating, especially information about the behind-the-scenes aspects of the city. Riley could have listened all day, but Coop was called away on conference business before they finished eating.

"I have to make a little speech tonight, so I won't be able to play tour guide," he said before leaving.

Riley flipped through her conference schedule to the page with that evening's events. Coop was listed as the keynote speaker. "Organizer and keynote? That's a bit unusual," she said.

Coop grinned at her. "I resisted, but the sponsors insisted."

"We're touring the White House this afternoon, so it's no

problem. I'm attending the reception tonight and ordering a pizza for Julia."

"Bring her. I'll make the arrangements. Would you like that, Julia, or do you prefer pizza over my boring speech?"

"Can I, Mom?" Julia's eyes pleaded for her to say yes.

"It's fine with me, but you don't have anything to wear."

"There's every shop imaginable within blocks of the hotel," Coop said. His staff member stood ten feet away, signaling to him. "I'd better go see to this life or death conference crisis. See you tonight. Say hi to the President for me."

"Are you sure you want to do this? It's just a boring dinner," Riley asked Julia after he left.

"I'll get a new dress out of it, and I'd rather go than sit in our room eating pizza."

Riley nodded. She liked the idea of having Julia by her side at the reception but wasn't sure they'd have time to shop between the White House tour and dinner. She scanned her schedule for the afternoon and decided the world wouldn't end if she missed her final seminar of the day.

She kissed Julia's forehead. "Fine. But finish your homework. I'll see you at lunch."

"Yes, Mom!" Julia said and did a fist pump as she grabbed her backpack and ran to the lobby.

Riley was exhausted by the time they took their seats in the ballroom for the reception that evening. They'd rushed from shopping to the tour to the hotel to dress without stopping to breathe. Getting around had taken twice as long because of the snow, which had piled up to eight inches. Julia looked a little peaked, and Riley hoped she wouldn't regret choosing to join her for the reception. Even Riley had gotten bored at similar events in the past.

All the guests at their table introduced themselves and compared notes from their classes and sightseeing excursions while they enjoyed the meal. Julia's eyes glazed over during the first two speakers, and Riley caught her trying to sneak her phone more than once, but she perked up when Coop stepped up to speak.

Riley noted that his hair was combed for once and his bowtie was straight. He was a strikingly handsome and captivating speaker. Every eye in the room was riveted on him, including Julia's. He spoke for forty-five minutes, but the time flew by. He came directly to their table as soon as the formal part of the evening ended.

"How'd I do? Still glad you came?" he asked Julia.

She blushed at the attention. "Yes, it was great. Thank you, Dr. Cooper."

The other guests at their table echoed her comments.

He bowed in thanks. "Riley, may I speak with you for a moment?"

She raised her eyebrows but stood to go with him. He led her into the hallway before reaching for her hand. Riley didn't resist.

"I haven't stopped thinking about you since last night. The offer for a drink still stands. I have some loose ends to tie up after the reception, but it will give you time to take Julia back to the room before meeting me at the club."

She hesitated before answering. Coop was clearly used to getting his way, and her brain cried out to say no, but she didn't listen. "I'd like that. Will thirty minutes be enough time?"

"Plenty."

He let go of her hand and walked back to the ballroom without waiting for her. If she was going to spend time with him, she'd have to get used to his abrupt departures without getting offended. She waited for her heartbeat to slow to its normal rhythm before following him into the ballroom. Julia gave her a look far too insightful for her age but didn't question her about what Coop had wanted.

Riley picked up her clutch. "It's late, and I should get you back to the room. Dr. Cooper wants to meet with me about my presentation tomorrow."

Julia said goodnight to the other guests at their table and followed Riley without a word.

Riley changed her outfit three times before realizing she was being ridiculous and settled on her most comfortable pair of jeans and a light hooded sweatshirt. The temperatures were below freezing outside, but the hotel was toasty.

When she was ready, she kissed Julia's forehead and said, "I'll be in the club downstairs and won't be more than an hour. Don't forget to bolt the door and keep your phone turned on so you can let me in. I'll keep mine on, too."

Julia gave her the same knowing half-grin and waved her off before turning back to her movie.

Riley was far more relaxed about leaving her than she'd been the first day and congratulated herself for making progress. She hadn't felt anxious for more than twenty-four hours, and the anticipation of seeing Coop was delicious. She couldn't remember the last time she'd allowed herself such feelings.

Her text alert dinged in the elevator, and her heart sank when she saw Coop's name on the screen, afraid he was canceling. She reluctantly opened the message and smiled as she read.

The club is too noisy and crowded. Meet me in the lounge.

A surge of relief and pleasure flowed through her. She hadn't been too happy about meeting at the club. She was too old for that scene. The lounge suited this thirty-five-year-old mother of three much better.

Coop was waiting for her in a quiet corner. He'd changed into jeans and a hooded sweatshirt, too, and for some reason, his hair was sticking up. She guessed it had stayed in place as long as it could. She slid into the booth next to him and hid her trembling hands in her lap.

"I have to be honest. I was shocked when you agreed to meet me. I've been expecting you to stand me up," Coop said.

Riley smiled. "I was shocked, too, but I'd never stand you up. I don't play games."

"I should have guessed that about you. Neither do I. You may have guessed that I'm an easy-going person who doesn't care much what others think, but when I see what I want, I go for it."

"I've noticed."

"The truth is, you're the first woman to spark my interest since Chelsey left me. When I saw that little redheaded dynamo smashing the lobby décor, I thought, that's the one for me."

Riley smiled. "So, that's what you look for in a woman?"

"Who knew?" Coop rested his arm on the booth behind her head without touching her. She felt his warmth and wished he had.

"You're the first man I've accepted an invitation from since Zach. If you knew more about me, you'd understand how monumental that is. I'm still not sure what I'm doing here."

"Don't overthink it. We're just two new friends having a drink."

Riley let out her breath and relaxed. "Fair enough."

They made small talk for the next forty minutes, until Riley started to yawn.

"I should get upstairs to Julia. Big day tomorrow. I'd like to review my notes before bed."

Coop took her hand and stroked the back of it with his thumb. "Not just yet."

She scooted closer and rested her head on his shoulder. "That feels nice."

He put a finger under her chin and tilted her head. "Can I kiss you, Riley?"

She leaned into him and pressed her lips to his in answer. He wrapped her in his arms and kissed her passionately in return.

Riley pulled away and met his eyes. "Just two friends having a drink? Is this how you treat all your friends?" Coop laughed and kissed her until she wriggled free of his arms. "As much as I want to stay here with you, I *do* have to go."

Coop reluctantly stood and offered his hand. "I'll walk you."

He kissed her once more outside her door.

"I wasn't sure I wanted this to happen, but I'm glad it did. I don't know what it means going forward, but I promise not to overthink it," Riley said.

"All I ask. See you at breakfast."

Part of her wanted to invite him in as she watched him walk away, but that was out of the question. Aside from Julia, she wasn't the type to hop into bed with a man on a whim. She and Zach married young, and most of her romantic education came from their relationship, but she was no longer an inexperienced girl in her twenties. She was a passionate and lonely woman, far hungrier for intimacy than she'd been willing to admit. She looked forward to exploring what else could reawaken with this man.

CHAPTER FOUR

RILEY SLEPT SOUNDLY and woke eager for the day. She dressed with care before hurrying to the dining room with Julia. Their breakfast with Coop was a repeat of the previous morning, except Riley convinced him that the buffet would be plenty, and he didn't need to order the entire menu. She made two trips through the buffet line before realizing she'd have to give up breathing if she ate another bite.

While they ate, she and Julia planned their day. Riley had freed up her morning so they could visit at least one of the Smithsonian museums before she gave her afternoon seminar. She had her heart set on the National History Museum, but Julia wanted to visit the Air and Space Museum. Since Julia was cooperating with being cooped up in the room, Riley let her have her choice.

While they were deciding what to see first, an alert sounded on the restaurant TV. Phone alerts started going off seconds later. Riley pulled her phone from the tote without taking her eyes off the TV screen. The cameras were pointed to an empty podium in the White House press room. When the Deputy White House Press Secretary stepped to the microphone, Riley's gut twisted into a knot. The president was traveling out of the country, and she feared he'd been assassinated or had a heart attack.

The restaurant quieted when the press secretary began speaking.

"I'm speaking on behalf of President Carlisle, who is unavailable to make this announcement himself. Please be assured that he is safe and well. He sends his respects."

Riley blew out the breath she'd be holding. At least they'd have a president to guide them through whatever was coming.

"One hour ago, scientists who monitor solar activity detected what is called a Coronal Mass Ejection or CME. CMEs are, and I quote, 'large expulsions of plasma and magnetic field from the sun's corona.' I've been informed that CMEs of varying speeds and sizes happen regularly. Most are harmless to our planet, but this CME that scientists have detected is quite massive and will collide with Earth in twenty-five hours."

He paused to let the information sink in. Riley reached for Julia's hand but was too anxious to muster a smile.

"While this situation should be taken seriously, there is no cause for panic. We anticipate no more than a four-day inconvenient loss of power. Scientists predict that while the entire Earth will be affected to some degree, most of the impact will be felt in North America. If we prepare properly and sensibly, the impact should be minimal. Electrical grids and devices powered by electrical power will be affected. Computer circuits, including those in motor vehicles, may also be impacted. With clear-headed planning, authorities predict power grids will function again within four to five days."

The press secretary continued to ramble about forthcoming instructions on the internet, TV, and radio, the National Guard and Reserves being called up, and the president declaring a national emergency. Riley barely heard him over her pounding heartbeat.

She stood and tugged on Julia's arm. "Come on. We're getting out of here."

Julia raised her eyebrows in confusion but stood to go with her. As they rushed out of the restaurant, Riley heard the press secretary say, "All air, train, and cruise travel will be suspended twelve hours before the CME is expected to arrive. Travel until that time is only authorized for previously purchased tickets departing before the ban goes into effect. Domestic and oceanic shipping will also be halted at that time. We advise you to stay off the roads as traffic signals and some vehicles may cease to function."

Coop caught up to Riley and Julia and stepped into their path. "Where are you going?"

Riley lifted her chin and crossed her arms. "Home. I'll drive the rental car all the way to Colorado Springs if I have to."

"Let's go back to your suite and discuss this rationally." He glanced at Julia. "We don't need to panic, remember?"

Riley brushed past him and headed for the elevator. She was disappointed to find the line of people already waiting.

"The man said we're supposed to stay inside, Mom. How can we go home?"

Riley gave up on the elevator and pulled Julia toward the stairs.

Julia broke free and came to a stop with her hands on her hips. "I'm not walking up ten flights of stairs."

"It'll be faster to wait for the elevator," Coop said behind them.

Riley raised her hands in surrender and walked back to Coop. She paced in front of the bank of elevators, reminding herself to breathe. Three minutes later, she was on her way to the suite and annoyed that Coop had been right. She raced to the room and started digging out their suitcases the instant she was through the door.

Coop gently put his hands on her shoulders. "Stop and think. How far do you think you'll get in twenty-four hours? Are you going to drive all that way with no sleep? What if the scientists have the timing wrong?"

She covered her mouth with her hand and said a muffled, "Oh, no," before hurrying to the bathroom. She leaned over the toilet and deposited her massive breakfast in the bowl. When the heaving stopped, she went to the sink and splashed cold water on her face.

Julia tapped on the door. "Mom, can I come in?"

Riley sank to the floor and pulled her knees to her chest. "Yes, sweetheart," she mumbled.

Julia sat next to her and put an arm around her shoulders. "We're going to be fine." She held up her iPad so Riley could see the screen. "I googled CMEs. It doesn't look like that big a deal, Mom. We just shut down electricity until this passes and then start it up again. It won't be any worse than the time we lost power for three days during that blizzard. That was kind of fun."

Riley took the tablet and read the article. The situation wasn't as dire as she'd imagined, but her only thought was of getting home to her other children. She handed the tablet back and rubbed her face.

Coop stepped into the bathroom doorway. "Mind if I join you?" Riley didn't answer, but he came in anyway. He sat across from her and reached for her hand. She thought he was going to hold it, but he pressed two fingers to her wrist to take her pulse. "Your heart rate is 120 and I don't like your color. Do you have a sedative?"

Julia climbed to her feet. "I know where they are."

"PTSD?" Coop asked. Riley stared at her trembling hands and nodded. "Thought so. I recognized the signs."

She wiped her mouth on a hand towel. "I guess tossing my breakfast was a dead giveaway."

"Among other things. I don't care, Riley. You deserve a little anxiety after what you've been through. I told you when we met; I understand trauma."

"This isn't just my anxiety. I need to be home for my family." Julia came in and handed her a pill and bottle of water. Riley swallowed the pill and wiped her mouth. "I'll get as far as I can before the CME hits. I'll drive ten hours today, sleep for six hours, drive ten more, sleep, and then drive until I'm forced to stop. I'll be close enough that if the car keeps working, I can load it up with food and keep going."

"What if the car dies and strands you on a barren road in the middle of Kansas in the dead of winter? Can you risk putting Julia in that kind of danger?"

"Then, come with us," Riley said. "I'll buy you a ticket to Chicago when this is over."

"How will my traveling with you prevent the car from dying? And I can't bail on the stranded conference attendees. You're not the only one desperate to get home, so take a breath, call your family, and do what you need to do to prepare. I'm going to talk to the hotel manager to see what they have in the way of provisions and generators. Julia can research what we need. You can work on your presentation for tomorrow."

"You expect me to give a seminar with the world ending? How will my presentation even matter?"

"The world's not ending. Don't be such a drama queen," Julia said. "I'm going to look at this like we're part of a big adventure." She offered a hand to Riley. "We have work to do, Mom."

Riley stared at her daughter in wonder, wishing she had even a fraction of her courage and optimism. She accepted her offered hand and got to her feet.

"If you're sure you want to stay, that's what we'll do. And don't worry, Coop, I'll be ready to present my seminar tomorrow or help with whatever else you need."

Coop kissed her cheek. "That's my girl. I'll be back as soon as I talk to the manager."

Riley's meds kicked in soon after Coop left. As her anxiety faded, she and Julia called to check on her parents and the children and assure them they were safe. Julia rambled on about their exciting adventure. Thomas said he had the generators ready and was stocked with food, firewood, and batteries. He'd even dragged out his HAM radio. Riley promised to see them in a week, even if she had to drive all the way to Colorado.

After hanging up, she turned on CNN. They were replaying the White House briefing and adding further details and information as they became available.

"Power companies will begin shutting down four hours before the CME strike, so plan to be in your homes by that time. Information on how to prepare generators and solar-powered homes will be forthcoming. In the meantime, charge your electronics and backup power supplies, then unplug anything that runs on electrical power. Those of you in colder climates, make sure you have a reliable heat source."

He stopped and wiped his forehead with a handkerchief.

"Please do not raid stores and gas stations to horde food and gasoline. Get only what you need to last a few days. If you know of anyone incapable of caring for themselves, please look after them if you can, or notify your local authorities. President Carlisle is preparing to return to the U.S. as we speak. Vice President Kearns is fully briefed and prepared to lead the nation until then. Let's take care of each other and weather this storm as I know we can."

Riley took notes while Julia searched for more information on the internet. Coop came back forty-five minutes later and handed her a stack of papers.

"I printed this downstairs. It's the latest information on preparations and what to expect after the CME. The hotel pantries are stocked with enough food for four days, depending on the number of guests that stay, and they're already collecting emergency supplies. Their generators run on natural gas and are what's called 'hardened' to withstand a nuclear attack, so they should function after this type of event. We'll be safe and warm here, so nothing to worry about."

"Sweet. The food here is awesome," Julia said. "We get to ride out the apocalypse in style."

"Get to? Lucky us," Riley said. "What about the conference?"

"I was mobbed by attendees the second I hit the lobby, but everyone calmed down after I reassured them we'd have food and heat. Most who drove here are gone, but about two-thirds stayed. The conference briefing is in the ballroom in half an hour."

"Then it looks like we have everything we need. All we have left to do is wait," Riley said and rubbed her forehead, feeling far less confident than she acted.

"Mom said I don't have to do homework, so I'm watching all the YouTube I can before the power goes out."

"Wish I could do that." He gave her a fist bump and winked at Riley. "See you in thirty."

Riley was impressed with Coop's composure during the conference briefing. He answered the barrage of questions calmly and had everyone laughing by the end. She hoped she could do the same during her seminar the following day. She packed away fears of the impending solar storm and practiced the presentation she'd been preparing for months.

Throwing herself into her work had always been her proven strategy for combatting anxiety. Helping mend broken bodies was deeply fulfilling, and she was confident in her abilities. She owed a large part of that to her father, who never missed a chance to praise or encourage her. He'd taught her to believe in herself and never quit. She'd reaped the rewards of those lessons as she progressed in her career.

She and Julia spent the afternoon in the suite while Coop

went scavenging for whatever water, food, and medical supplies he could get his hands on. He'd tried to convince Riley to join him, but she refused to leave her daughter's side.

For dinner, Coop arranged a casual conference meal in the ballroom, so Riley left Julia with pizza and a promise not to be too late. Julia planned to use the time to download every video she'd wanted to see until the memory on her iPad was full. Riley encouraged her to use the time more productively, but got a stony stare in return. She gave up with a shrug and went to meet Coop.

She took her laptop along so she could stay informed on what was happening as the country prepared for the CME. She insisted they take a table near an outlet so she wouldn't run out her laptop's juice. When their food arrived, Coop convinced her to close the lid and visit with the people at their table. She grudgingly complied, but was soon glad she did, enjoying the stimulating and animated conversation with their table-mates.

After the meal, Coop was sharing stories about trips to Africa as a boy with his father when suddenly lightbulbs above their table exploded and rained down shards of glass before the room went dark. Riley instinctively covered her head with her arms and jumped out of her chair when sparks blazed up her computer cord from the outlet. There was a loud pop when the sparks reached the adapter port, and flames shot out from the side of her laptop, catching her note papers on fire. Coop felt his way through the darkened room to a fire extinguisher hanging on the wall by the exit. He doused the flames as backup power kicked in, and soft emergency lighting flickered on.

A deafening bang rattled the ballroom walls seconds later, followed by squealing tires and a din of crunching metal on the street in front of the hotel. Ceiling tiles smashed to the floor, trailing clouds of dust. Riley crouched under the table with her hands over her ears and stared at her fried laptop in confusion. The CME wasn't supposed to hit for another sixteen hours.

When the frightened guests ran for the exits, Coop gave a loud whistle and raised his arms.

"Everyone, please, stay where you are while I find out what's happening. The last thing the hotel staff needs is panicked guests running around in the dark. Give me five minutes."

Most of the guests nodded and sank into their chairs. Ten or twelve ignored him and ran from the room. "Doctors, so terrible at following orders," he said, only loud enough for Riley to hear.

His joke brought her to her senses, and she caught his shirt sleeve as he started to go.

"I have to get to Julia. She must be terrified. I promise we'll lock ourselves in the suite until I hear from you."

Coop hesitated an instant before nodding, but it was long enough for her to read the fear in his eyes. She stayed close to him as they rushed down the crowded hallway to the lobby. He'd been right to tell the seminar attendees to stay put. It had only taken seconds for the hotel to erupt into chaos.

───────

Riley made a beeline for the stairs, not daring to go near the elevators, even if they were operating on backup power. Her room was on the eleventh floor, but she was an experienced hiker and runner, so a few flights of stairs didn't deter her. Even with being in shape, she was winded by the time she reached the sixth floor. Having to fight the panicked crowds jostling past her on their way to the lobby didn't help. She avoided making eye contact with them as she fought her own rising panic.

She swiped her keycard in the reader when she reached it, but the door didn't unlock until the third attempt, making her wonder how guests opened their doors when power was out.

She rushed into the darkened room, calling for Julia, but got no answer. She noticed the open balcony doors and headed that way. Julia was at the railing, taking in the spectacle instead of cowering in a corner, as Riley had imagined.

"There you are," she cried as she ran to her. "What are you doing out here? Get back inside."

Julia ignored her and continued to gaze out over the city. She reached for Riley's hand to pull her closer. "Have you seen this, Mom?'

Riley's simmering anxiety boiled over as she stared at the scene spreading before them. Fires blazed in several parts of the city, throwing up black plumes of smoke that mixed with the falling snow and obscured the cloudy sky. It looked like they'd been transported to a different world. The streets were choked with mangled cars and dazed people milled about aimlessly or clutched their injured loved ones. Riley counted at least ten broken bodies lying in the dirty snow.

Julia coughed from the toxic smoke, and Riley pushed her toward the doors. "Get inside, now," she ordered through her own choking coughs.

Julia obeyed without argument. Riley closed the French doors, checking to make sure they were tight, and ran to dig the evac bag out of her closet. She carried it to the sitting room and rummaged through it until she found duct tape.

Julia watched her with eyes as wide as saucers. "Is this the CME, Mom? Why is it here so early? They said it would just be a minor power outage, but it looks like the world blew up."

In trying to quell her own panic, she'd forgotten how terrified her daughter must be. She put the tape down and went to Julia.

Wrapping her in a protective hug, she said, "I wish I could tell you. Coop went to find out. He'll come tell us when he knows anything."

Julia stepped out of Riley's arms and gave her a weak smile. "I'm glad he's here with us, Mom."

"Me, too, sweetheart." Riley handed her a roll of tape. "We need to tape the windows to keep out the smoke."

Julia took the tape, and Riley showed her how to seal the doors. As she worked, she thought how ridiculous she'd felt packing that evac bag but had done it in memory of Zach. Carrying on his routine of preparing for any emergency made her feel closer to him. Considering the nightmare happening outside their walls, he may have inadvertently saved their lives. She wished she'd prepared better for the solar storm. *How could the scientists have gotten it so wrong?*

Someone pounded on their door just as she tossed the empty tape roll into the garbage. Julia ran to answer it, but Riley called out for her to stop. "Let me get it."

She stood on tiptoes to peer through the peephole and was relieved to see Coop standing in the hallway. She opened the door and hurried to keep up with him as he rushed into the room.

"Bolt and chain that door," he said, without turning to face her. He went to the balcony doors and examined her taping job, then nodded in satisfaction. "Smart to do that. Where'd you get duct tape?"

Riley ignored his question. "What did you find out?"

He glanced at Julia before turning to stare through the taped doors. "My guess is the astronomers are as good at predicting space storms as meteorologists are at predicting hurricanes. No one has a clue what's happening. Internet's down, cell service is down, we only have power because of the hotel generators."

Julia took out her cellphone and tapped Riley's contact picture. Nothing happened. Riley reached for the hotel phone but got no dial tone. A muffled explosion made the floors vibrate. Julia ran into her arms as the emergency lighting flickered for a moment.

"Are you sure we're safe here, Coop?" she asked over the top of Julia's head.

He turned toward them, the concern clear on his usually lighthearted face. "I won't sugarcoat this. Power won't be coming on in a few days. Those fires are from blown transformers, electrical surges, and natural gas explosions. People will get desperate in a hurry. We're safer inside the hotel for now."

Julia sat up and shook her head. "We need to leave like Mom wanted to do. I want to go home."

Riley held her hand. "Coop's right. Even with the fires, it's freezing, and people are panicking. Those streets in front of the hotel are impassable. The rest of the roads are probably the same. We have heat, food and a roof in the hotel. We'll wait here until it's safe to go home."

Coop nodded. "I'd estimate that about half the hotel staff has bailed already. We need to stay. We're doctors. They're going to need us. While we wait, we should round up all the food, water, and emergency supplies we can get our hands on before shelves are picked clean. I'm sure the looting has already started. There won't be anything left by morning."

Julia went to the faucet by the minibar and turned the handle. A weak but steady stream poured into the sink. "Water's still working, and we have the bottled water you brought earlier, so we don't need that."

"It's still pumping in the hotel, but the treatment plant might be down, which means the water is contaminated. It's fine for flushing toilets and showers, but don't drink from the tap. Those four flats of bottled water won't last long. You'll need at least six or seven more to start," Coop said.

Riley picked up the evac bag and held it out to Coop. "This is what Zach would have called a Go Bag. He was kind of a prepper and taught me never to travel without one. I have water purification tablets, basic first aid supplies, high-calorie protein bars, and walkies, among other things."

Coop rummaged through the bag, then put his hands on Riley's cheeks and kissed her. The blood rushed to her face as Julia giggled.

"You never cease to amaze. Wish we had ten more of these. I

need to get back downstairs, but I'll come back as soon as I speak with the manager. Add the contents of the minibar to your Go Bag. I don't think you need to worry about being charged for them now."

Riley walked him to the door. "I need to thank you for stopping me from running off this morning. Julia and I would be stranded on some unfamiliar road in this madness, or worse. We owe you our lives."

When she kissed his cheek, he gave a slight bow and left without a word. She bolted the door behind him and leaned against it with her arms folded. Julia grinned at her. The world was crashing down thirty feet beyond their door, but her daughter still found reason to smile.

"Go ahead, say it."

"You like him," she said in a sing-song voice, then took Riley's hand and led her to the sofa. "I'm glad. You're calmer around Coop, and I'm not as afraid with him here."

"Glad you approve, but it was just a little kiss. Don't make more out of it than it was." She kissed Julia's forehead. "Things could get rough in the next few days, and I'm glad Coop's here, too, but I'm even happier you're with me. I'll do whatever it takes to get us home. You have my word. I miss Emily and Jared, and your grandparents." She sat back and stared at the fire-lit world. "I wish we could get word to them that we're safe. I hate to think of them worrying about us."

"I miss them, too, and I trust you to get us home, Mom. You're tougher than you know."

She remembered her mother saying the same thing before they left for the airport. Everyone else saw a strength in her she didn't feel. If it existed, she needed to figure out how to tap into it before they were forced out into their frightening new world.

Four days earlier, the scariest thing in her life was the idea of boarding a plane. Now, she would have given anything to fly away from the terror raging outside.

Her stomach growled, so she got up and raided the minibar. She handed Julia a candy bar and kept the can of macadamia nuts for herself. She ignored the muffled sounds of mayhem drifting up from the street below as they ate. The saying about "fiddling while Rome burns" came into her mind.

"Might as well enjoy the moment while we can," she said. Julia smiled and gave her a fist bump. *This may be our last chance.*

Riley was trying not to notice that it was eleven o'clock and Coop hadn't returned. Julia had dozed off thirty minutes earlier while watching a video she'd downloaded before the Wi-Fi crashed. Riley helped her to bed, then sat in her room, struggling to organize the thoughts swirling through her brain. Leaving the hotel was out of the question, but how long could they hole up before the food and water ran out? How would they ever make it to Colorado if the entire country was in the same state as DC? Their only hope of reaching home was if the CME was localized to the East coast.

Fixating over a future she couldn't control was only making her feel worse, so she climbed off the bed and sat on the floor to do yoga and meditate. She'd spent the years since Zach's death training herself to live in the moment, but since the CME announcement, all she'd done was obsess about what was coming. Preparing for the disaster had been crucial, but her focus was on getting home, which could take weeks. For her and Julia's sake, she needed to let go and focus on surviving the next twenty-four hours.

She got into position and closed her eyes. As she slowly let out her breath, another more violent muffled explosion rumbled beneath her. The lamp wobbled, and her toiletries clattered on the bathroom counter. When the power cut out, she scrapped the yoga and ran toward Julia's room. Before she reached her door, the lights kicked on, and the rumbling stopped. She fell onto the sofa, crossed her arms over her face, and let the tears come. *This is one nightmare that wouldn't be conquered with yoga.*

Pounding on the door minutes later startled her out of her pity party. She wiped her face and shuffled to the door, dreading this next catastrophe. A bloodstained Coop waited in the hallway and rushed past her as soon as the door opened.

Riley followed him into the living room, frantically peppering him with questions. "Is that your blood? What are your injuries?"

He turned and ran his fingers through his hair. "Not my blood. Elevator's out. Wake Julia. I'm moving you into my first-floor suite."

"Hold on. Don't I get a say? I don't want to give Julia the wrong idea about us. We'll use the stairs."

He put his hands on her shoulders. "Listen to me. It's mayhem down there. I was in the elevator when the power cut out for a second. Scared the hell out of me. You can't be running up and down ten flights of stairs multiple times a day. What if the hotel catches fire? Have you looked outside?"

It was all she needed to hear. She rushed to Julia's room and flipped on the light. Julia groaned and pulled the blanket over her face. "What the hell, Mom?"

"Language. And how are you sleeping with the world exploding thirty feet from your bed?" Riley saw Julia's shoulders shrug under the blanket. "Get up and start packing. We're moving in with Coop on the first floor."

Julia sat up and rubbed her eyes. "What?"

Coop stepped into the doorway. "Hey, wake up, Champ. We need to move you and your mom downstairs before the power goes out for good."

Julia squinted at him. "Did you just call me Champ? And why is there blood on your shirt?"

Coop looked down at his bloody clothes and whispered, "I

should have changed first." Louder to Julia, he said, "I need a nickname for you."

Riley pushed Coop away from the door. "You barged in here like our room was on fire. Now, you're chatting about nicknames? Get up and get dressed, sweetheart," she called to Julia over her shoulder.

"Just trying not to scare her," he said as he backed into the living room. "I have two luggage carts in the hallway. I'll pack the kitchen and living room. You get your bedroom."

It took three harrowing elevator trips and running the gauntlet in the lobby to move their belongings into Coop's suite. Once they finished, Riley was relieved that she wouldn't have to step into those death traps as long as they were in the hotel.

Coop's suite was impressive. It was twice the size of hers and the décor even more upscale.

As Coop led her to what would be her room, she said, "This is more apartment than hotel suite. How many bedrooms?"

"Three. I have a master suite with its own bathroom. The two smaller bedrooms share the other bathroom, so there's plenty of room for all of us. It even has a patio."

She dropped the armful of bedding she'd taken from her suite onto her bed and turned to face him. "I'm sorry for arguing when you suggested we move in with you. It was a knee-jerk reaction from only knowing you a few days, but I guess the old rules no longer apply. You were right. I appreciate you taking us in."

He'd showered and smelled like lemons, so she didn't mind when he pulled her into his arms. "I hated the idea of you and Julia trapped up there if the worst happened, and if I'm honest, I wanted you closer." He brushed a curl of hair from her forehead and gave her a tender kiss. "But don't worry, I'll respect your boundaries and follow your lead."

"I appreciate that, too." She stepped out of his arms and leaned against the dresser. "What I need now is sleep, but first, you want to explain that bloody shirt from earlier?"

"When I saw the injured people stumbling in or being carried from the street, I grabbed any doctors I could find and set up a basic triage center in the ballroom. Patients have been streaming in nonstop. Some paramedics got word of the clinic and started bringing more patients. They located nurses to help us patch up the injured enough to transport them to any area hospitals still operating. It's only emergency field treatment, but it's better than nothing. Will you join us in the morning? It will mean leaving Julia on her own."

"I'd be willing if she's comfortable with it. I'll just be down the hall, and we have the walkies. I'll talk to her in the morning."

He kissed her again before heading for the front door. "I'm going to check on the clinic, then try to catch some sleep myself. See you bright and early."

CHAPTER FIVE

IT TOOK a few seconds to figure out what had happened to her hotel room when Julia opened her eyes. When she saw her mom sitting on the edge of the bed watching her, memories of their crazy midnight move to Coop's suite came rushing back.

"What time is it?" she asked in a hoarse whisper.

"Earlier than I want to be awake. It's six. I'm sorry to wake you, but we need to talk."

"If it's about you and Coop, I'm cool with it, Mom."

"Good to know, but it's not that. Coop and some of the other doctors have set up a clinic in the ballroom. They need me to help treat patients." She handed her a walkie. "I'll be close, and we'll try to communicate with these. If the walkies don't work. I'll check on you as often as I can." She hesitated before saying, "If you're uncomfortable with this and don't want me to go, I won't. It's your choice."

Julie toyed with the walkie. "Go, Mom. I'll be bored out of my mind, but I'm not scared. I'll find you if the walkies don't work or if there's an emergency."

"No, you won't. You can't leave this room unless it catches on fire, and then I want you to go to the patio."

"There's a patio? Nice. The walkies will work. The room won't catch on fire. You can chill, Mom."

"I'll do my best. Thank you for being so brave." Her mom kissed her forehead. "Turn your walkie to channel three. I'll call you on it when I get to the ballroom. If you don't answer, I'll be back in two minutes. Then you can go back to sleep for as long as you want. There's food for breakfast on the table."

———————

Riley's gut churned as she closed the door and headed for the ballroom. Leaving Julia alone was the last thing she wanted to do, but people could die if she didn't help in the clinic. It would have been selfish of her to stay in the room holding Julia's hand all day.

The lobby was deserted. It was eerie after the pandemonium of the previous night, but Riley preferred it. It meant the clinic might not be so chaotic. She stopped before entering the ballroom to call Julia.

She pushed the talk button and said, "Julia, it's Mom. Can you hear me?"

There was a moment of silence before Julia's voice came through clearly. "This is Warrior Princess responding. You're coming through five-by-five, Red Queen. Are you reading me?"

Riley snickered, despite her nerves. "Check. Lima/Charlie, Warrior Princess. See you in ninety. Love you. Red Queen out."

"Warrior Princess out."

She hooked the walkie on her belt loop and stepped into the ballroom. Her smile faded at the scene that greeted her. It was like something out of a World War I film. Mangled and bleeding bodies covered tables and every inch of floor space. She ducked to miss a paramedic who rushed past, carrying the limp body of a woman over his shoulder. All they needed was muddy foxholes to complete the picture.

She tried to take a step forward, but her feet wouldn't budge.

She tried again but could only stand in the chaos, frozen in fear. Someone tapped her shoulder and she flinched.

"Take a breath, Riley," she heard the soothing voice of a doctor named Nabhitha say. They'd met the first day of the conference and had taken an instant liking to each other. "You can do this. It's just a bit more disorganized than your operating theater back home."

Riley turned and hugged her. "No, it's impossibly more disorganized than my operating theater back home, but thank you. I'm glad you stayed. It's comforting to see a familiar face."

"Of course, I stayed. Where would I go?" After unwinding herself from Riley's arms, she placed a hand on the small of her back and gently nudged her toward Coop. "Time to go, doctor. You have work to do."

Riley took a breath and crossed to where Coop was treating a middle-aged man with a gaping abdominal wound.

While pulling on surgical gloves, he said, "Glad to see you made it, Riley. I was beginning to worry you'd bailed on me. Nabhitha, there's a clipboard by the door with a list of doctors who might still be in the hotel. Would you mind hunting them down? Bring anyone willing. Their room numbers are on the list."

Nabhitha pressed her palms together and gave a slight bow, then rushed off to retrieve the list. Riley scanned the room, picturing herself prepping for surgery in her OR back home. She was a skilled surgeon, capable of operating in any situation. She blocked out the background noise and focused on the task at hand.

Coop glanced between Riley and his patient. "Looking a little pale, Dr. Poole. You up to this?"

She squared her shoulders and nodded. "Put me to work, boss."

He gave a half-grin and went back to work on his patient. "Scrub up in the ballroom kitchen through that door to the left."

Riley followed his gaze and saw a doctor she'd met the day before coming out with a sterile cloth draped over her hands. She was an allergist, and Riley wondered how much help she'd be as a surgeon.

"Nurses are running triage in the south corner under the window," Coop continued. "They'll point you in the right direction. And please ask them not to admit any more patients. I hate to turn people away, but they're going to have to find somewhere else to go until we get ahead of this."

"Got it," she said, trying to sound far more confident than she felt.

After scrubbing, she ignored the groans and pleas from people scattered across the floor as she made her way to the triage station. She didn't envy the nurses having to decide which patients were top priority. They all looked equally severe to Riley.

"I'm Dr. Poole," she said when she reached the closest nurse. "Orthopedic surgeon. I'm ready for the next patient."

The nurse knelt on the floor, trying to stop the bleeding on a boy with a large laceration on his right thigh.

The nurse glanced up and wiped her forehead with the back of her sleeve. "Thank God. I'm Haley. This fine, ten-year-old young man is Jamaal. I just gave him morphine, so he's feeling fine. Aren't you, Jamaal?"

The boy nodded and gave Riley a goofy grin.

"There may be a nick on his femoral artery. He's lost a lot of blood, but the bleeding is slowing. Mind taking a look?"

Haley grabbed a box of gloves from the floor next to her and held it out to Riley. She put the gloves on and examined Jamaal's wound.

"The femoral artery looks intact. The bleeding is smaller vessels from the tissue damage. The femur looks intact. What I wouldn't give for an x-ray, though. Do we have sterile suture kits?" When Haley nodded, she said, "I'll close him up and move on to the next."

"Jamaal's not our most critical case. If he isn't in danger of bleeding out, that young woman on the table has a neck injury. She's next."

"She needs a neurosurgeon. Is Dr. Warren here?"

Haley pressed another dressing onto Jamaal's thigh. "I don't know who that is, but as far as I know, you're the only available surgeon."

Riley hadn't treated a cervical spine patient in years and wasn't sure what she could do for the woman, but knew there wouldn't be time to wait. "I'll need someone to assist. Where do you normally work, Haley?"

"Neurosurgery, as it so happens."

"First miracle of the day. Please, find someone to take over with Jamaal. You're coming with me."

Riley ran to Coop's table and explained about the neck patient. "Maybe Nabhitha will find Dr. Warren."

"Warren's gone. I heard he bolted for his private jet seconds after the insanity started. Imagine his surprise when the pilot couldn't get that jet off the ground. That's if he made it to the airstrip."

"Guess I'm neuro for the day. How'd your abdominal patient do?"

"Didn't make it. Organ damage was too extensive. He was the third I've lost today. This is tarnishing my perfect record."

"Nowhere to go but up, then."

Julia ran out of ways to entertain herself two hours after her mom left. She'd watched all the videos downloaded onto her iPad, and there were no good books to read. She tried to study, but her assignments seemed pointless. All she could think about was her family and friends back home and wonder if they were alive. She hated not being able to call them.

Someone pounded on the door as she got up to see if her mom had any games on her phone. She'd promised she wouldn't let anyone in but her or Coop, but she didn't say she wouldn't look through the peephole. She ran to the door and stood on tiptoes to see who it was. She kind of recognized the guy standing there but couldn't remember where she'd seen him.

"Who is it?" she called through the door.

"My name is Quinten. I'm here for Julia. Dr. Cooper sent me."

She only hesitated for half a second before opening the door. If the guy knew her name and room number and Coop's name, he must be legit. He stepped inside and flashed the most gorgeous smile she'd ever seen. He was tall with deep chocolate eyes and long brown hair. His arms were so ripped that Julia had to fight the urge to reach out and squeeze them.

"Hi, I'm Julia," she said.

Quinten carried a cardboard box that had a wine label printed on the side, and she wondered what he was bringing her.

"Hey, Julia. This is heavy. Where should I put it?"

"On the table." She ran ahead of him to make room for the box. "What's in it?"

"Dr. Cooper asked me to bring you some games, books, and puzzles from hotel storage. I wasn't sure what you like, but I did my best."

She stood there, grinning like an idiot while he unpacked the box. "Thanks, Quinten. Why do you look familiar?"

"I work in the hotel restaurant, but Dr. Cooper saw me helping in the medical clinic. He asked me to find out if you'd like some company?"

She glanced at him when he stopped unpacking the box. "So much. I'm going out of my mind locked up here alone."

"Excellent. I'll be right back."

Julia knew Quinten would never look twice at someone her

age, but that didn't stop her from admiring his firm behind while he walked to the door.

She finished unpacking the box and was happy to see he'd thrown in some snacks. She put them with the rest of the food and wondered who he was bringing for her to hang with. He came back five minutes later with a dark-haired girl who looked about twelve. She was thin, with doe-like eyes and pale skin. Julia thought she seemed fragile. Quinten introduced her as Hannah. She gave a quick bow of her head, looking like all she wanted was to crawl into a hole.

Julia smiled to encourage her. "Hi, Hannah. Are your parents doctors, too?"

"No," was all she said.

Julia looked to Quinten for help. "Her parents are missing," he whispered to Julia before turning to Hannah. "The hotel manager says you can stay here, and we'll take care of you until we find your parents. Maybe you can hang out with Julia."

"I'd love that," Julia said. "Coop won't care, and my mom will say it's okay. We have lots of room."

Hannah's eyes brightened as she looked around the room. "I can stay here?"

"Sure. Are you hungry? We have lots of food."

Hannah nodded and followed Julia to the kitchen.

"See you later," Quinten said, and practically ran from the room.

Julia let Hannah choose the food she wanted, then led her to the sofa. They ate for five minutes in silence until Julia said, "Do you mind telling me about your parents?"

"We're moving here from California. My parents left yesterday before the CME alert to go house hunting and never came back. I was with a babysitter they hired, but she said she was going to find out what was happening and left me alone." She covered her face and cried into her hands. Julia put an arm around her shoulders, not sure what else to do. "Can we go leave a note in my room, so they'll know I'm here if they come back?"

Julia shook her head. "I'm not allowed to leave the room, but as soon as Coop or my mom comes back, we'll go."

———

As patients came one after another, Riley lost track of numbers and injuries, but she didn't forget to keep tabs on Julia. She enlisted Quinten to check on her every two hours. He reported each time that she was fine and bored, which was what Riley hoped to hear.

She had vague memories of eating beef jerky, crackers and juice periodically, but beyond that, time passed in a mind-numbing blur. She almost passed out when someone placed a little girl with a partially crushed skull on her table and decided it was time to call it quits. She found another doctor to take the patient before curling up in an empty three-foot space near a wall. The next thing she knew, Coop was shaking her awake.

She sat up and rubbed her shoulders. "What time is it?"

Coop lowered himself to the floor with a groan and leaned against the wall. "Two in the morning. I just want you to know that you gave Julia and me a scare. I went to the suite looking for you, and when Julia said she hadn't seen you, I came back here in case I'd missed you. One of the orderlies pointed you out, buried under the pile of coats. I walked right past you the first time."

"I was so exhausted that this was as far as I got. Did you say Julia's still awake?"

"Yes. She's waiting up for you, and there's another surprise."

She could tell from his tone that she wasn't going to like it. "I'm not in the mood for surprises. What is it?"

He stood and extended his hand without answering. "I'll walk you to the suite. I don't want you collapsing in some random hallway where I'll never find you."

She accepted his hand and grimaced when she got to her feet. Every inch of her body ached. "Feels like my residency days."

As they wound their way to the door, she noticed that other doctors had taken their places at the tables. Most of the nurses had been replaced, too. Some of the others from earlier were scattered around the room in a dead sleep. She considered waking them to offer the sofas in Coop's suite but decided to leave them in peace.

Julia nearly bowled her over as soon as she came through the door. "You scared me to death, Mom. Where were you?"

Riley told her about the pile of coats. "I only planned to close my eyes for a minute. That was at midnight, but I'm here now. Sorry I left you alone for so long. Why aren't you in bed?"

Julia glanced at Coop. "I wasn't alone. Coop asked Quinten to bring someone here who needed our help."

Riley stared at Coop and said, "He did? Who?"

A girl with dark braids peeked her head out of Julia's bedroom. Julia waved for her to join them.

"Mom, this is Hannah. She's going to stay with us until her parents come back for her."

Hannah slowly inched closer. "Is that okay?"

Coop leaned closer and whispered, "Her parents are missing. She's alone."

Riley gave the poor, forlorn girl a smile. "Of course you can stay, Hannah. We'll make up the sofa bed for you."

"She's going to sleep with me," Julia said. "My bed's huge. There's room for both of us."

Riley wasn't comfortable with that arrangement but was too exhausted to argue and didn't want to hurt Hannah's feelings. "That's fine. You two should get to bed. I won't leave until you're awake in the morning, so I can say goodbye."

Julia led Hannah back to their room before going to brush her teeth.

Coop dropped next to Riley on the sofa. "What were you

thinking, letting Quinten bring a stranger into our suite? And are you ready to be responsible for other people's kids? I'm having a hard enough time keeping track of my own."

"Calm down, Riley. The hotel manager told me the poor thing spent the night alone in her room last night. She must have been terrified."

Riley got up and started pacing. "That's sad, but don't tell me to calm down. You should have cleared it with me. I'm Julia's parent, not you."

Coop got up and put his arms around her waist. "I didn't want to bother you, and there wasn't much time to think. But you're right, I was out of line. Hannah doesn't look too threatening, and Julia's safe, but I *am* sorry, Riley. Can you forgive me?" He moved his hands to her shoulders and massaged her muscles. "You're one big knot. Let me give you a back rub."

Julia came out of the bathroom before she could answer, and Coop lowered his hands.

"All set for bed?" Riley asked her. "I'll be there to tuck you in soon."

Coop dropped onto the sofa instead of going to his room, but Riley was glad despite the fact she was annoyed with him. She went and said a quick goodnight to Julia and Hannah, then hurried back to him.

"That offer for a back rub still good?"

In answer, he stood and motioned for her to follow him to her bedroom. She sat on the end of the bed and turned so he could reach her shoulders. The touch of his strong hands did more than relax her shoulders. He massaged her for ten minutes before moving her hair out of the way to kiss her neck. Her breath quickened, and she turned to face him.

They kissed tentatively at first, but their passion escalated rapidly. Riley couldn't have imagined thirty minutes earlier that she'd have the strength to do more than collapse into bed alone.

When Coop laid back and pulled her with him, she came to her senses and sat up.

"As much as I want this, the timing couldn't be worse. We both need to sleep. I'm too exhausted to think clearly and Julia could walk in."

Coop turned onto his back and put his hands behind his head. "We're just kissing, Riley, unless you had more in mind."

Riley crossed her arms and looked away. "I did. That's the problem. When and if anything happens between us, I don't want it to be because we're in the middle of Armageddon."

Coop climbed off the bed and stared down at her. "That's not what this was, but fine. You're the boss. Let me know when you're ready. See you tomorrow."

He gave her a quick kiss and was gone before she could get another word out. She considered going after him but changed her mind, not knowing if he was mad or honestly okay with waiting?

His odd behavior from the night they met flashed into her mind. *Maybe it's just his way,* she thought and rubbed her face, not sure it was behavior she cared to get used to. She changed into her nightgown and climbed into bed after she was once more left pondering what kind of man Dr. Neal Xavier Cooper III was.

CHAPTER SIX

JULIA WENT to the patio while Hannah was in the bathroom the next morning. The snow had stopped, and the sun was out, but the sky was gray from smoke rising over burned-out parts of the city. It was depressing, and tears stung at her eyes. The beautiful, shining city from a few days ago was gone, maybe forever.

She wiped her tears and checked her phone to see what time it was. Nine-thirty. Later than she thought. She wondered if her mom had left without saying goodbye after all. She went inside and inched her mom's bedroom door open and was relieved to hear her soft breathing. She never slept that late, but she'd had a long day and late night. Julia quietly closed the door and went to the kitchen to fix cereal for herself and Hannah with the last of the milk. They'd have to find milk in those little boxes that didn't have to be refrigerated. Julia thought that kind of milk tasted disgusting, but she'd have to get used to it.

Coop came through the front door and set the box he carried on the table. "Good morning, Hannah. Any word from your parents?" He frowned when Hannah shook her head. "Today will be the day," he said and glanced at Julia. "Is your mom up yet?"

Julia peeked over the rim of the box and said, "Still snoring away. What's in there?"

"Food and drinks. I went out scavenging an hour ago and found this. It's not much." He reached into the box and pulled out a package of donuts. "These are for you. Last ones in DC, I'd bet, so you'd better savor them."

Julia took a glazed donut and bit off a third of it before handing the box to Hannah.

Coop shook his head. "So much for savoring."

"What's with all the noise?" her mom asked as she shuffled toward them.

She was wearing the one ratty robe she'd brought, and her hair looked like a lion's mane.

Julia snorted and blew crumbs all over the table.

Her mom took a donut and shoved the whole thing into her mouth. With her mouth full of food, she said, "What are you still doing here, Coop? Shouldn't you be in the clinic?"

"I went on a scavenger hunt, but I'm heading there next." He gestured at the box. "Please, help yourself to the donuts."

She swallowed hard and reached into the box for another donut. "Any milk or coffee?"

Julia watched her mom and wondered what was wrong with her. She never let men see her looking so raggedy, especially not ones she liked.

"Milk's all gone unless Coop found some," Julia said.

"If you don't have coffee here, there's none to be found in the world." He kissed Riley's cheek. "Still planning to work at the clinic today?" She bit her donut and nodded. "Meet you there, then. See you later, *Champ*," he said to Julia and laughed his way to the door.

Riley rolled her eyes and turned to Julia. "Will you be okay here with me at the clinic all day?"

"I have Hannah to keep me company this time, and I did fine yesterday until you got lost under that pile of coats."

Riley kissed her forehead. "I'm going to get dressed before I devour the rest of the donuts."

Hannah watched her go and swallowed her bite of donut. "Coop's not your dad, is he?"

"No, we just met him at the medical conference. My dad died over three years ago."

Hannah stopped mid-chew. "He died? How?"

"He was a pilot and got shot down in Afghanistan."

She watched her for several seconds. "How did it feel? What was it like when you found out?"

Julia wasn't sure how to answer. It was the worst day of her life, and she couldn't imagine losing both parents at once, but she couldn't tell Hannah that. "I miss him every day, but I can think about him now without it hurting. I only remember the happy times, but at first, I thought I'd be sad forever."

Hannah lowered her eyes and picked at the donut crumbs on her napkin. "I will be sad forever if my parents are dead."

"Don't say that. It's just taking them a long time to get back because the roads are so bad. I bet they show up by dinnertime." Julia could tell Hannah didn't believe her, but she wanted to keep her spirits up. "I read about this secret underground bunker for government leaders. Maybe your parents went there and are just waiting for the right time to come for you."

Hannah perked up and watched Julia with bright eyes. "Is that true? My parents could be there?"

Julia was sure Hannah's parents were dead but would never say that to her. "Sure, why not? He works for a congressman, doesn't he?" Hannah nodded. "See, they're probably safe and cozy right now." To change the subject, she said, "Coop and my mom just met, but they like each other. I think it was love at first sight."

"That's nice for your mom. Too bad all this happened to ruin it."

"It's not ruined. Even in all this craziness, Mom's the happiest

I've seen her since Dad died. We're all lucky to have him, especially since he's letting us stay in his suite."

She watched Hannah finish her donut. She had chocolate icing on the sides of her mouth and seemed younger than twelve.

"It stinks that the babysitter ran out on you. What a jerk. We'd never abandon you."

"I was so scared by myself in the room all night. I didn't leave the room until morning when I was hungry and wanted to find out what to do. Dr. Cooper saw me and asked Quinten to bring me here. Can you ask your mom if we can see if my parents came back before she leaves? They won't know where I am."

"Sure, and I need an excuse to get out of this room for a minute. We'll go as soon as we're dressed."

Riley was stepping out of the shower when a deafening explosion shook the walls and the lights went dark. When two more explosions followed, she threw on her robe and ran to the living room. She shined her phone flashlight toward the girls, and they stared back, wide-eyed.

"Are you two all right?"

Julia moved beside her, and Riley put an arm around her shoulders. "What was that, Mom?"

"Nothing good," Coop said, as he came in the door.

Riley opened the patio curtains to let in the dull light. "How did you get in with your key if the power's out?"

"The card readers are battery-powered in case of power loss, fortunately."

"Good to know," Riley said. "Why are you back from the clinic?"

"To check on all of you. The ballroom was empty. I saw Nabhitha in the lobby. She said they finished with the last patient at six and closed up shop. She stayed in case anyone showed up but was leaving as I got there. I was on my way to get an update from the manager when the explosions happened. My gut's telling me the power's gone for good. If you're all safe, I'm going to see if the manager knows what happened."

Riley watched him go before turning to the girls. "You two bundle up while I get dressed. It's going to get cold inside in a hurry."

"I left my coat in my room," Hannah said.

Julia jumped up and headed for her room. "I'll take her to get it. We can get the rest of her clothes, too."

"You two are not going to go running around the dark hotel by yourselves. I'll take the message to your room and bring your belongings back with me. Write the note while I get dressed. What's your room number?"

"Thank you, Dr. Poole," Hannah said. "It's 923."

Ninth floor. Of course it is, Riley thought. "Since you're going to be a member of our family for a while, please call me Riley."

Hannah nodded as Riley went to her room and put leggings on under her jeans before layering a t-shirt and long-sleeved pullover under her heaviest sweater. Her bedroom was still warm, and the bulky clothing made her sweat. She pulled off the sweater and tied it around her waist, then put on a pair of wool socks.

She grabbed a walkie and gave Julia the usual warning about bolting the door before walking into the pitch-black hallway. She turned on her phone flashlight and took a breath to summon her courage. She was on a mission for that poor orphan girl who had spent a night alone in the hotel. If she was brave enough to do that, Riley could leave a note for her parents and retrieve her belongings.

The lobby was deserted and already growing colder, but at least gray light filtered in through the revolving door and front windows. She turned off her phone light to conserve the battery and considered going to find Coop to go with her to Hannah's room but didn't want to appear pathetic. She crossed to the stairs and flashed her light up the first flight. *This is ridiculous,* she told herself. *There are no monsters. It's just a stairwell.*

After making it to the room and leaving the note that she doubted Hannah's parents would ever see, she packed Hannah's clothes and other belongings. Since their suite was on the far end from the stairs she'd used going up, she descended the opposite stairway. When she rounded the corner of the second-floor landing, her foot bumped into a soft heap on the floor near the wall. She jumped back and dropped her phone, which clattered to the bottom of the stairs, leaving her in total darkness. The heap let out a low groan.

"Is someone there?" she whispered.

Another groan answered her. Switching into doctor mode, she knelt and ran her hands over the body to make an assessment.

"I'm Dr. Poole. Can you speak? Can you tell me what happened?"

"Riley?" the heap croaked.

She stopped the exam when her hands touched something sticky in his hair above his eye. "Coop? Don't move. Your head is bleeding."

She stripped off her three layers of tops and pressed her t-shirt to Coop's head. "Can you put pressure on this?"

"Yes," he said weakly.

She put her long-sleeved t-shirt back on and felt for more injuries. "Did you fall in the dark?"

It took several seconds for him to answer. "I raided the vending machines on the third floor and was coming to look for you when three men rushed me. They took my flashlight and box of food, then pushed me down the stairs. I think I recognized two of them as hotel staff, but it happened so fast. I'm not sure."

"We'll worry about who did this later. I have to leave you alone for a minute while I get my phone and whatever medical supplies I can scrounge from the ballroom." She covered him with her sweater. "I'll only be gone a minute. Don't move."

She raced down the stairs, grabbed her phone, and blinked in the daylight when she exited the stairwell. She searched the vacant reception desk and staff room for supplies, but all she found was a cigarette lighter, a small box of Band-Aids, and a travel sewing kit. She tossed them in a baggie and rushed to the ballroom. She passed the pool on her way and spotted what looked like a pack of glow-sticks sitting on a lounge chair. She went into the pool area and stuffed them into her pocket before taking the few towels left on the racks.

Once at the ballroom, she stopped in despair to see the shelves had been picked clean. She picked up the few unopened packets of gauze she found on the floor before heading back to the stairs. She lit a glow-stick while she made her way to Coop.

He was sitting against the wall, still pressing her t-shirt to his forehead. "I told you not to move," she scolded as she peeled the shirt from his wound.

"My neck and back aren't injured. I rolled into a ball as I fell, but my head hit the last step."

She knelt in front of him and held her phone close to his face to check his eyes. "Pupils are equal and reactive, so no concussion yet. That cut needs stitches. Can you make it to your suite?"

He gripped her wrist. "Riley, listen first." He closed his eyes and took a few breaths before continuing. "The hotel manager said an engineer told him the natural gas pipelines beneath the city have all been destroyed. That's what those rumbling explosions were before the hotel went dark. And the massive transformers that process the city's energy are all blown. The city's power isn't coming back. Not now, maybe not ever."

Riley switched out her t-shirt for one of the pool towels and ordered him to keep it pressed on his cut, then held out her hand. "My instincts have been telling me that, but I've tried to convince myself the lights would come back any minute. I'll freak out about it after I've stitched your head. Let's get you to your feet."

He took her hand, and after helping him up, she waited for him to get his balance before guiding him to the steps.

"Why would anyone do this to you? I get stealing your stuff, but why push you down the stairs?"

Coop swayed and grabbed onto Riley. "Maybe so I wouldn't follow or identify them. They were probably hoping they killed me."

"Over a flashlight and a box of food? People can't be that desperate already."

"I got the impression these weren't fine, upstanding citizens. People like them take advantage of any opportunity to get what they want, and hunger is a powerful motivator."

Riley was quiet for the rest of the walk to Coop's suite. She helped him to the sofa once they were inside, and the girls rushed them, asking a thousand questions at once.

Riley put her hands up to quiet them. "We'll explain after I've stitched his cut. Julia, please bring me that backpack next to the couch."

When Julia handed it to her, she took out a suture kit and Lidocaine to numb Coop's skin. She sterilized the wound with alcohol and sterile water before working quickly to suture the laceration before he lost more blood. She handed him ibuprofen and a bottle of water when she finished. He swallowed the tablets but immediately vomited them back up into a beautiful crystal bowl from the coffee table.

"Lovely," she said, while she rinsed it in the sink. "That bowl just became a little less priceless."

"Take me to my bed," he mumbled. Riley helped him down the hallway and got him settled. She sat on the edge of his bed, and when he tried to sit up, she put her hands on his shoulders, pinning him to the mattress. "With the city going dark, we need to get out of here by tomorrow morning."

"We'll discuss that later. I'll be right back with pain killers, antibiotics, and a saline drip."

Riley watched him while she started his IV and gave him the meds, trying to block out what he'd said about getting out of the city. He was in no shape to go anywhere, and she wasn't up to being in charge of him and two teenage girls. Conditions were deteriorating rapidly, but she still felt safest in the hotel, even without electricity.

She dropped into the recliner in the corner of his room. "I'll stay to monitor you. Try to sleep." *I predict an argument in my future,* she thought as she leaned back and closed her eyes.

She woke two hours later to Coop calling her name. She got up and opened the blinds. "You look chipper," she said when she saw him sitting up against the headboard.

"My headache is down to a dull roar, so that's a positive sign."

He flinched when she shined her penlight on his pupils. "I'm thrilled you're feeling better, but it could take a few days for a brain bleed or concussion to show up after the initial injury."

He gently pushed her hand down to get the light out of his eyes. "I'm a doctor, too, remember? I don't have a brain bleed. I'm too hardheaded for that. You and I need to find a truck today and fill it with as many supplies as we can scavenge before there's none to be found."

He swung his legs over the edge of the bed, but Riley leaned over him and said, "You're not getting out of that bed. You need to rest today. We'll go at first light."

"I need to pee if I have your permission. Remove the IV unless you want to join me in the john and hold the bag."

"You wouldn't be the first male patient I've had to help to the bathroom, but we should leave the IV in until we're sure you can keep food and liquids down."

In answer, he ripped the IV out. Blood immediately spurted from the open vein. He pulled tissues from the box on the nightstand and pressed them onto the opening.

She put her hands on her hips and glared. "You are the most impetuous person I've ever met. You could have warned me to have gauze ready."

Blood soaked the tissues in seconds, so he grabbed more and looked up at her sheepishly. "Do you have gauze and tape?"

She sucked her lips in to keep from laughing as she reached for the gauze. He was a contrite little patient while she taped him and helped him to the bathroom.

She stopped just outside the doorway and crossed her arms. "Sure you can manage in there by yourself?"

He grinned and closed the door. Riley shook her head and went to clean the blood off his sheets. She poured alcohol on a hand towel and scrubbed hard at the stains.

"Toilet won't flush," Coop called through the door. "Water pressure's gone. It was just a matter of time." He opened the bathroom door and showed her the trickle of water coming from the sink faucet. "Our situation just deteriorated by magnitudes. The tap water may not have been safe to drink, but at least we had it for the toilets and washing. Acquiring drinking water just rocketed to the top of our priority list. How much do we have left?"

"About a fourth of what we started with, so not nearly enough."

"The snow is too dirty to drink, but we can melt it for other uses. Grab me a pair of jeans and a sweater from the dresser, please. Have the girls fill every container we have with snow." When she saluted, he pulled her close and gave her a long kiss. "I'm proud of you. I know this isn't easy with your...issues. I like this new *take charge* Riley."

"I don't have the luxury of cowering in a corner if we want to survive. Maybe we've discovered the cure for PTSD: facing the end of the world. You're all depending on me. I can't afford to let you down."

"I gladly place my life in your capable hands."

She handed him his clothes from the dresser and said, "I'm not comfortable leaving the girls here alone while we're gone, but we can't take them with us. What if something happens to us? Or them?"

"We'll ask one of the other doctors or Quinten to check in on them. They'll be fine. Julia is the Warrior Princess, after all."

Satisfied with his idea, she gave him a quick kiss, then left him to dress.

Riley followed Coop into the hallway and waited for the sound of the bolt before proceeding in darkness toward the lobby. She switched on the flashlight and patted her pocket for her phone, which still had a small charge left. The backup chargers were all dead, so they'd have to rely solely on alkaline batteries and solar power. She was glad she'd remembered to put the other flashlights on the patio to charge before they left.

After hunting down her rental in the corner of a dank valet parking basement, she held her breath and pressed the ignition button. When the engine hummed to life, she and Coop sighed in relief.

"The circuits must have been protected from the CME by the garage structure," Coop said, as he climbed in and buckled his seatbelt. Let's just hope we can get out of here."

As Riley wound through the garage to the surface, she hoped the streets would be clear enough of debris and cars to navigate. She exited the garage and frowned at the sight of the one-way street blocked with mangled vehicles in the direction they needed to go.

"The other way is clear. Turn left," Coop said. "It's not like you'll get a ticket for driving the wrong way."

Riley made sure no one was coming before turning. She needn't have bothered. The only cars on the roads were twisted wrecks.

Reminding herself to breathe, she said, "I hope you know your way around. I'm useless without GPS."

Coop pulled a city map out of his pocket. "We'll have to do this old-school, as Julia calls it," he said and laughed as he unfolded the map. "I'm pretty familiar with the city and I have a freakish sense of direction. It's my superpower. It'll be easier to navigate if we get out of downtown."

"No argument from me," she said, eager to flee the shattered remains of the once glorious capital city.

Coop called out directions to her in an imitated GPS voice. She appreciated his attempt to distract her from the sight of decomposing corpses and burned-out buildings as they made their way to the interstate.

He directed her to the I-66 on-ramp. "We should be able to find most of what we need at an outdoor store just outside the city. If it hasn't been looted. There's a grocery store in the same shopping center."

Riley merged onto the interstate but was forced to slam on the brakes when they rounded the first curve. The destruction that met them was like a scene from *The Walking Dead*. Human debris was scattered around demolished cars and overturned buses. A car-seat hung from an open door, suspended by the seatbelt. Gratefully, it was empty. In the distance, she saw a commercial jet shattered into pieces and resting where the Iwo Jima monument should have been.

She shoved the gear into park and covered her face with her hands. "Still think it's a good idea to leave the hotel?" she whispered.

"This proves we need to get out of the city." Coop studied the map for a few seconds, then said, "Trade places. I'll drive."

She was about to object, concerned about him driving with his head injury, but she preferred to navigate rather than be forced to stare at the disaster stretching before them. He got out and ran to the driver's side while she climbed over the center console to avoid exiting the car. Coop put the gear in drive and made a U-turn to travel down the ramp.

He put his hand on her arm. "Want to go back to the hotel? Don't be ashamed if you do. Even I'm overwhelmed."

Riley was tempted to shout, "Yes!" but hesitated before answering. They'd been sheltered in the cocoon of the hotel and had only witnessed the devastation from a distance. She'd pictured their outing as an adventurous scavenger hunt, but after getting a glimpse of their terrifying new world, she wanted to run back to the girls and the security of the hotel walls.

She had to learn to function in this new existence sooner or later, so she swallowed her panic and raised her chin. "I can do this, but what's the point of going on? If all the roads are like this, we won't get far."

"Surface streets shouldn't be as congested. Let's give those a shot."

Coop wove the car along the surface streets like a professional driver. When they passed the occasional moving vehicle, he flashed the lights to get the driver to slow so he could ask what to expect up ahead. Most stopped, but a few ignored them and raced past. Riley didn't blame them. It took two and a half hours to travel twenty miles, and Riley estimated that they'd have just enough gas to get back if they didn't run into trouble.

She didn't relax her white-knuckle grip on the armrest until Coop pulled into a parking lot and turned off the engine. The outdoor store Coop had wanted to check out first had burned down. They'd passed countless stores after that, but most had their windows smashed or doors hanging by the hinges. Two others weren't damaged, but the shelves were empty.

Riley had given up hope by the time Coop spotted the sign for another outdoor store. If it was cleaned out, too, they were in trouble.

He rubbed the stubble on his chin. "The entrance doors are closed and intact, so that's a promising sign."

"Worth a try," she said as she unhooked her seatbelt.

She clung to Coop's hand as they slowly made their way past the now familiar crashed cars and dead bodies littering the ground on the way to the entrance. "I'm afraid of what we'll find inside."

"At least it won't be zombies," Coop said, and laughed.

She tried to smile but couldn't manage it. "Silver lining," was all she said.

Coop cupped his hands around his eyes and peered through the glass. "Looks untouched. We're in luck."

"Why do you think this store hasn't been looted? Did people around here know something we don't?"

As the words left her mouth, a gust of wind blew a store flier out of a garbage can near the door and dropped it at Coop's feet. He picked it up and read, then turned it for her to see. It was an announcement of the store's grand opening coming in three weeks.

He stepped back and pointed to a banner above the door. "My guess is people think the store hasn't been stocked yet."

Riley looked at the banner. "Hope you're right."

He shook the doors to see if they were open. "Not as lucky. We're going to have to smash our way in."

Riley stopped him as he searched for something to break the glass. "Can't you pick the lock? I don't want us to be like those looters you see on TV during a blackout."

He raised his eyebrows as he stared at her. "How exactly did you think we were going to get in? Did you think a salesclerk would be waiting for us with open arms?"

"I honestly didn't think about it."

"We have no choice, Riley. This is about our survival. Days of a leisurely outing to the mall are gone."

She put her hands on her hips. "Give me some credit. I just hoped the doors would be unlocked."

"And how were you planning to pay?" She lifted her pant leg to reveal a canvas money pouch strapped to her calf. "What is that?"

"I always carry cash for emergencies. I have $5000."

"You've been carrying 5K around all this time? Now who's insane?"

"I haven't been carrying it in the hotel. I had most of it hidden in a pair of socks in my drawer. I only brought $1000."

"That money is worthless. Nobody cares about pieces of paper when they're starving."

"It won't be worthless when power is restored. And what is it to you if I leave cash to pay for the things we take?"

Coop kissed the end of her nose. "Fair enough. No one but you would think to pay for looting. Each day with you is a revelation." He brushed the snow off a bent metal car part near the curb and picked it up.

"Here we go, our first criminal act."

Riley put her hands over her ears while he smashed the glass, then carefully reached in to unlock the door.

"I've always wanted to do that."

They turned on their flashlights and gingerly picked their way over the broken glass. Riley shined her beam over the shelves and was thrilled to see they'd finally caught a break. The store had everything they'd need, including kerosene heaters and the fuel to fill them. They took out their lists and began collecting the items. When they finished, she hid her wad of cash under the register, then surveyed the stack of goods by the door with satisfaction.

"Wish we had a truck instead of my car. Imagine how much we could take back with us."

Coop put down the two cases of water he carried and pointed to the opposite side of the parking lot. "What about that relic parked in front of the pet supply store?"

She covered her eyes against the sun and followed his gaze to the blue older model truck with a camper shell. "What if the owner's inside the pet store?"

"One way to find out," he said, and started off at a jog across the parking lot.

She followed at a slower pace, crossing her fingers that the truck was abandoned, and Coop could get it running. After peeking into the empty pet store, he opened the unlocked door and lowered the truck visor. The keys dropped onto the seat. The engine whined for a second when he turned the ignition, then went quiet. He tried again with the same result.

"Dammit." He banged his hands on the steering wheel, then got out to lift the hood.

Riley folded her arms and watched him fiddle with some cables like he knew what he was doing. "Think it might just be out of gas?"

"No, my guess is it's the battery. A truck this old wouldn't have computer circuits." He straightened and scanned the parking lot. "We need to find a similar battery and switch them. This is morbid but start checking some of these smashed trucks."

He told her what to look for before they headed in opposite directions. She avoided the more severely damaged vehicles, or ones containing bodies, and tried not to overthink their actions. If it meant getting more supplies back to Hannah and Julia, it was worth the sacrifice.

After twenty minutes, Coop called her name and waved her

over. By the time she reached him, he was already removing the battery from a full-sized SUV with its back end crunched into the back seats.

"This should work if the battery is the problem." He carried the battery to the truck and had it switched with the old one in another half hour. When he turned the key, the old truck chugged to life. He glanced at the gages. "Full tank. Get in and let's load up our haul."

She planted a celebratory kiss on him and climbed into the sagging passenger seat. They were in business.

Julia's gut had tightened when her mom told her she and Coop were going on a supply run, leaving her to take care of Hannah. She knew they didn't have a choice, but Julia had been a nervous wreck since they left, which wasn't like her. Her mom and Coop would probably have to start going out in search of food and supplies every day, so she'd have to get used to it. She squared her shoulders and pasted on a brave smile, then turned to face Hannah, who was curled in a heap under a pile of blankets on the couch. She looked as worried and forlorn as Julia felt.

Julia held up her iPad. "Want to watch a video until the battery runs out?"

"Not in the mood," Hannah answered softly. "Digging all that snow for water made me tired."

"Why don't you go to the room and take a nap? I can read a book out here."

Hannah got up without answering and headed for the bedroom but turned when she reached the hallway. "I'm glad to be here with you, Julia. Thanks for taking care of me."

Julia gave a weak smile and stretched out on the couch to watch a video. She had just pushed play when someone knocked on the door. She hurried to answer and smiled to see Quinten through the peephole. When she opened the door, he came in, followed by three boys she didn't recognize.

"Did my mom ask you to check up on me?" she asked.

Quinten shook his head and scanned the room with his eyes. "Just here to see if you need anything. Your mom and Dr. Cooper are gone?"

His voice sounded odd and made her uneasy. She hesitated before saying, "Yes, why?"

Quinten turned to the other boys. "Get the carts. Hurry."

While they followed his order, Quinten started picking up boxes of food and stacking them near the door.

Julia grabbed his arm to stop him, but he jerked it free. "What are you doing with our stuff?"

He ignored her and kept going. The boys returned with four carts and loaded the boxes and supplies onto them.

"Stop it," Julia said, and yanked Hannah's backpack out of one of the boy's hands. He pushed her aside and reached for the evac bag. "Quinten, please tell them to stop."

Quinten's eyes narrowed. "Shut up unless you want to end up like Coop. What's in the bedroom?" Julia ran to the hallway and stretched her arms and legs across the opening. He reached her in three strides. "Out of my way."

"Hannah, lock your door!" she screamed.

Quinten backhanded her in the eye before she could duck out of the way. The blow threw her off balance and the room started to spin. Her head missed hitting the wall by an inch on the way to the floor. Quinten sneered and stepped over her. Julia was desperate to get to Hannah before he did but was too disoriented to stand. She crawled to the couch, trying to use it as support to get to her feet, but it was no use.

The sound of Hannah shrieking came from down the hall before she ran into the living room five seconds later. She fell to her knees in front of Julia and screamed again when she saw Julia's face.

"What did they do to you? What's happening?"

Julia put her arms around Hannah. "I'm all right. Did he hurt you?" she whispered.

Hannah shook her head. "He just scared me and told me to get out."

"We need to stay quiet and not interfere. They'll be gone soon."

Hannah stared wide-eyed at Julia's face. Before Julia could stop her, she broke free and crawled to one of the carts which was stacked with medical supplies. She silently peeked into two boxes before reaching in and snatching an ice pack and was back at Julia's side before anyone noticed. She activated the ice pack and pressed it to Julia's eye.

Julia's vision darkened twice while Quinten and his gang robbed them of all their precious supplies, but she refused to lose consciousness. She fought to stay alert and protect Hannah at all costs. She threw a blanket over Hannah's shoulders and tried to shut out the sound of her whimpers. They huddled together on the floor until the boys left and the room was still thirty minutes later.

"Bolt the door," Julia said.

"Why? There's nothing left to take."

"Just do it."

Hannah obeyed and came back to help Julia onto the couch. "Your eye is swelling. Keep the ice on it."

Julia lowered the ice pack and stared at it in a daze. "It's not cold anymore. Did they leave any baggies?"

"They took everything. Everything. How could they do this to us? I thought Quinten was our friend."

Julia didn't have an answer. She was as hurt and bewildered as Hannah. Fighting back the tears, she said, "Find a towel and bundle some snow into it."

Hannah took a dishtowel to the patio and gathered ice with her bare hands. Her gloves had been in her backpack.

This is my fault, Julia thought as she watched her. *I'm such an idiot. How could I have let Quinten fool me?*

Hannah came back and handed the bundle of snow to Julia, then tucked her frozen hands into her armpits.

"Check in the bedrooms to see if they took our clothes. I think my mom has an extra set of gloves."

Hannah gave her a weak smile. "At least we won't have to dig for snow anymore. There's nothing to put it in."

Julia tried to smile back, but it hurt too much. Her sight was obscured by her swollen eyelids and her temple throbbed. She gently pressed the towel to her face and closed her other eye, doing her best to calm her rising terror.

———

The return trip took half the time since it was easier for Coop to retrace their route. Riley had never been so happy to see anything as when the hotel came into view. They'd survived their first run without incident and had come away with a heat source, water, and enough food to last for several days. She hoped it was enough to convince Coop they should stay put.

Coop drove into the parking garage and pulled close to a first-floor entrance. "Get the girls to help us unpack while I load up."

Riley grabbed a case of protein bars and went into the hall. When she got to the suite, she put the box down to knock. When several seconds passed with no answer, she tapped her knuckle on the door and said, "Julia, sweetheart, it's Mom and Coop. Open up."

Coop came up behind her with his arms full of boxes and raised his eyebrows. "Maybe they're out back getting snow or sleeping."

Riley banged hard as she could. "Julia, Hannah, where are you?" The door swung open, and Hannah faced them, looking pale and frightened. Riley rushed past her and said, "Where's Julia?" She came to a dead stop in the empty living room. "Where's all our stuff?"

"They took it all," Julia said, from where she sat bundled in blankets on the sofa.

Coop followed Riley in and whistled when he saw the cleaned out room. "Who took it?"

Julia buried her face in the blanket and burst into tears. "It's my fault. I let them in, and now we're going to starve to death."

Riley went to her and pulled her into her arms. She stroked Julia's hair while she sobbed. Hannah covered her face and cried in chorus with Julia. Coop guided her to a chair and squatted in front of her.

"Can you tell us what happened?"

When she shook her head, Julia sat up and said, "I will."

Riley looked into her face and gasped. Her eye was swollen shut, and an angry bruise spread from her temple to her cheek. "Holy hell, Julia! What happened to you?"

"Quinten hit me. He and his gang came about an hour after you left. I let them in because I thought you sent them. They stole all our stuff. I tried to stop them, but Quinten did this, so I let them go. They took everything but our clothes."

Riley took out her handy penlight and shined it into Julia's healthy eye before gently lifting the swollen lid on the other. "Coop, we need ice."

Hannah wiped her nose on her sleeve and pointed to the wet towel on the floor. "We've been using snow."

Coop took the towel and headed for the patio.

"Smart thinking," Riley said. She laid Julia's head in her lap. "How bad does it hurt, sweetheart?"

She sniffled and said, "Not as bad as it did, but I can't see out of that eye."

"That's from the swelling, but you should be fine in a few days. I'll see if those monsters left anything you can take for pain, but first, listen to me. This is *not* your fault. You had no reason to suspect Quinten. We all trusted him."

Coop handed Riley the snow-filled towel. "Your mom is right. No one is to blame but Quinten. I'm sick that he did this to you."

"Me, too," Riley said. "I'm sure we've seen the last of him. He thinks there's nothing left to take and doesn't know about the truck we brought back, filled with supplies."

Julia stared in disbelief. "We have food? We're not going to starve?"

Coop nodded. "We have more than just food. We'll unload the truck after we eat."

Coop and Riley prepared a meal of MRE beans and franks and reconstituted hot apple cobbler from a dehydrated mix. They splurged and heated the food with the small camping stove they'd found earlier. The girls weren't too fond of the MREs, but Riley gave each of them a double ration of cobbler to cheer them up and assure them that they weren't going to starve.

While the girls ate, Riley helped Coop drag the mattresses into the front room. They set up the heater and cracked the windows for ventilation.

"These things make me nervous. I wish we had a carbon monoxide monitor," Riley said. "Should we open the windows wider?"

"If we open them any wider, the heater will be pointless. I read the safety instructions carefully. We'll be fine."

She set the fire extinguisher next to the heater and reminded the girls for the third time to be careful not to knock it over.

"It's in a corner, Mom," Julia said. "Why would we even walk over there?"

Riley was glad to see the fight coming back into Julia, who had been despondent through dinner.

Riley hurried through getting the girls settled down for the night before escaping to her room while Coop carried the supplies inside. She'd held back her emotions for their sake, but once alone, she dropped to the floor and curled into a ball. Coop found her weeping in the dark thirty minutes later. He joined her on the floor and let her have her cry.

When she quieted, he said, "I came to tell you how impressed I was with the way you handled yourself today."

"Sorry to disappoint," she whispered.

"Not what I meant. I'd rather see you crying than debilitated by a panic attack. This is a natural response to what you've been through. You deserve a meltdown. I'm still impressed." He clicked on the battery-powered lantern he'd carried in with him. "Come here."

Riley scooted closer, and he put his arm around her. "If I hadn't left, none of this would have happened. I abandoned Julia when she needed me most."

"This isn't your fault any more than it's Julia's. It's the fault of some bad actors."

Riley wished she could agree but still felt responsible. She'd told Coop only days earlier that Julia was her top priority, but she'd failed her.

He gently stroked her shoulder with his thumb. "Do you see why we've got to leave? This is only a taste of what's coming. If grown men with weapons had broken in instead of unarmed boys, even you couldn't have stopped them. I'm regretting we didn't add a few more guns to the Glock I took today."

Riley sat forward and faced him. "Do you think you could shoot someone if it came to that?"

"If someone was trying to harm you or the girls? Without a second thought. Don't you think you could?"

"I'm not sure. Part of me wants to hunt Quinten down and make him pay for what he did to Julia, but the other part, the healer part, shrinks at the idea of causing harm. If someone or something threatened Julia or Hannah, I hope I'd be able to do whatever it took to protect them."

"Let's hope we're never forced to face that choice. You evaded my question about leaving."

Riley didn't know how to answer. She doubted Quinten would dare show his face again, and as far as he knew, they had nothing left to steal. There might be others inside the hotel who would gladly take their supplies, but even with the attack on Julia, the hotel felt like a more secure place for them. "I still think staying is the safest choice."

"And my instincts are screaming that we need to get out into the country. What about your uncle's ranch that you mentioned? Where did you say it is?"

"Outside Wytheville in southwestern Virginia, but it's over three-hundred miles from here. It took us hours to go twenty miles today and won't people outside the city be just as ruthless as city dwellers if they're starving?"

"Not likely. There will be smaller numbers competing for food and supplies in the countryside. Rural communities have stores of food and implements for survival and hopefully will be more willing to help strangers. You said once that your father has a small farm in Colorado. You must understand what I mean."

Riley wrapped her arms around him and rested her head on his chest. "My gut tells me leaving is wrong, and we can't both be right. I'm willing to put my trust in you. Don't make me regret it."

"Wouldn't dream of it." He stood and held out his hand. "We need to go tell the girls."

Riley reached for his hand and climbed to her feet, dreading breaking the news to Hannah. "This isn't going to go over well. You do it. They like you."

"And make me the bad guy? Chicken."

"It's your idea. "

Coop asked the girls to sit on the couch while he explained that they had to leave and why.

Hannah jumped to her feet before he finished and clenched her fists. "You're leaving? You promised not to abandon me."

Riley tried to put an arm around her shoulder, but she ducked out of the way. "We're taking you with us, Hannah. You're part of our family now."

She started to tremble. "I can't leave. My parents won't know where to find me."

"They're not coming back," Julia said without emotion. "They're dead."

"Julia, hush!" Riley said.

Hannah ran at Julia and pummeled the blanket with her fists while she screamed, "Why would you say that? You told me they were alive. You said they're waiting in a secret underground bunker. They're not dead. They're coming for me. Why did you lie?"

Coop wrapped his arms around Hannah's waist and pulled her kicking and screaming off of Julia before handing her to Riley on the couch.

"Don't listen to Julia," Riley whispered. "She's just in pain and upset about what happened with Quinten. We don't know anything about your parents. We'll leave them a map to where we're going so they can follow, but we have to go. Coop says it's too dangerous to stay in the city."

Julia sat up and wiped her tears before reaching for Hannah's hand. "I didn't mean it. I'm so sorry. I want you to come with us. You're like a sister to me. Forgive me?"

Hannah fixed her red puffy eyes on Julia. "How do I know what to believe?"

"Believe this," Riley said. "If your parents are alive, they'll stop at nothing to find you. That's my promise."

"Let's get that map ready for your parents. I'll take it to their room myself," Coop said. "Then we all need to pack and get a few hours of sleep. I want to be at least an hour out of the city by sunrise."

Hannah nodded and gave Julia a reluctant hug. Riley was disturbed by Julia's reaction and concerned about taking Hannah with them, but they had no choice. No matter what they faced when they left the hotel, she was sure of one thing. Hannah would never see her parents again.

CHAPTER SEVEN

THE TRUCK HIT a pothole and jarred Riley awake. She glanced at the digital sports watch she'd found at the outdoor store and frowned. Only an hour had passed since she'd fallen into a fitful sleep. Julia and Hannah rested peacefully in the back, ignorant of the horrors that lay just beyond their windows. The sliver of the moon provided dim light, but there would be no shielding the girls from reality once the sun rose.

"Sorry to wake you," Coop said softly. "I'm trying to avoid the bumps, but it's impossible to dodge them all with so much debris in the road."

Riley shifted on the seat in a futile attempt to get comfortable. "We're alive and the truck's running. Nothing else matters." In the beam of the headlights, she could just make out the shadowy outlines of demolished cars and frozen, contorted bodies scattered on the road. "Where are we?"

"Still on Route 29. It's been dicey, but I haven't had to divert to surface streets so far. We're about five miles from Centerville, Virginia."

She shined her penlight on the map. "We've only made forty miles in two hours?"

"Afraid so." The fatigue was apparent on his face. The poor man only had three hours of sleep in the past day. She clicked off her light and reached up to massage his neck. "Feels good," he said.

"Happy to help." She gazed into the darkness, watching their slow progress. "Are you sure we shouldn't go back to the hotel for another day? It's not too late."

He pulled into a grocery store parking lot just as the sun peeked over the horizon behind them. "No, Riley. That's not an option. I may be wiped out, but you can trust me. I already feel better just being out of DC."

She lowered her hand and stared at the smashed doors of the store entrance. *No point in going in there to scavenge supplies.* "Maybe the worst is behind us," she said, with more optimism than she felt. "It does feel good to be heading west. I may be nearly a continent away from Jared and Emily, but it's comforting to be traveling in the direction that brings me closer to them."

"Glad to hear that." He ran his hands over his face. "I need to sleep. Feel up to driving? The roads should become less congested as we get further into the suburbs, and the sunlight will make navigating easier."

She nodded and pulled the door handle. The door creaked as she pushed it open, and she cringed, fearing it would rouse the girls, but they didn't stir. *How would it be to sleep like the dead?* she wondered as she stepped onto the frozen asphalt.

The parking lot was half-full of empty cars waiting for owners that would never return. Other cars sat untouched where drivers had slammed into each other when the CME's magnetic pulse fried their onboard computers. Thankfully, the area was free of dead bodies. She hoped that meant the victims had walked away from the accidents. The sight was a stark reminder of the catastrophic disruption to millions of ordinary lives. A wave of sadness washed over her.

She shook off her dark thoughts and ran a few laps around the truck while Coop checked the oil and tires. She started for the driver's side when he closed the hood, but he caught her hand and pulled her to his chest.

She held him for a moment before gazing up into his face. "I didn't realize how much I needed that."

"Let's just stay here holding each other all day and let the world go to hell."

She lifted onto her toes and kissed him before reluctantly stepping out of his arms. "Wish we could, but the girls probably wouldn't enjoy it as much as we would. There will be plenty of time for that at the ranch. It's so tranquil there. You'll love it."

He stretched and yawned as he climbed into the passenger seat. "Take it slow. No more than thirty-five and stay alert."

She got behind the wheel and picked up the map. "Let's go over the route one more time."

Coop tapped his finger on their current position. "We're here on 29. Take it through Centerville and don't stop. It becomes more rural after that. Let's get as far as we can before stopping for breakfast."

Riley maneuvered out of the parking lot, keeping her eyes glued to the road. After the first mile, they passed a pile of neatly stacked bodies on the shoulder, and she wondered who'd been kind enough to move them. Vehicles and other debris hadn't been touched. Shoes, sweaters, schoolbooks, food wrappers, and other signs of everyday life littered the pavement.

"None of this makes sense," she said, breaking the silence. "Where's the military? Where are the local governments or community organizations? We haven't passed another living soul since leaving the hotel. We can't be the only ones who survived."

"Maybe it's the cold or people are too afraid to leave the security of their homes. The grislier answer is that enough time has passed that the population is dying of thirst and starvation.

Most people don't keep more than a few days' worth of food in the house, and water supplies are depleted."

"Zach always pounded it into our heads to be prepared for any catastrophe. Used to drive me nuts. Wish he was here so I could tell him he was right."

Coop studied her for a moment. "It would be small consolation. From what you've told me about him, I can't imagine he'd want to see his family suffering just for an *I told you so*."

"He wouldn't. Do you think the CME was a global event or a just regional one? If this area was affected so severely, why isn't the rest of the country or other countries stepping in to help? Is the entire world facing what we are?"

"I read before the CME strike that odds of a global event are minuscule, but even so, it would take massive coordination to mobilize a relief effort, even on a local scale. It may just be taking time for help to reach us. For all we know, rescuers are a day behind us."

"We can only hope." Coop's eyelids started to droop. "Sorry, I'm talking too much. I have these questions spinning in my brain and can't stop them. I won't wake you until we need to top off the gas." He fluffed a pillow they'd taken from the hotel and tucked it under his head. Riley smiled at how boy-like he looked. "Did you leave cash in the room for the things we took?"

Coop gave her a half-grin. "Yes, not that it matters. That place will be gang headquarters by sundown, and trust me, paper money won't be their currency."

"I know you think I'm ridiculous but paying for what we take feels like a lifeline to our former existence. Humor me until the cash runs out and we're forced to barter."

"Got it, boss," he said and squeezed her hand. "This will be a moot point by tomorrow. There's less than $500 left and I didn't exactly pay for the truck."

"Are we there yet?" Julia mumbled from the back seat.

Riley glanced at her in the rearview mirror. "No, sorry, sweetheart. Go back to sleep."

"Who can sleep with all the talking?"

Coop cocked his thumb at Hannah. "Her, apparently. You hungry?"

"Yes, and I need the bathroom."

"Porta-potty's in the back of the truck. Might as well pull over, Riley."

Riley was reluctant to stop but couldn't postpone the inevitable forever. She did a quick check for corpses before edging into an empty spot on the side of the road. Julia pressed her forehead to the cold window and stared at the post-CME landscape. It was her first look at the outside world beyond the hotel. She watched heartbroken, as Julia took in the charred remains of homes and businesses half covered in ice and snow, and streets clogged with demolished cars and garbage.

"Did the entire world end? I thought things would be normal after going so far," Julia whispered.

"We're only fifty miles from the hotel," Coop said.

"Fifty?" Julia whined. "It'll take a year to get to Uncle Mitch's."

Riley was relieved to hear her complain and reminded herself that Julia was more resilient than she gave her credit for. She really had handled the trauma of the past few days like a warrior princess.

Julia tapped Hannah's knee. "Wake up, sleepy. You've got to see this."

Hannah looked around in confusion. "Where are we?"

Julia crossed her arms and made a pouty face. "Practically down the street from where we started."

Hannah bolted upright. "Back at the hotel? Why?"

She seemed relieved, and Riley felt a pang of guilt. "Julia's exaggerating. Come see the fancy toilet Coop found for us."

Hannah nodded numbly and followed Riley out of the truck.

Julia opened her door and shrieked. Riley rushed to her, fearing a dead body, but only found a half-eaten deer carcass.

Coop dragged it into the grassy ditch. "Too bad. That would have made an excellent lunch." Hannah grimaced and vomited on his shoes. She wiped her mouth on her coat sleeve, and her lower lip trembled. He laughed and said, "No cause for tears. I've had worse, and I've always hated these shoes."

Julia laughed into her hand while Riley put her arms around Hannah's waist and nudged her to the back of the truck. Coop stripped off his soiled shoes and tossed them into the woods. Riley thought that was a bit rash. They'd be easy enough to clean, and he might need them down the road, but she kept her opinion to herself.

They rummaged through the stacks of boxes in the truck bed until they found a new pair of boots for Coop and their new bathroom. Coop had discovered a backpacking toilet with a privacy tent. That fortunate find would do as much to make the journey tolerable for the three women as any of their other provisions. Hannah's outlook brightened as they rigged the toilet, and each took a turn.

They got underway after stowing their gear and downing a quick breakfast of MREs. As Riley drove, she thought of Hannah's reaction to the carcass. If she was that disturbed over a dead deer, how would she react to a human corpse? Julia had taken the incident in stride, but that was her way.

Hannah had clearly led a sheltered and pampered life, and Riley wondered if she'd be strong enough to weather the trials to come. If her uncle's ranch was beyond the reach of the CME's destruction, at least life would have a semblance of normalcy, leaving Hannah to mourn the loss of her parents in peace.

They made slow but steady progress for the next two hours. Riley grew more adept at maneuvering around the wreckage as they went. Her anxiety subsided and she did her best to stay alert. She hadn't had much more sleep than Coop.

While Coop slept, Hannah and Julia chatted quietly about the drastic changes in the post CME landscape. Riley was relieved it distracted Hannah from thinking about her parents. The grieving process would take time, but the sooner she adapted to her new circumstances, the better her chance for survival.

Riley was imagining life as the mother of four children when she came over a rise and saw a traffic barricade blocking the road. She slammed the brakes, and the truck skidded to a stop inches from the barrier. Coop slid off the seat and banged his head on the dashboard. He climbed back up, rubbing his stitches.

"What the hell, Riley?"

She gripped the steering wheel with one hand and pointed a trembling finger at the barricade with the other. "I didn't see it until we were on it."

Coop grimaced. "No permanent damage. I'll go move the barricade." He made a check of the area before reaching for the door handle. "Stay in the truck and lock the doors."

"Are you sure you should go out there? Someone put the barricade up for a reason."

"No one's around. I'll be careful. Honk if anyone comes."

He was out of the truck before she could stop him. He had two sections of the barricade moved to the side of the road when three men in heavy coats came over the rise from the opposite direction. The one in the lead was of average build but had striking eyes and skin the color of dark, creamy chocolate. The one directly behind him reminded Riley of a short-haired Jason Momoa. The third was scrawny compared to the other two and reminded her of her dentist. He didn't appear too menacing, but it was impossible to tell if any of them carried weapons under their coats.

"Girls, get on the floor," she whispered. Hannah was out of her seat and curled up on the floorboard in a flash, but Julia didn't move. Riley flashed her fiercest stern mother look. "I said, get down."

"But, Mom, I want to see what's happening," Julia whined.

"Don't argue. On the floor, now!"

Julia slid off the seat just seconds before the dentist one turned toward the truck. Coop saw the men before she could warn him. He strolled up to them and called out a cheerful "morning" in that jaunty manner that magically made everyone like him. "Is the road out up ahead?"

Riley was too far away to hear the Jason Momoa character's response.

"What's happening? Are they going to hurt Coop?" Julia asked in a loud whisper.

Riley shook her head. "They're probably just warning people about some danger on the road past the barrier." She'd done her best to keep her tone light, but Julia's look showed she hadn't bought it.

As the conversation went on, the men became more agitated, and Coop's demeanor more guarded. She slipped the keys into her front pocket and reached into the glove box for the gun.

Julia peeked over the seat. "What are you doing? Do you even know how to fire that?"

"Hush. You two get under that blanket and do not leave this truck, no matter what happens. Do you understand?"

Julia sank down and pulled the blanket over their heads. "Yes, ma'am," they said in unison.

Riley stashed the gun in her waistband, zipped her coat, and settled in to wait, but Coop abruptly left the men and headed for the truck. He yanked the door open and slid in beside her.

"They won't let us pass unless we pay a 'road tax' of half our supplies. I tried to explain that we're just passing through and can't survive on fifty percent of our provisions. They were unimpressed. They say the streets and roads are barricaded for a hundred miles in every direction. I'm sure they're lying, but we can't know for sure. Give me a chance to stall and figure out a way out of this. No way they're leaving with our stuff."

Riley kept her eyes riveted on the men as she spoke. "Let's just back the truck up and go back the way we came. We'll find a way around them. The Jason Mamoa one is as big as a tree, and there could be more men hiding out of sight."

Coop raised an eyebrow. "Jason Momoa?" When Riley shrugged, he said, "I don't think they're just going to let us leave, and they might be packing. He opened the glove box. "Where's my Glock?" She lifted her coat and showed the weapon tucked into her jeans. He held out his hand. "Give it to me, Riley."

She crossed her arms and slid away from him. "No, you're too impetuous, and I can't risk you getting us shot. Let's just get out of here."

She was about to start the truck when a pickup came out of nowhere and pulled up, blocking their exit. The woman driving stayed at the wheel.

"There goes that plan," Coop said. "Look at the big guy."

The huge one lifted his coat a few inches to reveal a gun holstered at his hip just as the dentist one broke from the group and came straight for them and pounded on the window. "It's cold and we're tired of waiting, lady," he called out.

"Follow my lead," Riley said.

She climbed out and pasted on her most alluring smile to draw him away from the truck. Sauntering up to him, she said, "I was just zipping my coat. It's chilly out here. You wouldn't want a girl to get cold, would you?" He leered as she walked past him. Swallowing her disgust, she stepped in front of the leader, cocking her head and flashing a smile. "What can we do for you, gentlemen?"

The boss gave her an indifferent glance. "As I explained to

Coop, you're required to pay a fifty percent tax to pass through our territory."

She moved a foot closer. "That's a bit steep, don't you think? Even our greedy congress didn't expect fifty percent. We're just passing through on our way to family in the south. We'll be out of your hair in no time."

The pretty-eyed, chocolate one moved between them. "Flirt all you want, but it won't change a thing. Our children are starving, but you look well-fed enough." His eyes narrowed. "Adults in our community are starving. I'm starving."

"I've got this, Mason," the boss said. "Take Rogers and start loading their stuff into your truck."

Mason leaned his face an inch from hers. "I shouldn't leave you alone with these two," he said to the boss.

The boss gave Riley a disturbing grin. "I can handle them."

"You got it, Crawford." Mason backed away from Riley and she let out her breath. "Come on, Rogers."

The men jostled her as they passed, but she hardly noticed. She felt the cold metal of the gun against her skin and wondered how far she'd go to protect her girls. It would only take seconds for Rogers and Mason to discover the truck doors were locked and come demanding the keys.

She felt Coop eyeing her and hoped he'd read her thoughts. He moved closer to Crawford and held up his hands in surrender.

"Be reasonable, man," he said. "We'll share what we can spare. You don't have to take it by force."

Crawford patted the bulge at his hip. "This isn't a negotiation. We'll just take all of it and leave you here to die."

Coop backed away at an angle that drew Crawford's gaze from Riley. She inched her hand up under her coat and felt for the gun. When she almost had it wrapped in her fingers, Rodgers yelled, "Tailgate's locked. We need the keys?"

Crawford eyed Coop. "You have them?"

Riley let go of the gun and reached into her pocket for the keys. She dangled them in front of Crawford. "I do."

She turned to take them to Rogers, hoping for a way to distract the men so the girls could escape into the woods.

"You stay where you are," Crawford barked and drew his gun. "The woman's got the keys, Mason. Come get them."

Mason jogged over and ripped the keys from Riley's hand. She yelped in pain, and Crawford grinned at her. It was the first emotional reaction he'd made.

Coop straightened and inched toward him. "Is that how you get off, seeing women in pain? Or are you one of those that doesn't mind a little whipping now and then?"

Crawford fired a round past Coop's ear. Coop smiled and casually crossed his arms.

"You okay, boss?" Mason called. Crawford nodded slowly. "Just say the word if you need me to take care of Coop."

"Not how we do this," Crawford said, then turned his eyes on Riley. "Tell your man to shut it."

Riley swallowed her rising panic and tried to think. Coop was attempting to distract Crawford to give her an opening, and she had to play along. Crawford could have shot Coop if he'd wanted, but clearly wasn't ready to escalate the situation to that. Riley ignored the ringing in her ears and giggled.

"He's not my man. He's just some guy I picked up on the road. Do what you want with him."

Coop frowned. "I thought we had something special. Guess you think you'll take her for yourself, Crawford."

Riley heard the tailgate drop open and her gut tightened. She had to come up with a plan before they started searching the cab, but her mind was blank.

"On your knees," Crawford said, between clenched teeth. He leaned over Coop and held the gun to his temple. "Shut your mouth or I'll shut it for you."

Riley was trapped. If she drew the gun on Crawford, Coop

would be dead before she could get a shot off, but she couldn't risk what the men might do to Julia and Hannah when they found them. As a surgeon, she often made split-second decisions to save lives, but this time she wasn't the only one involved.

She was about to beg Crawford to release Coop when the cab door creaked. She swung around to see Mason leaning over the back seat with a creepy grin.

He pulled the blanket away and tossed it on the ground. "Look what we have here, Rogers. New breeding stock."

Crawford jerked his head toward the truck to see what was happening. Riley took advantage of the distraction and pulled out the gun as she used her best kickboxing move to slam her shin into the back of his knees. His legs went out from under him, and he toppled face down onto the asphalt. Riley stomped on his hand with her boot and heard the bones crack. When he groaned and released the gun, Riley kicked it toward Coop. He grabbed it and climbed on Crawford's back with the barrel pointed at his skull.

Riley fired a shot into the air and screamed, "Run, girls! Run for the woods. Don't stop."

Julia flew out of the opposite side of the truck and took off at full speed, dragging Hannah behind her. When Mason started after them, Riley shot at his feet. She missed, but it was enough for him to hit the deck. She rushed him and put a boot in the middle of his back.

"Put your arms forward, palms down on the ground."

As he slid his arms forward, she lifted his coat and searched for a gun but didn't find one.

"I'm not armed. Crawford doesn't trust us with weapons, but you didn't know that," he mumbled into the dirt.

She remembered Rogers and looked up in time to see him jump into the truck with the woman and speed off with their stuff. At least having him gone evened the odds.

Riley wasn't sure what to do next. Even with a broken hand

and no weapon, Crawford was twice her size and could snap Coop like a twig. They could tie him up, but if she took the gun off Mason to tie him up first, he could overpower her.

She turned to ask Coop what she should do just as he slammed the gun down on Crawford's head. He went limp, and Coop got to his feet. He trotted to Riley and took off his belt to bind Mason's hands.

When he finished, he held out his hand to Riley. "Give me your belt. I'll bind his feet."

She raised her coat. "I'm not wearing a belt."

"Socks will work." She climbed off Mason and started unlacing her boots. "We need to get the girls and get out of here before Crawford wakes up or Rogers comes back with reinforcements."

"What about me? I'll freeze to death out here on the ground," Mason muttered.

Coop kicked him in the leg. "Crawford can free you when he wakes up if he thinks you're worth it."

Riley knotted her socks together and handed them to Coop before pulling on her boots. "I'll look for the girls."

"Wait," Coop said, as she started for the woods. "You were brilliant back there. You never cease to amaze."

"I just reacted out of instinct to protect you and the girls. Guess those hours of kickboxing paid off."

———

Julia felt like her lungs were going to burst. Her mom said to keep running, but she didn't hear the bad guys following them and was afraid she'd die if took another step.

"Julia, stop, or I'll pass out," Hannah gasped.

Julia let go of Hannah's hand and bent over, gulping for air with her hands on her knees. She saw a large downed tree ten feet from where they'd stopped.

She pointed and said, "Let's hide over there."

They scampered over the trunk and crouched behind it. Hannah threw her arms around Julia. "I'm so scared. What if your mom and Coop are dead? Those men are going to kill us."

As scared as Julia was herself, Hannah's overreaction irritated her. Even Emily would have been braver. Hannah would have to toughen up if she wanted to survive.

"I didn't hear any more gunshots," she said, "and Mom took down that giant man before we ran into the woods. I saw Coop grab the gun and climb on his back."

Hannah's teeth started to chatter, so Julia pulled her closer. "Then we should go back to the hotel. Quentin and his gang are gone. The other bad guys probably are, too. I know there's no food left, but there's none out here now, either. It'll be warmer at the hotel, and we'd have a heavy door to lock people out. My parents might have come back looking for me."

"We left that map for them, Hannah. I wish we could have stayed at the hotel, too, but Coop said it was dangerous. I trust him."

"More dangerous than hiding from crazy men with guns in the freezing woods?"

She had a point, but Julia let it drop. A breeze kicked up, and she started to shiver as bad as Hannah. She was used to freezing temperatures from living in Colorado, but this was a cold that seemed to go right through her. They couldn't stay hiding under that tree much longer. She peeked over the tree to see if anyone was following them when she heard her mom calling.

"Did you hear that? It's Mom." She stood and cupped her hands to her mouth. "We're over here by the dead tree. Keep talking so we know where you are."

"I can see your coats. I'll come to you."

Julia helped Hannah to her feet. "See, we're going to be fine. Coop will find us somewhere warm to stay tonight."

Riley broke through the trees, and they ran to hug her. "Are you both all right? You're a long way out here."

"We kept running like you told us," Hannah said.

"We didn't stop until we were about to keel over," Julia said.

"Excellent job, warrior princess. Let's get back to Coop."

"Don't have to tell me twice," Julia said and took Hannah's hand to get her to walk faster as they headed for the road. She wanted to get back in the warm truck and forget about everything that had happened in the past few days.

Her mom started running when they came in sight of the road. Coop was standing near the truck holding a bloody towel to his face. The giant man was on the ground at his feet, but the other men were gone.

Her mom looked at the man on the ground and then lifted the towel to check Coop's face. "What happened? Where's Mason?"

Coop flinched. "Gone. I was loading the stuff they left on the ground when Crawford came to. I had my back to him and didn't see him sneak over to untie Mason. By the time I heard them, Mason was twenty-five yards down the road. Crawford came at me and smashed me in the head with a tree branch. He was still unsteady, so I was able to keep the gun from him and get him back on the ground. I injected him with Valium I found in the truck just to be safe, but we have to get out of here. Rogers and Mason are probably on their way here with backup."

Julia didn't wait to hear more. She jumped into the truck and hooked her seatbelt, waving for Hannah to join her.

"I need to stitch that," her mom said to Coop, but he waved her off.

"I'll slap a bandage on it until we stop. Get in and let's go."

He got in and started the truck. Riley reluctantly followed and said, "There's still some of our stuff back there."

"No time. We have to leave it."

He backed up to miss the giant man and did a U-turn back the way they'd come.

Hannah sat forward. "We're going back to the hotel?"

"Afraid not, but we can't go the way we were headed. Riley, find the map. Centerville is out. We need a way to bypass it."

Riley spread the map across her lap, and she and Coop talked about possible routes they could take. Julia listened for a minute, but the names of the roads didn't mean anything to her. She closed her eyes to try to sleep, but images of the giant unconscious man on the ground kept popping into her head. The incident at the barricade had terrified her. She had to come to grips with the fact that the world she knew was gone. They'd only been on the road for half a day and had already been robbed and almost shot. They'd gotten lucky. What would they face the next time?

Hannah squirmed in the seat and drew Julia from her thoughts. "What's the matter with you?"

Hannah crossed her legs and whispered, "I need to use the restroom."

"Use the restroom?" Julia snapped. "What are you, some pampered duchess? Do you still not get what's happened? It's about time you learned to take a dump in the woods."

"Julia, apologize to Hannah right now," Riley said. Julia ignored her and started to laugh. "That wasn't funny."

The look on her mom's face made her laugh harder. She laughed so hard, her laughter turned to sobs and the anguish she'd suppressed for the past three days poured out of her.

She was tired of babysitting prissy little Hannah. She was tired of danger around every corner, and she missed Emily and Jared. She missed her grandparents and her friends and envied them for being safe and warm at home. It wasn't fair that she had to be cold and hungry on some godforsaken road in the middle of nowhere.

Riley climbed over the seat and squeezed into the seat next to her. Julia buried her face into her mother's shoulder and wept harder than she had since her dad died.

Riley stroked her hair and whispered, "Don't fight it, sweetie. Let it out."

She didn't want to let it out but had no control. She was afraid she'd never stop, but in time, her sobs quieted.

When she could get the words out, she said, "I don't want to end up like all those dead people on the road or get shot or molested by bad guys. Is everyone out to get us?"

"We won't end up like the bodies on the road. Those people died immediately after the CME, and we'll be more careful if we run into strangers. We've survived this long, and we'll be at Uncle Mitch's tomorrow."

"But I just want to go home."

"Once we've had time to rest, we'll make plans to get to Colorado."

Riley handed her a paper towel. She wiped her face and blew her nose, mad at herself for breaking down and embarrassed for blubbering like a baby.

"I'm fine now. Just a moment of weakness."

"You don't have to be strong all the time. I fall apart if someone looks at me wrong these days."

Julia sat forward and shook her head. "Not anymore. You stood up to those bad guys like a tiny Wonder Woman."

"I only did that to save you. I'd do whatever it took to protect you."

"You couldn't have done that two weeks ago. You're turning into a badass, Mom."

"Language."

"Superhero then. Dad would be proud of you."

Riley turned her face to the window. "He would, but we have a long way to go, and who knows what's up ahead? I'm sorry for putting you in danger. If we hadn't come on this trip, we'd be home with family."

"I don't blame you or regret that we came. No one knew this

was going to happen. If we weren't here, we wouldn't have met Coop or been able to help Hannah."

Her mom's eyes glistened when she turned to face her. "Dad would be proud of you, too. So am I. Guess I'm not the only badass."

Riley kissed her forehead before unhooking her belt and climbing back into the front seat.

Julia squeezed Hannah's hand and gave her a weak smile. "I'm sorry for what I said. I keep shooting off my mouth, but this is harder on you than any of us."

"Don't apologize. I thought I was the only one who's scared. I'd be dead by now without you."

"You're stronger than you think, Hannah, and I'm glad you're here. Mom and Coop will take care of us. We don't need to be afraid."

"She's right," Coop said. "But enough mushy stuff. I know you two need a pit stop, but it's not safe here, so you're going to have to hold it. Try to get some sleep."

"Sure, Coop," she said half-heartedly.

She pressed her swollen eye against the cold window and watched the new world speed past them. She felt better after her cry but vowed to herself not to allow any more meltdowns. She needed to be strong for Mom and Hannah. There would be time to cry after they reached the ranch.

Coop drove for an hour after the barricade until his headache became too painful. Riley convinced him to stop so she could examine him and see if he needed stitches. She had to fight her tears when she retrieved the med-pack out of the truck bed and saw what was left of their supplies. The full gas cans, most of the med supplies, and the kerosene heater were gone. All they had were the tents, some of their clothes, a small first aid kit, and about thirty percent of the food, mostly MREs. Hannah was devastated when she found out the thieves had taken their wonderful porta-potty.

Coop picked up an empty five-gallon bucket by the handle. "At least they left us a pot to piss in."

"Great," Riley mumbled. "Turn it over and sit so I can check you out."

She took out her penlight and shined it in his eyes. He squinted and turned his head. "So glad they didn't get that blasted light of yours."

"It doesn't look like you have a concussion. I think you can get by without stitches, but I need to disinfect the wound. It'll leave a scar to match the one on the other side. At least you'll be symmetrical."

Coop grinned through his swollen lip. "It'll make me look tough."

"No, it won't," Julia said.

"Ah, the honesty of youth," he said. "I'm going to find the men's room. Back in a jiff."

He wandered off into the woods while the three of them made the best of the bucket and then stowed their gear before getting into the truck. Riley took a minute to review the map. They'd been forced to travel fifty miles out of their way, which had been the last thing they needed with their gas supply running low. They'd only made sixty miles since leaving the hotel twelve hours earlier, and it was getting dark.

Riley turned onto Route 29 once Coop was back and strapped in. She was relieved not to find a barricade blocking the road. There was less junk scattered across the road, so she sped up to fifty.

Coop and the girls were asleep within minutes and Riley was left with only the hum of the engine for company. She was skirting a muffler in the middle of the road when the sun slipped below the horizon. Moments later, brilliant swirling waves of green, violet, and red lit the sky.

She tapped Coop's knee. When he sat up and yawned, she whispered, "Look," and pointed to the sky.

"Incredible. I've wanted to see the Northern Lights since I was a boy. I never thought I'd get the chance in the middle of Virginia."

"Is that from the CME? We haven't been out after dark since it hit."

"The thick smoke and clouds would have obscured it anyway."

"What are you two jabbering about?" Julia grumbled. "Why can't you ever just let me sleep?"

"Because I didn't want you to miss this. Look out your window," Riley said.

Julia sat up and stared. "Cool!" She tapped Hannah's arm. "Wake up. You have to see this."

Hannah wiped her eyes and pressed her face to the window. "What is that?"

"The aurora borealis. Northern Lights," Julia said. "But we aren't far enough north for that."

"We think it's from the CME," Riley said, without taking her eyes from the spectacle.

Riley slowed to take in the stunning sight. The past several days had been filled with danger, death, and darkness, and her soul craved light and beauty.

She crested the top of a steep hill and gasped when the next spectacle came into view. The fractured remains of an enormous commercial jet lay sprawled across the road a quarter-mile ahead. The plane was split into two jagged pieces, one on each side of the highway with a thirty-foot gap between them. The right wing was still attached but severed in half. The left wing lay an acre from the fuselage. An evacuation slide hung like a giant tongue from the opening where the wing should have been.

In the light of the aurora, Riley made out the swath of

shattered trees where the plane had crashed through the forest on the edge of the field beside the road. A deep gash extended from the forest where the plane skidded on its belly before coming to rest on its side.

While keeping her eyes fixed on the wreckage, she said, "Do you see this, Coop?"

"How could I miss it?"

Julia peeked over the seat. "Is that a plane?"

Hannah popped her head up and gasped. "Do you think anyone's alive in there?"

Riley glanced at Coop. "No, honey," she replied.

"See that trail snaking through the wreckage? I think we can navigate through it," Coop said. "Just take it slow. I'll keep an eye out for debris."

Riley gripped the wheel and inched forward at fifteen miles per hour, trying to ignore the seats with bodies still belted to them strewn across the road. When they were fifty yards from the plane, she saw movement in the middle of the gap between the plane sections. It looked like a person waving their arms.

"Coop, get the binoculars. There's someone out there."

He took the binoculars out of the glove box and lifted them to his eyes. "It's a woman. She's holding a piece of cloth with writing on it."

Riley put the truck in park and took the binoculars from Coop. "It says SOS. We have to go to her."

She tossed the binoculars into Coop's lap and took off as fast as she could to still be able to maneuver through the debris.

"Slow down, Mom," Julia cried. "You're going to crash."

Coop put his hand on her arm. "Listen to your daughter, and don't think we're going to stop and get out of this truck. Just drive around her and keep going."

Riley got as close as she could before she was forced to stop in front of a six-foot pile of neatly stacked luggage blocking the road.

Riley reached for the door handle. "Looks like we don't have a choice. I'm going to see what she needs."

Coop grabbed her wrist. "I'm not letting you out of this truck."

She jerked her arm free. "I don't answer to you. She could be injured or dying of thirst and hunger."

"Please don't leave us alone again, Riley," Hannah cried.

Coop holstered his gun and opened his door. "I'm going to get out and move the suitcases. Stay here with the girls."

Riley picked up the gun they'd taken from Crawford and slipped it into her waistband. "Look, she's coming toward us. We can't just ignore her. Hannah, I'll be right over there where you can see me. Lock the doors."

Coop stared at her, then shook his head. "Riley, wait. I'm sorry for being so rough back there, but you need to think this through. We barely have enough supplies for ourselves, and have you forgotten what happened at the barricade? This could be a trap, and our own survival is my top priority."

"What you're saying makes sense, and this may not be the best tactical decision, or the most practical, but it's right, so that's why I'm going to do it. This is why I became a doctor. I'm smart enough to understand that we have to be cautious, but I refuse to start seeing everyone we come across as an enemy, especially on our first day."

Coop studied her with that maddening smirk she remembered from the first time she saw him. "I can't argue with that. I've got your back."

She and Coop got out, keeping her eyes on the woman as she approached. Riley guessed her age to be around forty. She was wearing a chic but dirty and tattered suit and tennis shoes that looked at least a size too big. Her hair was cut stylishly but hadn't been washed or brushed for days. She had healing cuts and bruises on her face and hands. She met Riley's gaze with eyes filled with fear and exhaustion.

Coop stepped in front of Riley as the woman picked her way

through the last pieces of luggage and approached them with her hands raised. "Stay alert. We don't know who's hiding in the plane."

Riley nodded as the woman reached them.

"You're the first people in a week willing to stop. Thank you," she said. "My name is Angeline Hughes. Angie. There's a man on the plane whose leg is severely injured. I've managed to keep him alive, but he's not going to make it much longer."

Coop stepped between her and Riley. "You've been living in that plane for a week?"

"Yes. It's been a hellish nightmare. Can you help us?"

"Who were the other people passing by? How many were there?"

"Mostly families or truckers, but there was this one group of thugs who were about to stop until I raised my shotgun at them, even though I'm out of ammo."

Coop stepped closer to her. "Where's the shotgun?"

Riley nudged him out of the way. "We'll do what we can. We're doctors, but most of our medical supplies were stolen from us earlier. Do you have any on the plane?"

Angie lowered herself onto a stack of suitcases. "You're doctors?"

"Surgeons," Coop said.

"It's a miracle. I took what I could from a pharmacy about two miles from here. I don't know if it's what you need."

"We'll find out," Riley said. "Come help us get what little we have from the truck."

She stood and wiped her eyes. "You're angels sent from heaven."

Riley glanced at Coop, but he wouldn't meet her gaze. They returned to the truck and loaded backpacks with anything that might be useful.

When they were ready, Coop said, "Hannah and Julia, stay

here until we come for you. Keep the doors locked and stay down under the blanket. You know the drill."

Julia nodded and covered herself and Hannah with a blanket. "Sure, Coop."

Riley patted her head. "Thanks, sweetie. This shouldn't take long."

"Do you mind telling us what happened?" Riley asked Angie as they made their way to the crash site.

"My husband and I were flying from Dulles to Paris for our anniversary when the CME hit. A smaller plane struck us, and we both crashed. My husband didn't make it." The last words caught in her throat, and she paused.

Riley put an arm around her waist. "I understand. My husband died in a plane crash three years ago."

Angie nodded and gave her a knowing look. "I have a teenage daughter and an eight-year-old son. I left them with my parents in Allentown, where we live. I haven't stopped thinking about them for a second since the crash. I've just been fighting to stay alive. I have to get back to them no matter what it takes."

Riley looked at the ground as they walked. "I left a son and daughter with my parents in Colorado Springs. It's torture being separated and not knowing what's happened to them."

Coop rubbed Riley's shoulder and turned to Angie. "What about the injured man? What's his name?"

"Kyle Bradley. He was flying to Paris on business. Kyle and I were the only survivors from either plane, as far as I know."

They reached the plane, and Riley groaned when she saw how far up they needed to climb to reach the cabin. She wondered how they were going to get up the evac slide when Angie grabbed hold of a rope dangling from the plane and started pulling herself up, hand over hand. Coop followed her, and Riley went last. It was a challenge, but she was grateful for her climbing experience. Her hands were burning by the time she climbed the ten feet to the top.

Most of the seats were gone, but the remaining ones were formed into two beds in the first-class section. Kyle Bradley was wrapped in blankets across one of them. Angie had cut and taped a life raft over the open door and another evac slide over the gaping hole in the fuselage where the tail section had separated. Riley was impressed with her resourcefulness.

Kyle moaned, and she snapped into doctor mode. His skin was gray and clammy, and it only took seconds to access how grave his condition was.

Riley gave Angie a weak smile. "Would you mind waiting in the truck with the girls while we treat Kyle? I don't like leaving them out there alone."

"I'd much rather be there than here," Angie said. "The medical supplies from the pharmacy are in that backpack on the floor next to him."

When Angie disappeared back down the evac slide, Riley said, "Help me get these bandages off. It doesn't look like we have much time."

She and Coop gently stripped off the makeshift bandages Angie had applied to Kyle's wound. The sight was far worse than Riley expected.

Coop scratched his head. "Open fracture and the tissue is necrotic. This is hopeless, Riley. It would be too late to save him, even if we had a fully stocked and functioning OR."

"Keep your voice down. He might hear you," she whispered.

"He's past hearing us, Riley. He'd have been better off dying in the crash."

"He would have died if that jagged edge of the femur had moved just millimeters to the left and cut the artery. Let's see what's in the backpack. Maybe we can at least ease his pain."

Coop opened the bag and placed the contents on the seat next to Kyle. Riley inspected each item but found little that would do Kyle any good. There were bottles of medications unrelated to Kyle's injuries, a few rolls of gauze, some anesthetic spray, and other miscellaneous first aid items, like the ones they already had in the truck. She sprayed the anesthetic on the wound, hoping it would numb any still living tissue.

Coop reached the bottom of the pack and said, "Bingo." He pulled out a vial of morphine and handed it to Riley.

She read the label and said, "How did anyone miss this when they raided the pharmacy? Pain meds are always the first to go. I don't suppose you have a syringe to go with it in that bag of tricks."

"No, but there may be one in carry-on luggage if there were any diabetics onboard."

Angie had emptied the overhead bins and piled the bags near the open end of the plane. Each bag was unzipped, and the contents scattered on the floor. Angie had rifled through them, but she wouldn't have been looking for syringes. Riley and Coop searched for fifteen minutes before she found a case with diabetic testing supplies containing two syringes.

"Got one," she said as they rushed back to Kyle.

She tapped Kyle's face to rouse him. He groaned, and his eyes fluttered but didn't open. Coop pressed two fingers hard against his sternum with no response.

"He's unconscious. Just do it."

She squatted next to Kyle and wiped the sweat from his forehead with a wad of gauze. "What if he's allergic? It could kill him."

"He'd thank us. If you want my opinion, you should double dose him."

She glared up at him. "That would be lethal."

Coop stared for a moment, then slowly nodded.

"I can't kill him. Time will do that soon enough."

Coop held out his hand. "Let me."

Riley crossed her arms and tucked the vial into her armpit. "First, you want to abandon a woman stranded alone in the middle of this chaos, and now you want to euthanize a patient. I'm finding it hard to recognize the revered Dr. Neal Xavier Cooper III I thought I knew."

"Don't judge me against these insane circumstances."

"I'm giving Kyle the prescribed dose, and we'll let nature take its course. That will save us from becoming murderers. Or maybe he'll surprise us and survive."

Coop closed his eyes and rubbed his forehead. "And people say I'm difficult to work with. Riley, it would take direct intervention from God to save him now. We wouldn't be murderers. Overdosing him would be the humane thing to do, but we don't have time to argue the ethics of euthanasia. We need to get moving."

Riley injected Kyle with the recommended dose. "He's so weak that even the normal amount might kill him."

"Then we'll know who was right soon enough. How do you plan to get him down that evac slide?"

Riley thought for a moment. "Let's construct a makeshift splint, then we'll put him on a blanket with the ends tied like a sling and gently slide him down."

"Could work, but we'll most likely kill him trying to get to the truck."

Getting Kyle down the evac slide was as harrowing as Coop predicted. They almost dropped him three times, but twenty minutes later had him settled in the truck bed. He never moved or made a sound throughout the ordeal.

She pulled Coop away from the others and said, "I'm going to ride in the back with him. I don't want him to die alone."

"It'll be a cold and rocky ride."

"We'll be fine. Wrap us in two sleeping bags."

"Suit yourself." He helped her into the truck and climbed in after her.

When he'd covered her and Kyle in the sleeping bags, she said, "What's the plan now?"

"It's late, we're low on gas, and we need to get Kyle to a warm, comfortable place, if such a thing exists. I was hoping to be much further by now."

"Me too. I'm going to try to sleep. Are you awake enough to drive?"

"I've had more sleep than you."

Riley did a quick calculation and realized she'd had less than eight hours of sleep in the past two days. "You may be right. Here's hoping we find a place where we can all get a good night's rest. None of us will hold up much longer if we don't."

Coop saluted. "I'll do my best boss."

Julia knocked on the back window of the cab. "What's the holdup? We're freezing in here."

"Coming," Coop said. He gave Riley a quick hug and kiss before jumping to the ground. "I'll avoid the bumps as best I can, but it's going to be rough until we're past the crash site."

"I trust you. Just get us there alive."

He ran his fingers along the window as he passed to the driver's side door. Riley thought of how close she'd come to saying I love you before catching herself. As she laid back against the few remaining boxes, she asked herself if she'd fallen in love with him or if it was no more than a bond born of shared trauma. Her head wanted to believe that was the case, but her heart wouldn't let it. She tucked the question into the back of her mind and closed her eyes. There would be time to seek her answers once they were out of danger.

CHAPTER EIGHT

THE CRUNCH of the tires on gravel drew Riley out of her stupor. She'd dozed off in the hour since leaving the crash site but was plagued by nightmares of rotting bodies half-buried in snow. That left her more exhausted, so she'd forced herself to stay awake the second hour and let her thoughts wander.

When Coop stopped the truck, she reached out from under the sleeping bag to take Kyle's pulse. His skin was ice cold. Kyle was gone. She drew in her breath, devastated by his death after how hard they'd worked to save him.

Coop, Angie, and the girls walked to the back of the truck. The girls stomped their feet and blew on their hands to stay warm while Coop opened the tailgate. Riley saw Angie through the window, standing apart and staring at the ground. Riley covered Kyle's face with his blanket before climbing out to go to her.

She quietly approached her and said, "Kyle didn't make it. There was nothing we could do. I'm truly sorry."

Light from the aurora glinted off the tears pooling in Angie's eyes. She turned her back and wiped them with her sleeves. "This is silly. I knew him for less than a week."

"A few days can feel like a lifetime in a crisis. You were kind to stay and try to save Kyle. No one would have blamed you for leaving him there to die."

She turned to face Riley. "I never could have done that."

Hannah ran to Angie and took her hand as she and Riley rejoined the group. "I'm sorry your friend died, Mrs. Hughes. You can be part of our family now. Coop and Riley will take care of you."

Riley was touched by Hannah's words, but she couldn't mistake Coop's thoughts on the matter when she glanced at him to gauge his reaction. They barely had enough to survive on with only four of them after what Crawford and his men took. Taking on another adult would tax their rations to the breaking point.

Coop closed the tailgate and shoved his hands in his pockets. "We'll take care of Kyle's body in the morning," he said, letting Hannah's comment drop. "Let's see if the occupants of the house are willing to put us up for the night."

They were parked in front of a quaint yellow house with an old model Buick in the driveway. The house and yard were well maintained and surrounded by a thick grove of trees.

"It's cute," Julia said. "Like a cottage from a fairytale."

"Let's hope there's not a wicked witch inside," Coop mumbled. "Riley and I will check first. The rest of you wait in the truck."

"Back in the truck," Julia grumbled as she opened the door. "I'm sick of the truck."

"Be grateful we have it," Riley said as she followed Coop to the front door.

He knocked politely and waited for a full minute before knocking louder.

"Maybe they're asleep," Riley said.

Coop knocked a third time. "Or even better, maybe there's no one here." He slowly turned the doorknob. It was locked, but he had no trouble kicking it open. "I'll go first."

Riley was more than willing to let him take the lead. He pulled

Crawford's gun from his coat pocket and flicked on his flashlight. The interior of the house was as well cared for as the exterior. From the crocheted afghans and outdated upholstery, it was clear the cottage belonged to someone elderly.

The house was freezing. Ashes in the fireplace were cold, even though there was a stack of wood on the hearth.

"Hasn't been a fire here in for at least a day," Coop said. "That's a sign in our favor. Check the kitchen, and I'll take the bedrooms."

He disappeared into the darkness of the hallway. Riley clicked on her penlight and headed from the small living room to the cozy kitchen. Unwashed dishes with the remnants of breakfast rested in the sink. An open newspaper from the day the CME hit lay unfolded on the table. The pantry was stocked with canned goods and other nonperishable foods. They'd hit the jackpot.

"Riley, you need to see this," Coop called from the opposite side of the house.

She followed his voice to a small bedroom at the end of the hall. His flashlight beam illuminated the body of an elderly man motionless on the bed. An oxygen cannula and tube attached to a concentrator lay next to him. Coop glanced at Riley, then shifted the beam to the body of an elderly woman crumpled in a heap on the floor.

"Explains why the cupboards are stocked," Riley said. "He must not have lasted long without his oxygen once they lost power."

Coop gently rolled the woman onto her back. "Doesn't explain what happened to her."

"She didn't starve or freeze to death. I found cases of water bottles in the kitchen. Makes no sense."

"Might not have been capable of caring for herself. Alzheimer's, maybe?"

"Doesn't matter now. What are we going to do with them?"

"I saw a shed off to the side of the yard. I'll see if there's room for them in there. Kyle, too."

Riley took an afghan from a rocking chair in the corner and covered the woman. "I don't like the idea of chucking them in the woodshed, but it's late, and the ground's too cold to dig graves."

Coop wrapped the man in the bedspread. "I didn't say chuck them. We'll put them there for tonight and figure it out in the morning."

The sound of the front door banging open made Riley jump. Coop grabbed his pistol off the bed and put his fingers to his lips.

"What's going on in there? We're about to freeze to death," Julia called.

Riley let out her breath. "I told you to stay in the truck. Don't come down the hall, sweetheart. Coop and I have something to take care of first, but you can start unloading the cab."

"Best news I've ever heard," Julia said, slamming the door behind her.

"Hurry," Riley told Coop. "We have to move Kyle's body before we can unload the truck bed."

They returned to the front of the house. While Coop pried open the frozen back door, Riley searched for mail or something else to identify the couple. A black pocketbook rested on a small table between the kitchen and living room. Riley hesitated to invade the woman's privacy, but she wanted their names to say a few words when they buried them in the shed. She found a large wallet containing a checkbook with the names Charlie and Elsie Stevens.

She was about to drop the wallet into the pocketbook when she noticed an insulin pen and an empty refill cartridge at the bottom. The mystery of Elsie's death was solved. She was diabetic and had run out of insulin. When Coop burst through the back door, stomping the snow from his boots, she turned her back to wipe away tears with her coat sleeve.

Without facing him, she said, "How's the shed?"

"Plenty of room. I found a hose to siphon gas and a few other supplies we need, but I'll pack them into the truck when it's light." When she didn't respond, he said, "What's wrong?"

She crossed the room and wrapped her arms around him. "I'm just sad for the Stevens. They look like nice people. I wonder if they had grandchildren."

Coop put his hands on her shoulders. "The Stevens?"

"That's the couple's last name. Let's get them moved so we can settle in and get some sleep. This has been the longest and most harrowing day of my life."

Every inch of Julia's body throbbed. After endless hours cramped in that stinking truck and multiple rounds of loading and unloading their supplies, she'd still had to help carry in their belongings while her mom and Coop took care of Mr. Bradley and the Stevens' bodies. She thought she'd drop right to sleep after their meal of canned stew and toast heated by the fire, but she was wide awake.

The five of them were snuggled up on mattresses in front of the fireplace in a small den at the back of the house. Hannah and Angie were out cold, and her mom was snoring like a lumberjack, which Julia had never heard her do.

Coop's mattress was near the door. She could see in the firelight that he was on his back, staring at the ceiling. While she watched him, she thought of how her mom, Angie, and Hannah had cried while Coop told them about the Stevens, but she hadn't felt a thing and worried she was getting numb to the sight of death.

Not wanting to be alone with her thoughts, she turned to Coop and whispered, "Why are you still awake?"

He rolled onto his side and propped up on an elbow. "I'm keeping watch, but I should be asking you that question."

"Wish I could sleep. I must be overstimulated. Mom always says that when Jared's wound up and can't sleep."

Coop chuckled. "Sounds like your mom. Try relaxation exercises. Picture your muscles relaxing and take deep, even breaths."

She closed her eyes and took a deep breath. "Can we stay here for a while, Coop? It's such a cute house. There's lots of food and it's so warm. I bet there's even a well, so we won't have to collect snow for drinking water."

"I didn't see a well, but there's a creek at the edge of the yard. I need to survey the property in the morning. If it checks out, we'll stay a few days if your mom agrees, but I know she's anxious to get to your uncle's ranch."

She took one more deep breath and let it out slowly. "Me, too, but I need a break before another day like this one."

Coop yawned and rolled onto his back. "Same here. Trust me, tomorrow will be easier."

She wanted to believe him, but he couldn't know for sure. None of them could.

The fire was getting low, so she got up to throw on a log. She left the screen open and stood on the hearth, letting the heat sink into her bones. She'd never experienced cold like she had that day, especially in the woods with Hannah. The warmth soothed her muscles, and she began to feel drowsy.

Coop's eyes were closed, and his breathing was deep and even when she climbed back onto her mattress. *So much for keeping watch,* she thought as she closed her eyes. She couldn't blame him. He must have been more exhausted than the rest of them put together.

The next thing she remembered was hearing a loud pop in the fireplace. She sat up as a shower of sparks landed on the ratty old rug in front of the hearth. Flames leaped up and licked the corner of her mattress. She sprang up and tried to smother the blaze with her blanket, but the fire was spreading too fast.

"Fire! Everybody up!" she cried.

The flames had covered a third of the room by the time the rest of them were on their feet. They swatted at the fire, but it overwhelmed them in seconds. It curved around toward the door, blocking their exit.

Coop yanked open the window, and the flames soared higher. "This way," he yelled over the roar.

Hannah reached him first. He thrust her through the opening, and Riley and Angie climbed out after her. Coop lifted Julia through just as a spark landed on the leg of her sweatpants and caught fire. He pushed her out and dove after her. Riley rolled her over to douse the flames in the snow.

They all scrambled to their bare feet and dashed to the street, twenty yards from the inferno. They stood on the frozen ground and watched in shock as the fire engulfed their sanctuary and the rest of everything they owned.

When Hannah started shivering, Coop ran to the truck and drove it up to the road. "Get in before you freeze."

The rest piled into the truck, but Julia stood on the edge of the pavement, hopping from foot to foot against the cold before taking off at a sprint toward the burning house.

"Julia!" she heard her mother scream but ignored her and kept running.

Coop was behind her seconds later and grabbed her arm to stop her from reaching the flames. "Julia, what are you doing? Come back to the truck."

"No," she cried, and struggled to free her hand. "Let go of me. The fire's my fault. I didn't close the fireplace screen, and now everything is gone. The fairytale cottage, our clothes, shoes, first aid supplies, and the wonderful food, all gone. I saw pancake mix and real maple syrup in the cupboard! We're all going to die because of me."

Coop took her by the shoulders and shook her. "Listen to me.

You're in shock. I won't let any of us die. Things can be replaced but you can't. I'd trade all of it for one of you."

Her eyes widened as his words sunk in, and she became still. "You mean that? After what I did?"

He put his hand to his heart. "Would I lie? Come back to the truck. Your mom's freaking out. You don't want to scare her more than she already is, do you?"

A wall caved in and sent sparks flying toward them. Julia jumped out of the way and took Coop's hand to let him lead her to the truck. He opened the door and helped her up to the seat beside Hannah.

Her mom opened her mouth to speak, but Coop said, "Don't ask." He pulled the truck closer to the house but kept a safe distance. "The fire will keep us warm until morning, so we won't have to waste gas running the heater. Once the fire's out, we'll see if there's anything we can salvage. If not, we'll move on and look for a new place to restock. In the meantime, I suggest we get some sleep."

There was a frightening crash as the roof crumbled and fell to the floor. Julia rested her head on the cold window and watched her fairytale go up in flames.

Sunlight crept over Riley's face, and she let its warmth sink into her skin before opening her eyes. The heat from the fire had kept them from freezing during the night, but the flames had faded, and the temperature inside the truck was dropping. She rubbed her face and sat up to check on the others. Angie and the girls were still sleeping, but Coop's seat was empty. She wasn't worried. He couldn't have gotten far on bare feet.

She needed to go to the bathroom and hoped the trusty bucket had survived. She tore up a sweater she'd left on the seat and wrapped her feet in the pieces before climbing out as quietly as she could and tiptoeing to the back of the truck. Coop wasn't there, but the tailgate was down, which meant he was nearby. The bucket was on its side in the bed, next to a tarp and tool chest. Angie joined her just as she reached in to grab it.

"I tried not to wake you," she said.

Angie shook her head. "You didn't." She looked at Riley's sweater-clad feet and raised her eyebrows. "Glad I sleep in socks, though they won't keep my feet warm for long. My bladder's about to burst. You don't happen to have a porta-john, do you?"

Riley held the bucket up by the handle. "Best we've got." She set the bucket down and leaned against the truck, staring at the smoking remains of the house. "Still glad we rescued you?"

Angie gave a half-grin leaned against the truck next to Riley. "Believe me when I say yes."

"I can't imagine what a nightmare it must have been living in that plane for a week."

Angie closed her eyes. "No, you can't." Riley put her hand on Angie's shoulder. "But that's over, and I'd like to use that bucket now, if you don't mind."

Riley pulled a dirty, half-used roll of paper towels from the truck and handed it to her. "All yours."

Angie crossed the road with the bucket and went into the woods for privacy. As Riley hopped onto the tailgate to wait her turn, Coop came up the driveway and stopped in front of her. He shook his head and stared at the ground.

"Nothing's salvageable. The fire incinerated everything. Even the shed got torched. Kyle and the Stevens were honored with a funeral pyre. We won't need to dig graves."

"Not sure if we can call that a silver-lining or not, but the way the house went up like a matchbox, we're lucky we didn't join them." Riley watched the rising swirls of gray smoke. "What happened with Julia last night?"

Coop rubbed his forehead. Without meeting her eyes, he said, "She was in shock and blames herself for the fire. She forgot to close the screen after she added a log and it sparked. If she hadn't been awake, we all probably would've died."

"Poor Julia. This is the last thing she needs." She rubbed her arms. "I need to get back into the truck after I use the bucket."

He kissed her cheek. "I'm going to make use of a tree, then we'll plan our next move."

She squeezed his ice-cold hand. "We're in trouble, aren't we, Coop?"

"Not a bit. You have me," he said, as he wandered off toward the woods.

Angie came back from the opposite direction and handed her the bucket and paper towels before getting back into the truck.

Riley set them on the ground. "This will have to do," she said to no one as she pulled down her sweatpants and squatted over the bucket.

When she was finished, she woke the girls and told them to hurry so they could get moving. Julia was the first to come back to the cab. She climbed in and hooked her seatbelt without uttering a word. Riley looked at Angie and rolled her eyes toward the door.

"I'll check on Hannah," she said, and left them alone.

Riley tried to brush the hair out of Julia's face, but she ducked out of the way. "Coop told me what happened with the fire. I know you feel responsible, but it was an accident. Stop blaming yourself."

Julia looked her in the eye. "Doesn't matter if it was a mistake or accident. It was my fault."

"Your fault or not, it's in the past. We can't change it, and the way I see it, you saved our lives."

Julia studied her for a moment. "I thought you'd be so mad at me."

"You thought I'd be angry over a mistake?"

Julia nodded slowly. "You're always telling me to pay better attention and not rush."

Julia shivered, so Riley draped one of the surviving blankets around them and rested her chin on the top of Julia's head. "I'm sorry I made you feel that way. It's important to pay attention, but after what we've been through these past two days, any of us could have made that mistake."

Julia pulled away and met Riley's eyes. "But I'm the one who did."

"What if it had been Hannah or me? Would you hold it against us?"

"Never, but I'm the one who has to be strong and take care of you and Hannah."

"Is that what you think?" When Julia nodded, she said, "You have that backward. I'm supposed to care for you. I know I haven't always been there since Dad died, but I'm the parent, and I promise to be there for you from now on. I do appreciate you being a big sister to Hannah, too, but you're not responsible for her. Let's put this behind us and face forward."

Angie and Hannah climbed into the truck, so Riley unwrapped herself from the blanket and motioned for Julia to cover Hannah. Julia gave her a knowing smile.

Coop emptied the bucket onto the glowing embers of the cottage and rejoined them after closing the tailgate. "Our top priorities in this order are shoes, warm clothing, water, and food. Do you all agree?" The four women nodded. "I got out of the fire with my gun and a full cartridge, but we lost the ammo, so we need to stay close and be alert. And let's avoid any more accidents."

Riley caught him glancing into the rearview mirror to give Julia a wink. She smiled and took a deep breath, reminding herself how lucky they were to be alive, and wondered how much longer that would hold true.

"That looks promising," Angie said, as Coop passed a pretty brick farmhouse missing a front door.

It was the twentieth house they'd seen that was still standing. The other nineteen had been cleaned out without a scrap of food, a drop of clean water or even a shoe left behind. Riley wondered why Angie thought this one would be any different.

"Didn't you notice there's no door, Angie?" Coop said.

"I'm not talking about the house. I meant that big workshop near the woods in the back," she replied.

Coop moved the truck so they could all see the large metal building that backed up to the tree line. It looked like a woodworking shop. A heavy padlock hung from the door handle.

"That's definitely worth a look," Coop said. "Riley, please grab the crowbar and come with me."

Riley's feet felt like blocks of ice, and the last thing she wanted to do was leave the warm truck, but they were almost out of gas. If there was anything in that building that would improve their dire situation, she had to try. She got out and opened the tailgate to get the crowbar as Coop ran across the grass with paper towels and grocery bags on his feet. She ran to the shed and peered in the window as he worked to break the lock. Trunks, cabinets, and boxes lined the walls. There had to be something of use to them.

She heard a metal pop, then stepped back as Coop slid the doors open. They went in and started opening the cabinets, drawers, and trunks. There was no food, but they found three cases of bottled water, two full gas cans and a siphon hose. Best of all were the old hunting clothes and boots. They'd be too big for the women but better than nothing.

"Get the others in here," Coop said. "Let's load up as much as we can and get out of here before anyone sees us. Then, we'll search for food. The girls must be starving."

Riley went to the edge of the yard and waved for the others to join them. Within minutes, the floor of the workshop looked like a weekend rummage sale.

"Look what I found," Julia said, showing them an old shotgun she'd taken out of a trunk. "It was wrapped in a towel, with three boxes of shells."

"Excellent," Coop said. "Add it to the pile."

The shotgun would come in handy if they were forced to hunt for food. A further search of the workshop yielded three small propane tanks, a rope, and a tarp. The items weren't top priorities, but they'd found enough to keep them alive until they could replenish their supplies. What they needed most were food and more fuel. Coop poured the gas they'd taken from the workshop into the tank and charted their course for Warrenton, the next town on their route.

CHAPTER NINE

"I won't be going on with you after Warrenton," Angie said as they neared the town.

Riley turned and peered at her over the seat. "You're staying?"

"Yes, if I can find someone willing to take me in."

"You can't leave us," Hannah said and grasped Angie's hand. "You're part of our family."

"Leave her be, Hannah," Riley said, without taking her eyes off Angie. "Mind if I ask why?"

She lowered her head and put a hand over her eyes. "I have to find some way to get home to my children. They don't know about their father or that I'm alive."

Riley recognized the anguish in Angie's face. Her thoughts raced back to the day she had to tell her children that Zach was dead. Her parents offered to do it in her place, but she knew the news had to come from her. As devastating as that had been, it was nothing compared to what Angie was suffering. She'd seen her husband die, and she had no way of knowing if her children were alive.

She swallowed her grief and said, "I understand that you're

anxious to get back to them, but is it worth taking up with strangers who could be dangerous?"

"You were strangers. There must be others like you. I'm banking on the hope that not everyone has turned evil."

"Don't count on that," Julia said and rubbed her bruised eye. "You're the only nice person we've met. Come with us to my uncle's ranch until it gets warmer. Then we'll help you get home."

"That's kind of you, Julia, and I appreciate all you've done to help. I couldn't have survived another night in that hellish plane any more than Kyle could, but you're heading too far in the wrong direction. Look how long it's taken you to get this far from DC. and you've been on the road for two days."

"Can't argue with that," Coop said. "We'll help you find a safe group for you to travel with, if you're right and such a thing still exists."

"I'll miss you," Hannah said and rested her head on Angie's shoulder.

Coop exited the highway and navigated toward the center of town. The streets were quiet and empty. Smoke rising from scattered chimneys was the only sign of life. They reached the main thoroughfare and passed a large church with a full parking lot.

Riley leaned forward to get a better look. "Why is the parking lot filled with cars that aren't wrecked?" She glanced at her watch. "It's Sunday. Do you think they're having church?"

Coop put the truck in park. "Unlikely but possible."

"What better place to gather in a crisis?" Angie said. "We should check to see if there are people inside. It could be an emergency shelter. They might have food."

Hannah sat forward and leaned over the front seat. "Can we check, Coop? I'm starving."

"Me, too," Julia chimed in. "And they could have cots and clothes that fit us better."

"Sorry to disappoint, but we can't take the risk," Coop said.

"It's safer to avoid large crowds. We passed plenty of shops full of clothes, and we'll find food somewhere else."

Angie unhooked her seatbelt. "Drop me off, then. I'm willing to risk it."

"We can't let you go alone," Riley said and touched Coop's arm. "We don't have to stay, but we should at least look. They could have useful information about what's ahead, at the very least."

Coop eyed her for a moment, then shifted into drive and turned into the parking lot. "On your heads be it. Girls, get down and wait here with the doors locked."

"We know the drill," Julia said as she pulled a blanket over her head.

Angie walked ahead of Coop and Riley, and when she was out of earshot, Riley said, "If the situation inside passes muster, would you consider staying? We need time to catch our breath and rest."

Coop stopped and turned with his back to Angie. "You just told Angie we can't trust strangers."

Riley stared at the large, intricately carved wooden doors of the church. "Reminds me of our church back home. It feels familiar."

Coop put a hand on her shoulder. "The people inside might not even be the members of the congregation. They could have come from anywhere, like us. No matter how safe it appears, we don't know who we can trust, just like you told Angie. Let's not make any judgments until we see who's inside."

Riley nodded. "Fair enough but keep an open mind."

"Fine, but my gut is telling me to be wary of any crowds."

Coop did a quick final inspection of his handgun before knocking. The door opened seconds later to reveal a tall Germanic-looking man with a kind, open face despite the shotgun resting on his shoulder. Coop's hand instinctively moved to his holster. The man stiffened until he noticed Riley and Angie.

He lowered the gun and stuck out a hand the size of a plate. "Brett Collins. Sorry about the gun, but we never know who we'll be facing when we open the door. Is it just the three of you?"

Coop stared at Mr. Collins' enormous proffered hand for a moment before shaking it without answering his question. "Neal Cooper. We saw the cars in the parking lot and thought we'd stop."

It was strange for Riley to hear Coop drop his doctor's title and nickname to call himself Neal. It signaled for her to be on her guard.

Brett gave their odd attire a look before saying, "Looks like you've had some trouble, but who hasn't these days? We don't have much. Come in and see what we can do to help."

Coop gave a restrained smile. "That's kind of you."

Riley stepped forward and offered her hand. "Dr. Riley Poole. Please, call me Riley."

She could feel Coop frowning behind her, but she saw no harm in being honest. Letting them know she was a doctor could be a valuable bargaining chip.

Brett smiled. "A doctor? Excellent news. We have sick and injured here and can really use your help."

"Coop's a doctor, too," Angie blurted out, and Coop's frown grew exponentially.

Riley tried to hide her smile. "This is our new friend, Angie Hughes."

Brett nodded and motioned for them to follow him down a flight of stairs to a large social hall beneath the chapel. The crowd grew quiet when they entered, and fifty pairs of eyes stared back at them.

"We have a few more friends to join us," Brett said. "These are Drs. Neal Cooper and Riley Poole, their friend Angie Hughes."

The occupants broke into action at once and crowded around them.

A slightly overweight middle-aged woman placed a stack of blankets and a pillow in Riley's hands. "Mercy Billings here," she said and pointed to the far corner. "We have three cots left. Just enough."

"Thank you," Riley said. "Are all of you members of the congregation?"

"Most, but some are transplants like you. We were preparing an emergency shelter as a precaution when the CME hit. We didn't think we'd all need to make use of it."

"How come you didn't stay in your homes and distribute food and supplies from here?"

"Safety in numbers. Some have stayed in their homes, but bands of mercenaries have started terrorizing residents in the area."

Riley nodded. "We've run into a few of those ourselves. You're smart to stay together."

She carried the blankets to the corner and put them on one of the cots. She bumped into Coop as she turned to go back for the girls. He was jumpy and kept nervously scanning the room.

"I don't like this. The room is overcrowded, and the only exit is up the stairs. We'd be trapped in a fire or an attack. Angie can stay if she wants, but we're leaving."

Riley crossed her arms. "I'm not going anywhere except to get the girls. Coop, we're exhausted and starving. It's been a helluva a few days. We need to stay. I never thought I'd be the one to say this, but you're overreacting. That's usually my department. It *is* crowded in here, but these people seem harmless enough."

He ran a hand through his hair. "I don't know what it is. Just a feeling."

Riley wrapped her hands around his. "Take a breath. Let's get something to eat and see to the sick and wounded. That will get us on their good side. After we've had a rest, we'll go in search of supplies. Come with me to the truck."

She tugged his hands to get him moving. He reluctantly allowed her to lead him through the crowd to where Brett stood at the bottom of the stairs.

"We left our teenage daughters in the truck, just to be safe," Coop told him. "We'll bring them down, then have a look at your sick and wounded."

"I'm grateful, and your girls are welcome. We have a nice group of kids here," Brett said. "And we'll see if we can find you some clothes."

Julia and Hannah practically jumped for joy when Riley told them what awaited in the church. Once they were inside, three girls their age hugged them and took them to find clothing and food.

Brett had been right about not having much to offer, but Riley's stomach growled at what there was. The food was mostly canned vegetables and meat with a few protein bars, cracker packs and granola bars. A teenage boy guarding the table handed her a can opener. She ate a small can of tuna, some corn and a granola bar. It felt like a feast.

With her hunger satisfied, she asked Mercy to show her who needed medical help. Coop joined them a few minutes later. Most of the patients had injuries like what they'd seen in the hotel; burns, broken bones and cuts. A few more had coughs from smoke inhalation or intestinal infections, most likely from drinking unsterilized water. Anyone with more critical injuries most likely would have died by that time.

She and Coop spent an hour doing what little they could to help them with the scant supplies on hand. They'd need a list of essential items to look for on their run even though odds of finding what they needed were slim.

Riley found Hannah and Julia regaling a circle of teenagers

with their harrowing adventure. She interrupted Julia and whispered that she needed to talk to her.

"We're going on a supply run. Get whatever you want to take with you. Coop's waiting."

Julia tugged on her arm to pull her away from the group. "Do Hannah and I have to go? These people are so nice, and Angie's here. We can stay with her."

"I'm sorry, sweetheart, but I'm not comfortable leaving you here," she whispered. "I'm sure these people are perfectly safe, but I want you with me."

Julia folded her arms and stuck out her lip. Riley caught a flash of her other daughter Emily in the mannerism and almost broke into the tears, but Hannah came up behind her and the moment passed.

Hannah glanced at Julia. "What's the matter?"

"She's making us go look for supplies with them. I asked her to let us stay, but she won't. We have to get back in that stupid truck."

"I'm glad," Hannah said. "I'm tired of being left behind."

Julia eyed her in surprise, then nodded. "Fine, but we'd better find some better treats. I'm still starving."

Riley saw Coop by the stairs, tapping his watch to get her to hurry. "Thank you, Julia," she said. "Say goodbye to your new friends, and let's go."

They raced up the stairs after Coop and found Brett back at his post by the doors.

He handed Coop a clipboard. "You need to sign out each time you leave. It helps us keep track of who's coming and going. Make sure to sign in when you return."

Coop scratched his signature onto the list, and said, "Will do," before rushing off to the truck with the girls in tow.

Riley signed her name and thanked Brett. "We were in dire need of help. We appreciate you taking us in. I don't know what we would have done."

"I should be thanking you for treating our people. We've lost several. I'm sure you understand."

"More than you know. We'll try to find more medical supplies."

"We'd be grateful."

She was about to ask who was in charge of the group when Coop honked the horn and signaled for her to come to the truck. She gave Brett a quick smile and rushed across the parking lot.

"We only have a few hours," Coop said when she got in. "I want to find a place to stay tonight before dark."

Coop's tension visibly diminished the farther they got from the church. He parallel-parked in front of a florist shop and drooped against the seat with his eyes closed.

Riley studied him for a moment, confused by his behavior. "What's going on with you? I wouldn't have pegged you as the claustrophobic type."

"I'm not. I wish I could say that it's sleep deprivation or a delayed reaction to the Crawford incident and the fire, but it's not that either. A hundred people crammed into that basement with only one exit feels like a recipe for disaster. You may be right that I'm overreacting, but I'm not spending a single night in that place."

"I like it there," Julia said. Riley glared at her, and she closed her mouth.

Riley took a beat to stop herself from blurting out her own thoughts. They'd found the first group willing to help them since the CME and Coop wanted to run in the opposite direction. They were all beyond exhausted and needed food and a safe place to rest. How could he ask her to walk away from that?

"I know your hunches have been right until now, and you've saved us more than once, but you're wrong this time. It would be irresponsible for me to drag the girls out of that church tonight. If you aren't willing to stay, you'll have to go off on your own, but I'm keeping the truck."

She noticed Julia fidgeting uncomfortably in the back seat. She would have preferred to have the uncomfortable conversation out of earshot of the girls.

Coop opened his eyes and stared at her. "Don't be so dramatic. We're not splitting up. How about a compromise? If I find a place where you'd feel safe spending the night, will you bring the girls and come with me?"

She hesitated to mull it over. She couldn't imagine finding a setup a good as the church, but if she agreed to his terms and he found another option, she'd be forced to go with him or separate from him.

Deciding to play the odds, she put out her hand and said, "I agree, but I decide what's safe."

Coop eagerly shook her hand. "Deal. Let's get to work."

They got out of the truck and surveyed the buildings along the surrounding blocks. Most were quaint shops, art galleries and local restaurants. The restaurants or markets would have been emptied days earlier, so there was no point in checking those, so they decided to widen their search.

Coop drove in ever-widening circles for over an hour until he found a quaint general store and café tucked off the road behind an antique store.

"Perfect," he said, as he jumped out of the truck and ran in through the unlocked doors with the other three on his heels.

Roughly two-thirds of the food shelves were empty, but there was enough left to fill four plastic bags with food. Riley found a box of cinnamon buns and handed it to Julia. She and Hannah sat down on a stack of laundry detergent boxes to devour them.

Riley found a one-pound bag of her favorite tortilla chips and a jar of salsa. She downed half the bag before handing to Hannah. "Carry me to the car if I fall into a food coma," she told Coop.

He laughed and opened a bag to show her his treasures; five cans of spam, six cans of sardines, and a box of bison jerky packets. "I can't believe no one took this stuff."

She wrinkled her nose. "Can't you?"

"Great sources of protein. You'll be thanking me."

"Doubt that," she grumbled.

"I'm going to check the back. You coming?"

She got to her feet with a groan and followed him to the storage room while the girls hunted for more sweets. Riley and Coop pushed stacks of empty boxes and ruined merchandise out of the way and discovered a large tent covered in dust, three army cots with sleeping bags, and two backpacks.

Riley picked up a sleeping bag. "Looks like these have been here since the Great War."

"They'll keep us just as warm. Add them on the pile."

They grabbed a few other odds and ends like thread, needles, pocket knives, and toilet paper, then enlisted the girls to help load the truck.

"Wish we'd found more food," Julia said, as Coop back onto the highway.

"Be grateful for what we have," Riley said. "We need to find a pharmacy next. I feel naked without medical supplies."

Coop rubbed his chin. "The chain pharmacies were probably already hit. A local independent pharmacy is our best bet."

"Shouldn't be too hard to find in a small town like this."

"What I wouldn't give for GPS right now."

They wove through strip malls and shopping centers for twenty-five minutes before they found a small local pharmacy. Coop broke the door open with the crowbar from the truck. They were all stunned when they saw the store was virtually untouched.

"I don't get it," Riley said. "It's like what we found in that outdoor store in DC. How did this windfall get missed?"

Coop shrugged. "Too out of the way? But that doesn't explain why people who live around here left it alone. And where's the owner? Dead?"

"Whatever the reason, it's another miracle. Hope we don't run out of those before we reach Wytheville."

For a full hour, they packed the truck bed and cab with medical instruments, medications, food, water, and other useful supplies. When there wasn't another inch of space to fill, Coop took Riley's last $500 from his pocket and left it on the counter.

"How did that survive the fire?

"I doubted anyone would want to steal it, so I left it in the truck."

Her eyes glistened as she kissed his cheek and said, "What a thoughtful gesture. I know you think I'm silly, but I'm grateful."

He tried to hide his blushing cheeks when the girls giggled as he climbed behind the wheel, but that just endeared him to her even more. She was finding out more every minute what a remarkable man he was.

As they rode in silence, Riley realized that Coop hadn't mentioned looking for somewhere to spend the night since they'd left on their scavenger hunt. She hoped he'd changed his mind, but when they were within blocks of the church, he pulled in front of an old theater and turned off the engine.

She was about to ask what he was doing when he said, "I want to see if this might be a good place to stay. No one would have reason to break into a theater. If the seats recline, it'll be comfortable for sleeping."

Riley frowned. He hadn't forgotten. "But why a theater and not a hotel with beds or another house with a fireplace?"

"Those types of shelter will be popular. It'll be chilly in here, but there aren't windows to make it too drafty or let people see that we're inside. We could even set up that tent we found."

His reasoning made sense but still didn't convince her that it was smart to abandon the church. She humored him and told the girls to stay in the truck while she reluctantly went around the building to a back door, crossing her fingers that it had been trashed. They went through a crowded storage room, and her heart sank when she saw the immaculate lobby. It appeared nothing had been touched since the last showing. Even the concession stand cases were filled with inviting boxes of candy. The girls would be thrilled about that.

They pushed through the doors into the pitch-dark theater. When Coop clicked on his flashlight, Riley instinctively reached for her penlight, but it had been lost in the fire. Just one more link to her pre-CME life gone.

Coop pulled a much smaller flashlight out of his pocket and held it out to her. "Not your penlight, but it was as close as I could get."

She took the light and cupped it between her hands. Embarrassingly, tears formed in her eyes. *Why am I getting emotional over a simple flashlight,* she asked herself, glad it was too dark for Coop to see. She turned it on and shined it around the room. The seats were the big cushy kind that reclined. They must have modernized the theater recently. She hoped they'd be able to adjust the chairs without electricity.

Coop turned to her and beamed. "This is perfect."

Riley pulled her coat closer and rubbed her arms. "I wouldn't say perfect. It's freezing in here."

"Maybe they have a heater at the church they'd be willing to lend us."

"We can't use it inside here. No ventilation."

"We'll crack one of the emergency exit doors."

Riley dropped into a seat. "The church is warm, they're willing to share food and water, and they have sick and injured who need our help. You say staying is dangerous. I think it's a mistake to leave."

Coop squatted in front of her. "I've asked you to trust me

before, and I am again. It's one night, Riley. If we get a good night's sleep, we'll leave in the morning and reach your uncle's ranch by nightfall. I want to get back to the girls, and we don't have time to search for somewhere else. You gave me your word."

Riley looked into his eyes. He was a good and kind man. He had their best interest at heart and had proven he'd do what it took to protect them. She pushed her misgivings aside and chose to trust him once more. It *was* only one night.

"We'd better get going then. We need to find more suitable clothes. Should be everything we need in those shops on the main drag."

Coop tenderly placed his gloved hands on her cheeks and gave her a tender kiss. "Do you know what this means to me? I'm in your debt."

She kissed the end of his nose. "Trust me, I plan to collect."

Julia was ecstatic to see Coop and her mom heading back to the truck. They'd been gone for so long that she was sure someone had jumped them in the theater. She'd been getting ready to ask someone to help her look for them. Hannah had slept through the whole thing, as usual.

Her relief faded when Coop announced that they'd be spending the night in the theater. She started to argue with her mom but stopped when she gave her *the look* and put her hands on her shoulders.

"Coop has his reasons and I trust him. Not another word about it.

"Well, if he has his reasons," she said sarcastically. "I've made friends at the church."

"Just do as I say. The church isn't far from the theater. I'll drive you over to visit in the morning."

"Whatever," she mumbled and slumped in her seat as they rode to the church.

When she and Hannah finished bundling up their few belongings at the church, they said a tearful goodbye to their new friends and Angie.

Julia gave her a tight hug. "Are you sure you won't come with us? It won't be the same without you."

Angie pulled away and wiped Julia's tears with her thumb. "I wish I could. I'll miss you, but I have to get home to my family, and you have to get to yours. Understand?"

Julia nodded. "We'll miss you, too."

Hannah hugged her and ran up the stairs, too overcome to speak. Julia dragged herself after her but cheered up when she remembered all the great stuff cram-packed in the truck. They weren't going to starve or freeze to death because of her. The thought made it easier to leave the church.

While they tried to find room for their stuff in the backseat, her mom came across the parking lot carrying what looked like a kerosene heater. It was smaller than the one they had at the hotel, but she was happy to see it even though she was still afraid of things that could catch them on fire.

When her mom plunked the heater on the ground, Coop said, "How did you talk them into giving us that? Brett was pissed when I told him we were leaving."

"I had to do some compromising. When we return it, we have to treat their patients and leave some of our medical supplies."

Coop put his hands on his hips. "How did he know we have medical supplies?"

"I told him. It was the only way he'd agree to this. What happened to Dr. Charming back there with Brett? You were acting like a petulant child."

Julia giggled, and Coop and Riley swung around to face her. "What? That's what you always used to say to me when I pitched a fit. It was funny to hear you say it to Coop."

Coop winked at her and smiled.

Riley continued to glare at her. "That's not funny, young lady. Coop, you need to work on your diplomatic skills if we're going to get through this."

"Brett said we owed them and were being selfish to leave. He wouldn't let it go and I lost my temper. We don't owe them anything. We treated their sick and injured in exchange for what they gave us. It was a fair trade. But your mom's absolutely right," Coop said to Julia. "I need to watch my temper. This isn't a game."

"Thank you," Riley said. "Now, get in the truck, you two. You'll have to hold the heater between you."

They squeezed into the truck, and Coop drove the two miles to the theater. When Julia stepped into the lobby with her first load of supplies, she cried, "Candy. Can we have whatever we want?"

Riley came in behind her and set the load she carried on the red-carpeted floor. "Yes, after the truck's unloaded."

Julia and Hannah rushed back and forth, hauling their new treasures into the theater. When they finished thirty-minutes later, they sat behind the concessions counter and feasted on movie theater treats. All that was missing was popcorn.

When they'd had their fill, her mom announced that they were going clothes shopping. "There are several shops nearby where we should find everything we need," she said.

Julia squealed in delight and pulled on her massive boots. When Hannah was ready, the four of them left on their shopping spree. As they strolled by window displays lit by the auroras, Julia remembered shopping with her mom for the conference reception. That day seemed like a lifetime ago but less than a week had passed. An overwhelming longing for her former life washed over her, followed by regret for taking it for granted.

Riley and Hannah turned and walked back to her when she stopped in the middle of the sidewalk.

"What's wrong, sweetheart? You look like you just lost your best friend. I thought you were excited to get new clothes."

"I just remembered something pre-CME. I'm fine."

"Shopping for your dress in DC?" Julia gave a slight nod, and Riley put an arm around her. "I was thinking about that, too."

"Wish I'd appreciated what I had back then."

"Me, too," Hannah said and stared at the ground.

Julia pasted on a smile. "Sorry for being such a buzz-kill. Forget all that and appreciate what we have now. It's like post-apocalyptic Christmas." Julia stepped between Hannah and Riley and took their hands. "We can have whatever we want for free."

Coop stepped into a men's store, and they passed a trendy women's boutique, but Riley kept walking.

When they passed the second one, Hannah said, "Why aren't we going in there?"

"We'll stop on the way back, and you can each pick out an outfit, but we need more practical clothes. There's a store on the next block with coats and boots. That's where we're headed."

"Great idea," Julia said, making a vow with herself to never complain again.

While they stocked up on as much clothing for themselves as they could carry, Coop came out of the men's store wearing a new coat and carrying only one small bag containing two pairs of jeans, one sweater, and five pairs each of socks and underwear.

Riley peeked into the bag and said, "That's all you're taking? You understand that we'll have to wash our dirty laundry by hand?"

"I'll wear each thing twice, except for the underwear."

"Glad to hear that," Julia said and laughed.

Coop set up the tent when they got back to the theater and heated up a meal of canned spaghetti and Bison jerky on Sterno cans. Julia wolfed hers down even though she'd stuffed herself with candy two hours earlier. After eating, Hannah and Julia changed into sweats in the tent and unrolled their sleeping bags.

"You should take the first watch, Mom," Julia said. "Coop didn't do so well last night."

"I won't argue," he said and laid his sleeping bag over the seat closest to where the kerosene heater blasted away by the emergency exit. "Give me three hours, then I'll take watch."

Riley guzzled an energy drink and put another on the floor next to her folding chair. "You've got it. If I feel myself getting sleepy, I'll run laps."

Julia hugged her and gave Coop a peck on the cheek before joining Hannah in the tent. She climbed into her sleeping bag, feeling safer than she had since leaving the hotel. She'd loved the little house she burnt down, but the theater felt impenetrable.

"Good night, Hannah," she whispered and drifted off in seconds.

———

Riley and Coop took their three-hour shifts during the night, but Coop woke her at four after she'd only been asleep for an hour.

"Is it the girls?" she asked after checking the time.

"No, they're sleeping," he said and put his finger to his lips. "Listen."

She waited a few seconds and was about to say she didn't hear anything when the sound of a barrage of gunfire broke the silence. It was followed by two more volleys, then stopped.

"What is that? Do you think it's near the theater?"

"That's been going on for a few minutes. I checked out front to make sure it wasn't close by. It's coming from the direction of the church."

"We need to go see." She turned on her flashlight and searched around her chair. "Where are my coat and boots?"

Coop dropped into a seat and propped his feet on the chair in front of him. "We're not leaving the theater."

"But there could be injured people. What about Angie?"

"It's too dangerous, and Angie made her choice. If it's safe in the morning, we'll offer to help."

Riley stared at him, hardly believing what she was hearing. "Isn't that a little heartless?"

"No, it's rational. What if it's Crawford's gang? Do you want to have another run-in with them? And what can we do to stop whoever it is? And what about the girls? Do we leave them here alone while we rush to the rescue?"

She sank into the seat next to him and rubbed her face. "If we aren't going to do anything about it, why did you wake me?"

"Just wanted to prepare you. Maybe it's just a shootout in the street over food. Trust me, I pray this doesn't have anything to do with those innocent people at the church."

She had no doubt he meant it but couldn't let go of the thought that people could die if they waited to go. On the other hand, rushing in could lead them into the middle of a war zone.

He reached for her hand and brushed it with his thumb. "I'm sorry, Riley. You don't deserve to go through all of this. Get some sleep if you can. I'll finish my shift."

She put her hand over his. "Thank you. I'll try." She went to the tent but turned before stepping inside. "You don't deserve this either."

Despite her middle-of-the-night scare, Riley felt more rested than she had in days when Coop woke her at nine. He unzipped her sleeping bag, snuggled up to her and started kissing her neck.

"Did you hear any more shots last night?" she whispered.

Coop signed and rolled away from her. "Way to kill the mood. I did not."

She sat up and wrapped her arms around her knees. "Sorry, welcome to the post-apocalyptic world."

He stood and helped her to her feet. Pulling her into his

arms, he said, "We might as well get ready to go, then. The truck is almost packed. We just need the tent and sleeping bags."

"Why didn't you wake me sooner?"

"I wanted to give you the same six hours I got. This could be another long day."

Riley stepped out of his arms and stretched. "Better than the last two, I hope."

He bent down to roll her sleeping bag. "Can't get much worse." They froze and stared at each other. "Wish I hadn't said that."

"I'll tell the girls it's time to go."

She couldn't shake her feeling of foreboding as they packed the last of their belongings. They both knew things could get worse, very much worse. Part of her wanted to drive away from Warrenton and never look back, but the other part knew she could never do that. She didn't want to risk conjuring bad karma, and as Coop said the day of the CME strike, they were doctors first.

Coop pulled into the parking lot ten minutes later and drove toward the front of the church but started to turn the truck when they were fifteen yards from the doors.

Riley unhooked her belt and sat forward. "What are you doing?"

"Riley, look at the doors."

She turned her head toward the front of the church and gasped. One of the beautifully carved doors hung at an odd angle on its hinges. The other was on the ground.

Julia leaned over Hannah to see what they were staring at. "Who did that?"

"Doesn't matter. We're getting out of here," Coop said.

He put the truck in gear and stepped on the gas just as Brett Collins ran out and waved his arms to stop them.

"Coop, wait," Riley cried. He stepped on the brake but didn't shift into park. Riley rolled down her window. "What happened? Are you hurt?"

Brett ran up to the car and leaned into the open window. "A gang of five men attacked us last night. They took at least ten of our people and killed or injured others. We need your help."

Riley reached for the handle, but Coop put a hand on her arm to stop her. "How many dead?"

Brett's voice caught as he said, "Eight."

Coop shook his head. "How long have they been gone?"

"Several hours. It happened in the middle of the night and was over in minutes. They killed the three men standing guard and took the rest of us completely by surprise."

Riley turned to Coop. He gave a slight nod and cranked the steering wheel. "I'll pull to the front. Tell us what you need."

Brett jogged alongside and waited for Coop to park. They dug out the medical supplies and heater, then Brett led them toward the stairs past three bodies covered in sheets.

When they neared the chapel, Riley paused and turned to Julia. "Put that box down, sweetheart, and wait for us in there."

Julia dropped her box at the top of the stairs. "Don't leave us, Mom. What will we do if those men come back?"

"They won't, but find a good place to hide, just in case. I won't be long, then we'll be on our way to the ranch. You'll be with Holly tonight."

Julia nodded and looked away. Hannah put her box on top of Julia's and eyed Riley. The fear in Hannah's eyes pierced her heart. The poor girl had already lost one mother that week. Nothing mattered more to her than protecting her girls, but she kept getting forced into abandoning them. It would kill her if anything happened to them while she was protecting strangers. She was tempted to hand over the med supplies and leave Brett's people to fend for themselves.

Julia reached for Hannah's hand and gave Riley a weak smile. "We'll be fine. Go help those people so we can get out of here."

Riley hugged each girl and kissed the tops of their heads. "Thank you for being so brave. I'm sorry I have to do this."

Hannah's voice tremored when she said, "We understand," and walked with Julia into the chapel.

"What injuries can we expect?" Coop asked Brett.

"Five with gunshot wounds in their limbs, one chest wound, a gunshot to the gut, and one in the back."

Riley's eyes widened. "They shot someone in the back?"

"A woman was trying to escape up the stairs with her baby. She fell and dropped him when they shot her. The baby didn't survive."

Riley rubbed her face as she fought back the tears. "Sickening. What kind of monsters were these?"

Brett stopped and faced her. "The worst kind."

She took a breath to calm her rising panic and switched into doctor mode. The scene in the church social hall was like the ballroom clinic in miniature. It was hard to believe they were in the same room they'd seen the day before. One end was sectioned off for the wounded. Small groups of people talked in whispers at the other end. Only about a third of the group remained.

Riley and Coop set up their supplies and got to work. She started with the grieving mother who had the wound to the spine. Coop took the man with the gunshot to the abdomen. There wasn't much either could do for their patients but clean their wounds and stitch torn tissue. The bullets had missed the major organs in Coop's patient, and he had a slim chance at survival, but Riley's patient wasn't so lucky. She would soon be reunited with her son.

When they'd done what they could for the others, they left care instructions with Brett.

He shook their hands and said, "We're deeply in your debt."

"You need to get your people out of here," Coop said.

Brett gave a slight nod. "Nowhere else to go. Best of luck to you."

"You, too," Riley said. "Coop, please, get the girls to the truck. I'm going to say goodbye to Angie."

"She's not here," Brett said.

Riley stepped closer to him. "Not here. Do you mean dead? Or taken hostage?"

"Not dead, and I'm not sure if she was taken. The attack happened fast, and it was absolute pandemonium. Some were taken, some ran. I didn't see what happened to your friend. I'm sorry."

Coop motioned for her to follow. "Come on, Riley. We have a long way to go."

She took one last look at the pale, terror-stricken faces and dragged herself up the stairs behind Coop.

Before they went into the chapel, she put her hand in the crook of his elbow. "Go ahead. Say it. You have a right to."

He raised an eyebrow. "What are you babbling about?"

"*I told you so*. I feel you thinking it."

He put his hands on her shoulders. "First off, even if I was thinking it, and I wasn't, I have too much class to throw that in your face. Second, it hurts that you think I would. Third, I get zero satisfaction from being right." He dropped his hands and moved away.

Riley stopped him. "You knew we shouldn't stay. How? Is seeing the future another of your superpowers?"

"It was coincidence, not a premonition. I'd bet my life this was Crawford's gang, but there will be more like them."

Tears brimmed in her eyes, and he pulled her into his arms. She rested her head on his chest and let his strength flow into her. "I was ready to rush into our deaths last night. I'm putting you in charge of all our decisions. No more arguments."

He stepped away and studied her for a moment. "I don't believe you for a second, and what would be the fun in that? Let's rescue those poor terrified girls and get the hell away from this place."

Riley passed a road sign showing they were twenty-eight miles from Charlottesville, so they'd made over fifty miles in three hours. If Coop hadn't been sleeping, she would have whooped for joy. They'd dodged a tragedy in Warrenton, no thanks to her, and escaped with enough gas to get them to Charlottesville. If their luck held out, they could stock up with enough to make it to the ranch by nightfall. She was beginning to see the light at the end of the long, horrifying tunnel.

She peeked at the girls through the rearview mirror. They'd been brokenhearted to hear about Angie but putting Warrenton behind them had buoyed their spirits. Each quietly read a novel they'd found buried under faded newspapers in the workshop.

"What are you reading?" she quietly asked Julia.

She looked up from the pages and smiled. "*The Hobbit.*"

"Your favorite. That was a lucky find. Don't you ever get tired of reading it?"

"Never. Do you get tired of *Pride and Prejudice?*"

"Good point. What about you, Hannah?"

Hannah glanced at the cover. "*The Sisterhood of the Traveling Pants.*"

"I love that movie," Julia said. "Never read the book."

Hannah shrugged. "I've never seen it or read the book. It's good so far."

Coop grunted and adjusted his pillow. "Too loud. Need to sleep."

She smiled down at him and whispered, "Sorry."

She winked at Julia and saw Hannah's eyes widen an instant before she let out a piercing scream.

"Mom, look out," Julia cried at the same time, but it was too late.

A truck-sized hunk of metal fell from the sky and landed on the road ten yards in front of the truck, sending up a wave of exploded asphalt that covered the windshield. Riley slammed on the brakes and cranked the wheel. The pickup flipped and rolled twice before coming to an upright stop, parallel to the metal object.

Riley gripped the wheel, unable to take a breath, then the world grew dark.

CHAPTER TEN

"RILEY, BREATHE," Coop called to her through the darkness, and she felt a sting on her cheek an instant later. She forced her eyes open and watched him jump out of the truck and run around to the driver's side. He yanked the door open and lifted the handle to recline her seat.

She did as he'd ordered and drew in a deep, cold breath. Her head immediately cleared. She started to sit forward, but Coop put a hand on her shoulder to stop her.

"No, you don't. Let me examine you first," he said. "I have to tear your sweater open."

She shoved his hands away. "I'm fine. Just knocked the wind out of me. I have to get to Julia and Hannah."

"We're fine, Mom. Let Coop check you," Julia said.

She struggled to sit up, but Coop pinned one shoulder to the seat and pointed at the dashboard. It was two feet closer to her than it should have been. Riley gasped, then looked at Coop. A stream of blood flowed from where the stitches on his stairwell injury were torn open.

She ripped off her sweater and handed it to him. "Tie this around your head before you examine me."

He touched his fingers to the cut, then pulled his hand away and stared at the blood. "Don't even feel that." He tore off a sleeve to wrap his head before leaning over to evaluate her injuries. He unhooked her seatbelt and pressed his ear to her sternum. After listening for two minutes, he said, "I could do this better with a stethoscope, but your rhythm is good, and the bone structure seems sound. You're going to have one hell of a bruise."

She pushed him out of the way and scrambled out of the truck. Julia and Hannah were already standing on the road, examining their cuts. Riley went to Julia first and started checking her injuries, beginning with her head. Aside from a few tiny lacerations from broken glass, she'd come through the accident unscathed.

Coop checked Hannah and found the same result. His cuts and scrapes were more serious, but by the look of the truck on the front passenger side, he was lucky to be alive. He had three lacerations in addition to his head wound that needed stitches yet again. Riley took the crowbar from under the front seat and got the girls to help her pry open the crumpled tailgate to get to the medical supplies. After digging out the med packs, she discovered the can of antiseptic spray they'd used on Kyle. There was just enough to spray his worst cuts.

"That's not going to dull the pain much, but it's the best I can do."

He cringed when she sprayed the cut on his forehead and said, "Don't suppose there's any morphine?"

"The vials shattered." She handed Julia a flashlight. "Shine that into the center of the cut, please." After swabbing the wound with alcohol, she poured some over the suture and needle. "Hold as still as you can, Coop. This isn't going to tickle."

Coop grinned and closed his eyes. "In med school, I sutured a cut on my leg after only one beer. I can handle this."

Riley was glad his eyes were closed so he couldn't see her

hand shaking as she raised the needle to his forehead. She stopped and closed hers, too, and took three deep, even breaths.

Coop opened his eyes. "What's taking so long? Get it over with."

"Fine," she said and jabbed the needle through his skin. He'd been smart to annoy her. It stopped the shaking.

A thin film of perspiration formed on his forehead while she stitched. He kept his eyes closed and panted, but he didn't cry out or complain. Riley was impressed with his restraint.

"Hannah," she said without taking her eyes from her work. "Look in that small first aid kit for some squares of gauze. When you have them, wipe Coop's forehead. We need to keep his sweat from dripping into the wound."

Before Hannah took a step, Coop reached up and wiped his head with his coat sleeve. "How's that?"

Riley sighed in exasperation. "Unsanitary. I forgot what a terrible patient you are. Hannah, I still need the gauze, please."

Their wounds were cleaned and bandaged thirty minutes later, including the duct tape Coop had insisted on wrapping around the cut on his arm. They hugged each other to celebrate the miracle of being alive, but the celebrating came to an abrupt halt when Riley got a good look at the truck. It was demolished. She sank to the ground and started to hyperventilate.

Coop bent over her and said, "Panic, or is this from the accident?"

"Panic," she gasped.

He wrenched the back door open and grabbed a baggy from the backseat. "Breathe into this."

She took the bag in her trembling hands and raised it to her mouth. Julia sat next to her and put an arm around her shoulder while Hannah sobbed into her hands.

Between breaths, Riley said, "Coop, we're doomed."

"Just breathe into the bag, Mom," Julia said.

Coop rubbed his gloved hands together. "I'll tell you what

we're going to do. We'll go on a winter backpacking trek to find a new truck. Hannah, stop blubbering and come help me unload our stuff." Hannah stared at him for several seconds before shuffling to the tailgate. "Julia, your mother's fine. Get over here and help. Riley, keep breathing."

Riley felt far from fine but nodded for Julia to go.

Hannah dropped the tent on the road and turned to stare at the giant steaming object that had caused all their trouble. "What is that thing?"

Coop straightened and stepped next to her. "Part of a satellite or other space junk would be my guess. The CME probably fried it."

"If that had landed on us, we'd be pancakes," Julia said.

"But it didn't, so we're good. What is it with you and pancakes?"

Julia shrugged and tossed a package of toilet paper on top of the tent. Riley watched the three of them dump their precious goods into random piles on the dirty pavement. After five minutes, she couldn't take it anymore and threw the baggie aside to get up and supervise the operation. She caught the wink between Coop and Julia and knew she'd been played.

They separated the supplies they needed for survival and left the rest. Riley saw *The Hobbit* sitting in the discard pile and snuck it into her backpack before Julia noticed. The extra half pound of weight would be worth it when she surprised her later.

Coop carried the big tent, two sleeping bags, and a fire-starting kit. Riley took the bulk of the food and the remaining first aid supplies while they split the rest of the food, two other sleeping bags and extra clothes between the girls. Each carried four bottles of water and purification tablets.

"If we keep up a three-mile per hour pace, we'll reach Charlottesville before sundown," Coop said. "If not, we'll look for a secluded place near water before it gets dark. The packs are heavy, and we're tired and sore, but the sooner we find another vehicle, the sooner we get to Wytheville."

Julia pulled her pack higher on her shoulders. "Just another adventure."

Hannah didn't even fake a smile. "I hate backpacking."

Riley squeezed her hand. "Think of it as carrying your books at school. We'll take breaks and not push ourselves too hard."

Hannah didn't look convinced. Coop turned on his heels to face west and marched off singing *Heigh-Ho, Heigh-Ho*, from *Snow White*.

Julia stepped into line behind him, followed by Hannah and Riley.

"Can't you find a better hiking song?" Julia asked.

"I always wanted to be one of the seven dwarves when I was little," he said.

Julia rolled her eyes. "You're so weird."

Hannah laughed, but Riley couldn't even conjure a snicker. Coop had warded off the panic attack, but her anxiety churned beneath the surface. They'd lost their only means of transportation and heat. Their odds of surviving had been cut by at least half. If they didn't find another vehicle, it would take weeks instead of a day to get to Wytheville, if they even survived that long.

She forced herself to join the others in their silly song and focused on putting one foot in front of the other.

They settled into an even walking rhythm and covered the first mile in eighteen minutes. Julia wanted to speed up, but Riley reminded her they had a long way to go and had to pace themselves.

Riley caught up to Coop, and as she fell into step beside him, another gigantic chunk of metal fell from the sky and landed a quarter-mile in front of them. A third crashed down two hundred yards to the south ten seconds later.

Julia covered her head with her hands and looked at the sky.

Hannah imitated her. "They're going to fall on us."

"We have time to run out of the way," Riley said, trying to sound more confident than she felt. "Why are they falling now? The CME was almost a week ago."

Coop followed another chunk with his eyes half a mile up the road. "It's taken this long to be pulled in by earth's gravity. I read once that scientists use gizmos to monitor orbital objects and keep them from falling to earth. These pieces must belong to a larger object that survived reentry through the atmosphere. Everyone, keep your eyes open."

"No, kidding," Julia said. "It's bad enough we have to watch out for bad guys and wild animals. Now we have to dodge giant space bombs," Julia said.

"The wild animals here aren't dangerous, and those aren't bombs," Riley said.

"Yet," Coop said over his shoulder. "And black bears do live in the area."

Riley scowled at him. "Can we please change the subject to something more pleasant? Let's look for a library in Charlottesville. I want to learn more about CMEs and wilderness survival techniques. Once we have another truck, we'll fill it with books."

"Only Mom would assign homework in the middle of Armageddon," Julia mumbled just loud enough for Riley to hear.

"My feet hurt, and they're freezing," Hannah whined.

"They'll be numb soon, and you won't feel them anymore," Coop said.

Riley elbowed his ribs and whispered, "Not helping." Coop gasped and sank to his knees, clutching his side. "What is it? What's wrong?"

He dropped his pack and tent and rolled onto his back. "Broken rib. Pneumothorax. Left side."

The girls ran to where he lay on the ground and stared down at him.

"What's a pneumothorax?" Julia asked.

Coop started to answer, but Riley shushed him. While she dug through her pack, she said, "A collapsed lung. He must have broken a rib in the accident. When I elbowed him, the bone probably punctured his lung."

Hannah knelt beside him and grasped his hand in both of hers. "Is he going to die?"

"No, because I'm going to save him," Riley said. "Breathing with his other lung will keep him alive for now. Julia, help me get his coat off and lift his shirt. Hannah, grab the cleanest chunk of snow you can find. Then I need you on the flashlight again. Shine the beam where I'm drawing this X."

The girls did as she asked while she scrubbed her hands with hand sanitizer and pulled on a pair of gloves. Coop groaned when she rubbed his side with the snow.

"You'll thank me," she said. "This is going to hurt a lot worse than stitches, but it's better than suffocating to death. The pain will be quick and done."

"Cardiologist, remember," he said between gasps.

"Don't move," she ordered. "Hannah, get that beam on the X. You can turn away if the blood bothers you, just keep the flashlight steady. Julia, get ready to hand me instruments, such as they are."

She pressed the scalpel to Coop's skin and made a half-inch incision. He let out a cry, but she shut it out of her mind. She asked Julia to hand her the small plastic tube she'd cut to the correct length and slid it between his ribs. The air that had built up in the cavity around his lungs rushed out, and he took a deep breath as his lung inflated.

"That got it," he said in a hoarse whisper. "I owe you."

Riley taped the tube in place and sat back on her heels. "This wouldn't have happened if I hadn't jabbed you in the ribs."

"Broken rib would have moved on its own. Glad it happened in daylight."

He tried to lift up on his elbow, but Riley held him down. "Stay where you are." She rechecked the tape and covered him with his coat before injecting him with an antibiotic. "When you can sit up enough to swallow, I'll give you ten milligrams of Oxy. We only have ten tablets left, so you'll only get five milligrams after that."

He turned his head toward her. "Just give me Tylenol and Advil. Save the pain meds. We might need them later, and I need to be alert."

"Not happening. With this and your other injuries, you'll be in too much pain to be any use to us, and you'll heal faster without the pain."

He closed his eyes and nodded. Riley got to her feet and asked Hannah to stay with Coop while she and Julia repacked the supplies.

Julia handed her the rubbing alcohol, and said, "Mom, we aren't going to make it to Charlottesville, are we?"

Riley zipped the pack and motioned for Julia to follow her to the edge of the road. She leaned against a tree and folded her arms. If their situation was critical before, it was grave now. It would take a miracle for Coop to walk twenty yards. She'd have to carry the tent and his pack as well as her own. It was after four. They'd need to set up camp before dark. With Coop out of the picture, she was left alone to plan their next move. She swallowed her dread and switched into take-charge mode.

"Where's the map? Let's figure out exactly where we are and find a safe place to spend the night. It needs to be as close as possible."

Julia found the map in Coop's pack and handed it to her. She racked her brain, trying to remember the signs they'd passed since the accident, but she'd been too focused on not getting flattened by space bombs. They couldn't have gone more than two miles past the twenty-eight miles to Charlottesville sign. She studied the map and did her best to estimate.

She hadn't noticed Julia wander off and was startled when she called to her from thirty yards down the road.

She pointed at a sign that Riley couldn't read. "Look, Mom, there's a campground over here. It says they have cabins and propane."

Riley jogged to Julia and read the sign. The campground was only a quarter-mile ahead. It was a promising option, but others may have had the same idea. She'd hoped to avoid other people, but given their desperate situation, it might be their only option.

Julia tugged on her sleeve. "Come on, it's perfect, Mom."

"Go back to Hannah and Coop while I look into it."

She covered the distance to the campground entrance at a full run. The gate across the gravel road was locked and had a "Closed for the Season" sign tacked to it, but the fence ended about ten feet to the left. She walked over and squeezed between the fencepost and a tree. She passed the check-in stand and trotted to the campground store. The propane cage was empty, but the store looked undisturbed.

She passed the store and reached the first cabin after another hundred yards. It was no more than a roof, four wood-plank walls and a window, but it would keep out the cold. There were two twin beds with worn mattresses resting on wire springs. There was another cabin, twenty feet past the first. It, too, was empty and had a queen bed. She didn't bother to go farther. She'd passed a cargo cart tucked behind the campground store. She took it and ran back to Coop and the girls.

She bent over to catch her breath, then said, "The campground's perfect. It's less than half a mile to the cabins. Girls, help me get Coop onto the cart, and we'll arrange our belongings around him."

Coop went pale and took quick, shallow breaths as the three of them gingerly helped him get situated on the cart.

Once their supplies were loaded, Riley gave the cart a gentle nudge to get it moving. "I'll have to take this slowly to keep from jostling you too much, Coop, but we should make the campground by sunset."

"You get no argument from me," Julia said. "Tell me if you need help pushing the cart, Mom."

Riley gave her a weak smile but kept moving, grateful they were on a gradual decline. She blocked out the little voice urging her to quit and repeated the phrase, *just get to the campground* in her mind.

Coop covered her hand with his and softly sang, "Heigh-ho, heigh-ho, it's off to camp we go."

Riley passed five empty cabins inside the campground and kept going.

Julia finally pulled the cart to a stop and put her hands on her knees. When she could get the words out, she said, "I'm about to pass out. What's wrong with that cabin or the last three you ignored?"

Hannah sank onto a tree stump at the side of the gravel trail and crossed her arms. "I can't go another step. Can't we stay here?"

Riley straightened and rubbed her hands on the small of her back. "I know you're exhausted, but it'll be safer if we get as far off the main road as we can. I want to avoid running into anyone else. You two rest here. I'll push Coop the rest of the way."

Julia stood and wrapped her gloved fingers around the cart handle. "I'm not staying here alone, and you can't push the cart by yourself over this gravel. If we can't all stay, we all go."

Hannah got to her feet with a groan. "I guess I can make it a little farther."

Riley nodded and put her hands on the handle. She hadn't wanted to leave them, but Coop was pale and shivering. She needed to get him to a cabin. It wasn't easy for her to drive the girls so hard, but safety had to be their top priority.

"Thanks, girls," she said. "One last push, and we'll have the whole night to rest."

Riley and Julia shoved the cart into motion. The right front wheel rolled over a small rock and Coop gasped, then pressed his hand to his ribs below the tube.

"Easy," he whispered without opening his eyes.

Riley squeezed his shoulder, then motioned for Julia to stop. She reached into the closest backpack for a flashlight. "It's getting too dark to see the bumps." She flicked the light on and handed it to Hannah. "Shine that in front of the cart. Hang on, Coop. Almost there."

Coop peered up at her. "You said that an hour ago. Why don't I believe you?"

Riley took out the tattered camp map she'd found and rechecked their location.

"Fifteen minutes. We can handle anything for fifteen more minutes." She re-pocketed the map and helped Julia get the cart rolling.

As they trudged along in silence, she made a mental assessment of their situation. She empathized with the girls. She was running on pure adrenaline, but her day would be far from over when they reached the campsite. Once they unpacked and settled in, she'd have to stay awake and monitor Coop throughout the night. She'd have no choice in the morning but to ask Julia to take over for a few hours so she could sleep, at least for a few hours.

Their next priority would be to find water and more food. She'd tested a few of the water spigots they'd passed, but the pipes were either frozen, or they worked on electric pumps. The map showed a stream that ran along the back of the campground. They'd have to use that and boil their water, but at least they wouldn't die of thirst while Coop recovered.

When they'd covered another three-hundred yards, they rounded a curve in the trail and the campsite came into view. Two cabins sat side by side and backed up to the woods. Riley wanted to drop to her knees and cry for joy, but she kept moving. There would be time to celebrate later.

Julia helped her maneuver the cart to the base of steps for the first cabin. "Wait here while I check the area," Riley told her.

The campsite was cleaner and better maintained than the ones closer to the entrance, so the extra effort to get there had been worth it. Like the other cabins they'd passed, one of these had two twin beds and the other a queen. Riley gave the girls the queen and took the twins for Coop and herself.

After inspecting the cabins, she surveyed around the outside. The water spigot in the common area between the cabins was frozen like the others. The sound of water flowing in the nearby stream floated through the trees. She was relieved it hadn't iced over and hoped it was accessible, but she'd have to wait for daylight to find out.

She rejoined the others and took a sleeping bag from the cart to spread on Coop's bed. When she finished, she squatted next to him to check his heart rate, respiration and the air escaping through the tube. Satisfied that he was stable, she felt his forehead for fever, but he was cool.

"I know you don't want to hear this, but you're going to have to walk up three steps to get to your bed. The three of us aren't strong enough to carry you. We might drop you."

Coop grimaced. "I'm not worried about the walking. It's getting off this rolling bone crusher that has me concerned."

"Logroll onto your right side and use your arm to push

yourself to a sitting position. It's what I tell my back-surgery patients. You won't have to use the muscles on your left side."

Coop frowned. "I'm familiar with the logroll maneuver. That doesn't mean it isn't going to hurt."

"No way around it. Let's get it over with."

Riley walked to his right side and extended her crooked arm. He gripped it and held his breath as he rolled. As cold as it was, Riley could still make out the beads of sweat on his forehead. Once he was upright on the cart, she told him to catch his breath and let his balance equalize. He nodded after two minutes and raised his arms for Julia and Riley to lift him to his feet.

Riley showed Julia how to lock her arms under his and lift without injuring him further. He wobbled once but righted himself and took three quick breaths.

Riley shined a flashlight on his face. He was gray and clammy but seemed coherent. "Ready to scale the steps or do you need more time?"

"Get that blasted light out of my eyes," he barked. "Makes me miss your puny penlight."

She handed Hannah the flashlight like before and nodded for Julia to help her get Coop moving. He took little shuffling steps, but they had him tucked into the sleeping bag five minutes later. She propped him on a backpack since it would be easier to breathe if he wasn't flat and coaxed him into taking four ibuprofen.

She kissed his forehead and smiled. "I'll quit pestering you and let you rest. You can take more Oxy in two hours but promise not to be a martyr. Tell me if the pain becomes unbearable, and I'll do what I can to alleviate it. I need to get the girls settled, but I'll only be a few feet away if you need me."

He caught her arm as she turned to go. "I can see in your face how stretched you are. You're pushing yourself too hard."

"No choice. I'll be fine. We'll have to stay here until you're recovered. It'll be a vacation after what we've been through."

"I hate that you have to do this alone."

Riley kissed his hand. "It's my fault you ended up this way, but just having you here makes all the difference. Rest and follow your doctor's orders. I need you well. You can't imagine how much."

He closed his eyes and sighed. "I'll do my best to be a model patient."

Riley spent one of the longest nights of her life keeping watch over Coop and the girls. She fought to keep her eyes open but couldn't help dozing off twice. Fortunately, the forest sounds soon startled her awake. She felt the weight of the world on her shoulders and had no one to share the burden. Her only hope was that a few hours of sleep in the morning would be enough to keep her from collapsing.

Coop moaned and tossed despite her best efforts to control his pain. He finally fell into a deep sleep around four-thirty. By the light of the aurora, Riley could just make out the even rise and fall of his chest. The air releasing from the tube had lessened, indicating that his lung had re-inflated. If so, she could remove it, and he could begin the healing process. Only time would mend the broken ribs.

When the first rays of sunlight peeked over the horizon, she left Coop sleeping peacefully and went in search of the stream. The map didn't show a trail or road leading to the water, so she risked it and wound her way through the woods toward the sound. If they'd been in different circumstances, she would have enjoyed her hike, but this time it was a matter of life and death. The snow had become shallower the further south they'd traveled. What was left was thin and dirty and wouldn't offer much in the way of drinkable water.

She'd been walking for ten minutes when the sunlight grew

brighter through the trees as she neared a clearing. She quickened her pace and broke through the woods to find not a stream but a river. The rocky edge where she stood was fifteen feet above the water, but the ground sloped away to a pebbly beach twenty yards upstream. She headed that way to find a quicker route to the campground and was rewarded with discovering a well-worn trail. The return trip took half the time.

She threw their empty water bottles and canteens into a pack when she got back to camp and was on her way back to the river when Julia poked her head out of the cabin doorway and yawned. Her hair was a tangled mess, and she had a smudge of dirt on her cheek, but her eyes were bright and clear. The bruising from her black eye had faded to almost nothing. She looked almost like the daughter Riley remembered.

Riley hugged her and whispered, "What are you doing up so early? There's nothing to rush off to for once. We're stuck here until Coop's better."

While Julia pulled her hair into a tie, she said, "The sun's blaring in my eyes, and I went to sleep at like eight. I don't think I've ever gone to bed that early in my life. Plus, I'm starving. Where's the backpack with the food?"

"In the corner in my tent. I found a river nearby. I'm going for water. Try not to wake Coop. He didn't sleep well."

"How about you? You look like hell."

"Thanks, sweetheart. Just what I needed to hear. I was keeping vigil over Coop. I'm going to sleep when I get back and leave you in charge if you wouldn't mind."

"No problem. Are there outhouses here? I'm about to burst."

Riley pointed at the two outhouses on the opposite side of the common area. "I'll be back in ten minutes. Don't wander off."

Riley took the trail at a slow jog and reached the river in five minutes. She was uneasy leaving Coop and the girls unprotected and wanted to get back as quickly as she could. A thin layer of ice had formed out five feet from the edge and slowed her down. She gathered a pile of rocks to break it so she could fill the bottles. She lost her footing once and almost tumbled in but was able to catch herself in time.

With the exertion and weight of the bottles, she was forced to walk on the return journey but still made it in ten minutes. Hannah was awake, and she and Julia were munching on protein bars.

"Morning," Riley said and hugged her. "Did you sleep?"

"Like the dead. If it weren't so sunny, I'd probably still be asleep. Can I have some water?"

"We have to boil it first. Start collecting wood and we'll get a fire going." She set the pack down and turned to Julia. "Any sound from Coop?"

"Sleeping like a baby." Julia stood and put her hands on her hips. "I'm ordering you to take a nap as soon as we get the water boiling. I'm worried about you."

"I'm fine other than needing sleep, but I won't argue. When I wake up after my nap, we'll go on a scavenger hunt."

She went into the cabin and checked Coop's vitals while the girls gathered wood. He stirred and opened his eyes for a moment before drifting off again. Riley was relieved to see him getting some good rest. Sleep would speed his recovery better than anything she was able to offer.

She helped Julia get a fire going and showed the girls how to heat water in the metal canteen cups on hot rocks ringing the pit. She was nervous about leaving them to the task, but she couldn't keep her eyes open another moment and had to trust them to manage. She went into their cabin and collapsed on Julia's bunk.

———

It felt like she'd only slept for two minutes before Julia was shaking her awake.

Without opening her eyes, she said, "What is it, sweetheart?"

"I'm sorry, but Coop needs you."

Riley sat up and glanced at her wrist, but she'd left her watch in the other cabin. "How long have I been asleep?"

"Over four hours," Julia said, as Riley got up and followed her out of the cabin. "You probably would have slept until tomorrow."

"Wish I could, but those four hours helped. I feel much better. Another good night and I'll be good as new."

"I think we'd all need a week of sleep for that."

Riley went into her cabin and found Coop sitting up, sipping something from one of the canteen cups. He gave her a half-grin and said, "Hello, Sleeping Beauty."

She smiled. "This is promising." He grimaced when she tapped her fingertips on the tissue around the tube before taking his pulse and respiration. She pressed her ear to his chest and listened for several seconds. "How's your pain?"

"Like I need more Oxy. Are there any left?"

"Two. I'll give you one and more ibuprofen. Is that water you're drinking?"

He shook his head and took a sip. "Reconstituted broth. Not too bad."

Riley handed him the meds. "An even better sign."

He swallowed the pills and leaned his head against the wall. "The lung is inflated and losing the tube will alleviate my pain considerably."

"Yes, doctor. Lucky for you, I agree. Finish your soup and let the meds kick in first. I'll eat and get ready."

Soup sounded good, so she dug a packet out of the backpack and took it to the fire-pit. There was a cup of hot water ready for her. She mixed the soup and sat on a warm rock to drink it. Hannah tossed another log in the pit and sat next to her.

"If we can find food, this will be a safe place to stay until Coop's better. Not as good as the theater, but better than freezing to death on the road."

Riley put an arm around her. "I'm glad you feel that way. We were lucky to find this. I hate to think what would have happened if we hadn't."

Julia came up with an armload of wood and dropped it on the growing pile. "There's lots of wood around here. Let's keep the fire going around the clock. It feels so good to be warm."

Riley was surprised to see Julia near the fire after the incident at the cottage. Another good sign. Their little band was growing more resilient with each crisis conquered, more than she could have imagined. What they'd accomplished the past few days had been almost superhuman. She'd been a quivering bag of fear less than two weeks earlier. It was hard to remember what had been so frightening in her old life.

Hannah held her hands out to the flames. "Wish we could have a fire inside the cabin." Julia flashed her a look and stomped off to get more wood. Hannah turned to Riley with a shrug. "What did I say?"

Riley shook her head and smiled over her cup, relieved to see Julia's healthy teenage reaction. Maybe they were just mere mortals, after all.

She allowed herself an hour of relaxing by the fire before going to remove Coop's tube. He was drowsy from the meds by then and didn't fuss when she packed a baggie of snow around the wound to numb it. He flinched when she slid the tube out but stayed quiet while she sutured him. She worked quickly and had the wound dressed fifteen minutes later. She gave him another antibiotic injection and left him to rest.

She found Julia and Hannah chatting quietly by the fire-pit and was glad Julia hadn't held Hannah's comment against her.

"Ready for that scavenger hunt?" she asked. In answer, the girls jumped to their feet in unison. "Grab any bags we can fill and put them on the cart. Keep your fingers crossed that they left something useful behind when they closed down for the season."

They started with the camp store. The shelves had been cleared, but stray boxes with odds and ends had been left in the storage room. They found travel shampoos, soaps, and sewing kits, but no food. They hunted for half an hour before gleaning all they could. Riley was disappointed but not defeated. The camp still had outbuildings to explore. She studied the map and found an area for group camps that looked promising. It was almost a mile from the store, but they had to make the trip even if it meant leaving Coop unprotected for longer than Riley had wanted.

The group camping area had a separate entrance that was too far to backtrack to, so Riley and the girls were forced to hike with their cart over rugged terrain. It took an hour to navigate, but it was worth the effort. The campground had a dining lodge and storage building with shelves stacked with pots and pans, cooking utensils, and boxes full of stale but still edible foodstuffs. They loaded up as much as they could carry and made the trip back to their campsite.

Riley checked on Coop the instant they returned, but he was sleeping peacefully, oblivious to the fact that they'd been gone for nearly four hours. She and the girls unpacked the haul and stowed it in their cabin. They had cornmeal, cooking oil, pasta, spaghetti sauce, large cans of vegetables, and, much to Julia's delight, pancake mix and syrup. There was even one case of boxed milk. Riley would have preferred more protein sources but figured they could find a way to fish and trap small game.

With the food crisis resolved, Riley sent the girls to gather wood while she fetched more water. By sunset, they'd settled into their new home. Coop was well enough to eat spaghetti and cornmeal cakes. All they lacked was a way to heat the cabins, but at least the sleeping bags prevented them from freezing.

After devouring her dinner, Riley watched the dancing flames and reflected on how their fortunes had flipped in twenty-four hours. She sighed in contentment and went to enjoy a much-needed night's rest.

CHAPTER ELEVEN

JULIA AND HANNAH had found a tattered blanket and hung it in their cabin to block out the morning sun. Julia pushed the makeshift curtain aside and rested her arms on the window frame to let the sun warm her face. For the past three mornings, she'd relished those first quiet moments in the sun before she got up to begin her chores. She loved their little camp, and if the nights hadn't been so freezing, she would have wanted to stay until summer.

The thought of giving up their sanctuary and getting back on the dangerous roads frightened her, but Coop was almost recovered and kept reminding her that if they found a vehicle, they could be to Uncle Mitch's ranch in a day. Each time they'd said that before, they'd ended up facing nothing but tragedy. Even her mom didn't seem to be in a hurry to restart their journey. They had enough food to last weeks. Julia saw no reason to rush.

On their second night in camp, Riley had presented her with the copy of *The Hobbit* she'd rescued from the wreck. Julia thought it would be fun to read together around the fire pit after dinner. Hannah said her family used to do that in summers on their houseboat at some lake.

Hannah stirred behind her, so Julia closed the curtain and stretched before pulling on her boots to go to the outhouse. She wanted to lounge around, but her mom had hammered in the importance of getting chores done early and going to sleep around seven, so they could make the most use of daylight and not waste the batteries in the flashlights. Julia felt like a little kid going to bed so early but understood that it was necessary.

"Is it time to get up?" Hannah mumbled.

Through a yawn, Julia said, "Afraid so. Mom's already building up the fire."

Hannah groaned and pulled the sleeping bag over her head. "Does she ever sleep?"

Julia pulled on her coat and smiled. "I've never seen it, but she's been perkier for the past two days."

Hannah sat up and rubbed her eyes. "That's probably because Coop's better."

"And we're not running away from catastrophes every two seconds. I'm going to the outhouse. You'd better get dressed."

She bounced down the steps and waved at her mom as she passed. She never thought she'd be happy to have an outhouse, but anything was better than that disgusting bucket. The cold temperatures and the fact that the toilets were mostly empty kept the smell down, so it wasn't too terrible. As she unrolled the toilet paper, she thought of how shocked Emily would be to see her cheerfully roughing it, but everyone has to adapt when the world comes to an end.

Hannah was with Riley at the fire-pit by the time Julia finished. Pancakes were browning in a pan and her stomach growled from the aroma.

She leaned over the pan and took a whiff. "I could eat ten of those."

"Go ahead," Riley said. "With what I brought back from the group camp yesterday, we have enough to feed an army."

She lifted the pancakes with a spatula and dropped them onto a plate for Julia, then poured about a cup of syrup over them. Julia shoveled a pile of the sweet gooeyness into her mouth. She followed it with a gulp of boxed milk.

"Almost perfect. If we only had some bacon." When Riley handed her a piece of pork jerky, she said, "Close enough."

Coop poked his head out of the cabin. "Do I smell pancakes?" When Julia held up a forkful to show him, he slowly descended the steps and joined them. Riley handed him a plate, and through a mouthful of pancakes, he said, "What's on the agenda for today?"

Riley sat on a stump across from him and held her hands toward the fire. "Are you up to going on that car hunt?"

"I feel great this morning. Slept like a rock. I'm up for anything. Where's the map?"

Riley cocked her head at the cabin. "In my pack. I'll get it when I'm done. Don't overdo it. Those ribs will take weeks to heal."

He winked. "Thanks, doc. I'll try to remember that."

Riley turned to the girls and said, "When you're finished, you need to make a water run. I want to stock up as much as we can, so we don't have to spend the day making trips. Take the cart and fill all the five-gallon containers."

Julia frowned. Of all her chores, getting water was the worst. It was freezing at the river, and each morning they had to break the new ice that had reformed during the night. It was hard to fill the containers without falling off the log they'd positioned in the water to they could reach further. She was determined to collect as much as they could that morning, so they'd get a break for a few days.

Her mom and Coop went into their cabin to study the map after they cleaned up from breakfast. She and Hannah bundled up and loaded the cart. She called out to let them know they were leaving and pushed the cart toward the trail. The path was pretty flat, much better than going to the group camp for supplies. She and Hannah wouldn't have any trouble bringing the water back.

When they got to the river's edge, Julia was annoyed to see the ice was twice as thick as the day before. "We're going to need bigger rocks," she told Hannah.

Hannah put down the jug she'd pulled off the cart. "We'll have to look farther away this time. All the rocks from around here are at the bottom of the river."

Julia leaned against a boulder and crossed her arms. "There's got to be an easier way to do this. Any ideas?"

"We could look for an ax and tape it to the end of a branch."

"Coop looked for an ax yesterday to chop wood but didn't find one, so that's out. We could make an ax with a flat rock and a piece of wood. See what you can find. I'm going to run back for duct tape. Stay away from the edge of the water while I'm gone."

Julia left Hannah searching for rocks while she ran to camp. She was surprised at how fast she could run. She'd always hated running, but all the hard work of survival was toning her muscles. She was starting to get why her mom loved running so much.

She bounded up the steps to her mom's cabin and caught Coop and her making out on his bed. Her mom shot up and blushed tomato red. Coop sat up and stared at his boots. Julia burst out laughing.

"That look was priceless, Mom, but you don't have to be embarrassed. I'm glad you're together."

Coop looked at her and grinned. "Glad to know we have your permission."

Her mom's blush faded, but she said, "That doesn't mean I want you bursting in on us. Knock from now on. What are you doing back here? You couldn't have gotten the water that fast."

Julia explained her homemade ax plan in a rush. "I need the duct tape. Where is it?"

Riley held up her hands. "I admire your initiative, but your idea won't work. Just use rocks for now and we'll work on inventions later."

Coop nodded. "Your mom's right. If you tried your rock on a stick plan, you'd just end up in the river. We're heading out tomorrow if I find a truck, so we won't need to worry about breaking ice."

Julia frowned. "Do we have to go tomorrow? I like it here, and it's too scary out there."

Riley put a hand on her shoulder. "I get why you want to stay. We've been through terrible things, and it feels safe here, but the ranch will be worlds better. We'll have a real house, heat, and water."

Julia studied her mom's face. Dark circles rimmed her eyes, and she had new creases in her forehead. She may have perked up the past few days, but she was exhausted. When they got to Uncle Mitch's ranch, she and Coop wouldn't have to carry the burden alone. It made sense that her mom wanted to get there as soon as possible, even if it meant facing the dangers on the road.

"Okay, Mom, we'll use the rocks to get the water, but I'm still going to figure out a better way to break the ice, just in case."

"Fair enough." She drew a full roll of duct tape from her pack and handed it to Julia. "Get back to Hannah. I don't like her alone at the river."

"And you two get back to what you were doing," Julia said and giggled on her way out of the cabin.

Hannah had a nice pile of potential ax rocks by the time Julia got back. She told Hannah about catching Riley and Coop in a make-out session, and they laughed until they cried.

When they stopped, Julia said, "They gave our ax idea a thumbs down, but after we get the water, we'll make it and prove them wrong."

Julia heaved a stone the size of a football onto the ice. The ice cracked, but the rock skidded across the top without breaking it. Hannah tossed hers and got the same result, so they moved closer to the river's edge.

"Let's try throwing them at the same time on the same spot," Hannah said.

They tried her strategy, but their rocks landed feet apart and ice didn't budge.

Hannah tapped her toe on the edge of the frozen river. "I could walk onto the ice. It looks thick enough to hold me."

Julia stepped in front of her. "No, Hannah. That's too dangerous. We just have to throw the rocks harder."

They collected the biggest rocks that weren't too heavy to throw. Julia picked up a bowling ball-sized one and heard a loud crack behind her. She spun around to find Hannah on the ice ten feet from the shore.

"What are you doing?" she yelled. "Come back."

Hannah had gone pale and began to tremble. "I'm afraid to move. The ice is cracking. Julia, what do I do?"

Ignoring her own fear, Julia frantically tried to think of a way to save her. The ice made another loud pop and reminded her of a scene from a movie. The person was stuck on the ice and laid flat to distribute their weight. "Hannah, slowly get on your stomach."

Hannah shook her head. "I can't. I'm too scared."

"You have to, Hannah. Do it now!"

Hannah swallowed and slowly lowered herself to her knees. As she pushed her legs out to get on her stomach, the ice opened, and she disappeared into the water. Julia screamed Hannah's name as she laid on the ice and inched herself toward the hole. When the ice started to pop and creak, she slid back to shore.

She ran along the river's edge for what felt like an hour before she spotted Hannah clinging to a small island of boulders twenty yards downstream.

She cupped her hands to her mouth and cried, "Hold on, Hannah. Don't let go. I'm going for Mom and Coop. Promise you won't let go."

Hannah yelled something, but the words were drowned by the rushing water and wind. Julia turned for the trail just as her mom and Coop burst out of the treeline.

Her mom ran straight for her. "We heard you screaming. What happened?"

Julia pointed to Hannah. "She broke through the ice. How are we going to get her?"

"Whatever we do, make it fast. Looks like she's losing her grip," Coop said.

Without a word, Riley stripped down to her underwear and plunged into the river. When she reached Hannah, she wrapped an arm around her and fought the current to swim her to shore. Hannah slipped away twice, and Riley had to go after her. She was shivering uncontrollably by the time they reached the side, but Hannah was limp.

Coop tore off his coat and handed it to Julia. "Wipe your mom down with this and help her get her clothes on."

Riley resisted, trying to get to Hannah while Julia dried her, but she ordered her mom to take off her wet underclothes. "Get dressed first, then help Hannah." Riley's teeth chattered as she changed into her dry clothes while Coop went to work on Hannah.

"No breath sounds or pulse. We need to start CPR. Julia, please, give me your coat."

Riley and Coop stripped off Hannah's wet clothes and covered her with Julia's coat. Coop kneeled near her torso to start compressions, but Riley shoved him out of the way.

"Not you. You'll rebreak your ribs and open your sutures. I'll do it."

Julia watched in horror as her mom performed CPR on Hannah and almost vomited when she heard the sound of her bones cracking from the pressure.

Without stopping compressions, Riley said, "Julia, do you remember how to do mouth-to-mouth?"

"Yes, Mom," she said, as she dropped to her knees by Hannah's head. She placed a hand under her neck and tipped her head back before prying her jaw open.

Coop put his hand on Julia's shoulder. "Breathe when I tell you."

Every thirty compressions, Coop told Julia to breathe twice. Julia closed her eyes so she couldn't see Hannah's purple face. She cleared her mind and focused on Coop's voice. She and her mother worked as a team as the minutes passed, but Hannah didn't move. Every few minutes, her mom stopped and listened to Hannah's chest, shivering violently as she did.

After the third pause, Coop said, "You're hypothermic and fatigued. Let me take over. Run back to camp and sit near the fire wrapped in a sleeping bag."

"I can keep going. I'm not letting you do this. I can't lose both of you today."

Julia climbed to her feet. "I can do it, Mom. I've been watching."

Riley stood and handed her watch to Coop, then traded places with Julia. She gave her a five-second instruction before they went back to work. Julia felt a rush of adrenalin as she pressed on her friend's chest and willed her to live. Hannah's color went from purple to gray to white, but she didn't breathe or move.

She caught Coop glancing at the watch. "Riley, thirty minutes. We need to call it."

"No. I refuse to give up. Julia trade back with me."

Julia didn't want to stop, but her mom slipped between her

and Hannah, forcing her out of the way. She moved toward Hannah's head, but Coop got there first and started giving her breaths. Sensing that Hannah was gone, Julia couldn't stand by and watch them torture her body another second. She blindly ran into the woods, not caring where she was going. Her only thought was to get away from the horrifying scene.

She wandered aimlessly until she found a hollowed-out oak tree. She climbed inside and pulled her knees to her chest, trying to shut off her thoughts, but the words *Hannah's dead, Hannah's dead,* played on a loop in her brain. It had all happened in a terrible flash. One second, they were collecting those stupid rocks. The next, Hannah was swallowed by the river.

She started to shiver and realized she didn't have her coat. *Will I freeze to death, too? Do I care if I do? Is there a point to fight to survive only to be wiped out in an instant anyway?*

While she pondered her life and death questions, the sound of Coop shouting floated into her hiding place. Not wanting to worry him, she crawled out of the tree and started for the riverbank, dreading what she'd find when she got there.

She didn't know which direction to go, so she stopped and closed her eyes, filtering out all the sounds but Coop's voice. She headed towards him, and the woods began to thin as she neared the river. She broke through the trees to find Coop with his arms locked around her mother's waist, dragging her off Hannah. She kicked and screamed, but Coop tightened his hold and carried her to the tree line.

"Stop this, Riley," he cried. "We've lost her. You have to let her go."

Riley quieted and went limp, so Coop loosened his grip. She wriggled free and took off at a full run into the woods. Coop dropped his arms to his sides and didn't go after her. He walked to Hannah and sank to his knees to gently remove Julia's coat from the body. He replaced it with Hannah's drenched jacket, taking care to cover her face. When he finished, he locked his fingers behind his neck and rocked as his body shook with sobs.

Julia stood frozen in place, just staring. She longed to join him, but her feet refused to move. She rubbed her arms, wishing for her coat, but it was in a heap on the frozen ground ten feet away. It might as well have been a hundred for her ability to reach it.

She'd seen hundreds of dead bodies since the CME and thought she'd become hardened to the sight, but this wasn't just another anonymous corpse. This was Hannah, her new sister, a part of their family. How could she go on without her?

An involuntary groan escaped her lips and Coop turned to face her. He stared for several seconds like he didn't recognize her, then stood and grabbed her coat. He tenderly wrapped it around her shoulders and pulled her into his arms.

"It's going to be okay, Julia. It was just a horrible accident. We need to put our grief aside for now and find your mom." He pulled away and looked into her eyes. "She's hysterical and I'm afraid she'll hurt herself. Can you help me look for her?" Julia nodded numbly and let him lead her in the direction her mom had gone. "Good girl. We'll come back for Hannah. Nothing can hurt her now."

Riley crashed into the woods, oblivious of the underbrush and branches clawing at her arms and face. All she knew was that she had to get away from the river. She ran until her lungs burned, begging her to stop, but she ignored them. After what felt like hours, she broke through the tree line to find herself on an outcropping above the river. She'd traveled in a half-circle.

She recoiled from the sight of the river and turned in the direction of the camp. Instinct drove her into the woods, but nothing looked familiar as she wandered in aimless circles. She kept moving, desperate to find their sanctuary and bury herself in the sleeping bag.

The ground leveled and the trees thinned. She was heading the right way. She increased her speed until she was moving at a full sprint. Just as she spotted the trail access to their campsite, her heel hit a patch of ice, sending her legs out from under her. The side of her head struck a tree as she fell. She sank down to the knotted roots and groaned as the world went dark. The last thing she heard was Julia calling her name.

Panic knotted in Julia's gut and drowned out her grief. She and Coop had been searching for her mom for almost an hour. Since her mom was wearing a yellow coat, Julia thought she'd be easy to spot. The woods surrounding the campsite just weren't that big and Julia had searched them ten times.

She stopped and leaned against a fallen log, calling her mom's name for the thousandth time. She began to wonder if she had abandoned them, but even if her mom had become crazy with grief, Julia couldn't believe she'd desert her, especially after what happened with Hannah. She heard Coop call her mom's name, and, not wanting to be alone, she headed in that direction.

"Coop, where are you?" she called. "Keep making noise so I can find you."

"I'm by the tree that looks like a trident," came his faint reply.

"A what?"

"A trident. A three-pronged fork. The thing Aquaman holds."

He's so weird, she thought as she walked toward what she and Hannah had named the fork tree. A fresh wave of pain washed over her at the memory. She stumbled but caught herself by grabbing the trunk of a massive tree next to the trail. As she righted herself, she saw a scrap of yellow in the underbrush ten feet away. She ran to the spot and found her mom, laying in a pile of broken twigs and branches.

"Coop, Mom's here," she screamed. "I found Mom."

"Where, Julia?" he called. "Tell me where you are."

Julia couldn't answer. The red stain spreading in the snow beneath her mother's head had left her speechless. Her mom was pale and not moving. Julia knew she should check for a pulse and see if she was breathing, but she was paralyzed.

"Julia, answer me!" Coop shouted.

The urgency in his voice broke her trance. She searched her surroundings to get her bearings.

"I don't know. Coop. Not far from the path. Mom's hurt. Hurry!"

She heard twigs snapping seconds later, and Coop smashed through the underbrush. He rushed to Riley's side and began examining her. Julia watched in horror, sobs racking her body. She couldn't bring herself to look and covered her eyes.

"Is she dead?" she whispered.

"She's alive but unconscious." Julia peeked between her fingers as he pulled a neckerchief from his pocket and pressed it to the side of Riley's head. "She's cut, but the bleeding is slowing, probably because her temperature is dropping. You found her just in time. We have to get her to camp as quickly as we can." He tied the neckerchief over her wound before putting his hands under her arms to lift her. "Get her feet."

Julia put her hands under Riley's calves and lifted, surprised at how heavy she was. They half dragged, half carried her to camp. Julia could barely stand by the time they got her on the bed but forced herself to keep going when Coop called for the med-kit to treat her mom's wounds. She sat on his bed and watched while he cleaned and stitched Riley's cut. Julia was relieved to hear her groaning.

When Coop finished, he tapped Riley's cheek. "Wake up, sleeping beauty. Naptime is over."

Riley moaned but didn't open her eyes.

Coop sat next to Julia and put a hand on her shoulder. "She'll respond once her temperature rises but she's going to have one hell of a headache. We know what that's like, don't we? She's the newest official member of the head injury club."

Julia couldn't bring herself to smile at his joke and started to weep silently instead.

"I thought Mom died," she whispered through her tears. "I thought she was invincible, but she's just like anyone else. Hannah's parents died. She was an orphan. I almost became an orphan. Any of us could die at any time. Nowhere is safe. We're never going to make it to Uncle Mitch's ranch."

Coop wrapped his arms around her. It felt good for him to hold her, but it didn't change the fact that they were all dead people walking.

"Listen carefully, Julia," he said. "Even before the CME, it was possible for any of us to die at any moment. Nothing has changed. True, chances are higher now, but life has always been unpredictable. I'm a cardiac surgeon. I've lost healthy, thirty-five-year-old patients who had sudden heart attacks that no one could have predicted."

Julia shook her head. "That was different. Most of the world is dead now."

"It is, but people still got in car accidents then. Children drowned in rivers or choked on hotdogs. Your dad died defending our country. We can't give up or stop living because we might die. We just have to be more careful and vigilant in this world. Can I promise nothing bad will happen to us? No, I can't. But I can promise I'll do whatever it takes to protect you, your mom, and myself. Hannah died in a tragic accident, but she'd want us to keep going. I bet she's rooting for us from the other side. Bet your dad is too."

"That's what I've told myself since he died, but I don't know anymore. This is different. I'm so scared all the time. I just want everything to go back to normal and I wish we'd never met Hannah. Then, I wouldn't have had to watch her die."

"But she wouldn't have had anyone to remember her or mourn her. The rest of her family doesn't know she's gone."

He stood and checked Riley's pulse and breathing. "She's warming up, and her pulse is strong and regular." He held his hand out to Julia. "Can you handle coming with me to give Hannah a decent burial? It's the least we can do."

Julia stood and kissed her mom's cheek before taking his hand. The last thing she wanted was to go back to the scene of Hannah's death, but her friend didn't deserve to have her body left rotting by the river. Once they finished burying her, Julia planned to climb into her sleeping bag, cover up her head, and forget that horrible day forever.

Riley woke in a dark room, wondering where the sun had gone. Last she could remember, it had been morning. She raised her wrist to check the time, but her arm was bare. *Where's my watch?* she wondered as she unzipped her sleeping bag and swung her feet to the floor. Her head pounded, her mouth was bone dry, and her bladder felt like it was about to burst.

She felt for her flashlight on the shelf next to her bed and pointed it at Coop's bed, expecting to find him asleep, but his sleeping bag was rolled and tied. She pulled her boots on and went to find out what had happened. As she descended the steps, she was relieved to see Julia and Coop sipping soup by a roaring blaze at the fire-pit. But where was Hannah?

At the thought, memories of the events at the river flooded over her. Her legs buckled, and she collapsed onto the frozen ground. Coop and Julia were at her side in an instant, talking at her, saying words she couldn't comprehend. All she wanted was to scrub the memories out of her head and go back to the oblivion of the dark cabin. Coop scooped her up and carried her to the fire-pit. He gently lowered her onto a warm, flat rock near the flames, then placed his palms on her cheeks and stared into her eyes.

"Do you know where you are?" he asked.

Stupid question. She brushed his hands away and glared. "In the campground where we've been for the past five days."

He gently pressed his fingertips to the back of her skull. She stared at him in confusion until a burning pain exploded on her scalp and traveled down her neck. She shoved his hand away and touched the spot with her own fingertips. There was a knot the size of a robin's egg and the rough edges of sutures. That explained the stupid question.

"What happened to me?"

Julia sat cross-legged on the dirt in front of her and took her hands. "You ran into the woods, and we found you unconscious. We think you slipped on a patch of ice and banged your head on a tree."

Julia's eyes were puffy and raw. When tears dripped onto her cheeks, she didn't bother to wipe them, which was strange because she hated for anyone to see her cry.

Riley studied her face, then squeezed her hands. "I don't remember."

Julia jumped up and wrapped her in a bear hug. "You scared me so bad. I thought you were dead like Hannah."

Riley turned her gaze to Coop. He folded his arms and stared into the fire with eyes as swollen as Julia's.

She unwrapped herself from Julia and patted the rock next to her. "Tell me what happened," she said.

Without taking his gaze from the fire, Coop said, "What's the last thing you remember?"

Her last memory was of him tearing her off of Hannah's body, but she couldn't speak the words. Saying it would make it real.

She wanted it to stay a terrifying nightmare she'd wake up from any minute.

"Hannah's dead," she whispered. "I could have saved her. You stopped me."

"We tried to resuscitate her for almost forty minutes. She was gone long before I stopped you. You need to accept that we did our best."

Riley pressed her knuckles to her eyes. "What would it have hurt to keep going? If you're right, we had nothing to lose."

Coop turned to face her. "Except for our sanity and her dignity. You were traumatizing Julia. We're not going to argue this now. You were incoherent and bleeding from your wound when we found you. We carried you here, and I stitched your cut, then I cleaned you up and put you to bed."

Riley looked down, ashamed to meet his eyes. "You carried me? With your broken ribs?" she whispered.

"I'm fine. My incision didn't reopen, and my ribs aren't even sore, so forget it. I wasn't about to lose you after Hannah."

"Sorry for making a traumatic situation worse. I owe you."

"Call it even."

Riley nodded. "Where's Hannah's body?"

Julia wiped her face on her coat. "Coop and I buried her under the rocks we'd collected, to keep the animals away from her. We're going to have a funeral tomorrow. We knew you'd want to be there."

Her words wrenched Riley's heart into a knot. She wanted to cry. Wished she could, but her eyes were as dry as her mouth.

She stood and dusted off her pants. "Coop, help me to the outhouse, please. Then, I'm going back to bed."

Julia got to her feet, too. "You should eat, Mom. You haven't had anything since breakfast."

"I can't. Not now. I'll try in the morning."

Riley scooted deeper into her sleeping bag when she heard Coop's boots pounding up the cabin steps. She felt him leaning over the cot and did her best to keep her breathing deep and even, so he'd think she was asleep.

He shook the bed frame with his knee, and said, "Decent acting but not quite Oscar-worthy. I've let you mourn for three days, Riley. It's time to get up and pitch in. Julia and I can't manage all the work around the campground alone."

She sighed and rolled onto her back. "I'm not ready. You and Julia are handling it just fine. You don't need me."

He unzipped the sleeping bag and uncovered her. "You're not the only one grieving for Hannah. Julia's traumatized, but she's not giving up like you are. She needs her mother. You're forcing her to cope alone. It's selfish."

"Guilt? That's the best you have? And Julia's not alone. She has you. She likes you better than me, anyway."

"Do you blame her? And do you think this isn't any easier for me? I'd come to care for Hannah like a daughter. We've all suffered a loss. The entire world is suffering. What makes you special?"

Riley sat up and glared at him. "Don't you think I know that? I just can't face it yet. It takes everything I have to drag myself out of this bed to go to the latrine. I'm sorry if that doesn't meet up to your lofty standards." She laid back and rezipped the sleeping bag, then covered her head. "I'll get up when I'm ready. Get off my back."

"Appears I'm caring for two teenagers. Julia and I are going to look for a truck. We might be gone all day. Get your own meals and keep the fire going."

"Take your time. I'll finally have peace for once," she called, as he stomped down the steps.

She waited until she heard Coop and Julia's voices receding before throwing off the sleeping bag and running to the outhouse. When she finished, she went to the fire-pit and planted herself on a rock to get warm.

She was disgusted with herself for the way she'd treated Coop, but since Hannah's death, all she could manage was the path of least resistance. He was struggling to keep the three of them alive despite his own pain. None of it was his fault, and he didn't deserve her anger, but she was too overwhelmed to control her outbursts. Crying would have eased her grief, but the tears still refused to come.

He'd been justified in calling her out for neglecting Julia, but his words had stung. Riley had been able to dig deep and face each crisis along their journey, but Hannah's death had broken her. Coop kept reminding her how close they were to Uncle Mitch's ranch, but the light at the end of the tunnel had gone dark. The thought of leaving the campground caused her physical pain, so her only defense was to crawl deeper into her cocoon and wish it all away.

CHAPTER TWELVE

JULIA SAT on Coop's bed and watched Riley sleep. In the four days since Hannah's death, her mom had only gotten up to go to the outhouse. She and Coop brought all her meals, but he told Julia that morning they weren't going to do it anymore to force her mom to get up or starve. Julia was afraid she *would* allow herself to starve. Her mom didn't care about anything anymore. Not even her.

Julia was starting to go from being worried to being pissed. Did her mom think they weren't destroyed over Hannah's death, too? Julia had found a way to keep going, with Coop's love and encouragement. They'd worked together to keep up with chores in the camp and find new supplies while her mom hid in her sleeping bag. It wasn't fair. Julia wanted to hide in her sleeping bag, too, but Coop wouldn't let her, and she was glad.

"I know you're not asleep," Julia finally said, softly. "Why won't you talk to me? Are you mad at me? What did I do?"

Without turning to face her, her mom mumbled, "I'm not mad at you, sweetheart. I love you. I'm suffering over Hannah and all the rest of the stuff we've been through. I just don't have the strength to cope. I need more time, but it has nothing to do with you."

Nothing has anything to do with me anymore, Julia thought. It was like Hannah had been her daughter and she loved her more.

"Coop and I found the perfect truck today. It's not very old and so much better than the one you crashed. We found gas, too, enough to get to the ranch. Coop says we're leaving in the morning."

"Oh, Coop says? He's in charge now? We all have to just do what he says?"

"Someone has to be in charge."

Riley rolled to face her. "I'm not leaving until I'm ready. I need time to grieve."

"Coop says we'll have time to grieve when we're safe at the ranch. He says, for now, we have to focus on getting to our destination."

Her mom sat up and glared at her. "Coop can do whatever he wants. We're staying."

Julia hopped off the bed. "I'm going. I'd rather be with Coop than you. Stay here and rot with Hannah."

"You can't talk to me that way! Coop is nothing to you. We didn't even know him three weeks ago. I'm your mother. You have to do what I say."

"Coop cares about what happens to me. You're the one who's nothing to me. I might as well not exist."

Riley stood and leaned her face an inch from Julia's. "How dare you say that after all I've done for you? Ungrateful little snit."

"I should have left you by that tree. You're so selfish, and I hate you. I should go jump in the river to get your attention. Maybe then you'll remember I'm the one who's your daughter, not Hannah!"

She heard herself screaming the words, but it felt like they were coming from someone else. She'd never raised her voice at her mother in her whole life. Shaking with rage, she turned and stormed out of the cabin, leaving her mother staring open-mouthed behind her.

She brushed past Coop, who was carrying a jug of water in each hand. "Julia, what's wrong?" he asked, as she raced up the stairs to her cabin.

"Nothing. Leave me alone!" she yelled and slammed the door.

———

Riley stood motionless in her cabin, reminding herself to breathe. She felt like she'd jumped into the frozen river herself and had the air ripped out of her body.

Coop bounded up the steps and put down the water. He stared for several seconds before saying, "So, Julia seemed pretty upset. Did you two have an argument?"

Riley dropped on the bed and covered her face with her hands. "She said horrible things to me, Coop, but nothing I don't deserve."

Coop sat next to her and rubbed her back while she told what Julia said.

He whistled when she finished. "Brutal."

"I was too self-absorbed, too consumed with my own grief and anger, to see how deeply Julia was suffering. I deserve it if she never forgives me. I'm the worst mother that ever lived."

"You won't be winning any Mother of the Year awards, but you're far from the worst mother ever. I tried to warn you. Julia's been doing her best, but it's been rough. She needs you despite what she says."

"You mean when she said she hates me and wishes I had died?"

"Teenagers say things. She's distraught. Go talk to her."

"What if she rejects me?"

Coop held out his hand and helped her to her feet. "I have clout. I'll get you in the door."

Riley dragged her feet as they walked the short distance to

Julia's cabin, afraid the words didn't exist to bridge the chasm between them.

Coop knocked softly. "Can we come in, Julia? Your mom has something to say."

"Tell her to go bang her head on a tree."

Riley pushed past Coop and opened the door. Julia was in the sleeping bag with her head covered. The sight of Hannah's bare side of the bed was like a knife in the gut, but Riley ignored it and inched herself onto the edge of Julia's bed. She uncovered Julia's head and tenderly placed her hands on her cheeks.

"Listen carefully to me, sweetheart. I will never forgive myself for what I've done to you. Everything you said is true. It was selfish and wrong of me to abandon you. We needed each other, but all I thought of was my own pain. I never stopped to consider yours. I have no right to ask, but I hope you will forgive me in time."

Julia sat motionless, watching her with tears dripping down her face. Riley searched her eyes and was amazed to still find love there.

"You are my world," she continued. "I love you more than my own life. Losing Hannah was almost more than I could bear but losing you *would* kill me. It terrified me when you talked about jumping in the river. Stay with me, sweetheart. We'll help each other get back to Emily and Jared together, and we'll be the family we used to be."

Julia threw her arms around Riley's neck and sobbed on her shoulder. "I'm sorry, too, Mom. I love you. I didn't mean it when I said I wished you died. That was awful. I just felt rejected and thought you loved Hannah more than me. I promise I'd never jump in the river or do anything like that. Let's forget this place and get to the ranch. I want to be with Uncle Mitch's family. Can we leave in the morning?"

Riley kissed her cheek. "Absolutely. I'm as ready as you to put this camp far behind us. Thank you for understanding and being the better person. I have so much to learn from you."

Coop wiped a tear off his cheek and did a fist bump before wrapping his arms around them. "We'll be the Three Musketeers, back on the road. We leave at sun-up."

Riley cupped the metal canteen lid in her gloved hands, letting the delicious hot liquid warm her numb fingers. She couldn't remember a time when she wasn't cold. Memories of her luxurious bed at the hotel felt like something out of a dream. She squeezed her eyelids and tried to count how many days had passed since the CME but gave up after a few seconds. The effort consumed too much of her dwindling energy. Logic told her it could be no more than two weeks, but it felt more like a lifetime.

She opened her eyes and watched the fire dance in the pit, wondering if her life would ever be so carefree again. Was the rift she'd caused with Julia truly healed? Would the day come when she, Julia, and Coop would be safe and warm? Would she ever see Emily and Jared again?

She heard Coop's boots crunch on the path. He walked up and took the rock next to her.

Putting his arms around her shoulder, he said, "Do you mind if I do that?" She snuggled closer to him in answer. "You looked a million miles away. Thinking about Julia?"

She shook her head. "Actually, I was trying to imagine what our future will be. I couldn't do it. Too many uncertainties. I'm afraid to hope we'll make it to Wytheville."

Coop turned her to face him. "We'll make it, but only if we work together and fight for it. I can't have you doubting our survival every step of the way."

She wrapped her arms around him and tucked her head against his shoulder. "I'll have to lean on your strength, then."

"You have my permission. Thank you for agreeing to go in the morning. You'll feel better once we're on the road." They watched the fire in silence for a few moments until he said, "I want to ask you something, but I'm afraid you'll freak out on me."

She sat up and looked into his eyes. "I don't ever want you to be afraid to ask me anything. What is it?"

"I'm trying to understand why Hannah's death pushed you so far that you were willing to risk Julia's safety. Losing Hannah was a tragic blow for all of us, and I can't believe how much I miss her, but we'd only known her for two weeks, but you reacted like it was Julia who died. Was it your PTSD? Did you reach your trauma saturation point? I wouldn't blame you if you did. I was only seconds from reaching mine. If I hadn't had to treat your injuries, I might have lost it."

Riley nodded in understanding and searched her mind for the words to explain. "If I tell you, promise not to make fun of me. It's a little nuts."

"I already think you're nuts, so you have nothing to lose," he said and gave her a half-grin.

"Not sure if you're joking, but I'll pretend you are. At some point, I'm not sure when, the idea formed in the back of my mind that if I kept Hannah alive, it meant Emily was alive. When Hannah died, it was like I'd lost her and Emily. I'd failed them both. That makes no logical sense, but that's how it felt."

Coop stroked his chin before responding. The hesitation made her nervous. Finally, he said, "You know better than I do that in a crisis, our minds play tricks as a defense mechanism. That's all this is. What do you believe now? You do know that Hannah's death has no effect on Emily, right?"

"It took time to get there, but yes, I do know. That hasn't changed the fact that I blame myself for Hannah's death. I'm ultimately responsible."

"How did you come to that insane conclusion? It was nothing more than a tragic accident."

She pulled away from him and looked him the eye. "No, I was the one who crashed the truck and broke your ribs. I elbowed you and punctured your lung, so we couldn't make it to Charlottesville and had to come here. You weren't able to collect water from the river, so the girls had to do it, and Hannah drowned. All my fault."

"That's the most irrational chain of logic I've ever heard! You didn't crash the truck on purpose or out of negligence. It was just as much an accident. If I follow your reasoning, it's my fault Hannah died because I made us leave the hotel. Why aren't you blaming me? Claiming you're responsible is just as absurd."

"Leaving the hotel isn't the same. We were in danger and were forced to go. I told you my reasoning was nuts. I just need more time to work through it."

"I hate seeing you punishing yourself for nothing, but I'll back off and let you figure it out. In the meantime, we pull up stakes and leap once more into the unknown. Tomorrow offers a clean slate, a fresh start."

Riley gave him a half-hearted smile. "How poetic." She stood and rubbed her stiff thigh muscles. "Julia told me about your shiny new truck. If we're leaving at sunrise, we'd better pack. You coming?"

Riley thought she was dreaming about the hand covering her mouth, but she forced her eyes open and realized it was real. She tried to suck in a breath and scream, but Coop put his lips to her ear and whispered, "Riley, don't make a sound. Someone's in the camp."

When she nodded, he carefully removed his hand. She listened to the sound of boots and male voices drifting in from the direction of the fire-pit. Through the haze of sleep and panic, her only thought was to get to her daughter.

She sat up and whispered, "Julia."

"Get your boots. We'll climb out the window and go around back."

While she silently laced her boots, Coop slid the window open a fraction of an inch at a time. When the opening was big enough for them to climb through, he tugged on the screen, but it was nailed to the frame.

"I need my knife. It's under the left side of my bed," he whispered, just loud enough for her to hear.

She lay across his bed and searched for the knife with her hand. Just as her fingers brushed against it, Julia let out a piercing scream. Riley grabbed the knife and climbed over the bed to get to the door.

"Riley, no!" Coop shouted.

She stared at him for an instant before racing down the cabin steps, ignoring the threat she faced from the intruders. All that mattered was Julia.

By the light of the fire, she saw two men dragging Julia toward the fire-pit by her arms. Julia cried out and struggled to break free, but she was no match for them. Two other men walked behind them. They were all at least six-foot with large builds.

Dreading what they had planned for Julia, Riley rushed them, grabbing a piece of firewood as she went. She gripped it with both hands like a baseball bat and aimed it at the back of one of their heads but missed. The target swung on her and pushed her to the ground. She scrambled to her knees, but he leveled his gun at her. She froze and slowly raised her hands.

"Stay still, and we won't hurt you," he said.

His partner had Julia pinned face down in the dirt with her arms twisted behind her back. The other two were forcing Coop to his knees five feet from Riley. There was no hope of escaping or overpowering them.

"Please, let her go," Riley begged. "She won't run. Right, Julia?"

"Mom, Coop, help me," she cried. "He's breaking my arm."

"Can he loosen his grip?" Coop asked the man holding the gun on Riley. "She's no threat to him."

He cocked his head at the one holding Julia. He moved off and jerked her to her knees. When he let go of her arm, she cradled it against her ribs with her other hand. One of the men with Coop got up and threw wood on the coals glowing in the fire-pit.

Riley caught Julia's eye and gave a weak smile to reassure her. "You all right, sweetheart?"

Julia straightened and nodded. In the moment of silence that followed, Riley assessed their situation, wondering if the men were part of Crawford's crew. Days had passed since the altercation with them, but they hadn't put much distance between themselves and Crawford's territory. What mattered more was what the men wanted with them. Riley was willing to give up all their possessions in exchange for Julia.

"You want our supplies?" Coop asked. "You're welcome to them. All you had to do was ask."

The man holding Coop said, "We've found out the hard way that asking politely doesn't work too well these days."

"Take what you want and leave us in peace," Riley said.

The man with Julia opened his mouth to speak, but a log popped in the fire-pit and shot out a spark that landed on his pant leg. When he reached out to flick it off, Julia got to her feet and ran for the woods. Without hesitating, he unholstered his gun and fired two shots in her direction. Julia spun, then collapsed in a heap. She thrashed on the ground like she was the one on fire.

Riley froze. It had happened in a flash and her brain was slow to catch up. Had that monster just shot her baby?

The man guarding Riley turned toward the shooter. "Jepson, you jackass," he yelled. "Why'd you do that? After what you did at that church, the Director's going to have your head for this."

Riley came to her senses and slammed her elbow in her

captor's crotch while he was distracted. When he doubled over, she stood and rushed to Julia's side. There was just enough light for her to see the dark stain of blood spreading under her upper leg.

She gently caressed Julia's forehead to calm her. "It's Mommy, sweetheart," she said in soothing tones. "I know you're in pain, but I need you to lie still so I can see what's wrong."

"That man shot me!" she shrieked. "It hurts, mommy! Help me!"

"I know," Riley said as she scooted to Julia's leg. "I'm going to fix you good as new." She ripped the leg of her sweatpants open where the bullet had pierced the fabric. Blood poured from the gunshot wound in her thigh. Riley stripped off her sweatshirt and pressed it to Julia's thigh. In the commotion, Coop broke free from the man holding him and dropped to his knees next to Riley.

Jepson ran after Coop and pointed his gun at Julia. "What are you two doing? Get away from her and back to the fire."

Coop ignored him and turned to Riley. "What's the damage?"

"The bullet may have nicked the femoral artery. From the angle of the wound, I'm almost certain it hit the femur. Do we have a clamp in the med-pack? If not, we have to find something else to clamp that artery, or we'll lose her."

When Coop got up and headed for the cabin, Jepson stepped in front of him, but one of the other men shoved him out of the way.

Jepson shoved back, and said, "What are you doing, Brooks? Get out of my way."

"You ordering me around now, Jepson? Don't forget who's in charge." When Jepson backed off, Brooks said, "I think they're doctors, you idiot. If we bring two doctors to camp, that'll be quite the prize. If she saves the girl, the Director might just let you live, so it's in your best interest to get out of the way and let them work."

Coop came back with the med-kit and started digging through it. Jepson didn't try to stop him, but he didn't lower his gun either.

Julia squirmed and wailed while Coop pulled three clamps out of the bag and held them up for Riley to inspect.

She picked the middle one. "It might be too big, but the others are too small and could cause more damage. We need gloves."

Coop grabbed the pack of gloves from the kit. Riley had to work fast before Julia bled out. She'd have to cut into the tissue to reach the artery and felt sick at knowing the intense pain she was about to inflict on her daughter, but there was no time to hesitate.

She pulled Coop's knife from her back pocket, and he handed her a sterile wipe to scrub the blade before dousing it with alcohol. The blade was thick and not as sharp as she wanted, but they were out of scalpels and had nothing sharper.

Coop cut off the leg of Julia's sweatpants and sanitized her skin with alcohol wipes. If Julia survived the blood loss and didn't develop clots, the next most serious threat was infection. They were as far from doing surgery in a sterile OR as they could get.

Once the knife was as clean as Riley could get it, she looked up at the men who had formed a half-circle around them. She pointed to one and said, "Shine a flashlight where I tell you." Brooks took out a heavy-duty flashlight like the one Zach used to carry. Riley indicated where she needed the beam. With the field lit, she pointed at the two standing behind the shooter. "You two get down here and help Coop hold her still. This is going to hurt."

One of the men knelt by her feet and grabbed her ankle. The other sat across from Coop and pinned Julia's shoulders to the dirt. With everything ready, Riley and Coop put on fresh gloves and went to work. Julia let out an ear-piercing scream that echoed through the woods when Riley made the first incision, then she went quiet.

"She's passed out from the pain," Coop said to the men

holding her. "That's a blessing for all of us, but don't let go in case she regains consciousness."

Riley tried to block out that she was operating on her daughter and let her training take control. She worked quickly, with Coop sponging the blood out of the field so she could check the artery for damage. It only took minutes to see that the bullet had only nicked it, but the femur was shattered. Julia would need extensive surgery to save the bone, but that would have to wait. She sutured the artery and began to work on tissue surrounding the wound.

Without looking up from her work, she said, "Coop, feel for an exit wound. I don't see the bullet, but we have to be sure."

He looked at the men. "I need another flashlight."

"Rawls, use yours," Brooks said.

The man at Julia's feet took a flashlight from his back pocket and held it out to Coop.

He shook his head. "You have to hold it for me. Get down here and shine it on the back of her thigh."

Rawls knelt on the other side of Julia and shined the flashlight while Coop gently slid one hand under Julia's leg to raise it slightly. He felt for an exit wound with the fingers of his other hand.

"Bingo," he said, after a minute.

Riley nodded. "Excellent. Where?"

"Roughly ten centimeters above the lateral condyle." He pressed a stack of gauze squares on the opening. "When you finish, we'll flip her to examine and close the wound."

Riley wiped her forehead with the back of her arm. "I'll be done in five."

Once the entry wound was sutured, she asked for a tarp or blanket to protect Julia's face from the dirt when they flipped her. Brooks ran to Julia's cabin and brought back her sleeping bag. Riley nodded her thanks, confused at why these men who had been brutes minutes earlier were so cooperative now.

She and Coop braced Julia's leg as best they could and carefully rolled her onto her stomach. Rawls pointed the flashlight where Coop showed him so he could examine the exit wound.

"Clean edges and not much bleeding. This won't take long," Coop said.

Riley let him take the lead while she became the assistant. When the wound was closed and dressed, they rolled Julia onto her back and fashioned a splint out of branches and strips of cloth so the jagged edges of the bone wouldn't move and cause more tissue damage.

Riley covered Julia with the sleeping bag, then put her hands on her hips and glared at Jepson. "If my daughter dies, I'm coming for you if it takes the rest of my life." Jepson raised his hands in surrender as he backed away. Turning to Brooks, she said, "She needs more surgery. You said you have a camp with a medic? What medical supplies do you have?"

Brooks shoved Jepson out of the way and stepped closer to Riley. "We should have whatever you need for the operation. If not, we'll get it."

"How far away is your camp?" Coop asked.

The men glanced at each other, but Rawls said, "Not far. Twenty minutes."

"Take us there," Riley ordered and started for her cabin.

"Not until we load all of your supplies," Brooks said. "You won't be coming back here."

Riley started to argue, but Coop motioned for her to back down. "Stay with Julia. I'll help them."

"And don't forget the keys to that fancy truck. That's going, too," Jepson said.

CHAPTER THIRTEEN

RILEY HELD Julia's hand as the cargo van bumped over backcountry roads. It was impossible to keep track of where they'd traveled in the darkness. Coop rode with Jepson in the truck. Riley hoped he'd been able to take note of street signs and landmarks so they could find their way back to the highway if they managed to escape.

When they hit a pothole, Julia moaned and Riley cringed. She'd done her best to keep Julia immobilized, fearing the bone fragments would shift, but it was impossible to protect her from every movement. She checked Julia's vitals with the blood pressure cuff and oximeter Brooks gave her when she climbed into the van. Riley tried not to think about how they'd acquired the instruments and prayed they'd have the equipment she needed to do a proper surgery on Julia. If they didn't, her odds of survival were slim.

The van approached a compound surrounded by metal fencing topped with barbed wire. Two men behind a gate unlocked it and waved for the driver to enter. They rode for five minutes before he slowed in front of a thirty-foot long tent. Riley had expected the camp to be small with a few Army tents scattered around the grounds, but it appeared to be as large as the campground.

When the van stopped, Riley climbed out and walked up to Brooks. "Where's the medical tent? I need to inspect your equipment and supplies so I can perform Julia's surgery, or she won't last the night."

Brooks stepped closer to her and crossed his arms. "We'll get to that in a minute. All new arrivals have to check in with the Director first."

"Screw your Director, whoever that is. My daughter is dying."

"The Director is the elected leader of this community. Nothing happens without his approval. He won't be happy about being woken up, so you'd better hold your lip, or your precious Julia won't be getting surgery tonight."

Riley reluctantly backed down. She'd do whatever it took to save her daughter. "Fine, but we need to hurry."

She was reluctant to leave Julia, but Brooks assured her she'd be safe. She had no choice but to believe him. They walked to a smaller tent adjacent to the one where the driver had parked. An armed man and woman stood guard in front of the entrance. Julia getting shot proved what these people were capable of, so Riley reminded herself to be on her best behavior. Coop came up behind her and put his arm around her waist. She felt his strength flow into her, and her anxiety abated slightly.

Brooks motioned for them to wait at the tent entrance while he went inside.

Coop leaned close and whispered, "How's Julia?"

"Her pressure's low and pulse is elevated, likely from the blood loss. She roused a few times, but she was out when I left her. They better have what we need to operate and be willing to let us use it."

"We'll make sure they do. What's the deal with this Director?"

She shrugged as Brooks opened the tent flap and stepped out. "I've explained the situation. The Director will see you."

He moved aside to let Riley and Coop pass. She ducked in first and found a man in pajamas and a terrycloth robe sitting in a camp chair with his legs crossed. He had an average build, glasses, and dull brown hair. He could have been any guy on the street and reminded her of the owner of the farming supply store her father used. He didn't look too frightening, and Riley wondered how he'd risen to power and why he evoked so much fear in his men.

"Welcome to camp, Dr. Poole, Dr. Cooper. I'm Director Branson. Since there isn't time now for your camp orientation, I'll just inform you that while you aren't free to leave, if you cooperate willingly, you can go about your activities in the compound without interference."

Her eyes narrowed as she stepped closer to him. "Do your goons know that? They shot my daughter for no reason. She's clinging to life. I need to operate, now."

"I apologize for the incident with your daughter. Some of my men are undisciplined hotheads. It's difficult to keep them in line at times, but I assure you appropriate action will be taken with those responsible."

Riley shivered at the tone of his words. He appeared calm and accommodating, but his eyes were cold and sterile.

"In the meantime," he continued, "you're welcome to anything you need to treat your daughter. All I ask in exchange is that you consent to act as head of our medical team. That means overseeing the needs of all members of our community. We'll make every effort to stock you with whatever supplies and medications you require."

"Agreed," Riley said. "Where do I sign?"

He stood and said, "A handshake will serve for the time being."

She shook his outstretched hand. It was as cold as his eyes despite the kerosene heater blasting in the corner. He locked his eyes on hers. She read the warning there.

"We'll prepare the required documents in the morning. Dr. Cooper, you also agree to our terms?"

Coop shook the Director's hand. "Yes, sir."

"Excellent. Brooks will show you to the infirmary. Come to my office as soon as possible tomorrow."

Riley was surprised to hear he had an office in addition to his personal tent. Even though they were captives, staying in the compound while Julia recovered might not be the worst thing. At least they'd be warm.

Brooks magically appeared to take them to the medical tent, but Riley stopped him. "We need to get Julia and take her with us. Do you have gurneys?"

Brooks turned and walked the opposite direction from the van. "She's already there waiting for you."

Brooks escorted Riley and Coop to a tent that reminded her of the set from M*A*S*H, right down to the bank of deep scrubbing sinks. Fortunately, the technology was modern. She was stunned to see a portable x-ray machine and a respirator, the exact equipment she needed to save Julia.

"Do you have the juice to run these machines?" she asked Brooks.

"Yes, we have several hardened generators and the fuel to run them. Plenty of power for whatever you need."

She nodded and moved into the adjoining room with Coop on her heels. Julia was on a gurney with what looked like clean bedding. Her eyes were open, and she turned at the sounds of Riley's footsteps. She reached out her hand and Riley cradled it between her own.

"Where am I, Mom? What happened?"

Riley brushed a lock of hair from Julia's forehead. "You were shot in the leg at the campground. Do you remember?"

Julia pressed her eyelids together, then gave a slight shake of her head.

"That's fine. The men who invaded our camp brought us here so I can operate on you. They have electricity and surgical supplies."

Julia's eyes widened, and her already pale face grew whiter. "It hurts. Am I going to die like Hannah?"

"No, sweetheart. It will take time to heal, but you're going to be fine. Coop and I are going to fix your leg. You won't feel a thing. I'm going to scrub up while Coop gives you happy juice to make you sleep. You'll feel much better when you wake up."

Coop stepped closer and leaned over Julia. "Hey, I came up with a nickname for you; WP, short for Warrior Princess. You're one tough lady. Ready for the happy juice?"

Julia nodded. "Hurry. I might be tough, but this is pretty painful."

He squeezed Riley's shoulder as he passed on his way to the supply room.

She kissed Julia's cheek and whispered, "I love you," then hurried to the small scrub room. Coop came in, and she held out her trembling hands. "I can't do this. Doctors aren't supposed to operate on family members."

Coop pulled her into his arms. She laid her ear against his chest and fought her tears.

"I'll take the lead if you want, but you're the ortho. It'll be a complicated surgery, and Julia needs the expert. She couldn't be in better hands than yours." As he gently stroked her hair, he whispered, "Take slow, even breaths. Forget the patient is Julia. She's just a teenage girl who needs you to save her leg and her life. You're a skilled surgeon, and I'll be at your side the entire time."

Riley pulled away and squared her shoulders. "Thank you. Let's get to work. I've wasted enough time. "

Riley curled up on a gurney next to Julia and watched the steady rise and fall of her angel's breathing. She would have cried if she'd had the strength. *At least she's alive. All three of us are for now,* she thought and covered her face with her hands.

The surgery had been grueling but successful. The bullet hadn't severed the femur completely, and there were fewer bone fragments than she and Coop anticipated. They wired her femur together like a puzzle and repaired the damaged tissue. In pre-CME days, she would have had access to better hardware for the reconstruction, but given what they'd had to work with, Riley was hopeful Julia would survive and have full use of her leg in time.

Coop tried to coax Riley to go to her tent after the surgery, but she insisted on staying with Julia. She didn't trust anyone else with her post-op care. She'd managed to steal a few moments of rest but needed hours of uninterrupted sleep.

She was too exhausted and traumatized to consider any option but to surrender to their fate. Events had unfolded in rapid-fire succession since leaving the hotel two weeks earlier, and they'd been carried along on the swift current of momentum. Julia was clinging to life and wouldn't be able to walk unaided by wheelchairs and crutches for months. They were captives to thugs waving guns in their faces. She couldn't envision a route of escape.

She climbed off the gurney and stretched before venturing to look for Coop. As she passed a small office at the infirmary entrance, a young woman came out and asked to have a word with Riley. She flashed a brilliant smile as she shook her hand. She wasn't sure what anyone had to smile about in their insane world, but Riley was grateful. It was impossible not to cheer up in the sheer radiance of it.

Her dark eyes were rimmed by thick lashes and her brown

skin was as smooth as caramel. Someone had woven her hair into a beautiful system of braids, looking like she'd just stepped out of a salon. Riley wondered who'd done that for her and how they'd had the time. Life at the compound was clearly different than what she, Coop and Julia had lived.

"My name is Dashay Robinson. I'm one of the five nurses in camp. Mendez filled me in on Julia's surgery. I'd be happy to take over her post-op care so you can rest."

Riley rubbed her eyes. "Mendez?"

"The camp medic. I thought he said you met."

"Right. I'm still groggy. I appreciate the offer, Dashay, but I was going to find Dr. Cooper."

"He's sleeping and asked me to tell you not to disturb him." When Riley frowned, Dashay flashed another smile. "I'm just the messenger."

Coop was as desperate for sleep as she was, and it wouldn't be fair to wake him. She didn't like leaving Julia in the care of strangers but standing vigil around the clock wasn't viable. Riley saw no choice but to turn the reins over to Dashay. Her gut told her she could trust her. After updating her on Julia's care, she asked Dashay about her background and experience.

"I'm an RN with a bachelor's from Johns Hopkins. I worked for an oncological surgeon for six years. I'd been visiting my family in Charlottesville with my boyfriend for the holidays. We were on our way back to Baltimore when the CME hit. We got in an accident. He didn't survive. I walked away without a scratch."

Another life tragically impacted. "I'm deeply sorry. I'd love for you to tell me about him sometime. How did you end up here? Were you taken hostage, too?"

"No, I'm one of the few who came here by choice. After the accident, I started walking with no idea where I was headed. Some of Director Branson's people stopped and offered me a ride to their camp. I had nowhere else to go, so I joined them. Glad I did. It's good to be needed and it distracts me from thinking about Darian, but most of the other camp residents would rather be anywhere else."

"I appreciate you telling me and for your offer to tend to Julia. If I don't get sleep soon, I'm going to fall down where I stand. I leave my daughter in your capable hands."

Dashay promised to stay by her side until Riley or Coop came to relieve her. Riley thanked her and stepped into the bright sunshine to go in search of her tent.

The infirmary was in a central square of the compound adjoining the big tent Riley had seen the night before. There was another long tent on the opposite edge of the courtyard she didn't recognize. The area was clean and well maintained. Riley was baffled at how they'd been able to construct the compound in such short order. Her only conclusion was that Director Branson had sinister methods to wring obedience out of his minions.

As she wandered the paths between tents, people stopped and stared. At first, she thought it was because she was a newcomer, but after the sixth or seventh person, she glanced down at her clothes. Stains of Julia's blood covered the fabric. She quickened her pace and was relieved to see Brooks walking toward her.

"I was just coming to show you to your quarters." He studied her for a moment gave a small grin. "Looking a bit grisly. You might want a shower and change of clothes. Your belongings are in your tent."

"The shower can wait until I've had some sleep, but I'll be glad to change. Is there somewhere to get something to eat?"

"I put in an order to have a tray delivered to your tent. Should hold you until dinner." He pointed to the large tent next to Director Branson's personal quarters she'd seen the night before. "That's the dining facility. The showers are thirty feet to the right. My quarters are directly behind The Director's." He stopped in front of an average-sized tent. This is you. Dr. Cooper is next door. You know where to find me."

He gave a slight bow and strode off without another word. It reminded Riley of when she first met Coop, but she wasn't sorry to see Brooks go. He'd been kind to her since Jepson shot Julia, but she had a feeling he would not become a friend.

She ducked into her tent and was happy to see her backpack and other belongings. She'd only owned them for a week, but they felt like old friends. She changed into a clean pair of sweatpants and a long-sleeve thermal shirt, then surrendered to the sleep that overpowered her the instant her head hit the pillow.

It was dark by the time Riley woke six hours later. She grabbed her backpack and headed for the showers before going to check on Julia. It was pitch black inside the showers, so she clicked on her flashlight to look for a light source. She found what looked like a searchlight mounted to the wooden frame. She pulled the dangling chain and was nearly blinded when the bulb lit up.

There was a line of six shower stalls that reminded her of summer camp as a child. Neatly folded white towels were arranged in stacked wooden crates. Bottles of body soap and shampoo lined a narrow shelf on the opposite side. All she lacked was a razor to shave the forest growing on her legs and armpits.

She stepped into a middle stall and pulled the chain. Glorious warm water poured from the showerhead and flowed over her bruised and aching body. If it hadn't been for Julia, she would have stayed there luxuriating for an hour. As it was, she let go of the chain and soaped up before doing a quick rinse. She was reluctant to leave the peaceful little sanctuary until she reminded herself that she could shower whenever she wanted now.

She dressed quickly and headed for the infirmary. Dashay was on a metal folding chair next to Julia's bed. She put down her book and smiled when she saw Riley. She returned the smile before going to Julia.

"How is she? Has she been awake?" she asked, then felt Julia's forehead and checked her pulse.

"She's been awake for short periods, but she's weak. Dr. Cooper came in and was able to get her to respond to stimuli for a few minutes."

Riley nodded, relieved Coop had been in to see Julia. She studied her daughter's face for a moment. "I'm concerned about her color."

Dashay stood and moved next to Riley. "She may need a transfusion."

"We'll see how she does through the night. Do we have the equipment to run blood tests?"

"Yes, a centrifuge and microscope. We're short on tubes, strips and slides, but we should have enough for Julia. Director Branson sends teams on scheduled runs to scavenge for med supplies. The next one should be at the end of the week."

"Like a well-oiled machine," Riley mumbled. "Thank you for staying. I'll take over now."

"My shift ends in ten minutes. Claire, the night nurse and Mendez will be in to replace me."

"Who else do you have on the medical staff?"

"We have three other nurses and a dentist, but she's been too ill to be much help."

"What's wrong with her?"

Dashay shrugged. "Dysentery, but she refuses to let us treat her."

"I'll see about that. We need everyone with medical knowledge on staff."

Dashay nodded. "Happy to have you here. See you tomorrow."

Riley watched her go before scooting the chair closer to Julia and lowering herself into it. She watched a beetle climbing up the opposite tent wall.

"Didn't you get the memo that it's winter and the world has gone to hell?" she asked him. She considered tossing him out into the cold but decided if he'd managed to survive so long, he deserved a cushy life in the warm tent.

A tall, broad-shouldered redhead of about Riley's age came in, followed by Mendez. The red-head walked directly to Riley and extended her hand.

"Dr. Poole, I'm guessing. I'm Claire O'Brian. Pleased to meet you. Can't imagine how happy we are to have you here. How's the lass?"

Claire had a booming voice to match her frame and a strong Irish accent. Riley felt stronger just being in her presence and took to her at once. Between Claire and Dashay, their medical staff was shaping up nicely.

Mendez gave a slight nod. "Evening, Dr. Poole."

He reminded Riley of the thousands of Airmen she'd seen pass through the base back home. He had a faint Spanish accent.

"Evening, Mendez. I wanted to thank you for offering to help with Julia last night. I don't want you to feel like we're pushing you out the way. I hear you've been doing an admirable job running the medical staff here."

He ran his hand through his closely cropped brown hair. "Well, someone's lying, then. I'm just a lowly Army medic with no idea how to run a medical clinic. You and Dr. Cooper are a godsend."

"Glad you feel that way. We'll still need your skills."

Claire stepped between them and put her hands on her ample hips. "Enough with the pleasantries. How's that girl of yours?"

"Barely hanging in there. She needs a transfusion, at the very least. She's O-neg. That will complicate things."

"Excuse me for saying so, Dr. Poole, but you look like hell. We'll keep tabs on your little angel. Go get some food and rest. She's in good hands."

Riley chuckled. "Thanks for the compliment, but I am

starving. I'll be in the mess tent if there's any change. I'll try to round up some blood donors before I return."

Claire gave a snort. "Good luck with that crew out there. They aren't exactly the giving kind."

Riley let the comment pass and kissed Julia's forehead on her way out to get dinner. As she crossed the square, she saw a bedraggled group huddled around a campfire. Coop waved and joined her to walk to the mess tent. He kissed her cheek and asked about Julia.

"Sleeping. Stable but weak. Thanks for checking on her earlier," she said. "She's lost too much blood, Coop. Since neither of us are the right blood type to help her, do you think these people would be willing to donate? They look so frail themselves, but I'm not sure Julia will survive without a transfusion."

"They are malnourished, no thanks to our captors stuffing their faces in the mess tent, but I've heard they were awed by the way you ordered Branson's men around last night. You're a bit of a hero. That might soften them up but give them a minute to meet you before asking for blood."

"Noted, but I'm no hero, just a momma bear desperate to save her cub. Have you eaten?"

"Yes, such as it was. With an outfit like this, I'd expected bigger portions. I hear Branson is generous with his staff but holds out on any who refuse to kiss up to him. Looks like we might be going hungry."

"I'll welcome anything at this point. Go back to the fire. I'll join you after I eat."

"I'll save you a seat," he said, then walked back to the fire-pit.

She entered the mess tent and was pleasantly surprised at how warm it was until she saw a large wood-burning stove in the center of the room. She wondered why the group at the fire hadn't stayed inside like Branson's people at a long wooden table near the stove.

She found the cafeteria-style serving area and went to get her food. The young woman behind the rough-wood counter served her soup in a metal cup and two pieces of dry bread. She carried her meal to a smaller table near the stove to eat. Even though the soup was mostly broth, it was steaming hot and smelled delicious. It was the first hot meal with fresh meat that she'd had in weeks.

She sipped the soup between bites of bread and watched Branson's people. The group consisted of fifteen men and women, mostly men. They had a much bigger dinner piled in front of them and laughed and chatted like they didn't have a care in the world. Riley's stomach growled at the sight of their plates steaming with food. She was tempted to assert her authority as medical chief of staff and demand more to eat but knew it wouldn't be fair to the others at the campfire, so she lowered her eyes and stared at her soup.

She finished eating as quickly as she could, then reluctantly went to join Coop outside, hoping she could convince him and the others to come inside the warm mess tent. Being in the heat would be healthier for them than shivering outside, even if they had to share the space with Branson's people.

Coop caught her eye as she came out and pointed to the chair, he'd saved for her. She was grateful since it meant she wouldn't have to sit on one of the stumps set in a circle around the fire. A man she didn't know handed her a thin blanket. She nodded in thanks and arranged it over her legs as she studied the people seated around her. Most of them looked like she felt; frightened, scared, exhausted. They were probably no different than her before the CME, average Americans going about their ordinary existence before being thrust into this nightmare world.

Riley counted twenty men, fifteen women, and eight children. Four boys who looked to be Julia's age, and one girl who looked around nine, stood behind the adults. A boy and a girl each about Jared's age sat with their parents. The youngest was a boy of about three. Riley wondered how he'd survived. He was sitting at one of the women's feet, drawing in the dirt with a stick, seemingly oblivious to what was happening around him. Maybe that was the solution to survival: selective oblivion.

Coop introduced her to the group, but the names and faces were a blur. She should have paid better attention since this could be her collective for months to come, but all that mattered was saving Julia.

"Riley's daughter needs a blood transfusion, so we need donors," Coop said after the introductions. "We know it's a lot to ask. We'd use our own blood, but Julia's type O-negative and can only receive that type of blood. Riley and I are both A-positive, so we're incompatible. Are any of you type O-negative and willing to donate to save Julia?"

Most glanced at each other or stared at the ground. A few shrugged.

The woman with the little boy raised her hand. Riley thought her name might be Kelly. "I'm willing to help, but I don't remember my blood type."

"Me, either," a man named David said. He looked like he was in his mid-fifties but seemed fit and healthy enough. "I used to know in my Marine days, but that was years ago."

"How many of you know your blood type?" Riley asked. Only five raised their hands. Of those, only two looked healthy enough to spare their blood. She turned to Coop. "I forgot to ask Dashay if we have a blood typing kit."

"I'll ask Mendez. He'll know."

As he left for the infirmary, an image of hospital cabinets back home stocked to the brim with every kind of medical device or kit imaginable flashed in Riley's mind. She added it to the list of things she'd taken for granted in the pre-disaster world. Would something as simple as the lack of a blood type kit cost Julia her life?

She took a breath and stood to address the group. "If we obtain testing kits, are any of you others willing to donate?"

The adults avoided her eyes, but one of the teenage boys raised his hand. "I'll do it."

Riley was about to thank him when a man stepped between them. "That's generous of you, son, but I won't allow it. You need to keep up your strength. Sorry, Dr. Poole."

Riley stepped closer and stretched her tiny frame to appear menacing. "How about you, then? You look healthy enough."

He held her gaze without flinching. "Why should I? When our daughter died, no one stepped in to help us."

Riley relaxed her shoulders and stared at the ground. In her desperation to save Julia, she'd forgotten that hundreds of thousands, if not millions had died. Every person in that group had probably lost a loved one. How could she expect them to sacrifice for a stranger?

"I'm sorry. Tell me what happened, Mr...," she said softly.

"It's Marcus. She was Type I diabetic. We begged and pleaded for insulin everywhere we went. No one helped us. She slipped into a coma and died in my arms."

"Has the whole human race gone mad?" she whispered and closed her eyes for a moment. "What was your daughter's name?"

"Cassie."

"You have my deepest sympathies. We've suffered tragedy as well. Losing Cassie might help you understand what I'm going through. If Julia dies, it won't bring Cassie back to you. Refusing to help will make you like the people who refused to come to your aid. Do you want to become what they are?"

He lowered his head and put his hands in his pockets. "I don't. If you find a testing kit and I'm a match, I'll donate to save your daughter."

Riley walked to him and extended her hand. He ignored it and pulled her into a hug. A few others circled around them and offered to donate.

A woman stepped from the shadows beyond the fire. "I'll donate if I'm compatible."

Riley recognized the voice, but it took a moment to match it to her face. "Angie!" she cried and threw her arms around her friend. "We thought you were dead. We went to the church, but no one knew what happened to you."

Angie stepped away and wiped her eyes. "Mystery solved. I've been a hostage here since that horrible night. So, one of these monsters shot Julia? Let me guess, Jepson? He has a reputation around for being trigger happy."

"He's the one. We were able to repair the damage, but she's lost a lot of blood and needs a transfusion. Do you know your type?"

"I think I'm O-positive, but I'm not sure."

"Angie, thank God," Coop said, and gave her a tight hug. Riley caught his eye, hoping for a positive answer about the testing kits, but he shook his head. "They used the last of the supply two days ago. We need to get our hands on a test kit."

"Our benevolent jailers might have what you need," a man called from behind Riley.

She swung around to see who'd spoken. A small, balding man of about forty sat on the ground twenty feet from the campfire. He slumped against the tree he was tied to, wrapped in a thin blanket and visibly shivering.

"Who's that and why is he tied to a tree like a dog?" Riley asked as she started for him.

Marcus put his hand out to stop her. "Leave him be." He cocked his head toward the mess tent. "That bunch won't like it if you help him."

"Why? What did he do?" Coop asked.

"That's Dr. Adrian Landry," Angie said. "He knew hell was about to rain down on us and didn't tell anyone. Our captors weren't too happy to hear that."

Riley walked past Marcus' outstretched arm and grabbed two blankets from one of the camp chairs. "Another doctor? We can use him. I don't care what he's done."

She marched up to the man and held the blankets out to him. He stared but didn't move to take them. Riley squatted and draped the blankets over his legs and chest. She hesitated when she saw his bound hands folded in his lap. The skin on his wrists was raw and festering. Riley felt him watching her and raised her eyes to meet his. She expected to see pain and humility, but his look was one of challenge.

The patch of ground where he sat was clear of snow, so Riley sat facing him with her legs crossed. She pointed to his wrists and said, "Did you do that trying to escape?" He nodded without taking his eyes off hers. "Do you have other injuries?"

Dr. Landry lifted his shirt to expose his bruised torso. "They nearly beat me to death."

Riley's eyes widened at the severity of his bruising, fearing he'd suffered internal bleeding. "What did you do to warrant this?"

"I did nothing. That's the problem."

Riley reached forward and gently untied the rope holding him before climbing to her feet. She held out her hand to help him up. "I'll listen, and I'll treat your wounds. I'm a doctor, too. Can you stand?"

He didn't move. "The rest will turn on you if you help me."

"Let them try."

"What's going on?" Coop asked and pointed his thumb at the group behind them. "They got agitated when they saw you untie him."

"Why? He's too weak to hurt anyone. Help me get him to his feet. Careful, he's injured."

Riley and Coop lifted Dr. Landry to his feet. He was so weak they practically had to carry him to the infirmary. Riley ignored the angry stares from the others as they passed. No matter what the doctor had done, no one deserved to be tied to a tree in the dead of winter.

Riley and Coop worked quickly to clean and examine Dr. Landry. When she was satisfied that they'd done what they could to get him warm and stable, she pulled a chair next to his cot and sat facing him with her arms folded.

"Coop, would you mind checking on Julia?" He nodded and walked to the other end of the makeshift recovery ward. "Now, tell me why they think you deserve to freeze to death tied to a tree, Dr. Landry."

"Please, call me Adrian." She smiled and motioned for him to continue. "The first thing you need to know is that I'm not a medical doctor. I'm an astrophysicist."

"Disappointing. Another set of skilled hands would have been invaluable. If you're an astrophysicist, tell me why the CME struck twenty hours early and was far more destructive than predicted."

"You won't like the answer. That's how I ended up like this." He pointed to his bandaged torso.

"It can't be worse than what I've been through in the past few weeks. Just tell me."

"I was working at the Goddard Space Center outside of DC. before the solar storm began." Adrian rubbed his face and sighed. "I'm a solar specialist. I was the first person to spot the second CME. Tragically, I was so focused on that eruption that I failed to see the first CME until it was too late."

"I'm confused. First CME, second CME. There were two?"

"The second CME was the one the world was warned to expect. The first CME was twice the size, but due to mass, position, and strength, it reached Earth in sixteen hours instead of thirty-six."

Riley jumped to her feet. "Sixteen hours? Why weren't we warned like the other one?"

He waved for her to sit. She hesitated before sinking back onto the chair. "I alerted the director the instant I spotted the first CME. He alerted Vice President Kearns since the president was out of the country. Her response was to order me to the White House."

"Couldn't you have told her what she needed to know over the phone?"

"She wanted to interrogate me in person and needed a scapegoat. She was far more concerned with political fallout than saving lives."

"That's harsh. She's always seemed like a decent person to me."

Adrian stared at her with cold eyes. "You weren't there."

"Fair enough. Continue."

"The last place I wanted to be was the White House. I wanted to go to my family and warn them, but who can refuse the vice president? I FaceTimed my wife and kids and told them how to prepare. I drove to the White House, fearing I'd never see them again."

Riley could relate. She'd have given anything to know that her last video chat with Emily and Jared was the final one.

"Why are you here and not with them?"

"I was trying to get to them when I was captured and brought here. I made the mistake of telling these lovelies my story, Dr. Poole."

"Please, call me Riley. Did you make it to the vice president?"

"I was taken directly to her office. She spent the first fifteen minutes dressing me down for not discovering the first CME sooner, as if I have control of the sun. It was then I realized I was to be her fall-guy."

"She wasted time chastising you instead of alerting the public? Just to have a fall-guy? I refuse to believe that."

"Refuse all you want. It's the truth. She'd been in communication with the president while she waited for me. He was aboard Air Force One, trying to reach U.S. soil before the CME hit. He wanted to warn the world of what was coming, but

VP Kearns advised against it. She said it would just cause mass panic. By that time, only seven hours remained until the CME strike. It was too late."

"Didn't you tell her she was wrong? Those hours could have saved countless lives. Did you ask to speak to the president?"

"She refused the first time I asked, making it clear that it was her call. I was about to ask again, but an aid came in to tell her they'd lost communication with the president. I think she was glad. By that point, I agreed that alerting the public would only cause panic. My final crime was in telling Kearns that once the CME hit, covering her ass would be the least of her worries because there wouldn't be a country left to govern."

It took all of Riley's restraint not to jump up and strangle the man. She leaned closer to him, taking quick, shallow breaths. "You knew? You knew and did nothing?"

He nodded and looked down at his hands. "To my dying shame. Now, you understand my injuries. I kept my mouth shut like a coward. I could have contacted colleagues or news networks on my own or spread the word on social media, but I stayed silent."

Riley slumped in her chair, stunned at his confession, and furious that their leaders were more concerned with protecting their reputations than saving lives.

"Acting could have saved millions, maybe even your own family."

"I told you I alerted my family. I told my wife to warn our friends and extended family," he whispered.

She wrapped her arms tightly around herself to stop the trembling. "What happened next?"

He gave an eerie chuckle. "Kearns alerted leaders of allied countries, making sure they knew how futile it would be to alert their people. Some did anyway but communications cut out before word spread. When she'd waited as long as she could, she rounded up her family and all the top DC. brass to scurry off to some secret bunker in Pennsylvania. She shipped me off with an Air National Guard convoy. No one gave a damn about me, so I escaped in the chaos following the CME."

"And your family?"

"They were gone by the time I reached home. My wife has family in St. Louis, so I assumed that's where she headed. I was trying to find a way to follow them when our cordial hosts *invited* me to this lovely establishment." He watched Riley's reaction for a moment before saying, "You think I got what I deserve."

"No. I was thinking what a difference those hours would have made for Julia and me. I'm sure the same is true for thousands. I need to go back to my daughter. Get some rest. I'll have food brought to you."

Adrian laid back and covered his eyes with his arm. "Don't bother. I seem to have lost my appetite."

Riley was still reeling from Adrian's story when she went to see Julia. She did her best to suppress her shock and focus on her top priority, her daughter's survival. She wove her way through the infirmary to the area she and Coop had blocked off with makeshift walls for Julia's privacy. She'd hoped to find Coop there and fill him in on what Adrian told her, but Julia was alone.

Her color was worse and her pulse thready. They were running out of time. Time she shouldn't have wasted on Adrian, who didn't seem to care if he lived or died. *Maybe he* did *deserve to die.*

A commotion in the infirmary interrupted her thoughts. She left Julia to find Coop helping Jepson onto a gurney. They both had blood-stained shirts and hands. Jepson was cradling his right arm against his chest. Riley forgot Adrian and switched into doctor mode. Jepson had shot her daughter and could end up being her murderer. Still, Riley had an obligation to treat every patient. So, as she had done during Julia's surgery, she pushed her emotions aside and got to work.

She gloved up, stepped next to Coop and said, "Catch me up."

Coop finished injecting Jepson with morphine before taking Riley by the hand to drag her the far side of the room. He let go of her and bent over with his hands on his knees.

"It was the most sickening scene I've ever witnessed," he said, between breaths. "Branson cut Jepson's right index finger off for shooting Julia and killing those people at the church. He said it was to cure Jepson's itchy trigger finger. He did it right in front of me.

"What?" Riley gasped. "Do you have the finger? Can I reattach it?"

He shook his head. "Branson tossed it right in a garbage can next to his desk like a candy wrapper, then ordered me to bring him here and treat him. Said he didn't want him to die, just make an example of him."

She forgot about her sterile gloves and ran her hand through her hair. "Coop, we have to escape from this nightmare of a place. But how? Julia's too sick to move."

"We're going to lie low and bide our time. We'll reassess Julia's condition once she's had a transfusion. Then, we'll plan our exit strategy. For now, Branson wants to see you. Watch yourself, Riley. Remember Julia and don't ruffle his feathers. The guy's psychotic."

"Don't worry. If Branson's capable of this, I promise to be on my best behavior. Stay with Julia once you finish with Jepson. I want her under guard around the clock."

She gave him a quick hug before rushing out of the infirmary, not wanting to keep Branson waiting.

Branson's tent was decorated like a regular office, right down to the beautiful cherry wood desk. It was so out of place in the shabby tent. Branson was clearly making a statement that he was in charge. *He and the VP would have made great friends*, Riley thought.

One of Branson's thugs leaned against the wooden tent frame and watched her before shoving her in front of the desk. Branson ignored her and continued to write on a yellow notepad.

Riley recognized it as an intimidation tactic, but she didn't play into it. She folded her hands and waited calmly for him to address her. He wrote for another thirty seconds before slowly laying his pencil on the desk. He interlocked his fingers and stared at her over the top of his glasses.

Without moving his gaze from her, he cocked his head at the thug in the corner. "Warner, have some manners and get Dr. Poole a chair."

Warner grabbed an upholstered leather chair from the far side of the tent and set it in front of the desk before going back to his corner. Branson motioned for Riley to sit, so she slowly lowered herself into the chair.

"I hear Julia needs a transfusion," Branson said, as if he hadn't just severed a man's finger. "There's no need to test anyone's blood. I'm O negative and I'm willing to donate what you need. Despite what I'm sure Dr. Cooper told you just happened here, I'm not an evil man. It's just difficult to keep a community this size in line without the proper motivations. You may not approve of my methods, but they're effective."

Riley stared at him in stunned silence. In the same breath, he was justifying his psychotic actions and offering to save her daughter. She'd do anything for Julia but wasn't sure she wanted Branson's blood coursing through her veins. He studied her, waiting for an answer, but Riley couldn't make her mouth form the words.

"Do you want my help or not? If not, I have other matters to attend to."

"Yes, thank you," she muttered. "Are you available to come to the infirmary with me now? Julia's running out of time."

He nodded and came out from behind the desk, gesturing for her to lead the way. Stepping from the warm tent into the freezing air cleared her head. Despite her disgust for the man, she had one duty, save Julia. Blood was blood.

The infirmary was quiet when they entered. Jepson was sleeping on his back with his bandaged hand propped on his chest. Riley led Branson through the recovery area and asked Claire to prep him for the transfusion.

When he was ready, Riley hesitated before sticking the needle into his arm. "You're sure you're O negative? If you're wrong, it'll kill her."

"I'm certain. I have no desire to harm your daughter."

She wasn't convinced of that but slid the needle into his vein and watched the life-saving blood flow into the collection bag. When she had as much as was safe to take from him, she bandaged his arm and told him to eat and get plenty of fluids.

"My daughter may need more blood, but you can't donate again. We need blood typing kits."

"We're running low on other med supplies as well. Once Julia is stronger, you'll accompany Brooks on a supply run." She nodded and handed the blood to Claire. "Come to my tent when you're done here," he said. "We still need to discuss your responsibilities."

"Yes, sir," she said as she watched him go, grateful that he'd helped save Julia's life but terrified of what being in his debt would mean. They needed to find a way to escape ASAP.

The transfusion worked wonders for Julia, and she woke, asking for pancakes. After joyfully fulfilling her daughter's breakfast wish, Riley went to check on Adrian. He was showing signs of improvement as well, and despite her personal feelings about the man, she was relieved to have been wrong about the internal bleeding.

She watched him sip his chicken broth with a thousand questions churning in her brain. He was the one person on earth who could answer them.

He caught her eye and said, "Ask your questions. I'll tell you whatever you want to know."

She wanted to ask how he could live with himself after betraying the human race but pushed those thoughts aside to focus on more pressing matters.

"I appreciate that," she said. "We've been running blind since this madness started. The government claimed the CME would cause no more than a weeklong inconvenience."

"If we'd only been hit by the second CME, that would have been the case. The first CME was a very different beast."

"Since we weren't warned about the first CME, thanks in no small part to you, can you tell me what to expect going forward? How long before power can be restored? Was the rest of the earth hit as hard?"

"The first and most crucial point you need to understand, Riley, is this was a global event. Only hardened solar, wind and hydroelectric systems will still operate. They make up a minuscule fraction of the energy produced in the world. I'd estimate that ninety percent of energy-producing capabilities were destroyed worldwide. They won't be restored for five to ten years, if ever."

"What do you mean ever? We mortals are smart and innovative. Why can't those systems simply be repaired?"

"Because backup and spare parts don't exist, and even if they did, there are very few people left alive who know how to repair them." Adrian put down his broth and leaned on his elbow to face her. "You have to understand, the human race has been decimated. I estimate that only three billion people survived, and that's a generous estimate."

"What?" Riley gasped, feeling like he'd stabbed her in the gut. The entire planet was dark and lost. Those left alive were suffering just as they were. She'd held out hope that her children and parents were safe and waiting to hear from her, but Adrian's words killed that hope. Were they even alive? And if they were, how would she and Julia ever get back to them? They could be looking at years of separation.

Her chest tightened as she struggled to breathe. Their world was gone. Humankind had been transported back to the eighteen hundreds, only worse because they weren't prepared to live in such a world. There would be no manufacturing of medications or medical supplies. They'd have to grow or raise their own food and make their own clothes. She didn't know how to garden or sew and couldn't Google or YouTube to learn how.

The tent spun, and she grabbed the side of the cot to steady herself.

"Riley, are you all right?"

"How can you ask that?" she cried. "Our world has ended. How can you sit there so calmly?"

"Now you understand why I was tied to that tree, and why I don't care what happens to me. What is there left to live for?"

She took a deep breath and tried to stand. The ground tilted for a second before she got her bearings. "I have to find Coop. This changes everything."

CHAPTER FOURTEEN

JULIA PEEKED AT DASHAY, trying to hide that she was awake. She liked Dashay and was glad she offered to sit with her whenever her mom or Coop couldn't, but she wanted some time alone to think. Life since the CME had been one long string of nightmares. She needed to process all of it.

Hearing her mom and Coop describe how close she came to dying had freaked her out. Getting shot had been her own fault. If she hadn't panicked and run, none of it would have happened. After the way her mom reacted when Hannah died, Julia hated to think what she might have done if the gunshot had killed her.

Coop had scolded her for blaming herself, saying it was no one's fault but the bad guys'. She wanted to believe him, but it was hard. Getting shot wasn't like what happened when the cottage burned down. That had just been a stupid accident. She'd chosen to run away from Jepson. Her mom told her to forget about blame and put her energy into getting better.

She was glad she'd get to recover in the camp, even if they were hostages. The compound was the best place they'd had since leaving the hotel. She wanted to get to the ranch but hoped they could stay until spring when her leg was strong enough to walk without crutches and it was warmer outside. She was sick of freezing all the time.

Most of all, she wanted time to grieve for Hannah and for her former life. A week had passed since Hannah drowned, but it felt more like a day. Losing her new sister had left a giant hole in Julia's heart and made her miss Emily and Jared even more. She was getting afraid she'd never see them again, and that tore at her heart even more.

Feeling tears sting her eyes, she shook off her dark thoughts and listed all the things she had to be grateful for. Her mom and Coop were alive and loved her. They were together in a warm, safe place. She'd survived getting shot and had food and clean water. What else did she need?

She was about to ask Dashay for help with the bedpan when she heard the canvas wall rustle. She rolled over to find Angie poking her head through the opening.

"Angie, you're alive! How did you get here?" she cried as the other woman came in to hug her. Dashay stepped in Angie's way, but Julia waved her off. "It's safe. Angie's my friend."

Angie sat on the edge of the bed and took Julia's hand. "I was taken hostage at the church. Coop and your mom told me about your ordeal. I got off easy. I'm so sorry about Hannah. She was such a sweet girl."

Julia tried to will her tears away, but they refused to obey. "It was so horrible, Angie. The worst day of my whole life. It still doesn't seem real that she's gone."

Angie brushed a tear from Julia's chin. "I feel that way about my husband sometimes and wish it was all just a nightmare I could wake up from. Glad we didn't lose you. How are you feeling today?"

Julia beamed at her. "Better now that I know you're alive. My leg hurts pretty bad, but I have the best doctors in the world."

"That's true," Dashay said. "Your mom's an amazing person, Julia. She never left your side those first two days."

Julia nodded. "Coop told me. I never knew how awesome my mom was before the CME. Coop's pretty great, too. I'm lucky." She turned to Angie and said, "What's this place like?"

"If we have to be hostages, the compound's as good a place as any, I suppose. It's safer than on the road, as you know."

"I was scared all the time. I hope Mom says we can stay until my leg's better."

"Leaving may not be up to her," Dashay said. "We're all trapped here, remember?"

"I keep forgetting. The pain meds make me dopey."

Angie kissed Julia's cheek and stood to go. "I'm on kitchen detail, like I know how to cook. I'll come back after my shift. Get some rest."

"I will. It'll be easier knowing you're here. Thanks for visiting me."

Angie smiled and gave a quick wave as she left.

"Guess I need to hear her story," Dashay said, as she reached for the bedpan.

"We have lots of unbelievable stories, but hers is pretty incredible. She survived a plane crash."

Riley rushed across the compound from Adrian's tent to the infirmary. Coop was there doing morning rounds. She waited for him to finish reviewing Claire's notes on a patient with dysentery and severe dehydration before grabbing his arm and pulling him to a secluded corner.

She paced the small space, rubbing her temples. "I just left Adrian. I have news. Literal earth-shattering news."

"I really couldn't care less if Adrian withheld the warning about the first CME. We can't alter the past."

"Don't you think I know that?" she snapped.

"Don't bite my head off." He moved closer and laid his hands on her shoulders. "We need our escape plan," he whispered.

She scanned the room and found Mendez watching them. Lowering her voice, she said, "This isn't about Adrian. It's about our future, but we can't talk here. When you finish rounds, find Angie and meet me in my tent. I'm going to check on Julia. Is Claire with her?"

"No, Dashay is. Are you sure we should include Angie? She made her choice in Warrenton."

"She will when she hears what I have to say."

"Breaking three of us out of here is going to be tough enough, especially with Julia's condition."

"If Angie wants to go along, we'll figure out a way."

Coop picked up the stack of folders he'd set on an empty tray and flipped through them. "Here's Julia's chart. I was going to examine her after I finished my other patients."

She took the file from him. "I'll do it. See you in thirty. Make sure to bring Angie."

Coop and Angie sat facing Riley on a cot in her tent, eager to hear her big announcement.

"How can what you have to tell us be more life-altering than what we've already been through?" Coop asked.

Riley sat in a lawn chair across from them. "Not life-altering. I said earth-shattering. The world has ended."

Angie crossed her arms. "Yeah, we noticed. Cut to the chase. I have to get back to the kitchen."

Riley leaned closer. "No, I mean, the CME struck the entire planet. It's not localized to this area. Adrian estimates there are only two or three billion people alive in the whole world. From what we've seen, I'd say even fewer than that."

Angie sprang off the cot. "The whole Earth? They said that wasn't possible."

Riley huffed. "Turns out it is, and it gets worse. Power is out everywhere and won't be back on for years, if ever. Adrian's exact words. If ever. No help is coming. This disaster is impacting our families and friends, everyone we know."

Angie swayed for a moment before lowering herself onto the cot. "If that's true, my family may be dead. It's even colder in Pennsylvania than here. I have to get out of here."

Coop squeezed her hand. "We all do. We started planning to escape after what Branson did to Jepson. That guy's a lunatic. We'll help break you out, Angie, but you're on your own once we're free. We're still heading south."

Riley slapped her thigh to get their attention. "Yes, we have to escape, but you're ignoring the big picture. The world has been thrust back to the pre-industrial eighteen hundreds. That means no medication production. No vaccines. No antibiotics. Worse, it means no food processing plants, heat, or fuel production. Once the gas runs out, that's it. No more cars. We won't even have clean water without wells, and most of those function on electric pumps."

Coop ran his hand through his hair. "I've only been focused on surviving until the rest of the world stepped in to help. This means we're all starting from scratch."

Riley fell back in the chair and closed her eyes. "It's been generations since humans lived without electricity. How will we survive?"

Coop got up and peeked through the tent flap to make sure no one was listening. "As devastating as this is, it doesn't change our immediate dilemma. How are we going to get out of the compound with Julia?"

"I might have a solution," Riley said. "You're not going to like it, Coop, but it's our best shot. Branson wants me to go on a med supply run with Brooks tomorrow. I'll find a way to take Brooks out while we're gone and come back with the truck after dark. In the meantime, gather supplies and find an unguarded area along the fence. We'll sneak our stuff and Julia out before anyone knows we're gone."

Coop glared at her. "Are you insane? Take Brooks out? He's twice your size. Are you planning to kill him?"

"Of course not. I'll knock him out or drug him."

"We can't let you do it, Riley. It's too dangerous," Angie said.

"I'll convince Branson to let me go, instead," Coop said.

"That might alert Branson or make him suspicious. And he's not the type to change his mind. It has to be me."

Coop let out a weary sigh. "Branson's not the only one who never changes their mind."

Riley rested her hand on his shoulder. "Brooks seems to like me, and he helped us with Julia. Coop, figure out how to get Julia out of the infirmary without raising any alarm bells."

Coop put his hand over hers. "How will you know where to meet us? I can't exactly text you."

Angie stood and smoothed her pant legs. "I can help with that. I'm in a tent with three other women. One of them snores, and I'm having trouble sleeping since…events. I've been taking walks at night, so the guards are used to seeing me wandering around the camp. There's a long stretch of fence at the far east side that no one patrols. It's heavily wooded, and the access road doesn't reach that far. It'll be a hike to get Julia and the supplies to the truck, but no one will see us."

Coop got up and hugged her. "I'd forgotten about your husband. Let's meet behind the infirmary tonight at around three to scope it out."

Angie gave a quick nod. "Thanks, Coop. It's been a hell of a time for all of us. I have to get back before they miss me. Like you said, we don't want to alert Branson."

She hugged Riley and hurried out of the tent. Coop sat on Riley's cot and pulled her onto his lap. She wrapped her arms around him and rested her chin on the top of his head. Coop sighed and Riley felt his shoulders sink.

"I get that we don't have many options, but this plan scares me. If you get hurt or worse, I'll never forgive myself for letting you go."

"Nothing will happen. I have to do this for Julia. I'm more worried about what will happen while we're trying to get her to the truck. If one of Branson's goons to see us, it's all over. I wouldn't put it past him to execute us."

"He won't. We're valuable commodities, but that doesn't mean he won't punish us and put a tail on us round the clock. We can't get caught. We won't."

"If all goes according to plan, in less than twenty-four hours, we'll be back on our way to the ranch."

Coop laid her on the cot and gave her a lingering kiss. "I love you, Riley Poole, more than I've ever loved anyone. I can't lose you now. If you don't find the perfect opportunity to take out Brooks, just come back with him. We'll find another way to escape."

She brushed her lips on his cheek. "I will. I love you, Coop. I never thought I'd love anyone after Zach. You've changed my life in ways you can't imagine. Even if the world has gone to hell, we'll face it together and build a new one."

He leaned down to kiss her again but stopped when he saw a shadow outside the tent door. He got up and helped Riley to her feet.

"Who is that? Get in here."

Warner came in and flashed Coop a lewd grin. "Getting a little afternoon snack?"

Coop gave a fake chuckle. "Jealous? What do you want?"

"Director Branson wants a word with the little doctor."

Riley stepped up to him with her hands on her hips and stared him down. "That's Dr. Poole to you. What does he want?"

Warner looked amused at her attempt to stand up to him. "Didn't bother to ask, but don't keep him waiting, *Dr. Poole*."

He bowed and backed out of the tent. Riley was tempted to throw a boot at his head.

"Miscreant. What do you think he was doing before World's End?"

Coop shook his head. "Drowning kittens."

Riley was relieved when Branson only wanted to see her about planning the supply run with Brooks. She said she'd have a list ready and meet him at the truck after breakfast. Once they'd finished, she did her afternoon rounds and spent the rest of the day with Julia. They chatted about Angie's visit, how much Julia liked Dashay, and how nice it felt to be warm. Riley listened and gave short responses whenever Julia stopped to take a breath.

Not wanting to disappoint Julia about having to leave the compound or burden her with their secret, she held back about the escape plan. She hated being forced to take her weak, injured daughter on the road but was convinced it was their best hope for survival.

She reminded herself that they'd be in Wytheville in two days. Uncle Mitch had probably rigged solar or wind power the day after the CME. Barring that, he had wood-burning stoves and cords of firewood stacked for winter. There would be well water, livestock and shelves lined with canned goods. All she and Coop had to do was get Julia there.

During Riley's meeting with Branson, she'd politely asked for an increased food ration for Julia. Branson had readily consented. At dinnertime, Claire brought a tray loaded with enough food for three people. Julia's appetite had returned, but she was weak and couldn't eat her usual amount. Riley was tempted to down the rest of the food but instead ate just enough to satisfy her hunger pangs. When Julia drifted off, Riley stuffed the leftovers into clean sample bags and hid them in her backpack.

After leaving instructions with Claire and Mendez, she went to her tent to sleep until she had to meet Angie to inspect the fence. Coop came in around ten and asked to climb into her sleeping bag.

"As much as I'd love to have you snuggle in with me, I won't sleep if you do, and I need to be sharp tomorrow. One more day and we'll be able to share a bed every night. You can take Julia's cot if you promise to be quiet."

He kissed her before getting into the other sleeping bag. "This is getting old. How much longer do I have to wait to be with you? And what about the age-old tradition of a night of lovemaking before going into battle?"

Riley rolled over to face him. "Those are always twenty-year-old men, not exhausted thirty-five-year-old mothers. Just keeping my priorities straight here, and I *am* exhausted."

"Just yanking your chain, Riley. I'm no twenty-year-old boy either, and I've hit the end of my reserves, too."

"I set my watch for a quarter to three. That gives us five hours. I'll wake you if you don't hear the alarm. Goodnight. Love you, Coop."

He yawned and whispered, "Love you."

They didn't run into any trouble during their inspection of the fence. Angie had sneaked short-handled bolt cutters out of the maintenance hut and brought them along for Coop to cut the fence.

While he worked, he said, "Memorize landmarks. It won't be as easy to remember the route under pressure in the dark, and we'll only have a short window to get Julia out safely. We'll wheel her on the gurney as far as we can, Angie, but you'll have to help me carry her after that."

Angie was pulling the fence apart as Coop cut but nicked her finger on a jagged edge. "I'll do whatever you need. I'm tougher than I look," she said, as she stopped to shake off the pain.

Riley stepped into her place and tugged on the unattached part of the fence. "You don't have to tell us. We've seen what you're capable of. This will be a cakewalk compared to surviving for a week in that crashed plane."

Coop finished cutting an opening big enough to fit two of them carrying Julia. He moved back to admire his handy work before pushing the fence back into place and handing the cutters to Riley.

"Hide those in your pack. They'll come in handy later. Thanks for taking the risk to sneak them to us, Angie, and for joining us in escaping. A hundred things could go wrong on this little adventure. It might be smarter to stay."

Angie shook her head. "I know the risks, but I've got to get back to my family. I don't care what it takes."

"I'll wait for you in Julia's room in the infirmary until midnight. If you aren't there by then, I'm going alone. Riley, do your best to be here by one."

"I'll aim for that, but I can't guarantee what time I'll be back. You'll have to be patient. If I'm not here by four-thirty, get Julia back to the infirmary."

They all agreed and went through the plan once more to make sure they hadn't forgotten any details. Coop and Riley left inconspicuous signs such as broken branches and marks on trees along the path on their way back to the compound. Only someone looking for them would notice.

Coop was asleep the instant he hit the cot, but Riley couldn't turn off the thoughts churning in her brain. She tried relaxation and deep breathing exercises, but nothing helped. She couldn't stop worrying that the risk was too big this time. They weren't in a movie or a game. Most of Branson's men acted like hardened prison guards, and for all her bluster with Warner, she was afraid of him. Despite all of this, staying in the camp was out of the question.

A few hours of sleep and the chilly sunshine brightened Riley's outlook in the morning. She was more confident about their plan when her alarm went off for the second time that day. She pulled on her boots and hurried to the infirmary to say goodbye to Julia. Coop was already there doing rounds.

"Any second thoughts?" he asked her while they pretended to consult on a patient. "Not too late to back out."

"I have to go on the supply run either way, so I might as well see it through. I promise not to take unnecessary risks. I want to pull off this mission as much as you do."

He pulled her close and gave her a sloppy kiss without caring who saw. "I'll be waiting at one. Be there."

He stalked off before she could respond, so she went to explain to Julia about the supply run.

"Don't go, Mom," Julia pleaded. "It's too dangerous. Can't someone else go?"

Riley brushed Julia's hair aside and kissed her forehead. "The director of the camp is insisting I go. I don't want to leave you, and I tried to get out of it, but Coop and Angie are here, and the infirmary staff will take care of you. I'll be fine. You don't need to worry. I won't be back until late, so don't wait up for me. I love you, sweetheart."

Julia sniffled, but Riley could see she was trying to be brave. "Love you, Mom. See you tonight."

She hurried out before breaking down and went for a quick breakfast before going to meet Brooks.

Riley pushed her anxiety aside and focused on procuring provisions for the infirmary. Brooks was stamping his feet to keep warm when she got to the armored military Humvee they were using for the run.

He opened the driver's side door and grumbled, "About time."

Riley tossed her pack in the back seat before hoisting herself up into the passenger side. "I couldn't leave without saying goodbye to my daughter. You never know when you might not return from one of these runs."

He started the engine and grinned. "I have every intention of both of us returning in one piece. I do this twice a week. Piece of cake."

"That's comforting. Our luck hasn't been as favorable, as you know."

As the truck rumbled along the dirt road leading away from the compound, Riley tried to keep up the small talk in the hope that Brooks would lower his guard. He'd been less harsh with her than other members of Branson's staff and had come close to what Riley would call kindness. She sensed decency hiding under the bravado, which was more than she could say for the others.

She waited ten minutes before asking about his life before the CME. He frowned at her, then turned his attention back to the road. "What does it matter?"

His reaction caught Riley off guard. "I'm not trying to pry. If we're going to be alone in this truck for hours, I thought time would pass quicker if we chatted."

"I'm not used to *chatting*. Branson's not one for conversation, and I have nothing to say to those other lugs."

Riley crossed her arms and turned toward the window. "Makes sense. Never mind."

"Not what I mean. I'm saying I'm not used to it. I don't mind talking while we ride. I managed the supply chain for a farm equipment company. Worked with a good group of people. Wonder where they all are?"

Riley sighed in relief after envisioning riding in silence for hours. She thought about his comment about the people he'd worked with. She hadn't had time to think about her colleagues back home. They were good people, most of whom she'd call close friends. They had families and full lives. She wondered how they were faring in the aftermath of the disaster.

"That's one of the hardest parts, no communication. Instant contact has become so ingrained in us. I miss just taking out my phone and immediately connecting with someone." She hesitated a moment before saying, "I have two younger children with my parents in Colorado Springs. It's torture not knowing how they are or what's happening to them. I'd give anything to hear their voices one more time. Do you have children?"

Brooks gave her a quick glance. "I do, but I'm divorced, and my wife has majority custody. I see my three boys as often as I can. They live two hours away, so it's not easy. The oldest was supposed to graduate high school in June, then he was planning to go into the Air Force. The other two are fifteen and thirteen. Good kids."

"My husband was in the Air Force. Pilot. His helicopter was shot down three years ago on the Pakistan border."

"Sorry to hear that. Guess my boy won't have to worry about such things now."

Riley watched him, sensing his despair at being separated from his sons. She could relate and felt a bond sprouting between them but couldn't allow that to happen. Feeling compassion for him could make her hesitate when it came time to take him down, so she changed topics.

"How'd you get hooked up with Branson?"

"He lived in the same county as me and came asking for volunteers to help set up a safe community at an abandoned Boy Scout facility. I was alone, hungry and freezing, so I thought, what the hell. I've worked hard and kept my head down, so he's given me more responsibility."

"Do you regret joining up with him?"

Brooks rubbed his beard and thought for a moment. "If you'd asked me that before the incident at the church and what he did to Jepson, I'd have said no regrets. I didn't always agree with his tactics, but he hadn't done anything to cross the line. I don't like that he feeds us better than the other people in the camp. There's no reason for it. We have plenty of food for everyone. It's a power play. I sneak food to families with children when I can get away with it."

Riley was surprised by his answer, but said, "And since the church?"

Brooks shot her a quick glance. "I've been questioning my loyalty to him, not that I have much choice but to stay if I want to stay alive. Branson has changed since the attack at the church. We were just supposed to threaten the group and grab some people as laborers, but Jepson started shooting, and the others joined in. I stopped it as fast as I could, but the damage was done. We got the hell out in a hurry. Branson was furious and warned Jepson, but that was the end of the punishment until he shot your daughter. You know the rest."

"Agonizingly well."

"I'm no fan of Jepson. He shot an unarmed mother carrying her infant in the back. He deserved more than losing a finger, but the way Branson handled it was disturbing. Seemed like he enjoyed it."

"Dr. Cooper said the same thing. I have to admit I'm torn over it. Jepson almost killed Julia, but Branson's brand of wild-west justice is alarming."

"When I signed up with Branson, he talked about elections and fair government, but he's turned into nothing more than a mafia boss or petty dictator."

Riley was concerned to hear Brooks speak so candidly about

Branson and wondered what he'd ask in exchange for her secrecy, but since she'd already opened the flood gates, she decided to go with the flow.

"Do you plan to do anything about Branson? Who knows how far he'll go if no one stands up to him?"

"What can I do? The guards are armed to the teeth, and I don't know who to trust. I'm hoping Branson will come to his senses. I'm putting together a proposal for how we can form a democratic government if he's still willing."

She had no doubt that his proposal would fall on deaf ears. It's impossible to reason with a sociopath, and it was far too little, far too late.

She steered the conversation to less controversial subjects for the rest of the drive and was relieved when the medical supply warehouse on the outskirts of Charlottesville came into view. Brooks pulled up to a door with a broken chain dangling from the handle.

She got out and followed him. "How did you find this place?"

"Dashay told us about it. She's been the driving force behind getting the infirmary set up and stocked. Mendez, too, but we couldn't have done it without her. Finding you and Dr. Cooper was the last piece of the puzzle."

Finding us? You mean stalking us and dragging us against our will into forced servitude?

Brooks pulled the chain out of the handle and took a set of keys from his belt loop to unlock the door. She followed him through a set of metal double doors to the central part of the warehouse. Her jaw dropped at the sight of rows upon rows of twenty-foot high shelves loaded with every kind of medical implement imaginable.

Brooks picked up an empty bin and held it out to her. "Get your list and stay on task. Let's finish this so we can be back before it gets too late. I don't like traveling these roads in the dark."

Riley took out her two lists. One was for the infirmary, and the other was to stock the truck for their escape. She felt a pang of guilt, knowing the infirmary would have to go without until Branson sent someone for Brooks and to get more supplies. She planned to be long gone by then.

She studied the warehouse map to get her bearings before telling Brooks which supplies she wanted him to collect. She kept him in sight while she ran through scenarios of the best way to incapacitate him. He had a handgun holstered at his hip, but she wanted to reserve that as a last resort.

After working for an hour, she told Brooks she needed the bathroom and picked up her pack on the way to the staff restroom. She locked the stall and took out the syringe and vial of Midazolam she'd lifted from the infirmary that morning. She filled the syringe with a big enough dose to give Brooks a blissful nap that he wouldn't remember and recapped the needle before stashing the syringe in her front pocket. She'd worried about getting close enough to him to administer the drug, but he'd relaxed with her and hopefully wouldn't notice when she moved in for the attack.

Brooks had their lunch laid out on an empty sorting table when she returned. He talked comfortably while they ate, and she considered reaching under the table and stabbing the needle into his thigh but was afraid he'd choke on his food. She'd have to act soon to make it back to camp in time for the rendezvous, so she psyched herself up to inject him when lunch was over.

When Brooks shoved the last bite of sandwich in his mouth and stood to repack the lunch containers, Riley picked up a plastic container with leftover pear slices and popped the lid on it. "I'll do this while you work on the second page of the list. We still have a lot to get."

As he turned to head back to work, she whipped out the syringe and sank the needle into his neck just above the clavicle.

"What the hell?" he said and took a swing, but the medication was kicking in, and he missed her by two feet.

Riley reached out to catch him as he started to go down, but he weighed more than she'd estimated and slipped through her hands. The crown of his skull struck the sharp edge of the table on the way down. Blood immediately pooled into a gruesome halo around his head.

Riley stared at him and debated what to do. The logical thing would be to turn and run to the truck, leaving Brooks to bleed to death, but she couldn't bring herself to do it. Even though he was her captor, he was a decent guy. She wasn't Branson and couldn't let herself descend to that psycho's level, no matter the circumstances.

She rolled Brooks on his side to examine the wound. The cut was substantial and would need extensive suturing. A quick glance at her watch told her she needed to hurry. She pressed gauze to the laceration before gathering the required tools to stitch him. She worked at a record pace to close his wound, then propped him against a support column so he wouldn't aspirate if he vomited. She checked his vitals and covered him with sterile blankets before laying food and water within his reach.

"Thank goodness you won't remember this when you wake up," she said, as she fished in his pocket for the keys.

She left the outer door unlocked and was on her way with a full stock of medical supplies ten minutes later. If she broke her thirty-mile-per-hour rule and sped back, she'd make it to the compound in time to meet Coop. Her plan had worked, and they'd soon be free.

Julia was getting worried. She'd had dinner more than three hours earlier, but her mom still wasn't back. She glanced at Claire snoring in the chair and sighed as she reached for the stack of books Dashay had left for her. She was contemplating knocking the books on the floor to wake Claire when Coop came in and held out his hand for a fist-bump.

She crossed her arms and slumped against the bed. "Where's Mom? Shouldn't she be here by now?"

"She won't be back until after eleven. It's only nine, and you know how these things go."

"I do and that's why I'm worried. Did Mom really say she'd be back after eleven?"

He pressed his fingers to her wrist to take her pulse. "Why would I lie?"

"To keep me from worrying."

"You know that's not my style. I'm too honest. Your mom says painfully honest."

That was true. Coop had a way of blurting out whatever came into his head. Julia had the same problem sometimes, and her mom was always telling her to think before she spoke.

"No need to worry. Your mom's in an armored truck with Brooks. She'll be fine."

"Brooks? Isn't he one of the guys who kidnapped us?"

"Yes, but he also stopped Jepson from killing you. He's not a bad guy."

Claire snorted herself awake and looked around in confusion.

Coop gave her a half-grin. "Nice job keeping an eye on Julia."

Claire jumped up and smoothed her disheveled hair. "Sorry, Dr. Cooper. I've been here since morning and I'm not as young as these other nurses."

"Relax, Claire, I'm not going to fire you. In fact, I need your help." He reached through the makeshift door and picked up a pair of crutches. Holding them up to Julia, he said, "I have something to take your mind off your mom. It's your 'get out of bed free' day."

Julia shifted away from Coop to the far side of the bed. "You want me to stand up? I'm not ready. Does Mom know?"

He rested the crutches against the bed and crossed his arms. "Her idea. You need to get up to prevent blood clots and pneumonia, and we don't want your muscles to atrophy. Goodness knows you're going to need them the way things are nowadays. If you'd been your mom's patient at home, she'd have had you up the morning after surgery. But don't worry, I'm not going to make you walk a marathon. We're just going to get you standing and see how you do." He took a filled syringe from the tray and uncapped it. "You need this first."

Julia frowned. "More drugs? I don't like those. They make my stomach hurt and I get all goofy and sleepy."

Coop winked at Claire. "She's the only patient on the continent refusing pain meds. You'll want this, Julia, trust me."

She pushed up her sleeve and held her arm. "Like I have a choice."

Coop brushed her arm with alcohol and gave her the injection.

She jerked her arm back and unrolled her sleeve. "That burns."

"Give it a second. Then, you won't care about anything."

Coop was right. Once the meds circulated into her system, everything was hilarious, and she couldn't stop giggling. Coop nodded at Claire, and they turned Julia, so her legs were sticking over the edge of the bed. He handed her the crutches and gave her quick instructions on how to use them.

Julia held up her hand to stop him. "Don't bother. I broke my ankle when I was eleven. I'm a pro."

"Perfect. Put your good foot flat on the floor, but don't put any weight on your bad leg. We'll help you push yourself off the bed. Go slowly. Your body needs to adjust to you being upright."

Julia ignored him, grabbed the crutches, and lifted herself to a standing position before they could stop her. She beamed at

Coop until burning pain like a knife twisting hit in her thigh, and the room started to spin. Coop and Claire put their hands on her arms and shoulders to steady her.

Claire shook her head. "He told you to take your time. Why do kids always think they know everything?"

Julia didn't feel like giggling anymore. "I'm going to barf."

Coop lowered her to the bed while Claire grabbed the trash can. Julia leaned over it and deposited her dinner. They got her settled back under the covers after the heaving stopped.

Coop handed her a pill. "Put this under your tongue and let it dissolve."

Julia stared at the small white tablet. "What is it?"

"For nausea. Claire, go back to your tent and stay there 'til morning. You need rest. I'll keep an eye on WP. I grabbed a nap earlier."

Julia watched Claire practically run out of the room before turning to Coop. "Sorry. That medicine made me feel like I could do anything. Guess not."

Coop grinned at her. "Do you know how to play chess?"

He had a dizzying way of flitting between topics. She scrunched her eyebrows and said, "What?"

He took out a travel chess set and laid it on the bed. "Have you played chess?" She shook her head. "Then, it's time you learned. Playing chess hones your brain and teaches logic. You'll care about that when you get old like me."

She shrugged and watched him set up the game. Her brain was still fuzzy, and her gut was doing somersaults, but at least playing a game would distract her. She tried to focus as Coop rattled off the rules, but his face started to fade and finally went dark.

A voice called Julia's name from far away and ordered her to open her eyes. She willed her eyelids to lift, but they wouldn't budge.

"Julia, wake up right now," the voice said, louder this time.

She took a breath and focused all her energy on raising her eyelids. When her vision cleared, she saw a man was leaning over her.

"Daddy," she muttered groggily.

"No, sorry, it's only Coop."

Who's Coop, she thought, still trying to clear her brain. *Stupid pain meds.* "Stop that, Coop, whoever you are. Let me sleep."

Coop chuckled and patted an ice-cold hand on her cheek. "I know you're confused, but you need to fight to wake up now. You can sleep soon."

Julia rubbed her face, then opened her eyes wide, but everything was pitch dark, and she thought she'd gone blind. Seconds later, a cold rush of air hit her in the face. She tried to get off the gurney, but her legs wouldn't move.

"Why am I outside and who are you? I want my mom."

She yelped when she felt a searing cold sensation in the center of her back. Her breath caught, but her head cleared, and memories of her bum leg and Coop flooded over her. None of that explained why he'd had dragged her into the forest.

Coop leaned closer to her, and said, "Awake now?"

She pushed him away and frowned. "Yes. Why are you torturing me in the woods?"

"I drugged you to get you out of the infirmary. We're making a break for it. Your mom will be here soon with a truck to take us to freedom."

"Escaping? But I need to be in the hospital, and I like it in this camp. There's food and it's so warm."

Coop unstrapped the bands binding her legs and chest, then raised the head of the gurney until she was in a sitting position. "There are dangerous people here who want to hurt us. We have to go. We'll explain everything in the morning." He pointed to a fence ten feet away. "See that hole? I need to carry you through that. Put your arms around my shoulders and hold on tight."

She did as he said, grunting at the pain when he slid his hands under her to lift her off the gurney.

"We have to work together to keep your leg immobile, but it's going to be tough moving over the uneven ground. Breathe through the pain and try not to tense your muscles."

She closed her eyes and focused on her breath. It helped but didn't block out the stabbing heat in her thigh.

To take her mind off it, she said, "Is Mom waiting for us? Have you seen her?"

"She'd better be there or we're going to freeze to death."

"We could die?"

He slowed his pace and propped himself against a tree. "Don't worry. We'll have at least five minutes before that happens." She stared at him in shock until he said, "Only kidding. We'll have ten minutes, at least."

She rolled her eyes and smacked his shoulder. "You said you never lie."

"That was a joke, not a lie. I need to take a break. I'm going to sit you on that big ass log over there." Julia gritted her teeth while he lowered her onto the broad trunk of a fallen tree. Coop straightened but held onto her ankle to keep her leg level. "You're heavier than you look."

"Is that an insult or a compliment?"

"Hush," Coop whispered. "Did you hear that?"

Julia listened and heard the faint sound of footsteps crunching on the snow.

They leaned their heads together, and Coop whispered, "That could be your mom or one of Branson's men. We need to hide."

"How am I going to hide?" she asked in a harsh whisper.

"I have a dark blanket in my pack. I'll throw it over you. Scoot forward while I lower your leg. Rest your heel on that rock."

Julia stifled a whimper, but once her leg was still, the pain faded.

Coop put his lips to her ear. "I'll be in the underbrush right behind you. Breathe quietly and don't move."

She heard him scuffle into the bushes and did her best not to move, but she was freezing and terrified. Her whole body started to shake. She prayed whoever was coming wouldn't notice.

After what felt like hours, she heard a woman's voice whisper, "Coop." It was too muffled with the blanket covering her ears to tell if it was her mom. "Coop, Angie. It's Riley."

Julia threw the blanket off and said, "Mom, over here."

"No, Julia," Coop said in a harsh whisper.

"Julia!" Riley cried. She ran to her and pulled her close. "I was so afraid I wouldn't find you. How are you? How's the leg?"

Coop jumped out of his hiding place and threw his arms around both of them. "Thank God it's you, Riley. Julia, you should've waited until we could see her. It could have been someone impersonating her."

Julia freed herself from her mom's grasp. "Don't you think I know my own mom's voice? I'm glad to see you too, Mom. I was so scared. My leg's killing me, but it's fine. Coop's being careful."

Coop straightened but kept his arms around Riley's waist. "You're early," he said.

"No, you're late. I got lost and was afraid I'd miss you." She turned her head and searched the area. "Where's Angie?"

Coop rubbed his chin. "Didn't show. I waited as long as I could. She must have lost her nerve."

Riley shook her head. "She was dead set on getting out of here."

"Maybe she'll catch up with us at the truck. We better get moving. Branson's men were getting antsy. They came to Julia's room and grilled me over why you weren't back yet. I put on a good show, but I'm not sure they bought it."

"Men came to my room?"

Riley and Coop carefully lifted Julia off the tree stump. She was so cold and happy to see her mom that she didn't notice the pain in her leg. She put her arms around their shoulders and dug her fingers into their coats. She wasn't going to let them drop her, no matter what it took.

Between breaths, Riley said, "I think the truck is only a half-mile from here. I'm not sure because of all the wandering while I was lost."

"Good to hear," Coop said between puffs. "Although this is much easier with two of us."

"Mom, Coop called me fat."

Coop raised his head and eyed her as he walked. "That is so not what I said. I said she's heavier than she looks. That means you *don't* look heavy."

Riley chuckled. "Don't bother, Coop. For future reference, avoid the word *heavy* around teenage girls. Or any woman for that matter."

Coop nodded. "Noted."

"I can hear you," Julia said, but she wasn't upset. She was glad to have just the three of them on their own again. As much as she'd wanted to stay at the compound, she trusted Coop and her mom. If they'd gone to so much danger to get out of camp, they must have a good reason. It sounded like they had another truck, which meant they had a chance to make it to Uncle Mitch's, and she wouldn't have to worry about walking. Best part, trucks came with heaters.

———

Riley felt like she was about to pass out by the time the Humvee came into view. She was thrilled they'd found it, but as they got closer, her relief was replaced by disappointment that Angie wasn't there. It was only three, so they had a small window before they'd be forced to leave. Coop started the truck and blasted the heater while she got Julia settled into the backseat. Then, all they could do was wait.

Coop whistled when he saw the stacks of boxes filling the back of the Humvee.

"Did you empty the entire warehouse?"

"I wish," Riley said. "You should have seen that place. It was enormous and had every medical device and supply imaginable. It was hard to narrow down what to take. I wanted all of it."

She handed Coop a protein bar. He took a bite and said, "So how'd you get away from Brooks? I want the juicy details."

She cocked her head at Julia, who was munching away on caramel corn. "Not now, but Brooks will be fine."

He raised his eyebrows. "Will be? I'm intrigued."

Julia drifted off once she was warm and full. Riley felt herself getting drowsy but needed to stay alert. She'd had little sleep the past two nights, and they were facing a long day, so she downed an energy drink she'd taken from Brooks' pack. Coop knelt on the back seat, rummaging through boxes like a kid at Christmas.

Riley reached over Julia and tapped his shoulder. "I'm going to search for Angie," she whispered.

He climbed out of the truck and motioned for her to follow. "There's no way I'm letting you go look for Angie."

"Let me go? You're not my father."

"Didn't say I was but going after Angie's too risky. There's a reason she didn't show. Branson may have uncovered our plan and might have had her tortured for information. His goons could be on their way. We should be long gone by now."

"Maybe she got lost wandering the woods like I did. We might be her last hope of getting out of that camp alive. We can't just run off and abandon her."

"We will if we have to. I don't like this any more than you, but our first priority is Julia and ourselves. Angie's tough. She can look after herself."

"You were wrong about stopping at the plane crash. If I'd listened to you, she would have died there."

"I was wrong then but not this time. I'm sick at the thought of leaving Angie, but we can't risk our lives to save hers."

Riley knew he was right but wasn't ready to give up yet. "Let's give her a little more time. We owe her that."

Coop hesitated before slowly nodding. "You're too kindhearted. It's what I love most about you, but in this world, wanting to save everyone could be a curse."

She kissed his cheek and made a 360-degree sweep with her flashlight before getting back into the truck.

Coop was patient for another thirty minutes, but after that, he insisted they go. As they bumped along the track running the perimeter of the camp, Riley kept her sights locked on her side mirror, hoping to catch sight of Angie.

"We're going to pass close to the main gate of the compound soon," Coop said, drawing her from her vigil. "This truck is so loud everyone within a two-mile radius will probably hear us coming."

"They might think it's Brooks and me returning, but we're close enough to the main road now that you can speed out of here if anyone sees us."

When they were twenty yards from the gate, he said, "I have to gun it. Is Julia strapped in?" Riley did a quick check and nodded. "Hang on."

Riley glanced in the mirror as Coop pressed the accelerator. In the beam of the security lights, she saw someone who didn't look like one of Branson's guards running toward the gate. She took off her seatbelt to search for binoculars and found a pair in a compartment under her seat.

Coop gave her a quick look before turning toward the road. "I told you to hang on. What are you doing?"

"Coop, stop," she cried. "It's Angie."

Without reducing his speed, he said, "You sure?" When she

glared at him, he took his foot off the gas and put the truck in park. "Let me see." She handed him the binoculars, and he twisted around toward the compound. "She's almost to the gate."

He gave Riley the binoculars and shifted into drive.

She lowered the binoculars and stared at him. "What are you doing? We have to go back for her."

"We're not going near that gate. I'm going to pull behind that stand of trees. She saw us. If she makes it through the gate, we'll get her and be out of here in two minutes."

When Riley looked again, Angie was ten feet from the gate and running like an Olympic sprinter. "She's reached the gate."

Angie was fumbling with the chains and locks when two guards appeared from behind the guardhouse and barreled toward her. They each grabbed an arm and dragged her from the fence. Riley watched in horror as she opened her mouth to scream for help.

"The guards have her, Coop. We have to rescue her."

Coop picked up the binoculars and, after watching for a second, tossed them on the seat and pressed on the gas.

Riley unzipped her backpack and started digging through it. "I have Brooks' gun."

"That gun won't do any good. We're out of range. We're making a run for it, Riley." She dropped the gun and grabbed at his hands to pull them from the wheel. He swatted her away and kept driving. "Stop this. It's too late to help Angie."

She fell back on the seat. "How can you do this? They'll kill her, and it'll be your fault." Coop reached for her hand, but she tucked it under her arm.

Julia sat up and rubbed her eyes. "What's with all the yelling?" When she saw Riley crying, she said, "Mom, what's wrong?"

Riley was too distraught to answer. She pulled her sweater sleeves over her hands and covered her face.

Without moving his eyes from the road, Coop said, "Your

mom's just upset about having to leave Angie, but everything's fine."

As furious as she was with him, Riley was glad he hadn't told Julia the truth. Knowing what happened to Angie wouldn't save her and would only upset Julia. As they sped away from the compound, Riley added Angie's death to her growing list of failures.

CHAPTER FIFTEEN

COOP DROVE FOR FOUR HOURS, only stopping for bathroom breaks and to fill the gas tank. The roads surrounding Charlottesville became more congested with cars and debris as they got closer to the city. It was a relief when they passed south of the interstate. Coop charted their course over narrow, deserted country roads to assure Branson's people couldn't track them.

It felt like they were driving in circles to Riley, but she kept her opinion to herself. She hadn't said a word to Coop since escaping the compound. She'd slumped in her seat and silently wept while Julia slept.

Coop pulled to the side of the road ten miles from Roanoke. "We're on our last gallon of gas. I need to fill the gas cans before we go any further. It's starting to snow, and we don't want to get stuck on a lonely road in the dark with an empty tank."

Riley unhooked her belt. "Do what you need to. I'm going to stretch my legs and get Julia up on her crutches for a few minutes."

Coop silently watched her before going for the gas cans. When he slammed the liftgate, Julia said, "What really happened at the camp, Mom? You've been crying all day and haven't said two words to Coop."

Riley climbed between the seats and sat next to Julia. As she stroked her daughter's hair, she said, "It's mostly about Angie. The rest is between Coop and me. There are some things I can't share with you. Grown-up things."

Julia made a face. "Then, I don't want to know. Whatever it is, work it out soon. We have enough garbage to face. We need each other. I'm sad about leaving Angie, but I don't want that to come between us."

"You're very wise, but nothing could ever split you and me apart. You're my world, sweetheart. Don't worry about Coop. We'll figure it out."

"Good because I'd love to have him as my new dad. I know you love him, and he's so into you. I see the way he looks at you."

"I'd rather not talk about that right now. Let's get you up on those crutches before it starts to snow harder."

"Fine, but please don't give me whatever Coop gave me. It made me toss my dinner."

Riley knew she was talking about Midazolam. Coop had used it so Julia would be out when he snuck her out of the infirmary. Riley wouldn't have minded a dose of the drug herself at the moment.

"Don't worry, sweetheart, I won't give you that. What's your pain level now?"

Julia shifted her leg a few inches. "Not bad. About a three."

"That's excellent. It means you're starting to heal." She took a Percocet from a bottle in her backpack and handed it to Julia with a bottle of water. "Take that just in case."

After Julia swallowed the pill, Riley helped her get up with the crutches. Julia did well, but it was snowing so hard that they couldn't see the other side of the road. Riley let her take a few steps before making her get back in the truck.

"I don't like this," Julia said through chattering teeth. "Where's Coop?"

"I'm sure he'll be here any minute."

The temperature inside the truck was dropping fast. Riley searched the multitude of compartments for hand-warmers or something to generate heat. As angry as she was with Coop, she didn't wish anything terrible on him, and she was getting as worried as Julia. They were looking at a full-blown blizzard and he was in unfamiliar surroundings.

She didn't find hand-warmers but did find insulating blankets and MREs with Sterno cans. If they got desperate, she could light them for heat. She covered them with the blankets and asked Julia about the book she'd been reading in the infirmary to take her mind off Coop. She'd only read three chapters and didn't have much to tell. She started explaining how Coop tried to teach her chess, but the pain meds kicked in, and she dozed off.

The sky darkened as the blizzard raged. The odds of Coop finding his way back to the truck plummeted with the temperature. She didn't even know if he'd taken a flashlight. She did her best to fight off the panic threatening to rear its head. She had to stay in control for Julia.

She was settling in to meditate when someone pounded on the window. She started the truck and cracked the window.

"Who's there?" she shouted to be heard over the wind.

"Riley, it's Coop. Unlock the door. Hurry!"

She unlocked his door and held it open while he climbed into the seat, then slammed it behind him. He was shaking uncontrollably, so she helped him strip off his wet, snow dampened clothing. When he was down to his dry undershirt, Riley cranked the heater and rubbed down his arms and legs.

He held his fingers to the heater vent, and said, "It's a nightmare out there. Thought it was the end of me."

Riley grabbed a solar blanket and wrapped it around his shoulders. "How did you find us in the storm?"

"Freakish sense of direction, remember?" He took her hand and held it to his chest. "You're talking to me now?"

She pulled her hand free and rested it in her lap. "This doesn't change anything, but I still love you and didn't want you freezing to death."

He gave her that infuriating cocky grin of his. "Glad you don't want me dead."

She wanted to kiss and strangle him at the same time, as she'd wanted to do from the moment they met. She looked down at her hands so he couldn't see her smile. "Did you find any gas?"

"I filled three of the five-gallon cans, enough to get us half-way to the ranch, but we're not going anywhere in this blizzard. I'll fill the tank and we'll keep the motor running so we don't freeze. Hopefully, it will clear soon. What I wouldn't give for my Weather Channel app."

"We have heat and food for the night. This four-wheel-drive tank will get us over the roads once the storm clears. Things could be worse."

"Truer words were never spoken."

Coop reached over and covered her hands with his, and she let him, remembering the first time he held her hand in front of the Lincoln Memorial. Were those two the same people now stranded in a blizzard in the middle of nowhere? It didn't seem possible. She hadn't known anything about him that night when he took her hand. After the hardships they'd faced, she knew him about as well as was possible in so short a time. Yet, he'd left Angie to die without a second thought. How could she love a person capable of such a thing?

She ran through their chain of catastrophes and dissected Coop's behavior. He'd tried to prevent her from stopping for Angie at the plane crash. He'd wanted to euthanize Kyle. He'd opposed her on nearly every decision, but he'd often been the one in the right. He'd risked his life for her and Julia multiple times. She didn't doubt that he would die for them.

Her emotions swirled in a tangled rope of confusion. There were no easy answers in their post-apocalyptic lives. She'd always considered herself a competent judge of right and wrong, but her dividing line had already started to blur. Was it right to abandon her morals just because their circumstances had changed? She'd been forced to steal, wound and maim to protect Julia. Gratefully, she hadn't been forced to kill, yet. Could she make that choice in the moment as Coop had done?

He tapped her shoulder and she flinched. "You were far away. Thinking about Angie? I'm sick about leaving her, too, but you know what would have happened if I'd gone back for her. Nothing good."

Riley put her hands over her ears and shook her head. "I don't want to talk about it. Leave me alone."

As her tears resurfaced, he put his arms around her and pulled her to his chest.

While he gently stroked her hair, he whispered, "I'm sorry. We're free of Branson and the compound. We're only hours from safety. Rest now. The world will look brighter in the morning."

Desperate for comfort, Riley silenced her doubts and surrendered to his tenderness. She relaxed against his warm body as he rocked and caressed her. But was she just postponing the inevitable? A day would come when she'd have to decide if he was a man worthy of her trust and devotion, but this was not that day.

***

Sunlight streamed in through the windshield the next morning. Riley blinked her eyes open and stifled a smile. Coop had predicted the world would look brighter in the morning. Why did he have to be so damned right all the time?

She stretched and peeked over the seat at Julia. She was sitting up, snarfing down a cinnamon roll and grinning at Riley with white icing coating her lips.

"Morning, sleepyhead. I wondered if you were ever going to wake up."

"Where'd you get that cinnamon roll? And I want one."

Julia held the box out to her. "Coop found them yesterday. They taste like heaven." Riley took three and ate as fast as she could swallow. "Easy there, Mom. You're not used to the good stuff."

Riley guzzled a bottle of water and wiped her mouth on her sleeve. "I suppose we should have protein bars. Your muscles won't heal eating this garbage."

"Stop being my doctor for one minute and enjoy yourself. You've earned it. We'll have protein bars for lunch."

"And maybe Aunt Beth's homemade shepherd's pie and stewed peaches for dinner." She closed her eyes and breathed in the imaginary aroma of the food.

Julia cocked her thumb at the window. "Coop's out there trying to dig us out. He said it snowed three feet. Maybe you should help so we can get out of here faster." Riley started bundling up and pulling on her boots. "Mom," Julia said.

She stopped and turned to face her. "Yeah? You need something? The bedpan?"

She shook her head. "Coop already helped me with that. I just wanted to say how happy I am that you're back to your old self. You had me worried yesterday."

Riley squeezed her hand. "Sorry, sweetheart. Rough day. Rougher week. Nightmare of a month. I'll try to do better."

"Don't apologize. I totally understand. Thanks for saving me and keeping me alive. I know it's been hard."

"I'd do it all again and more. As I said, you're my life. See you in a bit."

She kissed her cheek and hopped out of the truck. Her legs sunk in up to her knees as she stared in awe at the transformation to their little part of the world. Snow glittered under a brilliant sun hanging in a crystal-blue sky. Being from Colorado, she was used to the aftermath of blizzards, but she hadn't expected such a scene in Virginia. It was a welcome sight after the darkness of the past few days.

Coop was digging out the snow in front of the truck with a small foldable spade. He'd hardly made a dent. At that rate, they'd be stuck on that road for a week.

She stuck her gloved hands in her coat pockets and trudged over to him. "You're going to need a bigger shovel."

He stuck the shovel upright in the snow and leaned on the handle. "Thanks for pointing that out. It was all I could find. You look chipper this morning."

"A few hours of sleep and three cinnamon rolls helped. Let me make use of the lovely bucket, then we should unload the boxes and see if there's a storage compartment in the back."

"I had the same thought. There's a tarp we can spread on the snow to keep the boxes dry."

Riley followed in Coop's footsteps to the back of the Humvee. After handing her the bucket, he spread the tarp and started stacking boxes on it.

She watched him for a moment before saying, "Thanks for helping Julia and letting me sleep."

He stopped and straightened to face her. "Of course, Riley. She's like my own daughter. I'd do anything for her, or you."

"I believe that. I just wanted you to know I appreciate it. She told me yesterday she thinks you'd make an awesome father."

He stared at her for several seconds without speaking. When the silence became awkward, and she fidgeted, he said, "That's humbling. Please, don't thank me for doing what I should. It's what families do."

The conversation was taking an uncomfortable turn, so Riley changed the subject. "What are we going to do about getting her up and walking? She can't do that on crutches in three feet of snow."

"That problem will be solved when we reach the ranch."

"Hadn't thought of that." She smiled and picked up the bucket. "Be right back."

They found two larger shovels in a compartment with the jack. It still took an hour to dig out enough snow to get the Humvee moving, but once they did, they were amazed at what a mighty beast it was. Coop had to go cautiously to keep track of where the road was, but they made progress for the first time in days.

The depth of the snow eliminated the debris issue. The tops of cars stuck out enough that Coop could maneuver around them. Even so, it would be impossible to reach Wytheville before dark. Riley didn't relish spending another night in the truck, but it was better than freezing to death in a tent.

Two hours after getting on the road, they passed a sign indicating the ramp to I-81 was ten miles ahead. Coop stopped to check the map they'd found in the glove compartment.

"I think it's safe for us to risk getting on the interstate. It's the most direct route, and other cars may have made a track we can follow. Branson will have given up on us by now. We're not worth wasting men or valuable resources."

Riley folded the map and tucked it between the seats. "For once, I agree. I'll drive to give you a break once we're on the interstate." She turned and smiled at Julia. "We're on the home stretch. Our twenty-four-hour journey that turned into weeks is almost over."

Julia cringed. "Don't jinx it, Mom."

Riley smiled and went back to watching the road. They were heading due west, and she was concerned to see the bank of dark clouds blowing toward them at a fast clip. Ten minutes later, the clouds were directly overhead. The first flakes fell and melted on the windshield. She *had* jinxed it when they were so close to their goal.

Coop rounded a curve in the narrow highway and slammed on the brakes. The weight of the Humvee propelled it across the snow and came to rest inches from an enormous fallen tree blocking the road.

He gripped the wheel and tried to catch his breath. "Everyone all right? Julia?"

"I'm fine. We're lucky that didn't end up like the space-junk crash."

Riley stared through the thickening snowfall at this latest blow. The base of the trunk was at least three feet in diameter. It would be impossible for her and Coop to budge it. To their left was a rock face that rose twenty feet above them, and the right fell away to the valley below. Going around wasn't an option.

Without taking her eyes off the tree, she said, "Time for one of your brilliant ideas, Coop."

He unhooked his seatbelt. "You didn't happen to see a chainsaw hiding in the back of the truck?"

She shook her head. "Not even an ax."

"Don't lose hope. We'll conquer this beast. Julia, you stay here."

"Funny," she said, as Riley and Coop climbed out into the cold.

They lumbered through the deepening snow to the tree and stared at it for several seconds. The trunk looked even bigger up close.

Riley brushed the two inches of new snow off her jacket. "How much do you think that thing weighs?"

Coop stroked his chin. "Several tons, at least."

Riley gazed up to the top of the rock wall. "It came from up there?"

He pointed at a deep opening along the ridgetop. "See the gouges in the rock and the displaced soil? The roots must have been weak. The wind and weight of the snow toppled it."

"Still waiting for an idea."

"Let's try pushing the tree out of the way first. That Humvee's a brute. It could work."

Riley had her doubts. She'd seen enough fallen trees in Colorado to know that one this size would be impossible to move without chopping it into pieces, but she pasted on a smile and said, "Can't hurt to give it a shot. First, we need to get Julia out of the truck."

Coop nodded and helped Riley spread the tarp on a low bank above the road and cover it with blankets. They carefully carried Julia to the bank and gently lowered her to the tarp. Riley covered her with another blanket, then tucked it around her.

"Whatever you're doing, make it quick before I get buried in snow," Julia said.

"We'll do our best, WP," Coop said and climbed behind the steering wheel.

Riley directed him through the blowing snow until the bumper gently tapped the trunk, then jumped onto the bank beside Julia.

"Cross your fingers," she shouted to Julia above the howl of the wind and roar of the engine.

Coop rammed the bumper against the tree and gunned the motor, but all that got him was spinning tires. He tried three more times with the same result.

He got out and ran to Riley and Julia. "What next?"

"The Humvee has a winch and a tow cable," Riley said through her chattering teeth. "Hook the cable around the tree and wrap the winch cable around a boulder or another big tree."

Coop looked skeptical but jogged off to try her plan. She went after him to help. The storm was intensifying, and they were running out of time. They worked in a rush to rig the cables, then Riley rejoined Julia.

"I know," Julia said, brushing snow off her blanket. "Cross my fingers."

Riley held her breath when Coop powered the winch. When

the line tightened, the tree shifted a few inches then stopped, but Coop kept the winch running. The tree creaked and shivered but refused to move. Seconds later, the cable tore off the tree it was anchored to and whipped up, missing the windshield by inches. The tow cable came loose, and the Humvee careened toward the fifty-foot drop off on the far side of the road.

Riley couldn't watch. She threw her hands in front of her eyes and waited for the crash of Coop plunging to his death, but the only sound was the wailing wind. She peeked through her fingers and saw the truck resting parallel to the cliff with its tires three inches from the edge. Coop climbed out and inspected the damage before waving her over.

"That tree's not budging and moving it isn't worth dying for. Let's get Julia back inside the truck, then I'll search nearby houses for saws or axes. Should be something this close to the interstate."

Riley put her hand on his shoulder. "Wait until the storm passes. We have enough gas to keep the engine running for hours. You were lucky to make it back yesterday. Don't push it."

"No, we can't wait. If the snow gets too deep, we'll be trapped, even with the Humvee. I won't wander far, and I'll be prepared this time."

"It's your neck," Riley said and headed back to Julia.

The snow was so thick that Riley couldn't see the fallen tree by the time Coop left on his crusade. Julia was sick with worry, and Riley thought desperately for a way to distract her.

"Why don't we create our own game?" she said. "Or play twenty questions?"

Julia's eyes brightened and she straightened in her seat. "Coop had a travel chess game. Check his pack."

"He took his pack with him."

"But he dumped everything out and repacked it before he left. Look behind the seat."

Riley didn't think Coop would have bothered with something so frivolous as a game when they escaped the compound, but she peeked over the seat to humor Julia. It only took seconds to find the chess set perched on top of the contents from his pack. And lying under the game, Julia's book. Riley smiled and ran her thumb over the cover. She'd never figure out that man.

"I have a surprise," she said, and held the book up for Julia. She squealed in delight and snatched it from her. "I found the chess set, too."

Julia set the book in her lap and helped Riley set up the chessboard. "Do you know how to play?"

"Yes, but it's been years. I'll read the rules and tips. It'll come back to me as we go."

They soon became engrossed in the game and stopped obsessing about Coop. Riley was impressed at how quickly Julia picked up the strategy. Riley had always been a good chess player herself and must have passed the ability on to Julia. She remembered playing engrossing matches with her father on long snowy nights and hoped to start that tradition with her daughter if they ever stopped running long enough.

Three hours passed before Coop pounded on the window. Riley got him in quickly and went through the same routine as the day before to get him warm.

When his teeth stopped chattering, she said, "Did you find a chain saw?"

"Something better. There's a perfect cabin not half of a mile from here. It's stocked with shelves of canned goods, a fireplace and cords of wood, so I imagine we'll find an ax. It didn't look like anyone's been there for ages, and with the snow and CME, I don't think we need to worry about the owners showing up tomorrow. It'll be a rough go carrying Julia, but the snow is slowing, and we can chop up the tree after the storm."

Riley looked to Julia for her opinion. "We can't live in the truck, Mom. If the gas runs out, we'll freeze."

"Good point, WP," Coop said. "After she's settled and we get a fire going, we'll make trips for the most crucial supplies."

Riley chewed her lip while she weighed their options. She didn't like putting Julia at risk, but they'd already done that by taking her from the infirmary. Staying with the truck was likely more dangerous than being in a cozy cabin. She just hoped they were strong enough to make it without getting lost or freezing first.

Riley zipped her coat and pulled up her hood. "We don't seem to have a choice. I'm ready."

They bundled up as much as possible and laid Julia on the tarp and blanket. Riley covered her with one of the solar blankets to keep her dry and piled the crutches on top. Coop faced forward and reached for the two corners of the tarp near her head. Riley took the ones at her feet.

"Ready," she said. "On three."

With both of them carrying her, Julia wasn't as heavy as Riley expected. Plodding through the deep snow was a challenge, but the wind had quieted, and her legs were strong. The last bit of the trek was an incline, but when the cabin came into view, Riley felt like she could run.

"Guess I worried for nothing," she called to Coop.

Julia laughed. "Why should today be any different?"

They stomped up the steps to the front door and laid Julia on the small porch while Coop undid the latch. Once the door was open, they lifted Julia and set her on a small couch across from the fireplace. It was dark and frigid in the cabin, but Riley had a roaring fire going within ten minutes.

She took off her wet coat and draped it on the back of a chair she'd pulled close to the fireplace. The rush of adrenaline she'd felt coming up the last slope had drained her, and her legs felt like cooked spaghetti.

"Give me a minute to rest and get warm before we go for the rest of the supplies. That wore me out more than I thought."

Coop sat in front of the hearth and stripped off his boots and socks. "No argument from me."

Riley collapsed in a dusty old easy-chair next to the couch and sat back with her eyes closed, letting the heat warm her bones.

"I thought we were doomed to die in that truck," Julia said.

Coop laid on the floor and folded his hands behind his head. "That thought crossed my mind when I saw that gigantic tree."

"I've thought we were doomed to die twenty times since we left the hotel," Riley said. "Once the snow melts, we'll be a two or three-hours' drive from Wytheville. Am I foolish to hope we might actually make it?"

Coop rolled on his side and smiled at her. "I'll make sure we get there."

"Why did we risk escaping instead of staying in the compound until my leg was better? What did those bad guys do to make you want to run?"

"We'll tell you the whole story once we've had time to rest, sweetheart. In the meantime, we'd better go for the rest of the stuff." When he didn't respond, Riley said, "Coop?"

In answer, he let out a snore, and Julia giggled. "Guess the stuff will have to wait."

"A nap's not a bad idea. I'm going to check the bed situation." Riley got up and handed Julia the crutches. "Want to join me?" Julia took them and was off the couch in seconds. "Careful. You aren't used to being upright."

"I've been lying around for days, Mom. It feels good to move."

"Just take your time."

Riley made her do two circuits around the small front room before they went to tour the rest of the cabin. There was a tiny rustic kitchen with a gas stove. Riley wondered if there was a propane tank that still might have fuel and planned to check that first thing in the morning.

Down a short hallway were two bedrooms and a bathroom with a sink, toilet and shower. One bedroom had a bunk bed. The other had two twins.

"We'll take the room with the twins," she told Julia. "Coop can have the bunkroom."

"I'd love sharing a room with you, but why aren't you going to stay with Coop like you have been doing?"

She dropped onto one of the twins and sighed. "That was partly because of Hannah, and I had to keep an eye on Coop. Now, I need to be close to keep an eye on you. You're still in the early days of your recovery, and these aren't exactly ideal circumstances."

"As long as it's not because something happened between you and Coop."

Riley gave her a weak smile and let the matter drop. She found some dust-covered blankets and sheets in a small closet and made their beds. She was about to climb into hers when Julia said, "I'm not tired and it's too cold in here. I'm going to sit on the couch and read. I saw some books on a shelf by the kitchen."

Riley walked her to the living room and read off the book titles. Some weren't appropriate for Julia, but there were two or three Riley felt would be fine. The last book in the stack was *The Sisterhood of the Traveling Pants.* She held it in her hands for a moment and fought back her tears as she pictured Hannah with the book, grinning at her from the back seat of the old truck.

"What's that, Mom? What's wrong?"

Riley tucked the book under the others. "Nothing. That book reminded me of something, but you wouldn't like it. You have plenty of others to read, and I'll bring your book from the truck tomorrow."

Julia's look told Riley she wasn't buying the lie, but she wasn't ready to face the emotions that surged up with her discovery of the book. She kissed Julia's forehead before going to her new room with hopes of falling into sweet oblivion.

Riley woke in another dark room, in another strange bed and wondered how many there'd been since the Hotel. She counted the cottage and theater before convincing herself it was better not to dwell on it. What mattered was making sure this would be the last unfamiliar room before reaching the ranch.

She glanced at her watch and was surprised to see she'd slept three hours. The darkness wasn't from clouds. It was after sundown. She dragged herself off the rickety mattress and went to the bathroom. They'd gotten spoiled with functioning toilets at the compound, and she frowned when nothing happened after pushing the handle. They'd have to use buckets of water to flush this one, but she was glad they wouldn't have to use buckets as a toilet.

Julia was alone in the living room, reading her book by flashlight. Boxes of their supplies were stacked against the wall by the door.

"Where's Coop? Has he been making runs to the truck by himself?"

"Yes. He only slept for an hour. This is his last trip. He'll be back in a minute."

As she spoke the words, the door swung open, and Coop stomped in carrying five boxes wrapped in a rope on his back. He unloaded them before locking and bolting the door. After hanging his coat on a hook, he went to get warm by the fire.

"That's it for tonight. It's snowing hard again, and the wind is whipping. If the storm passes by morning, we'll get the rest and start working on that tree. I found two good axes in a small shed behind the cabin. I would have preferred a chain saw, but we can't get greedy."

"Why didn't you wake me? We might have been able to get everything."

"We have more than what we need for the night, and I want you rested when we attack that tree. Hungry?"

Her stomach growled as he said it. All she'd eaten that day were the cinnamon rolls that morning.

"Starved. What do we have?"

"Come with me. I have a surprise in the kitchen." He lit one of the stove burners and grinned like the first human to discover fire. "I found a propane tank out back and figured out how it works. I don't know how much gas is left, but hopefully, it'll last the few days we're here."

They made a stew of canned meat, tomatoes, and potatoes with seasonings they found in the cupboards. They polished off the rest of the cinnamon rolls in front of the fire for dessert.

Coop groaned and rubbed his stomach. "Not used to so much food. Why didn't you stop me from eating that last roll?"

"You were done before we blinked," Julia said.

Riley slumped in her chair and sighed. "Our stomachs have shrunk. We need to pace ourselves."

"I don't know why you're complaining," Julia said. "I ate as much as you, but I'm fine."

Coop glared at her. "That's because you're young. Don't rub it in."

Riley pushed herself out of the chair. "You need to rest, Julia. Come on, I'll help you get ready for bed."

"But it's only eight-thirty. I'm not tired."

"Your body needs strength to recover, and you've been awake all day. You can read until you fall asleep."

She made a face but grabbed her crutches and got up to follow Riley. "I wish that shower worked. I feel disgusting."

"You wouldn't be able to use it if it did work because of your brace and stitches," Coop called after them.

"He's right. I'll boil water and give you a sponge bath."

Julia scrunched her nose. "Better than nothing, I guess."

While Riley bathed her, she said, "Tell me why we had to leave the compound. It can't be worse than the other stuff that's happened."

Riley studied her for a moment, deciding how much to tell her. Before their trip to DC, she'd viewed Julia as a child, but she was a young woman. The horrors they'd experienced since the CME had forced her to grow up in a hurry. She'd seen more death and pain than most teenagers would know in multiple lifetimes. Julia continued to amaze Riley every day with her resilience and wisdom. There was no way of predicting how the trauma would affect her in the future, but Riley believed she'd weather it fine. She chose to tell Julia the truth.

She gave her the details of the aftermath of the attack and what happened to Jepson.

"He was one of the ones who shot those people at the church. He's an evil person, but Mr. Branson is equally as dangerous. After what he did to Jepson, we knew we had to get you out of that compound."

Julia grew quiet. "I've seen stuff like that in movies but knew it wasn't real. It's scary to know there really are people who'd do those kinds of things."

"Dangerous people have existed in the world since the beginning of time. Events like the CME can bring out the worst in some, but there are far more good people, like Coop and Angie. Don't ever forget that."

"I won't. Thanks for getting me out of there, Wonder Woman." Riley rolled her eyes. "That explains why you cried at leaving Angie. That must have been so hard."

Riley stopped soaping Julia and stared at the floor. "Hardest thing I've ever had to do."

"Maybe they'll just put her in their jail for a while or something. What could they do to a person just for wanting to get back to their family?"

Riley knew what Branson was capable of, but she said, "I'm

sure you're right. Let's get you dried off. I need to change your dressing and check your sutures."

The sunlight turned the snow into a glimmering field of diamonds the next morning, but Riley wasn't buying it. The same had happened the day before, and they'd ended up with another foot of snow. Even if they got the tree cut, they weren't going anywhere until the weather warmed enough to melt the snowpack. Even another foot or two could trap them in for weeks.

After a breakfast of reconstituted powdered eggs and protein bars, she and Coop suited up to start chopping up the tree. Riley wasn't thrilled to leave Julia alone but knew it would be impossible for anyone to get to her in a hurry.

"I'll come back every ninety minutes to feed you and help you to the bathroom," she told her as they got ready to leave. "Promise not to get off this couch until I'm here."

Julia crossed her heart. "I won't move a muscle."

"That's my girl."

Coop went down the slope in front of the cabin first to forge a new route for Riley to follow. The snow reached up to her thighs. She had a hard time keeping up with him and was relieved when she saw the opening to the road where the truck was stranded.

"This would be much easier with cross-country skis or snowshoes," she said when they were ten feet from the road. "Did you see any in the shed?"

"I didn't notice. Not what I was looking for. We'll check when we're done."

They broke through the treeline and trudged around the last curve, then stopped and stared at the empty spot where the Humvee should have been. Visible tracks led in the opposite direction. Riley dropped onto the tree trunk and covered her face with her hands. Their one hope of getting to Wytheville was gone.

Coop put his hand on her shoulder. "It's not like we were going anywhere today. At least we don't have to chop the tree."

She pushed his hand away and jumped to her feet. "Is everything a joke to you? Do you know what this means? Unless we find another truck, we're stranded for weeks, if not months until Julia's leg heals. And what happens when the food runs out? There are no stores or other food sources within miles of this place."

Coop stepped closer and leaned his face inches from hers. "I'm aware of our situation. I use humor to mask my anxiety and find hope in dire circumstances. Would you rather I go around growling and sobbing like you every time things don't go our way? I know we've been through a crap storm of trouble but acting like we're on the edge of death every minute doesn't solve our problems."

Riley had never seen Coop angry. She stepped away from the intensity of his reaction and toppled backward over the tree. She scrambled to her feet and dusted herself off before turning toward the cabin. Coop stepped in front of her. She tried to move around him, but he wouldn't let her.

"You're not running off this time. I'm sick of you arguing with everything I say and blaming me for whatever goes wrong. I've risked my life for you and your daughter more times than I can count, yet you treat me like I'm the enemy whenever there isn't another one handy. I'm on your side, Riley. I love you and meant it when I said I'd do anything for you, even die for you. If you can't see that by now, there's no hope for us."

Riley was glad she was too angry to cry and give him the satisfaction. She shoved him in the chest, but he didn't budge. "You killed Angie! You saw her calling for help, but you drove away like it was nothing. How can you be so cold?"

She stopped to take a breath and was shocked to realize she was yelling. She'd never raised her voice at anyone in her life. She moved back to the tree with her head lowered. Coop sat next to her but didn't attempt to touch her. She felt empty and was at a loss where to go next.

She and Zach had had their petty arguments like any married couple but never screaming matches. He'd never gotten her fired up the way Coop did. As infuriating as he was, she had to admit it made life interesting.

"Riley," he said calmly, "I'm sorry for losing my temper. I've never done that, not even with my cheating ex-wife, and I'm as shocked as I can see you are. I put it down to the hideousness of these past weeks. Please, forgive me."

"I was the one screaming. I've never done that either. We're both in foreign territory here."

"If you ask, I'll go and leave you in peace. I won't force myself on you."

"Julia would never forgive me if I let you go."

"That's not an answer. I wagered on getting you and Julia out, alive and safe. I wanted to help Angie, but I couldn't do both. It was an impossible choice, and I don't regret the one I made. But this isn't just about Angie."

She raised her eyes to meet his. "What are you saying?"

"You're angry about Hannah, Julia getting shot, Angie, and you're blaming yourself for all of it. But it's not your fault. It's not my fault. It just is. So, I ask again, do you want me to go?"

She felt like he'd cracked her brain open and peeked inside. Or was she just that transparent?

"If I had been strong like you and Julia after Hannah died, we could have left the campground when you wanted. Instead, I spent three days wallowing in my selfish fear and misery. That caused Julia to get shot. It caused us to be taken captive and may have cost Angie her life. What you said about me was right. You're not the monster here, I am."

"Stop this, Riley. What I said was out of anger. It was cruel and it's not true. You're the most amazing person I've ever known. The fact that you're taking responsibility for the cosmos conspiring against us proves that."

"I want to believe that it's not my fault, but it isn't that simple."

"Why not? I'm painfully honest, remember? You can trust whatever I say." She gave him a weak smile. "Forget what I think. Believe Julia. She loves and trusts you without reservation. She doesn't blame you and has too many other traumas to face to add your guilt to the mix. Julia needs you strong and whole."

"Can't remember the last time I was strong and whole, but I understand. I'll give it my best, but don't expect overnight change. And don't you dare leave us."

"Done. Can we put this behind us and go back to our cozy cabin to figure out how we're going to get the hell out of here?" When she held out her hand, he ignored it and lifted her into his arms. He pressed his lips to hers, then whispered, "No monsters here."

CHAPTER SIXTEEN

RILEY PUSHED the shovelful of snow off the porch and watched it tumble down the steps. She had to restrain herself from throwing the shovel after it.

"This is pointless," she yelled at the endless drifts of white spreading in every direction. "Go away and leave us alone."

Julia opened the door and maneuvered onto the porch. "Who are you yelling at, Mom?"

Riley huffed and shoved more snow off the porch. "Not who, what. I'm yelling at the snow."

Julia closed the door and propped herself against the doorframe. "As long as you're not expecting it to answer."

"I was ordering it to go away and leave us alone. How many times have Coop and I shoveled this porch in the past two weeks?"

Julia shrugged. "Seems like a hundred."

"Every time we clear it, another storm comes. That's over five feet of snow out there, mocking me. I'm sick of you," Riley shouted and her words echoed off the hills.

"My diagnosis: cabin fever."

Riley glared at her. "Thanks, doctor."

"How do you think I feel? I can't even go past the porch. At least you have your little ski outings. I'm stuck inside with these stupid crutches."

A smile crept up Riley's face. "You just gave me an idea. Where's Coop?"

"He said he was going to work on the tree. He's chopped enough wood to last if we're stuck here for three years."

"Bite your tongue," Riley said and pretended to spit three times on her knuckles to ward off evil spirits as her grandmother used to do. "He's determined to chop up that entire tree. It may take him three years." She snapped on one of the pairs the cross-country skis they'd found in the shed. "Go inside. I'll be right back."

"Where are you going?" Julia called after Riley as she skied down the hill.

Cross country skis weren't made for downhill, so she made her way to the road in a switchback pattern. Getting back uphill would be tricky, but at least she had a way to travel across the snow since it was as deep as she was tall.

She glided around the bend to where Coop was lopping away at the tree and slid to a stop. When he saw her, he buried the ax blade in the trunk and straightened, wiping the sweat from his forehead.

"What's up? Julia okay?"

"She's fine." She looked at the wheels of trunk sections and split pieces scattered on the snow. "Why are you bothering with this? We don't need the wood, and there's an opening big enough for a tank."

"It's very satisfying and keeps me from going stir crazy in the cabin. I have to take advantage of breaks between storms." He pulled the ax from the tree and held it out to her. "Want to take a whack at it?"

"I'll pass, but I might have a more constructive way for you to pass the time. Let's build a sled for Julia. I feel terrible that she can't leave the cabin, and it might come in handy when we're ready to leave."

He grasped her shoulders and gave her a peck on the cheek. "Brilliant idea. I was thinking we need a way to leave since our food stores are getting low, but I didn't know what to do with Julia. A sled would solve that problem. Let's go draw up the plans."

He sat on the trunk and strapped on one of the pairs of snowshoes they'd found in the shed with the skis. Coop had the advantage of ascending the incline to the cabin, but Riley did a decent job keeping up with him.

When they told Julia their plan, she squealed in delight. Coop spread three pieces of paper he'd torn from an old notebook on the table. "Don't get too excited. None of us has ever built a sled, and we may not have all the tools and supplies we need."

Riley sketched out a detailed design and proudly held it up for Coop to admire.

After studying it for three seconds, he said, "Perfect if you're hiding a scroll saw and the electricity to power it. You need to think more *Man Versus Wild* than *Pottery Barn* here."

She balled up her design and tossed it in the fire. "I got carried away for a minute."

Julia, who'd been listening from the couch, said, "Couldn't we take the legs off the coffee table, turn it upside down and nail the snow shovel to the end of it?"

Riley and Coop turned and stared at her, wondering why they hadn't thought of that.

"Aw, the nimble mind of the young," Coop said. "We'd need runners to lift it off the snow, but yes, that might work."

They had a workable design an hour later. Coop stood and stretched. "My brain's melted. I'll see you both first thing in the morning."

While Julia made her way down the hall, Riley leaned close to

Coop and whispered, "Wait for me in your room after Julia's asleep."

He raised his eyebrows, then winked. "With pleasure."

Riley gave Julia a sponge bath and ran through physical therapy exercises with her before tucking her into bed. She sat next to her and brushed a wisp of hair from her face.

"I'll give you a haircut tomorrow and let you try out the hot shower system Coop rigged. I'm not making any promises it'll work, but your scar is healed enough to try it."

"A hot shower sounds heavenly, but not until we build my sled. I'm sick of the view from the porch."

Riley kissed her forehead. "After we build the sled, then. It's late. No reading tonight."

Julia yawned big enough for Riley to see her tonsils. "I'm too tired to read. Love you, Mom."

She rolled over to face the wall, and Riley waited until she heard her soft, even breathing. She was glad Julia had fallen asleep so quickly, but she also felt a pang of jealousy. Sleep was much harder for her to come by.

She tiptoed out the room but hesitated before tapping on Coop's door. She'd been cordial since their encounter at the tree but had kept him at arm's length while she worked through her tangled mess of emotions. His patience and consideration had helped, along with the diminishing supply of Xanax he'd stolen from the infirmary. She'd been tapering her dose down and felt more like her old self.

As her anxiety faded, her desire to be close to Coop grew. While the memory of Angie still stung, she'd come to believe he'd made the right choice to leave without her. Attempting to save Angie would have put them all at risk. She still clung to the hope that Branson had been merciful with Angie, but it was hard to accept that they'd never know her fate.

Her love for Coop had gradually reignited, and she was ready to commit to him. Julia had easily embraced him as part of their family. She was willing to do the same, but it wasn't just his love she desired. She pushed his door open without knocking and drew in her breath when she saw him sitting propped up and shirtless on the bed.

"I'm ready," she whispered as she kissed his neck and chest. "And you've waited long enough."

Riley lay awake with her head resting on Coop's chest, listening to the rhythm of his heartbeat and reflecting on their lovemaking. She never imagined anyone could satisfy her the way Zach had. Coop's style was different but every bit as pleasurable. She snuggled closer to him, almost able to forget they were trapped in a cabin at the end of the world.

Her only concern was how to explain their relationship to Julia. Riley had made a point to impress upon Julia the importance of waiting for marriage to have sex. She knew it was an unpopular concept and that Julia likely wouldn't heed her advice, but she hoped it would get her to postpone sex until she was in love.

As a doctor, Riley had seen the damage a promiscuous lifestyle could wreak, especially on teenagers, and wanted to shield Julia from that. She'd seemed receptive to Riley's advice and planned to follow it, but she was young and with the world was on its head, who knew what kind of romantic future Julia would face?

Riley pushed thoughts of her daughter aside and allowed herself to enjoy her minute of contentment. Those times were a rare commodity in their new lives.

Coop shifted and opened his eyes. When he saw her lying on him, he smiled and tightened his arms around her.

"What are you doing awake? Have you slept?"

She smiled up at him. "I'm just savoring the peaceful moment.

That was incredible last night, Coop, and it feels so right to be with you. I'm sorry I wasted so much time."

"You chose a time that wasn't an impetuous act of desperation when we could die at any second. This was worth the wait."

"Thank you for saying that. I was worried you'd resent that I put you off for so long."

"I wouldn't have done that." He picked up his thermal shirt, and Riley moved so he could put it on. "It's freezing in here. We forgot to stoke the fire last night."

Riley eyed him seductively. "Oh, we stoked the fire last night."

Coop feigned shock. "Dr. Poole, I never expected to see this side of you."

She blushed and rolled on top of him. "Me, either."

He put his warm hands on her waist and pulled her closer. "I hope to see more of it."

She gave him a sensual kiss and whispered, "Trust me, you will."

Julia was surprised to see her mom's empty and tidy bed in the morning. She woke before her mom most mornings, but even when she didn't, her mom put off making the bed until Julia was up so she wouldn't bother her. She hoped it meant that she and Coop had gotten an early start on the sled.

She was about to call out to her when she heard her giggle coming from Coop's room.

She frowned and wondered if she'd slept on the top bunk or with him. It was gross to think of her mom and Coop that way, but once she got over being creeped out, she was glad they were together.

Her mom had acted weird toward Coop since they got to the cabin, and Julia was afraid he'd get fed up and leave. She was relieved her mom finally remembered she loved him and was lucky to have Coop in their lives. It meant they could be a real family, minus the whole wedding thing since it wasn't like her mom and Coop could run to city hall. All that mattered to Julia was that her mom had found someone who made her happy.

As she reached for the crutches to go to the bathroom, Coop came out of his room and saluted her.

"I'll build up the fire, and we'll start on your sled after breakfast."

"Sounds good," she said as he hurried down the hall to the living room.

She shuffled to the bathroom, imagining how incredible it would feel to take a hot shower.

Her mom tapped on the bathroom door a few minutes later. "Need any help in there?"

"I'm good. How are you this morning?" she asked in a singsong voice.

Her mom hesitated a full ten seconds before saying, "Doing great. Thanks for asking. I'll be in the kitchen, so call if you need me."

Julia laughed and finished washing her face with the ice-cold water from the bowl on the counter. When she was done, she went to the kitchen and caught her mom blushing but didn't tease her, afraid it would scare her off from being with Coop.

She took one of the two kitchen chairs and leaned her crutches against the table. "What's for breakfast? Let me guess. MREs and canned peaches."

Coop pulled up the other chair and sat next to her. "Be glad you have that much. Our stores are getting pitiful. If we get another stormless day tomorrow, I might venture out to see if there are any food sources within walking distance. If not, I'll have to try hunting. I've seen rabbit and deer tracks. It won't be easy with the range of the Glock, but it's the best we have."

Riley set a bowl of peaches in front of Julia and dried her

hands on a raggedy dishtowel. "As long as you don't run into a bear. Are there bears in Virginia?"

Julia shoveled a spoonful of peaches into her mouth and said, "Who knows? I forgot to Google local wildlife before the CME."

Coop mussed her hair. "Snarky. Black bears live around here, but they're hunkered down this time of year, especially with the cold temperatures. Even if they are out, they usually stay clear of humans. Nothing to worry about."

Riley finished her protein bar and tossed the wrapper in the bin. "Good to know. I've had venison but never rabbit. How do they taste?"

"I make a mean rabbit stew."

Julia crinkled her nose. "Sounds disgusting."

"You'll be grateful when it's all you have to eat."

They cleaned up the few dirty dishes and got to work on Julia's sled. It was an uncomplicated design but wasn't simple to build without the right tools. Julia watched from the couch as they pulled the legs off the coffee table, making sure to save the nails and screws. With that done, Coop brought in the extra pair of skis to use as runners.

The table was wider than the snow shovel, so he trimmed off three inches with a dull, rusty saw he found in the shed. While he worked, Riley poked holes in the shovel with some medical instruments. They made matching holes in the table after Coop finished trimming it.

"What are those for?" Julia asked.

"We're going to lash a rope through the holes to hold the shovel to the table edge, so it won't cause friction in the snow. If we only used nails or screws, they'd tear through the plastic, so we'll use both."

Before they added the shovel, they nailed the skis to what used to be the top of the table, then wove a rope through the holes.

Coop pounded the rest of the nails they'd scavenged through

the shovel and stood back to admire their work. "Not bad. Won't win any prizes, but it'll work for Julia and for carrying supplies."

"Hope that table wasn't a family heirloom," Riley said.

Coop chuckled. "Couldn't be too precious if they stuck it away in this cabin."

Julia clapped and got up to give the sled a try. Riley and Coop lowered her onto it in a sitting position with her back toward the shovel. "Perfect fit! When can we take it for a test run?"

"How about right now?" Coop said, seeming as excited to try it out as she was. He turned the door handle, and a gust of wind tore it from his hand and sent snow blowing into the room. He shoved the door closed and turned to face her with a frown. "We'll have to wait until after the blizzard."

Her mom groaned and covered her face with her hands. "It's like living in the Rockies backcountry. Is much snow normal for this area?"

Coop shook his head. "Not for at least a hundred years."

Her mom helped her off the sled and said, "Adrian Landry said he suspected the CME might affect weather patterns."

Julia reluctantly crutched back to the couch and lowered herself onto the cushions. "Who's Adrian?"

Coop glanced at her mom, then back at her. "We didn't tell you about Dr. Landry?" Julia shook her head. "You aren't going to like this."

She listened in shock while Coop and her mom told her about the physicist they met at the compound and what he'd said about the CME. She felt sick by the time they finished.

"The entire world is like this, even at home? Do you think Emily and Jared are okay with Nana and Papa?"

Her mom sat next to her and put an arm around her. "I'm sure they're fine. Papa has everything they need at the farmhouse, and he and Nana are very resourceful. I'm not worried about them."

"Now, I know you're lying. You worry about everything."

"I'm telling the truth. I trust Nana and Papa, and I bet your Aunt Lily and Uncle Kevin are with them, and Miles, too. They have everything they need to survive comfortably."

Julia wiped the tears dripping off her chin. "Not my friends, though. I bet they're all dead."

"We're not dead. Why would your friends be?" Coop asked.

"That's true," she said, encouraged by the thought. "Except for Hannah, we're still alive after all the horrible stuff we've been through."

"And you even got shot," her mom said. "That'll be an awesome story to tell your friends when we get home."

"Home," Julia whispered. "How will we get home? It's taken a month to go a few hundred miles."

"We'll stay at the ranch until you're recovered, and the weather improves. Uncle Mitch has trucks we can use and horses. Plus, the chaos will have died down by then. People will start to rebuild their communities."

"Like on *The Walking Dead*," Coop said. "But we don't have to deal with zombies."

Julia crossed her arms. "Mom doesn't let me watch that show."

"Smart woman. Let's just say they had it way worse than we do, and they were able to start rebuilding *their* communities."

Her mom kissed the top of her head. "We shouldn't have told you."

Julia turned to face her. "I'm glad you did. I had to find out some time and I don't like it when you keep secrets from me. Now, we all know what we're facing, and we'll do it together."

"Are you sure about this?" Riley asked as she watched Coop pull on his snowshoes two days later. "There's at least a foot of fresh powder and it's still snowing."

"It's just flurries, and what choice do I have? The food's almost gone, and who knows how long we have before the next blizzard? It's too bad the owners of this place didn't think to leave a *Farmer's Almanac*. It's surprising how accurate their forecasts are."

"Promise to stop and head straight back if the storm gets worse. We can ration for a few days if necessary and can give trapping rabbits another go. The ones you cooked weren't that bad."

"You looked like you were trying not to throw up while you ate that stew. I give my word that I'll turn around if the storm gets worse. I'll be back before dark, if not sooner."

Riley hugged him for a full minute before reluctantly letting go.

Julia gave a half-hearted wave as he went out into the cold. "I don't like this, Mom. I can eat this couch leather if it'll stop him from going."

Riley was glad her back was to Julia so she wouldn't see she felt the same way. Their food stock was low, but not gone, and the snow had to stop sometime. She'd warned Coop when they were alone that it was reckless for him to venture out when it was already snowing. She shouldn't have wasted her breath. He was too impetuous and stubborn. She watched him snowshoe down the slope until the top of his hood disappeared below the drifts, then pushed the door closed and pasted on a smile.

"Coop's smart and has that freaky sense of direction he's always bragging about. How many times were we sure he wasn't coming back just to have him pop up at the last second?"

"Say whatever you want, Mom. I see in your face how worried you are."

"That proves nothing. I'm always worried, remember. Let's play chess. I'm leading in the tournament and want to see if you can catch me. Or are you chicken to take me on?" Julia mumbled something under her breath. "I didn't catch that."

Julia gave an equally fake smile. "Nothing. I'd love a game of chess."

Julia silently watched Riley while she set up the board. She'd been in a funk since they told her about Adrian and the global-CME, and Riley wished they hadn't. She'd promised not to keep secrets from Julia, but maybe she was too young to hear some truths.

She perked up some as they got into their game. Riley was doing her best to let Julia win without her knowing. They played for hours to distract themselves, only stopping to eat the last of the MREs and for Julia to take her hourly five-minute walks around the cabin. Neither mentioned the howling wind, the rapidly falling snow, or the fact that Coop had failed to return.

Riley's panic began rising as the hours passed and she felt powerless against it. She'd taken her last Xanax the previous day and had no other sedatives. If a blizzard hadn't been raging outside, she would have gone for a vigorous hike, which usually worked to calm her. By sunset, she was suffering a full-blown panic attack. Julia did her best to help calm her, and she tried yoga and deep breathing, but nothing worked.

The worse her attack got, the more agitated Julia became, and the more furious Riley was with herself for not being able to stay in control. The attacks weren't her fault, but she'd done so well keeping them at bay since the day they got the alert about the CME. She couldn't figure out why this one was overwhelming her.

By eight, Julia was in tears, and Riley was relentlessly pacing the room. Her legs ached, and her head pounded, but she couldn't stop.

Julia was lying on the couch, weeping with her arms covering her face. "Coop's never coming back, is he, Mom?"

Riley was so out of breath that it was a chore to talk, but she managed to say, "We don't know that. Maybe he's holed up somewhere until the storm passes."

Julia sat up and blew her nose on her sweatshirt. "How could he abandon us? We needed him more than food. If he comes back, I'll never forgive him."

Riley knew that wasn't true but didn't bother contradicting her. "I don't want to talk about Coop. Read to me. It'll help both of us."

"I can't stop crying. How do you expect me to read?"

"Julia, I'm begging. Please, help me."

She stared at Riley before getting her crutches and going to the stack of books in the corner.

"Fine, but I want a different book. The one I was reading is boring." She flipped through the stack before Riley could stop her and picked up *Sisterhood of the Traveling Pants.* She brushed the smooth cover with her fingers before raising her eyes to Riley. "Why did you hide this from me?"

Riley paused her pacing. "I thought it would be too painful for you to see it. I should have thrown it out into the snow."

"I'm glad you didn't. I want to read it. I love this book, and it makes me feel like Hannah's with us. That comforts me."

Riley nodded and started moving again. "Go ahead."

Julia read until eleven when she started to yawn, and Riley's legs finally refused to take another step.

"Let's go to bed. We'll pick up where you stopped in the morning."

Julia followed her down the hall. "I don't think I'll be able to sleep."

"Me either, but we need to try. Even resting will be good for our bodies, and my body is screaming for rest."

They climbed into their beds, fully clothed. Despite her worry, Julia was sleeping soundly thirty minutes later. Riley rested against the wall with her knees pulled to her chest as she listened to the wind. She forced herself to imagine Coop safe and warm in an abandoned cabin like the one they'd found. It didn't stop her panic, but it helped her stay still. She stoked the fire every few hours and waited for the blessed light of dawn.

The storm quieted sometime around sunrise, and they woke to a brilliant, cloudless sky. Riley's anxiety had also calmed to a dull roar. She was exhausted but hopeful that Coop would make it back before nightfall.

She got up to stoke the fire but discovered they were out of wood. When she opened the back door to bring in a load from the woodpile, a mound of snow spilled into the cabin. The doorway was covered by a drift that reached halfway up the frame. At least three new feet of snow had fallen in the past twenty-four hours.

Since they'd used their only shovel for Julia's sled, she dumped the trash out of the kitchen garbage can and used it to dig a trail. It took three hours of backbreaking work to reach the wood stacked against the shed and another two to carry in enough wood to last three days. Julia woke up just as she'd finished filling most of the kitchen and half the living room with logs.

The exertion had burned off her anxiety and blocked her mind from obsessing about Coop. She changed the subject whenever Julia brought him up to stay in control, so she soon got the hint. At noon, they ate the last two protein bars. That left them with a jar of canned beef and a few cans of peaches and green beans. If Coop didn't come back with food, they might be forced to eat the couch after all.

They passed the time as they had the day before by playing chess and reading. When they grew tired of that, they played twenty-questions, I Spy, and tic-tac-toe. At three, Julia begged Riley to take her for a sled ride until Riley relented and opened the front door. Julia went to the doorway and peeked over the top of her head.

"How deep do you think that is?"

"I'd guess close to seven feet. We measured it last week, and it was five. Some melted, then we got this. No sled ride today."

Julia sank onto the couch and crossed her arms. "What did people in the olden days do to keep from going out of their minds in the winter?"

"They did chores, like shoveling, chopping wood, drawing water, and cooking. At night, they sang, read, and played games like we've been doing. They had to take care of livestock, too. They went to bed early and got up early to work hard all day. Once we get settled, that's what our lives will be until someone figures out how to get electricity running."

"At least there won't be pollution. What about solar and wind power?"

"I'm sure the world that emerges from the ashes won't look much like the one that existed six weeks ago."

"As long as someone figures out cell phones and the internet, I'll be happy."

"People are going to be far more concerned with the food at first. The rest will come later, but not for years or decades. It'll be your generation that grows up in this new world and finds ways to innovate. It's exciting to think about."

"That's if we survive. It'll be a miracle if we make it out of this cabin."

"We will, sweetheart."

They sat lost in their private thoughts for several minutes until Julia said, "I'm hungry, Mom."

"Me, too, but we have to ration. It'll take a few days for our stomachs to shrink."

"If mine shrinks any more, it'll disappear."

"I could slice you a piece of couch."

Julia rolled her eyes. "I'll pass."

"Ready for another game of chess?"

Riley slept for seven hours after her day of digging, hauling wood, and gathering snow for water. When she woke to another cloudless day, every muscle ached, but she felt refreshed. To distract Julia from her hunger and Coop, she cleared the snow from the porch and dug a short path in the snow so that she could pull Julia on the sled. It took her until two to finish, but it was worth it to see the happiness on her daughter's face for the first time in days.

She pulled Julia past the shed to a little break in the trees above a frozen creek with a waterfall. It was fascinating to see the falls frozen in place.

"That's beautiful," Julia said softly. "Wish I had my phone to take a picture."

"We'll have to take pictures with our minds." She was about to turn the sled and return to the cabin when she spotted movement in the woods. "Quick, hand me the binocs."

Julia dug through the emergency supplies they'd put in the sled and handed the binoculars to Riley. She raised them to her eyes and searched the woods, hoping to see Coop, but there was nothing. She lowered the binoculars and sighed.

"I must have been imagining it."

"No, Mom, look. It's a deer."

Riley shifted her gaze to where Julia pointed and saw a huge buck step out between two trees. "Wish we had the gun, but Coop took it," she whispered.

"How can you think of killing him? He could be Bambi's dad."

"Because in two days we're going to starve if we don't find some food. Bambi's dad would feed us for the whole winter."

"Didn't think of that. Is there another way to catch him?"

Riley raised her eyebrows. "Catch him? He's not a dog." Their conversation became moot when the buck bounded down the hill. "He might come back. I'll try to think of a way to lure him closer to the cabin, and maybe we can trap him. Wish we had grain of some kind."

"We shouldn't have eaten all the popcorn."

Riley reluctantly turned the sled and pondered how to trap the buck as she dragged the sled back to the cabin. If Coop didn't show up soon, it was up to her to make sure they didn't starve.

Riley was dreaming she was at a luxurious banquet with Coop when an earth-shaking crash startled her awake. Julia's screams followed seconds later. Riley had moved to Coop's room around one when Julia's snoring was keeping her awake, so she grabbed a flashlight and raced back across the hall.

Chunks of plaster and wood littered the floor, and Julia's door hung by the hinges. She ducked through the opening and found Julia on her crutches staring at the side of the room where Riley's bed should have been. It was buried under the collapsed roof and mounds of snow. Julia repeated "*Mom, mom*" in a daze.

Riley shined the flashlight in her direction. "I'm here, sweetheart. I was sleeping across the hall. I'm not hurt."

Julia let out a cry and nearly fell off the crutches in her rush to get to Riley.

"I thought you were dead, and I was left alone in this demolished cabin with no food and a bum leg. I love you, Mom."

Riley unwound herself from her daughter's grip and looked into her eyes. "I love you, too, sweetheart. Are you hurt?"

Julia checked her arms and patted her torso. "I'm good."

"Excellent. We have to get out of here before the rest of the roof crashes in on us. Go to the living room while I grab the emergency supplies. We're going to take cover in the shed."

Julia went toward the living room, carrying her boots by the laces while Riley gathered what they needed to survive the night.

She ran toward Julia when she was ready but stopped in shock at the sight of the living room. The entire left side of the roof was on the floor. All that remained was a narrow opening between the roof and the woodpile. It was just big enough for them to get to the back door. The couch and the rest of the supplies were buried.

Riley cautiously led Julia to the door but had to yank on it with all her strength to open it. She lowered Julia into the sled and pulled her toward the shed, grateful she'd kept the trail to the woodpile clear.

She left Julia outside while she shoved rubbish out of the way so Julia could maneuver inside the cramped space inside the shed, then she helped Julia to a wooden crate. She covered her with a sleeping bag before turning to leave, but Julia grabbed her wrist to stop her.

"Don't leave me, Mom."

"I have to go back to the cabin. We need more supplies and blankets, or we'll freeze to death."

"What if the rest of the roof caves in and crushes you? I'll die out here alone."

"It won't. The roof has stopped falling. I have to hurry, Julia. Please, let go of my arm."

Julia put on her brave face and released her. Riley gave her a quick nod and dashed back into the night. She was terrified of going back inside the cabin but knew she had to or there was no chance they'd survive. She loaded every blanket and article of clothing that wasn't buried into the sled and went back for their last bit of food.

The boxes of med supplies and tools were blocked by a fractured support beam, so she had to let those go. As she took the sled handle and started for the shed, the section of the roof over Coop's room collapsed. She ran to Julia as fast as she could across the packed snow.

"I made it. I'm safe," she said, as she unloaded the sled and wrapped Julia in blankets.

"I knew you would be. You're Wonder Woman."

Riley cuddled up next to her for warmth and struggled to catch her breath. "Wish I had an invisible jet. I'd take us to get our family, then fly to the warmest spot on the planet that has lots of food."

"Sounds amazing." She was quiet for a moment, then said, "Mom, what are we going to do?"

"Give me a minute to make a plan. Don't worry, I'll do whatever it takes to make sure we make it through this. I know you're cold but put your head on my shoulder and try to sleep. You're going to need your strength."

Julia leaned against her and closed her eyes. Riley stroked her silky hair and fought the wave of panic rising like a tidal wave. They'd faced impossible circumstances on their rabbit hole journey, but she had no clue how she was going to save her daughter.

"Mom, snap out of it," Julia shouted. "You have to save me."

Riley was desperate to answer but couldn't move her mouth. She was barely able to breathe and didn't know where she was.

Julia shook her by the shoulders. "You can't do this to me. I need you or I'll die."

When she still didn't move, Julia slapped her hard on the cheek. Riley bolted upright and looked around in confusion. They were in a tiny, dark, freezing room. She rubbed the spot where Julia had slapped her.

"Where are we?"

Julia lowered herself onto a wooden crate and broke into sobs.

"The cabin caved in. We're in the shed. I woke up and you

were just staring at nothing. I shined the flashlight in your eyes, but you didn't move. You scared me so bad. I thought you had a stroke or something." She wiped her face and took a deep breath. "It's morning, and it's starting to snow. We have to get out of here before the shed roof caves in, too."

Memories of the night before flooded over Riley. She must have hyperventilated and passed out. She stood and hugged Julia before opening the shed door. The wind was calm, and the storm didn't feel like a blizzard, just an average snowfall, but Julia was right. They had to get moving before a worse storm hit.

Their sources of shelter and food were gone. She'd have to make a rope harness and tie it to the shovel handle on the sled to pull Julia. Getting her down the hill would be a monumental challenge, but once they were on the road, the going would be more manageable.

She rubbed her gloves together. "Time to load the sled. You're going to get that adventure you've been begging for."

"What if Coop comes back?"

Riley had little hope of that. Three days had passed since he left. They had to face the fact that he was gone.

To appease Julia, she said, "We'll leave a note. Do you see paper or a pen?" They searched the shed but found nothing useful to write a message for Coop.

"Scratch a message on the door with a nail, Mom. That way, it can't get wet or be erased."

"Right. Start packing while I do that."

Riley hadn't dug a path to the front door from the shed, so she went to the back of the house and pulled her skis and poles from the wreckage, then skied to the porch. She scratched a message telling Coop they were headed for I-81, then carved the address to the ranch in case he didn't catch up with them before they made it to Wytheville.

She skied back to the shed to help Julia finish the packing and rig a harness. When they were set, Julia climbed into the sled, and Riley arranged their meager supplies around her. The sled was heavy in the powdery snow but didn't sink in too far for Riley to pull it. She didn't know how far they'd get before her strength gave out but was determined to power on until they found safe shelter. Their lives depended on it.

CHAPTER SEVENTEEN

RILEY STABBED her ski-poles into a drift and lifted her goggles as she toppled into the snow. Flakes landed on her lashes, but her arms were too tired to brush them away.

"Why are you stopping, Mom? You told me not to let you stop, no matter what."

Julia's muffled voice came from under the layers of blankets covering her face. Riley barely heard her over the wind.

"I can't go on. My legs won't move."

Riley pushed up her sleeve to check the time. She'd been pulling that sled for five hours. By her estimation, they should have reached I-81 an hour earlier, but it was nowhere in sight. She hadn't seen a sign or mile marker and wasn't even sure they were traveling in the right direction.

Her muscles screamed. Their food was gone and her energy drained. They were out in the open, exposed to the elements. She'd searched for signs of any structure they could hole up in while she rested, but she was too short to see over the drifts lining the road. Her only solution was to kneel in the snow and wait for death. Julia yelled at her, coaxing her to get on her feet.

When Riley didn't respond, Julia gave up and sat weeping in the sled.

Riley hated herself for failing her daughter, for failing Jared and Emily, and for failing herself. Millions had died since the CME, but she'd deluded herself into believing they'd survive. Was she more deserving of life than they?

She unhooked her skis and crawled to Julia. If they were going to die, at least they'd do it together.

As Riley closed her eyes and rested her head on Julia's leg, a man's voice said, "Riley Poole, on your feet."

Riley lifted her head and turned in the direction of the voice, but no one was there.

"I never pegged you for a quitter," the voice chided. "I said, on your feet."

She didn't bother to look the second time, knowing she was hallucinating or losing her mind. That sometimes happens with people in dire distress, and after her bizarre episode that morning, it wouldn't surprise her.

"You're so close, Riley. Just a little further. Don't quit yet."

Relief poured over her as she recognized the voice. Was it Coop? No, not Coop. Zach. She hadn't heard his voice in such a long time. It took a moment to remember the sound. That proved she'd lost her mind? Zach was dead.

"You're stronger than you know, Riley. Julia needs you. Emily and Jared need you. Get off that snow and start walking."

Julia reached her hand out from under the blanket and tapped Riley's shoulder. "I'm not ready to die, Mom. I know the sled is heavy, but you have to keep going. We'll find somewhere to stop soon."

Riley squeezed Julia's hand before tucking it back under the blanket. She and Zach were so confident she could make it. Could they be right? And what did it matter if she died walking or curled up in the snow? She'd be just as dead, either way.

She snapped on her skis and struggled to her feet. Julia

clapped as she slipped into the harness and slid her ski across the snow. *One step at a time, Riley Poole. Just keep going, one step at a time.*

———————

She kept up a lively conversation with Zach as she slowly glided along for what felt like an eternity. It was fortunate no one could hear her ramblings, or they would have locked her in a padded room. *On second thought, a warm padded room sounds lovely,* she told him and giggled.

She trudged along, numb and insane until she heard what sounded like an engine. She wondered if it was one of Branson's gang coming to drag them back to the compound and realized she didn't care. She'd find out Angie's fate, and she and Julia would be warm and full. She could hang out with Branson, one psycho to another.

She laughed at her hilarious joke and pulled the sled to the side of the road to await their fate. The truck pulled alongside them and slowed to a stop.

Julia threw the blankets off her head and cried, "That's our truck. These are the guys who stole our truck."

"Hush," Riley said. "Keep quiet. I'll handle this."

A strikingly handsome lumberjack of a man climbed out of the driver seat and walked around the truck to Riley. He wasn't one of Branson's men. She would have remembered him.

He held his hand out to her, but Riley didn't move. "I'm Bryce Casper. What are you two doing out in this storm?"

Riley straightened and crossed her arms. "Where did you get that truck?"

"We found it abandoned by a fallen tree. Finders keepers these days."

"That's my truck. Return it immediately. I'll drop you off wherever you want."

A man in the back seat had rolled down his window to listen. He stuck his head out and said, "Prove it." Riley glared at him and rattled off a list of everything she could remember that they'd left in the Humvee, down to Julia's book. The man nodded and turned to another passenger. "It's her truck."

As Riley was about to demand again that they return it, the world spun, and she crumpled onto the snow. Bryce went into action, unhooking her skis and lifting her into his arms like she was a toy. As he carried her to the truck, he ordered the two other men and a woman to load Julia and the sled into the Humvee.

"Watch my daughter's leg. She's injured," Riley said, as Bryce lowered her into the back seat.

One of the men laid Julia next to her, then climbed into the third row of seats with the other man. The woman sat in the front with Bryce.

"This is Laura," Bryce said, cocking his thumb at the woman. "Those two in the back are Tyson and Lance. Mind telling us who you are?"

Riley met his gaze in the rearview mirror and said, "I do. Where are you taking us?"

"There's no reason to be afraid of us," he said. "We won't harm either of you."

Riley lowered her eyes. "Then you'll be the first."

"Are you hungry?" Tyson asked. "Looks like you haven't eaten in a while."

"Starving," Julia said. She turned and looked through the compartment on her door. "Where's my caramel corn?"

"Sorry, I ate it," Lance said sheepishly. "We have other food." He picked up a pack at his feet and fished out energy bars and packets of dried bananas. "Will these do?"

They gladly accepted the food along with bottled water. When Julia started to wolf hers down, Riley warned her to eat slowly, or she'd get sick. Riley took a bite of her bar and chewed several times before swallowing.

She felt Bryce watching her through the mirror and glared at him. "Stop staring at me."

"I'm sorry, but there's something familiar about you. Have we met?"

"I'd remember you. I don't mean to sound ungrateful, but please, tell me where you're taking us."

"We've established a community at a senior independent living facility about ten miles from here. We discovered it shortly after the CME. Most of the staff had bailed, and many of the residents died, but we've helped the rest as best we can and have brought others to join us. We have power and limited stores of food. We were on a supply run when we found you, and when we found your truck last week."

His explanation sounded too good to be true, but he seemed honest. If he was telling the truth and they didn't run into another Branson, it would be the perfect place to recuperate until they were ready to leave for Wytheville.

"Have you come across a man who goes by Coop?" she asked.

"Not that I remember, but I don't know everyone at the center. We get new people every day. Any of you guys hear of Coop?"

The others shook their heads.

Julia put a handful of bananas in her mouth and said, "You'd remember Coop if you met him."

Riley gave her a sad smile and turned toward the window.

"Now, it's your turn," Bryce said. "Why were you out in a snowstorm with your injured daughter on a homemade sled?"

Julia opened her mouth to answer, but Riley held up her hand to stop her. "That's a long story, but to sum up, the roof of our cabin caved in from the weight of the snow. We had to abandon it."

"Is that how your daughter got hurt?" Lance asked.

Julia washed down her bananas with a gulp of water and said, "No, I got shot."

"Julia, please," Riley said, disappointed that her daughter still hadn't learned when to keep her mouth shut.

Julia shrugged and took another gulp of water. Riley silently watched the snow-buried world pass by in slow motion until Bryce pulled into the plowed parking lot of a lovely complex with a welcome sign reading "Blue Ridge Meadows Senior Living Center." It reminded her of similar facilities in Colorado where she'd treated patients. Her hope that they'd found safe harbor soared.

They climbed out, and Lance ran inside to get Julia a wheelchair. Bryce offered his hand to help Riley out, but she waved him off. The energy bar had kicked in, so she was able to make it under her own power. He led her into a spacious lobby where small groups of people sat in luxurious chairs scattered around the room. They stopped talking and stared at the sight of Riley and Julia.

"Meet our newest residents," Bryce said, before turning to Riley. "I'm sorry. I didn't catch your names."

Riley scowled at him before turning to the expectant group. "I'm Riley Poole. This is my daughter, Julia."

Bryce stared at her like he'd seen a ghost. "Are you Dr. Riley Poole?"

"How do you know that?" she asked when she'd recovered from her shock.

Laura, Tyson, and Lance stepped behind Bryce and came to attention as Bryce lifted his hand in salute. "Major Bryce Casper, United States Air Force. It's a pleasure to meet you, ma'am. I had the honor of serving with your husband."

The others followed his salute. Riley felt her legs go weak. Bryce jumped to her side and helped her to a chair.

Julia rolled the wheelchair next to them and stared wide-eyed at Bryce. "You knew my dad?"

"I did, and more. I considered him one of my best friends. He talked about you all the time. I'll tell you about it later, but first, I'll take you to your quarters so you and your mom can clean up and rest. Lance, get Dr. Poole a wheelchair. Tyson, find someone to help unload their belongings. Bring them to room 1224 in the south wing."

Lance hurried down a hall past the lobby and returned with a wheelchair. He and Laura wheeled them behind Bryce as he led them to their room.

Julia stared in awe at the elegant decor and said, "This reminds me of the hotel."

Riley was subdued and bewildered as she thought how close she'd come to dying and the odd coincidence that had led her to that particular road just as Bryce was passing. Logic and science told her that hearing Zach's voice had been nothing more than delirium, but she couldn't discount the possibility that it could have been something more. Julia would have whole-heartedly believed it was. But whether hallucination or intervention from the great beyond, Riley was just grateful she was alive to wonder.

After eighteen hours of the best sleep Riley had enjoyed in years, she took a warm shower using lavender soap in her sparkling bathroom and dressed in the cleanest of the three outfits she'd been able to rescue from the cabin. Satisfied that she was presentable, she twisted her hair into a tidy knot and went in search of Julia.

Riley wound her way through various corridors until she found the hallway leading to the lobby. The room was empty, but she found a map of the facility and located the main dining room. Marvelous smells of bacon and bread grew stronger as she moved through the halls to the dining room. The growling in her stomach transformed into a roar. She'd eaten next to nothing for the past three days and hoped they'd have enough food to satisfy her.

She found Julia talking to a dark-haired boy and a blond girl who looked to be about her age. When Julia spotted her, she smiled and waved her over.

"I thought you were never going to wake up. You missed dinner. I thought you'd miss breakfast, too, but Laura said to let you sleep. Isn't this place totally amazing? This is Mallory and that's Dane. They've been here with their families since a few days after the CME. Can you believe that? They have no idea how terrible it is out there. I told them about getting shot and how we almost died yesterday, but I don't think they believe me."

Dane gave a small wave and Mallory smiled. "Nice to meet you, Dr. Poole. Is what Julia said true?"

"Unfortunately, yes. Have you eaten, Julia?"

"Yes. They have a ration system here, but Bryce said we could eat as much as we want today. I had ten pancakes. I think that's a family record."

"No doubt it is," Riley said and looked around the busy dining room. "Where is Bryce? I need to speak to him after I eat."

"He said to tell you he'd be busy all day, but he'll meet you here for dinner at six."

"Trays are over there," Dane said and pointed at the serving area.

Riley thanked him and made her way to the counter, worrying she'd faint before she reached it. A bright-faced young woman smiled and served her food. Riley carried her tray to an empty table and took a spoonful of oatmeal with brown sugar, savoring the warm ambrosia. She dumped her cup of chopped almonds and raisins into the oatmeal and shoveled the food in as fast as she could swallow. When the bowl was empty, she wolfed down five pancakes.

Just as she finished, Laura came in and offered to give her and Julia a tour of the facility. The tour ended at what was named the

Community Exchange, where residents shared what they didn't need and took what they did. She and Julia each found a few changes of clothes and other necessities.

After the tour, Laura and Mallory took Julia to the makeshift schoolroom while Riley did their laundry and unpacked their few belongings. With her chores out of the way, she took the time to relish her peaceful solitude.

She marveled that less than a day earlier, she'd been on the verge of death but now was living in luxury. While it was an effort to trust these new acquaintances, her gut told her she had nothing to fear. This community would be a temporary stopping place, but there couldn't have been a better one left in the world. All that was missing to make it perfect was Coop.

Riley and Julia were getting ready to go to dinner when Mallory stopped by their apartment to invite them to eat with her family.

Julia looked at Riley and grinned. "Can we, Mom? We should get to know the people here."

"Thank you, Mallory, but I have a meeting with Bryce. You go ahead, Julia. I'll stop by and meet your family later, Mallory."

Julia went off as fast as her crutches would carry her. Riley followed at a slower pace to have time to gather her thoughts. While she knew Bryce wanted to talk about the clinic, Riley was anxious to question him about Zach.

Bryce rose out of his chair when she walked into the dining room and hurried to his table. He took her outstretched hand in both of his and shook it enthusiastically before pointing to the table covered with food.

"I wasn't sure what you like, so I got a little of everything."

As he said it, her thoughts raced back to her first breakfast with Coop when he'd done the same. The meal that morning had been a banquet but compared to the meager fare Riley had been consuming lately, the food Bryce offered was a feast. There were bowls of tomato soup with crackers, tuna sandwiches with actual bread, oatmeal raisin cookies, but it was the fresh apples that caught her attention. She hadn't seen fresh fruit since leaving the hotel.

She took her seat and smiled. "This is unbelievable. Two days ago, Julia and I were considering eating the sofa."

He laughed a deep, genuine laugh that melted her cares. She understood why Zach had gravitated toward him.

"I'm glad we spared you that." He gestured at the food. "Please, eat first, then business."

Riley watched him as they ate. He was at least six-three, Zach's height, with fair skin and broad, confident shoulders used to bearing responsibility. He wore his light-brown hair clipped short but longer than a military cut. His most striking feature was his blue eyes, the color of calm Caribbean seas. He had open, easy manners and was oblivious to how attractive he was. She wondered if he'd ever been married or had children.

When her hunger was satisfied, she sat back, watching the residents eating and chatting in happy contentment, ignorant to the whirlwind of chaos raging beyond their walls. If they'd had Wi-Fi and cell phones, life wouldn't have been much different than before the CME.

"You're shocked that a place like this exists, aren't you?" Bryce asked, drawing her out of her thoughts.

She nodded. "How is this place possible? Where are you getting power, food, water? Who's in charge?"

"I've spent time on the road. I understand your bewilderment. This facility belongs to a chain of 'green' senior centers around the country. The owners built them with hardened, off-grid solar power so that they won't be dependent on local power companies. It's a massive investment upfront, but they make it back in savings on electric bills. The well water pumps are solar powered as well, so we have clean water."

Riley stared at him in wonder and said, "Incredible."

"The facility was well stocked with food when the CME hit. Our stores are running low, but we've been augmenting with what we find on supply runs. That's what we were doing when we found you."

"And we're infinitely grateful you did. I wouldn't have lasted another hour. It's a tragedy more people don't have access to conditions like this."

"We bring in anyone we find who's willing to come, but not many are left out in the open these days. What few there were, the snowstorms took care of." Riley nodded in understanding. "Having you here is a boon for us. I wanted to ask if you'll serve as our medical clinic director."

"I'm more than willing to help in any way I can while we're here, but this is a temporary stop for us. Once the snow melts and Julia is stronger, we'll be moving on to my Uncle's ranch about an hour's drive south of here. I was hoping you'd be willing to return our Humvee."

He crossed his arms and frowned. "I'm sorry to hear that you're planning to go. You'll be the first wanting to leave. Is there any way I can change your mind?"

She shook her head. "We've been making our way to Wytheville from DC almost since the CME hit. What you have here is a miracle, but we need to be with family."

He watched her quietly for a moment. "I can't return the truck. It will be a huge help for the community, but I'll make a deal with you. I'll drive you to your family's ranch if you promise to return with me if you don't find things to be what you hoped. Or maybe your family will want to join us."

"Not likely, but you have a deal. Until we leave, I'll run your clinic." She held out her hand to shake on it.

"With that settled, do you mind if I ask what you're doing here? Aren't you from Colorado?"

She told him about the conference and a few of their

harrowing experiences. She mentioned Coop but left out the personal details.

After telling him about Branson's compound and how Julia got shot, she said, "I feel terrible about the people trapped there and wish we could have rescued them. Maybe when the snow melts, you can take a group to free them."

"I'll mention it to the council, but that would expend a lot of resources. People are suffering all around us. As much as we want to help, we can't save them all, especially in an armed compound of that size."

Coop had told her the same more than once. It made logical sense but broke her heart, especially when she remembered Angie.

"I appreciate your willingness to ask. Now, I have some questions for you. Why are *you* here? Were you stationed in the area?"

He gave a slight nod. "At Andrews with Laura, Tyson and Lance. We were in convoy escorting VIPs out of DC With the chaos in the CME aftermath and breakdown of communications, it all went to hell. We kept it together as long as we could, but this scientist we were babysitting told us the CME was global."

"An astrophysicist? Dr. Adrian Landry?"

Bryce's eyes narrowed, and his jaw muscles tightened for an instant as he tried to contain his shock. "You know Landry?"

"He's in Branson's compound if he's still alive. He told me the whole story about the CME. Unfortunately, he told everyone in the camp, too. They didn't take the news well. I treated his wounds from the beating he got as a result."

"Small world," he mumbled. "After Landry's bombshell, it was every man for himself. When the good doctor gave us the slip, and the rest of our unit scattered, the four of us considered returning to Andrews but figured there wouldn't be anything to return to. We went in search of a place to call home for the winter and found Blue Ridge Meadows."

"I should be stunned that your unit deserted, but after what we've seen, nothing shocks me anymore. It does break my heart, though. I'm glad you've found another way to serve." She took a breath for the courage to ask her most burning question. "How do you know Zach?"

"Ah, I wondered when you'd get around to asking that. Let's go somewhere more private."

She walked beside him as they wound the hallways to what could only be described as an old-fashioned game room. The room was deserted, so she and Bryce took the wing chairs in front of the wood-burning fireplace.

"I feel like we've transported into a nineteenth-century novel. My grandfather would have loved this."

"Suitable for the previous clientele. The youngest one here is seventy-eight. We have four residents in their nineties. There's a group that meets here to play bridge every afternoon."

They watched the flames in silence for several minutes, until Riley turned to him and said, "Please, tell me about Zach."

He kept his eyes on the fire and stroked the stubble on his chin. "Still hard for me to talk about even after all this time. He was one of the best men that ever lived."

Riley's eyes glistened as she said, "Yes, he was."

"We were at the academy together. We kept in touch and crossed paths over the years until we were stationed together at Bagram."

She studied him for a moment. "I think he told me about you. Didn't give your name, of course. He was excited to be stationed with one of his oldest friends."

The corner of his mouth curled. "That would have been me."

"He told me about some of your extra-curricular activities. Was there anyone that didn't fall victim to your pranks?"

"Just the CO. We used the pranks as a way to keep up morale. It was rough over there." He took a breath and slowly released it. "I was with him that morning before he left on his final mission.

He'd just gotten off a video chat with you and the kids. It was all he could talk about, how much he missed the family. He thought the world of you."

Riley wiped her cheeks and wondered if she'd been wrong to ask him about Zach after getting her grief to a manageable level. Why re-open the wound? But it was nice to hear about him from a new perspective. Bryce was the only person she'd spoken to who knew him on a personal level before that fatal mission.

Bryce leaned forward and put his elbows on his knees. "I'm sorry. I'll stop if this is too difficult."

"No, please, go on."

"Zach was flying troop transport in a Chinook near the Pakistan border when the enemy fired on them. All hands lost. It was a tremendous blow for everyone on the base. We dealt with death and violence every day in the field, but I took the news hard. I'd lost a brother." He hesitated before saying, "I tried to get leave for the funeral, but the Air Force had other plans."

Riley placed her hand on his arm. "Thank you for telling me. I know it wasn't easy."

"Glad I got the chance. Finding you and Julia on that snowdrift was a miracle. Sure I can't talk you into staying?"

She leaned back in her chair and sighed. "We can't. I need to get Julia to my family. There's something you should know. Wytheville isn't my last stop. I'm going to leave Julia there and ask my uncle to lend me a few ranch hands and horses to take me to Colorado. I need to know if Emily, Jared and my parents are alive. Then, I'll find a way to come back for Julia."

"You're going to travel across the entire continent after it took you weeks to get this far, almost dying multiple times? Forgive me, but that's downright insane."

Riley chuckled. "Don't hold back. Give me your honest opinion." Growing serious, she said, "You joined the Air Force and risked your life for the benefit of others. How is this different? Because I'm a woman?"

"How can you ask that? Some of the bravest people I've served alongside are women. Women like Laura. She has a warrior's heart."

Riley smiled at how his eyes brightened when he said Laura's name. She put her hand over her heart and bowed her head. "My apologies for making assumptions. Do you have children, Bryce?"

"Never had the chance. I'd always hoped to be a father, but now? Who could think of bringing children into this world?"

"Then, you can't understand why I have to get back to mine. They're my whole life, my reason for fighting to stay alive. I'm painfully aware of conditions out there, but I'm holding out hope that life will self-correct given enough time. Look what you've built here in such a short time. Others will do the same."

"Zach was right about you. He said you were the pluckiest person he'd ever met. Speaking of children, we have a resident due to give birth any day. I told her you'd examine her."

"Gladly," she said, happy to change the subject. "Laura gave me a tour of the clinic. It's impressive. I'll start work in the morning." She stood and took his hand in both of hers. "You can't know how much hearing about Zach meant to me. He was lucky to have you as a friend."

"I was the lucky one. I hope I'll be able to call you a friend, too."

"It would be my honor."

CHAPTER EIGHTEEN

THE STORMS and snow left as quickly as they came. The snow had melted within three weeks of Riley and Julia arriving at Blue Ridge Meadows, or BRM as they affectionately called it, and temperatures had risen to the low sixties. The first week after the thaw, the grounds were a swamp, but the sun soon dried the excess water, and shoots of grass and flowers broke through. With the first signs of spring, Riley's hope for the world's renewal soared.

She'd asked Julia to meet her in the enclosed garden one Saturday after lunch. They stretched out on lounge chairs and soaked up the sunshine.

Riley sighed and closed her eyes. "Isn't this glorious? Hard to believe that we almost died in a blizzard three weeks ago."

Julia pulled the Nationals cap Bryce had given her over her eyes. "Some days, I forget the cabin ever happened."

Wish I could, Riley thought. She hadn't seen Coop for nearly four weeks, but he was always in her thoughts. Not knowing his fate tore at her heart.

One consolation was that Julia was thriving and her leg was getting stronger by the day. Riley estimated she'd be walking without crutches in a week. But she had mixed feelings about how well Julia was settling in at the center. She and Mallory had become inseparable, and Riley caught the way her eyes lit up whenever Dane walked into the room. All of that made the conversation she needed to have with her more difficult, but she couldn't postpone it any longer.

She swung her legs to the ground and sat up facing Julia. "We need to talk."

"I knew this was coming," Julia said, without looking at her. "You want to leave BRM."

"It's more than wanting. We *are* leaving. Bryce and Laura are driving us to the ranch on Tuesday. That gives you three days to say goodbye to your friends."

Julia pushed the cap up and glared at her. "Go if you want. I'm staying."

"You can fight me or come willingly, but you're coming either way."

"I don't get a say in my own future? That's not fair."

"You'll have plenty of years to decide your own future. Until then, I get the final say in what's best for you. This is what's best."

"Like leaving the hotel was best? Like breaking out of the compound and abandoning Angie was best? Like going to the cabin was best? Every choice you make almost gets us killed."

She had a point, but admitting that would derail her point, so she changed tactics.

"Have you forgotten Coop? Aside from wanting to see how our family is, we need to find out if he made it to the ranch. I scratched that note on the cabin door. What if he saw it and went to the ranch expecting to find us? He'd be worried sick and thinking we're dead."

Julia looked down at her hands. "I haven't forgotten him," she said softly. "Do you really think he could have made it to the ranch?"

Even though she had her doubts, she didn't hesitate before saying, "I do."

A tear rolled down Julia's cheek as she raised her eyes to Riley. "I don't want that. I miss Coop, Mom, but what if we get to Uncle Mitch's and he's not there?"

"I hope that doesn't happen, but at least we'd know. It would still be worth it to find out about our family."

"But what about Bryce?"

The question caught her off guard. "Bryce? What about him?"

"Isn't there something going on between you?"

"I don't know why you think that, but no, there isn't. He's more like a brother, and he's got his heart set on Laura."

Julia's eyes widened, then she smiled. "Laura? That's cool."

Riley moved next to Julia and put her arm around her. "I should have talked to you about this before now, but I'm in love with Coop. I never thought I'd love another man after your dad, but I do. I don't know if he's alive, but even if he's not, grown-ups don't change their feelings from one person to another that quickly. I know it's different at your age. I'll never stop loving your dad, and I'll never stop loving Coop. I miss him more than you'll ever know."

"I'm sorry for being selfish and not thinking of your feelings. I've tried to pretend we never met Coop because it hurt too much to remember him. It's like I lost two dads."

Riley kissed the top of her head. "I know, sweetheart, and I get that it's hard for you to leave your new friends. Maybe when the roads become safer, you can come for a visit. This doesn't have to be goodbye forever."

Julia's eyes brightened. "That would be awesome. Can I go tell Mallory?"

Riley nodded and watched Julia zoom off on her crutches. Their conversation had gone better than she'd hoped. All she had left to do was prepare herself to face the worst, just in case.

Riley made her final rounds of the four patients in the hospital. She'd successfully delivered the baby two days earlier. They were both thriving, and she felt confident releasing them to their quarters. Another patient was an elderly man with pneumonia. He hadn't responded to antibiotics, but Riley still hoped he'd turn the corner. She left him in the hands of the skilled respiratory therapist they were fortunate to have.

The next patient was a young mother recovering from an appendectomy. Riley had performed her surgery the old-fashioned way, with a big incision since they didn't have access to laparoscopy. Her patient was improving rapidly and would be well enough to be discharged in a day or two.

The last patient was an eleven-year-old-boy who'd sustained a compound fracture when he tried to skateboard down the front steps of the center. Performing surgery on him brought back poignant memories of Julia's surgery and her practice at home.

After leaving detailed instructions with the nurse practitioner who was taking over for her, she said her goodbyes and loaded the last of their belongings in the Humvee. Julia and Mallory stood on the steps, clinging to each other and sobbing like they'd known each other for years. Riley finally had to drag Julia to the truck. As Bryce shifted into drive, Dane stepped on the landing and blew Julia a kiss. She pressed her face to the window and sobbed harder.

Bryce winked at Riley through the mirror, and said, "Don't despair, Julia. If the roads are safe, I'll ask Dane and Mallory's parents if I can bring them for a visit."

Julia turned her red, swollen eyes to him and said, "You'd do that?"

"Gladly. It'll give us a chance to visit with your mom, too."

Julia wiped her face on her hoodie and sat back with a smile before asking how long it would take to get to the ranch.

"I'd estimate three hours, but that will depend on how clogged the roads are," Laura said. "At least we won't have to contend with snow."

"Thank God," Riley mumbled.

Not in the mood for small talk, she turned to the window and watched the landscape speeding past. A glance at her watch and some quick math told her ten weeks had passed since the CME strike. She'd fought through those seemingly unending weeks toward one goal, getting Julia to safety at the ranch. Now that she was mere hours away, she was terrified of what they might find. What if the property had been overrun and her family was gone? Would it be the end of her hopes of going on to Colorado? As much as she trusted Bryce and his people, they weren't family. Could she trust them enough to leave her precious daughter in their care, possibly for years?

When she felt a twinge of panic in her gut, she shook off her dark negative thoughts and tapped Julia's elbow. "I was too anxious to sleep much last night. I'm going to try to nap. Wake me when we're close."

"I will. Everything's going to be fine, Mom. You'll see."

Riley rallied the best smile she could, hoping for both their sakes that Julia was right.

Riley woke fifteen miles outside Wytheville. She was rested, but no less anxious. Julia was asleep with her mouth hanging open and drool dripping from her chin. Riley shook her awake and handed her a handkerchief.

Julia blushed and wiped her face before looking out the window. "Where are we?"

"Almost to your aunt and uncle's house," Bryce said. "It's been a smooth, uneventful trip."

"First time for everything," she said.

Riley recognized some landmarks and directed him to the ranch as best she could. "I haven't been here in years, and I had GPS last time, but this looks right."

It was comforting to be in familiar surroundings for the first time since leaving home. Beth and Mitch had friendly neighbors and were respected in the community. She hoped that had been enough to protect them.

Bryce turned onto the gravel, tree-lined lane leading to the gate, and Riley's gut twisted into a knot. When the arched sign reading Dogwood Run Ranch came into view, she started to hyperventilate.

Julia handed her an empty baggie from her lunch and whispered, "Breathe into this, Mom. It'll be fine."

She did as her wise daughter instructed and struggled to regain control. As Bryce pulled the Humvee up to the gate, three men with raised rifles stepped in front of them. Riley breathed harder into the bag.

Bryce lowered the window. "We're here to see Mitchell and Elizabeth Dunne. We have their niece, Dr. Riley Poole, and her daughter, Julia, with us. May we pass?"

One of the men lowered his rifle. "Let me clear that," he said and jumped on a horse tethered to the fence.

Riley lowered the baggie and took a slow breath. If her aunt and uncle were gone, the man wouldn't have bothered to check if they could allow them through the gate. They probably would have sent them away or killed them, but she told Julia to duck just to be safe.

Bryce closed the window. "How far to the house?"

"No more than a quarter of a mile. This shouldn't take long."

"It's reassuring that they're taking safety measures," Laura said.

That comforted Riley, too, but also made her wonder what had happened to make Uncle Mitch institute them.

A red pickup truck came bouncing over the gravel five

minutes later. Riley threw her door open when Mitch climbed out and told his men to unlock the gate. When she ran to him, he lifted her in his arms and spun her around like he used to when she was a girl.

He wiped his eyes and said, "My little Riley Kate. Never thought I'd see your freckled face or fiery locks again. We've heard horrifying stories about conditions in DC."

"It's as bad as you've heard, but we left there months ago. It's been an adventure getting here."

Julia got out of the truck and raced up to Mitch on her crutches. He hugged her before stepping back to give her a good look. "Bet there's a story behind that, Miss Julia Mae."

"You won't believe it. Where are Holly and Aunt Beth?"

"At the house waiting for you. Aunt Beth nearly fainted when she heard you were here. Who are your friends?"

Bryce and Laura stepped out of the truck and joined them.

"This is Bryce Casper, a longtime friend of Zach's." When Mitch raised his eyebrows, she said, "Long story. This is Laura Kittleson, our new friend."

Mitch shook each of their hands. "Follow us up to the house," he said, before helping Julia into his truck. He shook his head while Riley climbed into the front seat. "I can't believe it's really you. We were sure you two were dead."

"We almost were, lots of times," Julia said.

"She's right. We almost didn't make it." Mitch pulled in front of the house and opened his door, but Riley put her hand on his arm to stop him. "We were traveling with a doctor named Neal Cooper. Is he here? We got separated, and I left him directions to the ranch."

"We haven't seen him. I'm sorry, Riley."

Julia whimpered quietly in the back seat.

"It was a long shot," Riley said, doing her best to hide her devastation.

Mitch studied her and smiled with understanding. "This man

was important to you?" She nodded and turned away. "How long since you got separated?"

"A month."

He put his hand on her shoulder. "Don't lose hope. Look how long it took you to get here."

"True. And he has a way of popping up when we least expect him."

"Let's go in. It's like Christmas in there."

As he spoke, her aunt burst through the door and hugged Riley so tightly she couldn't breathe. Holly followed her out and shrieked when she saw Julia. The girls hugged each other and cried until Beth shooed Holly away so she could have a turn hugging Julia.

Uncle Mitch moved the reunion inside where their daughter, Kathryn, and two sons, Russell and Jesse, waited with their families. Kathryn and her husband, Clint, were Holly's parents. They had another daughter, Rosie, who was four years younger. They were staying in the main house while Russell and Jesse had their families in two guest houses on the property.

Riley introduced Bryce and Laura, and Beth insisted they stay the night.

"It's too dangerous on the roads after dark. We have plenty of room."

"I was hoping you'd ask," Bryce said with his best smile. "I'll bring our things out of the truck."

He and Laura hung back while the family got reacquainted. Riley knew they would have preferred to get back on the road, but she was glad they agreed to stay until morning so she wouldn't have to worry about them getting stranded in the dark.

After an extraordinary meal of roast chicken, potatoes, vegetables, and freshly baked bread, the family begged Riley to tell them about their trip to the ranch. She gave them all the details, holding nothing back, and Julia interjected from time to time. The family stared in shock or amazement and asked an endless stream of questions. Even Bryce, who hadn't heard the whole story, listened in awe. Riley was exhausted by the time she finished two hours later.

Beth wiped her eyes and said, "Providence brought you to us. There's no other explanation."

She thought of Zach urging her on through the snow and nodded. "I'd have to agree."

Mitch stood and gestured at the grandfather clock in the corner. "That's enough for tonight. You need rest." He lifted his water glass. "To Riley and Julia. Welcome home."

CHAPTER NINETEEN

RILEY WAITED for three days before approaching Mitch with her plans to leave for Colorado. She found him in the stables feeding the horses after breakfast and felt a pang of sadness as she passed the empty stalls. Mitch told her they'd lost five horses out of twenty-five to people stealing them for meat. He understood what a powerful force hunger was, but the horses were like his children, and he was devastated to lose them.

He looked up and smiled when he heard her coming. "What brings you out here?"

She patted the horse's neck and said, "I have something I need to discuss with you if you have a minute."

He turned an empty horse feed bucket over for her to sit on and dropped onto a stack of hay bales. "I always have time for you, Riley Kate."

She smiled at his use of her middle name. He'd called her that for as long as she could remember.

"I was wondering if you could spare a few ranch hands, horses, and provisions for me to travel to Colorado Springs. I'm desperate to know what's happened to Mom and Dad and my children. I'd leave Julia with you and come back as soon as I could. It could take as long as a year."

He stared at her in disbelief. "Have you lost your mind? How can you even consider a journey like that after what you and Julia went through to get here?"

"We made it, didn't we? The world is stabilizing. People are resilient. They'll settle into a new normal with time. I'm not saying it will be easy, but people traveled across the country long before electricity and cars."

Mitch stood and took off his baseball cap. Scratching his head, he said, "And half of them died."

"Please, sit down and listen." He reluctantly lowered himself onto the hay. "That was before they knew about germs or had the knowledge of medications and surgical procedures we do. I know I can do this. I've learned how to survive in the past few months."

"Even if I could spare men, horses or supplies, which I can't, I'd never agree to this. I owe it to your parents to keep you and Julia alive."

"What good does it do for me to be alive if they'll never know?"

"Undertaking a trip like this would be suicide. My answer is no, Riley."

She was about to protest, but he put his cap on and stalked out of the stable. She stood and kicked the feed bucket. The horse whinnied and stamped her foot. Riley stroked her neck as she frantically tried to figure out her next play. She hadn't expected Mitch to warm to her plan immediately, but his reaction had seemed definite. Staying was out of the question. She was determined to find a way back to her younger children.

Beth and her cousins gave her the same reaction when she asked them to convince Mitch to change his mind. She considered driving to Blue Ridge Meadows to talk Bryce into going with her, but he'd thought her idea was as crazy as her family did, and Mitch would never agree to let her take one of his trucks. Short of stealing one, she was stuck.

Deciding her best option was to back off and give the family time to get used to the idea, she threw herself into helping around the ranch. She treated the occasional cut or cough, but other than that, there wasn't much call for a full-time doctor. Jesse was a vet, so he took care of the livestock. She assisted him occasionally, but he managed just fine without her.

Russell was an electrician by trade and was also trained as a plumber. Kathryn had a master's degree in education and took charge of instructing the children. Mitch had his ranch hands who cared for the horses and helped patrol the ranch boundaries for intruders. Everyone had responsibilities to fill their days but her, and she didn't handle idleness gracefully.

One welcome distraction was having Uncle Mitch teach her how to operate his HAM radio. They'd been able to contact some distant relatives but hadn't reached Thomas. When Riley showed concern, Mitch told her not to read too much into it, that maybe Thomas' radio was plugged in when the CME struck and got fried. She took his word for it and threw herself into learning all she could as it might prove to be a way to communicate with Julia when she was traveling to Colorado.

One night at the end of their third week at the ranch, she asked Mitch and Beth to assign her tasks that needed doing.

"I'm strong and like hard work. I can't take this thumb-twiddling."

Beth chuckled and said, "We have an endless list of chores. We wanted to give you time to recuperate and didn't want to burden you. I'll have plenty of assignments ready for you by morning."

Mitch held up his hand. "Hold up, Beth. I get first crack. I need someone to take care of the groundhogs in the east meadow. It's the horses' favorite place to graze, but the groundhogs dig holes that can break their legs. That means having to put the horses down and we can't afford to lose any more."

Riley crinkled her nose. "What do you mean, take care of the groundhogs?"

Russell grinned at her. "He means to trap them and shoot them with a pellet gun."

"That's right," Mitch said. "It solves the hole problem and makes good meat for the dogs."

Julia giggled, but Riley felt like she was going to be sick. She'd expected him to ask her to lug hay bales or mend fences.

She shivered and said, "That's disgusting. I don't even know how to use a pellet gun."

"You were going to kill that deer when we were starving in the cabin, Mom," Julia said. "Taking care of a little groundhog should be easy."

Mitch leaned back in his chair and crossed his arms. "All part of life on a horse ranch. Meet me on the front steps at seven. I'll drive you out to the meadow and show you what to do."

"Terrific," Riley said and frowned.

"Welcome to my life," Katheryn said. "Still glad you asked for chores?"

Three days of trapping groundhogs hadn't lessened Riley's disgust for the task. She understood the need but would have preferred any other chore. Mitch taught her how to poke the ground with a stick to check for holes, then set the traps and wait. She'd convinced him to have someone else dispatch the little buggers after she shot one in the eye, and it didn't die. Mitch had teased her, calling her surprisingly skittish for a surgeon.

Riley failed to see how slaughtering groundhogs compared in any way with performing complex surgery on humans.

As she aimlessly wandered the meadow, poking that ridiculous stick into the grass, she struggled to find a way to travel to Colorado but came up empty. She stopped at noon for lunch, and as she unwrapped her jam and butter sandwich, Mitch's truck rumbled up to the meadow and stopped twenty yards from where she sat. Her gut tightened as she stood and dusted off her jeans, fearing what could bring her uncle to the meadow at that time of day.

A man who wasn't Uncle Mitch jumped out of the truck and started toward her. Visions of bad guys attacking the ranch raced through her mind. As the man approached, something in his gait sparked recognition in Riley. She tossed her sandwich in the grass and sprinted for him, tackling him to the ground and kissing every inch of his dirt-smudged face.

He rolled her onto her back and buried his face in her hair. "Is it really you, Riley Poole, or is this some cruel dream?"

"It's no dream, Coop," she whispered. "I'm as real as you."

He raised his head and flashed that smug grin she'd missed every second since he disappeared. "I love you, and I promise never to leave your side again for as long as I live."

She wove her fingers into his hair and said, "Let me see you try."

He leaned down and kissed her with a hunger to match her own. When he rolled onto the grass in exhaustion, she propped on her elbow and took a good look at him. He was as thin as a scarecrow and his clothes were worn and filthy.

Resting her hand on his chest, she whispered, "Tell me what happened to you."

"Can that wait until I've eaten and had a long shower? Please, tell me they have food and clean water here."

She brushed her lips on his. "We have *everything* you need here."

He took her hand and pressed it to his cheek. "Truest words I've ever heard."

Julia was in the family room doing schoolwork with Katheryn and her cousins when her mom poked her head into the doorway, grinning like the Cheshire cat. "I have a surprise for you," she said and moved aside to let a man in ratty, stained clothes step past her. Julia crinkled her nose at his smell and wondered who her mom had dragged in off the street. As she studied his face, he smiled, and she let out a shriek as she ran to him, nearly knocking him over.

"Coop, you're not dead! How did you get here? Where have you been?"

Riley threw her arms around them and said, "He'll tell us all about it after lunch and a shower."

Coop stepped back and wiped his eyes. "Look at that face. And no crutches."

She did a little spin and beamed at him. "This is the best day of my life."

He swayed and grabbed the back of a chair to keep from falling. Julia braced her hand on his elbow and said, "Come on. You need to eat. You're too skinny, and Aunt Beth makes the best food ever."

Her mom took his other arm as they helped him to the kitchen. Julia couldn't take her eyes off him as he wolfed down his food despite her mom's warning that eating too fast would make him sick. Having him sitting at their table was a miracle.

She hated to let him go when he finished eating, but he was filthy and stinky and begging for a shower. She waited at the bottom of the stairs until he came down looking like the old Coop, only skinnier. Her mom introduced him to the family, then insisted he take a nap. Katheryn herded the kids back to the family room, but Julia was too antsy to study. Coop showing up was the best thing to happen since Bryce rescued them.

At dinner, the family peppered him with questions until her mom shushed them, and said, "Let the poor man speak. Coop, start from the day you left the cabin to go searching for food."

He swallowed his bite of apple pie and said, "I'll start by telling you I should have listened to you, Riley, and not gone out into the snow. I've learned my lesson. I'll agree to whatever you say from now on."

"Like today, when I told you not to eat so fast, or you'd get sick, and you got sick?"

Julia waved for her to be quiet. "Let him talk, Mom."

"The storm started an hour after I left the cabin, and I couldn't see ten feet in front of me. I stumbled on to an abandoned gas station with a damaged roof, but it provided enough cover and heat for me to survive the night. I woke to a clear sky, so I decided to risk pushing on instead of returning to the cabin."

"Wish you hadn't done that," Riley said.

"Me, too," Julia said.

"I make three. I walked for hours without passing a single house or store until I came to a small cottage with smoke rising from the chimney. I knocked, and an emaciated elderly woman answered. When I explained who I was and asked if she'd let me in, she started to cry and hugged me. She was living there with three other elderly women. They hadn't eaten for two days and were almost out of wood. Their families had been looking out for them until the snow started, but they hadn't seen any of them for days."

Julia watched him as he rubbed his forehead, knowing what a hard decision he'd had to make. He'd probably wanted to get back to the cabin more than anything but never could have abandoned a house full of old ladies.

He straightened and took a breath. "I promised to stay and help in exchange for lodging. After chopping enough wood to last that day, I went to search for food. The women were all lifelong residents of the area and knew where to direct me. I scavenged enough canned and boxed goods from an old diner to get us by for three days."

Julia nodded her approval. "You did the right thing."

Coop gazed at her in silence before going on. "That third morning, one of the lady's sons and grandson came bringing boxes of food. They thanked me for my help and gave me enough food to last on my journey back to the cabin. I hiked back that day, only to find the cabin collapsed and buried in snow. I was sure Riley and Julia were dead inside."

His voice caught, so he stopped and took a breath.

Julia put her hand on his arm. "But didn't you see the message Mom scratched on the door?"

"Not at first. I blamed myself for your deaths and seeing no reason to go on, I collapsed in the snow to wait for mine. Luckily, the weather warmed that afternoon, and all I got was wet and cold. When I got up to go to the shed, I saw Riley's note carved into the door. With renewed hope, I salvaged what I could from the cabin and went back to stay with the friendly grandmas until the snow melted."

Riley wiped her eyes and smiled. "So like you."

"After that, I followed the trail of the fiery little red-haired doctor, hiking and hitching rides with kind strangers. I ran into an enthusiastic group of college students who'd taken it upon themselves to form a rescue squad for anyone in need. They drove me to Wytheville and dropped me on Main Street. I asked anyone I passed for directions to the ranch, and here I am. By the way, Mitch, Pastor Bennett says hello and hopes to see your family in church on Sunday."

Mitch chuckled. "We'll see, but I'll be sure to thank him for directing you to us."

Julia's eyes brimmed with tears. "You almost died like us. Another miracle."

Riley squeezed Coop's hand. "Carving the note on the door was Julia's idea,"

Coop pulled Julia into a bear hug. "Brilliant. You saved my life, WP."

"WP?" Beth asked.

Julia pulled away and smiled through her tears. "Warrior Princess. That's Coop's name for me. I owed you, Coop. How many times have you saved me?"

"Let's call it even," he said. "I want to thank all of you for welcoming me into your family. I didn't know what I'd find at the end of this trail. It's better than I could have dreamed."

Mitch stood and shook his hand. "Glad to have you, son, if for no other reason than to see Riley and Julia smiling."

———

Riley and Coop stayed awake long into the night filling in the gaps of their harrowing adventures and took their time getting up the next morning. Riley woke before him and watched him sleep, trying to convince herself that he was alive and lying in her bed.

Not wanting to disturb him, she wrapped herself in an afghan and moved to the window seat. Her window faced west, and each morning she'd savored the grandeur of the Blue Ridge Mountains spreading in majestic rows as far as her eyes could see. That morning, they held a new promise.

Since recovering from the shock of Coop's return from the dead, her hopes of going to Colorado had sparked to life. She wouldn't have to travel alone. She'd have the man she loved by her side and the only obstacle would be convincing him to leave the comfort of the ranch to face a harrowing cross-country journey.

She heard Coop stir behind her and turned to him with a warm smile, delighted to see the contentment in his face.

"You weren't just a dream, then. What are you doing way over there?" He threw the covers back, and she returned to the bed, snuggling up beside him. He brushed his lips on her neck and said, "Do I even want to know what you were thinking so hard about by the window?"

She gave a small laugh. "You can't read my thoughts yet?"

He stopped kissing her and looked her in the eye. "You're evading. Spill it."

"I was wishing I had a way to tell my family in Colorado about you. They would love you as much as Julia and I do. And I miss my babies, Coop. I begged Uncle Mitch to lend me men and horses to make the trip home, but he unequivocally refused. The whole family thinks my plan is insane. Bryce agrees. But that's all changed now that you're here. Look at what we each survived to get this far. I know we could make the journey together. All I need is for you to agree to join me."

He rolled onto his back and tucked his hands behind his head. "Riley Poole, I haven't been here for twenty-four hours, and you're asking me to turn around and leave on a cross-country trek?"

"I'm not asking you to leave today. Two or three weeks would give you time to put weight back on and get your strength back. It would also give us time to secretly gather supplies and plan our strategy."

"Because our plans are always so successful? And what do you mean secretly gather supplies? You're not going to ask for them?"

"Uncle Mitch will never agree to outfit us. He just found five horses abandoned on a nearby ranch to replace the ones he lost. They're in bad shape, but he says they'll survive. If I take three of his healthy horses, he'll have more than enough to run the ranch."

"Who have you become? You've gone from making us leave cash for supplies we took to being a horse thief. They used to put people to death for less."

"I'm not stealing them, just borrowing. I'll return the horses when I come for Julia. It tears me apart to do it, but I have to leave her here. I can't dare put her in danger a second time, and she's safe and loved here."

"You think you'll be able to just walk away from her?" Riley looked away, not sure she could say yes. "She'll never forgive you for leaving."

"She will when I show up to take her home. She may be off the crutches, but she'll have a limp for months, if not permanently. My options are to either forget Emily and Jared in Colorado, living out my life, never knowing their fate, or leave Julia here with a loving family. I've had months to ponder this, Coop. As gut-wrenching as it is, my choice is clear. You may have to throw me over your shoulder and haul me away when the time comes, though."

He studied her for a moment and sighed. "I gave my word yesterday that I'd agree to whatever you said from now on, but more than that, I'd move heaven and earth for you. I've learned the hard way what hell it is being separated from you. I can't go through that again, so I'll take you to Colorado, against my better judgment. And how else am I going to ask your dad's permission to marry you?"

Riley gave him a playful slap. "What are you talking about, silly man?"

He wrapped the sheet around his waist and knelt on the bed. Taking her hand, he said, "Those weeks we were separated were the worst of my life. Only the hope of seeing your face again kept me plunging ahead, day after excruciating day. Now we're together, I want us to be a real family, committed for life. So, Dr. Riley Kate Poole, will you marry me?"

"That was a moving speech, but who do you imagine would perform the ceremony? And are you planning to wait until we get to Colorado when you can ask Dad for my hand?"

"Pastor Bennett has already agreed to marry us, so no, I don't plan to wait until we get to Colorado. I'm sure your dad will grant me leniency for asking after the fact, given that the world's gone to hell. Marry me before we leave, if your answer's yes."

"You know how much I love you and the whole idea's absurd, but if it makes you happy, Dr. Neal Xavier Cooper III, yes, I'll marry you."

He bounded off the bed and started rummaging through one of the drawers Riley had given him in the dresser. When he found what he was searching for, he jumped back onto the bed and held up a gorgeous two-carat diamond ring set in what looked like platinum.

"Think this will fit?"

Riley raised an eyebrow. "Who did you steal that from?"

"Not stolen. One of my sweet grandmas named Mary gave it to me one night when I told her about you. She said she didn't have anyone to pass it on to and wanted you to have it."

Riley stared at the ring for several moments in stunned silence. When she was able to speak again, she said, "I thought this was one of your seat-of-your-pants, impulsive acts, and I didn't take it seriously. Way to go and melt my heart. So, let me answer again. Coop, it would be my honor and greatest pleasure to become your wife." She raised her hand for him to slip the ring on her finger. "Perfect fit."

"Just like us."

Julia was beside herself with joy when Riley announced her engagement to Coop, but Riley got the bigger surprise when Holly showed her their notebook full of wedding plans. Their ideas were a little elaborate, given the state of the world. Riley relented when they pestered her to ask Russell for a ride into town to search for a wedding dress. Mitch jumped into action to make the arrangements with Pastor Bennett. The good pastor only agreed to perform the ceremony on the condition that Mitch start bringing his family to church. He grudgingly agreed.

Riley was plagued by guilt as the family enthusiastically prepared for the first happy event on the ranch since the CME disaster. She and Coop manufactured a fake honeymoon at Uncle Mitch's fishing lodge when in reality, it was a way to deflect suspicion as they made their getaway on their wedding night.

Mitch agreed to loan them three horses to carry their food, water, and gear, so Riley and Coop spent the two weeks leading up to the wedding concealing provisions near the gate that they'd retrieve on their way out of the ranch. With their exit strategy in place, all that was left to do was wait.

After a tender and unforgettable ceremony in the garden behind the house, the family enjoyed a lavish spread that Beth had orchestrated, right down to the beautifully decorated cake. As the sun began to set on the gathering, Riley slipped away to Julia's room. She fell on the bed and buried her face in the pillow, soaking it with tears and imprinting the smell of her precious daughter on her brain.

Leaving Julia behind was torture but Riley had no choice. It was Julia's only hope for a stable future in a safe place surrounded by a loving family. Taking her on the road with them would be irresponsible.

When Riley had her cry, she replaced the pillow and picked up the envelope she'd carried in with her. Her hands shook as she pulled out the letter tucked inside and began to read.

My dearest Julia,

This is the most difficult letter I've ever had to write. For reasons I hope you'll understand someday, I've been keeping a secret from you. By the time you read this, Coop and I will be many miles away on our journey to Colorado Springs. I've planned to go home since the day of the CME strike. I need to do whatever it takes to find out what has happened to Jared and Emily, and let them know we're alive. After seeing everyone thriving at the ranch, I have to hope that they are, too.

Leaving you is tearing my heart in two and is the hardest thing I've ever had to do. If you don't believe me, ask Coop when you see him. And you will see him again. We've shared so many extraordinary experiences on this journey, my sweetheart. I couldn't have survived them without you by my side. You've been my spirit guide and warrior princess. Please believe it when I say you are one of the most remarkable young women in the world.

As soon as I get to Colorado, I'll start making plans to return to you. (Please tell Uncle Mitch I'm sorry for taking his horses and that I promise to bring them back.)

Be brave! Be happy. You are my heart and my life. I love you more than you'll ever know.

With my deepest love and devotion,

Mom

She replaced the letter and slid the envelope between the covers, hoping Julia wouldn't find it until she and Coop were long gone. She kissed her fingertips and pressed them to the pillow, praying her angel girl would forgive her someday.

Coop found her in their bedroom, changing into her clothes for the road. She lovingly hung her wedding dress in the closet with tears streaming down her face. Coop came up behind her and wrapped his arms around her waist.

"There's time to change your mind. It's your call." Shaking her head, she turned and quietly wept on his shoulder. He gently stroked her hair and said, "You're the unhappiest bride I've ever seen."

She gave a teary laugh and blew her nose on the handkerchief she'd tucked in her shirt pocket.

"Don't take it personally. I just needed to get that out of my system. I'm overjoyed to be your wife, and leaving Julia is right, but that doesn't mean it's easy."

He nodded and kissed her forehead. "We'd better leave if you're determined to travel tonight."

Riley shouldered her backpack and made one last check of the room. "I *am* determined. Let's head to the stables before I lose my nerve."

The horses were calm while Riley and Coop saddled them and tied down their gear. Riley spoke softly to them, giving the horses a chance to get reacquainted with her. They'd be family on the long journey ahead and had to learn to trust and rely on each other.

When they finished in the stables, they led the horses to the hiding place near the gate to retrieve the rest of their belongings. With the supplies packed, they mounted and rode the horses down the gravel drive. Cheerful sounds from their wedding reception floated on the breeze. Riley turned, resisting the urge to gallop back to the house and give Julia one last hug.

Coop reined his horse to a stop next to her. "I know you're torn, but we either go now or wait at the fishing lodge until morning."

In answer, Riley, filled with fear and determination, snapped the reins to get her horse trotting away from the ranch. They faced months of travel on dangerous roads masked in shadow. With the hope of reuniting her family as her driving force, she sat taller in the saddle and turned her face to the west.

END

The story continues...

HUNTING DAYBREAK
Shattered Sunlight Series Book II
Available Now!

ABOUT THE AUTHOR

E.A. Chance is a writer of award-winning suspense, historical and post-apocalyptic women's fiction. She has always cherished books that influence her writing and her life. She hopes to create the same experience for readers and thrives on crafting tales of everyday superheroes. Her debut novel, Arms of Grace (under pen name Eleanor Chance) is a finalist in consideration for production by Wind Dancer Films, a silver medalist in the Readers' Favorite Awards, and a recipient of the B.R.A.G. Medallion.

She has traveled the world and lived in five different countries. She currently resides in the Williamsburg, Virginia area with her husband and is the proud mother of four grown sons and Nana to one amazing grand-darling.

She loves hearing from readers. Connect with her at:
www.eachancebooks.com
e.a.chance@eachancebooks.com

Made in the USA
Las Vegas, NV
26 July 2025

25430782R00204